HORSE
LATITUDES

Jay Merrick has travelled widely, having lived in the Far East and California. More recently, he has spent time in South America and Africa, where he has examined and written about environmental issues.

HORSE
LATITUDES

JAY MERRICK

FOURTH ESTATE • *London*

This paperback edition first published in 2000
First published in Great Britain in 1999 by
Fourth Estate Limited
6 Salem Road
London W2 4BU
www.4thestate.co.uk

Copyright © 1999 by Jay Merrick

10 9 8 7 6 5 4 3 2 1

The right of Jay Merrick to be identified as the author of
this work has been asserted by him in accordance with the
Copyright, Designs and Patents Act 1988.

A catalogue record for this book is available from the
British Library.

ISBN 1-85702-915-1

Typeset by Avon Dataset Ltd, Bidford on Avon, B50 4JH
Printed in Great Britain by Cox & Wyman Ltd, Reading,
Berks.

In memory of Honor Jean Partlow

Everything is broken up and dances
Jim Morrison

Prologue

I MUST begin with the image, so stark and convenient, that Freyn seeded within me: truth and artifice locked together in the sharply cut reliefs of a distant frieze, telling the story of a violent disorder.

'You have to imagine,' he said that day, with the rain rattling against the cardboard walls of his hovel, 'the sailors on deck under the spars, the deck slippery with water. There is a repetitious thump and sizzle of head-on seas across the bows. Fix that firmly in your mind: ship and sea. Let's say it is 1874 and the ship is rigged for sail but also equipped with a coal-fired engine to make progress into the wind, or in dead air. The sails have been reefed. A wavering line of sooty smoke is wandering aimlessly away from the crown of the thin black funnel. The passengers are on deck. No, I need to be more precise. The inhabitants of second class and steerage are assembled along the port rail; first and cabin class passengers are on the aft deck looking down at them. However, they have one thing in common. Both groups look expectant. And why not? They are to witness a jolly nautical pantomime.

'There would have been laughter as the contrivance was hauled across the deck. Contrivance? Really, how very dry of me. I mean an effigy of a horse made out of anything the hands could find – sackcloth, cushion stuffing, stuff that could be lashed together to produce the right shape; and all of it tarred so that this sudden, strangely limbed creature was as sleek and shining as it could be. Its tar barrel body would have been packed with combustibles. And then this bogus horse would have been set on a bogey and carted round the deck, mounted by one of the mates dressed as a jockey. And all this to mark the fact, symbolically, that the sailors had worked off their first month's pay at sea and were due another instalment.

'I can see the ship's captain clapping his hand down hard on the bridge rail and calling the auction to order. His voice under the whipping furls of the sails must have been loud; but louder still comes the laughter and hurrahs of the crew and passengers as he recites the creature's pedigree. More laughter as the captain accepts the hilariously penny-pinching bids for the beast's ownership: the coppers, leavened with the odd piece of silver from the soft, pale fingers of a well-dressed stranger on the aft deck, would later be distributed among the rum-soaked tars.

'And then – it must have been so, and in mock judicial tones – the captain's voice: "Raise the horse!" Imagine the creak of the ropes as the dreadful thing gets pulled up and out along the yard arm. So there it is, dangling over the ship's side, ugly, laughable. It turns first one way and then the other. Think of it as a compass point struggling in a deranged magnetic field. No north, nor south, just the flexing of an uncontrollable power.

'Now then. Passengers and crew braced against the rails, waiting, ignoring the spindrifts of spray. And the captain again: "Set the beast afire!" And the crew reaching for long poles, tipped with bulging wraps of tarred cloth; the balls of flame and the poles thrust heartily at the wobbling horse; the first trembling smear of flame and more hurrahs; the sizzle of the tar on the barrel body and a strange tearing sound as the flame engulfs the neck. And then the whack of an axe-blade into the securing rope, its sudden cartwheeling drop into the sea, the ship's bow-waves rocking it as if it lay in some infernal cradle.

'The water would have hissed around the burning shape as the ship passed on. Sea birds may have circled it incredulously. Its form would gradually have been lost in the flames on the water; bit by bit its existence as a horse of convenience would have become something else. The slats, the roping, the crudely sawn lengths of pole, the whole mess of it would have degenerated into the charred, unidentifiable remains of an illusion, the smouldering bits and pieces separating and either sinking or floating away, unmarked, going nowhere, some of it washing up on a coast in the dark years later – centuries perhaps.'

That was the first of Freyn's asides which struck me as significant. Of course, this is not the story of a contrivance that burned at sea in the middle of the nineteenth century; it is not quite the right drama to recount. Like the tarred horse, that story is the bones of another story, Freyn's story. I should emphasise that. I tell you of it simply because the images meant something to me. Not that I can compare myself to Freyn. His sensibility is beyond me. Yet the way he told the story made me see things: the flaring object, the skew-limbed fall into the swell. You don't have to be a Freyn to feel something from it.

Freyn's history lesson is not entirely pointless. You could even imagine him as one of the remnants of the burning horse, flotsam grounding on the shingle of an abandoned shoreline. I will do a Freyn, then. I'll say to you: 'You have to imagine that you are nowhere – that is, that you are in a place that is considered to be nowhere.'

It is not easy to be nowhere, but – like the remains of the seared barrel, the stolid trunk of the creature – that is where I found Freyn, an exile from the past who had been excluded from the future. He was separated even from the insistent, almost jagged stench of the Moist Delta Section, known simply as the Delta. Freyn's separation or self-exclusion is a paramount point. Now that I come to approach his story I find myself wondering how much he existed; no, not how much, but why he persisted.

It is the nature of Freyn's being, the ancillaries rather than the blunt fact, that offers some weight to the whole. It seems odd to say it, but without that sense of the ephemeral which suffused him everything else could only have been false. Without it, the story could not have happened and the incidents that drove him

3

into exile could only have been a dream or visions in a fever.

Freyn would never have started his story like this, incidentally. He would not have fumbled with qualifications and disclaimers. Even when he expressed a doubt he did so in a way that made that doubt seem concrete, something hard and nuggety. The nerves and haziness are mine alone.

I don't know why he chose to tell me about Luchenne and the horses. It is as if I've been handed something unidentifiable, a shape that will not quite fit the palm however long is it handled. What he told me is certainly of historical interest – yet it might also be something precious; or the reverse, an intellectual infection of some sort, a shady thing, difficult to shake off. I am troubled by his . . . I guess I could call it his discourse. I can risk that description; I am not a philosopher and can therefore use it casually.

There is nothing creative in the pages that follow – nobody wants anything too raw or uncontrollable these days. So I simply recorded everything he said, applied myself to the necessary additional research and distilled the information. Like I said, you can't make things up nowadays, can you?

Assuming you are not familiar with the nature of habitation in the Delta, I shall describe Freyn's home. Picture a large cardboard box about seven feet square on all sides, providing an internal volume of about six cubic metres. It is daubed with splotches of black market NuCote water repellent and smears of bitumen tar. Its precise location in the Delta is irrelevant in such an amazing metastasis of shelters and free market biological activity. It is surprising how many of us seem to be ignorant of the Delta's presence; eleven hundred hectares of degraded cellulose and vinyl refuse spreading south-west towards London from the remains of Stansted airport, which as you know was destroyed by the Void Templar architectural terrorist cell in 2012. The Delta is easy to miss, cloaked as it so often is in a temperature-inversion fog – the Delta Dimmer as outsiders know it.

I don't mean to parade my specialism, but I really do know

about the Delta. I monitor spontaneous microfloral crudescences there, and the incidence of acid-loving lichen in particular. It is not a subject I expect others to be interested in. Freyn was certainly not interested, though it gives me some small satisfaction to think that, however accidentally, my subject area led me to him.

I had just finished taking a laser back-bearing – I was well into the Delta, near to where runway three used to be – when I noticed an unusually large growth on the side of a large well-maintained cardboard box. Some chance! Freyn's box in particular among that welter of objects and decayed shapes in a wild geometry of sodden planes, angles and wind-flayed sheeting.

What had formed him? How exactly did he exist? At first, he gave the impression of not being aware of much around him; and yet when he spoke he gripped me. I am swept up in his thrall even now. He spoke first. I did not have to listen: I could have pointed to my epaulet, the orange and green double chevron signalling enforceable non-response privileges; but something made me respond. It's a contractual thing, conversation, no matter how one-sided and I grew increasingly happy with our terms as time passed between us.

I'm jumping ahead. I'm not used to presenting data in a narrative form. I'd better explain the precise circumstances of our meeting. After noticing the lichen growth I began to collect a sample of the lichen encrustation. It is hardly noisy work but he must have detected the gentle scrape of my spatula, a well-used Grimaldini Flexor. A few seconds later the curtain covering the box's front opening was slowly drawn aside. Freyn's face appeared. After scrutinising me for what seemed half a minute, he crawled out on all fours and then rearranged himself on his haunches, one palm on the ground to steady himself.

And I remember thinking: this man is very old, he must be at least ninety. I was almost twenty years adrift on that assumption, as it turned out. Freyn wore a filthy dark brown tweed overcoat belted over flannel pyjamas, the pyjamas surmounted by a padded waistcoat that may once have been of a plum red colour. Other items included integrally belted plastic overtrousers, luminous green; the kind that sports licensees wear to induce sweating. Freyn wore them to keep the rain off and had clearly possessed them for some time because they were streaked with sulphuric discolorations.

It was hard to tell Freyn's size and I'm still not sure of it. Like all Delta dwellers he moved mostly on his hands and knees, or in a crouching gait. His knees were padded externally with a succession of bits and pieces of semi-durable matter: wads of felt, crapulous sponges, skilfully folded newspapers. His knuckles were padded with arthritic lumps. The wrists were well enough formed, though their bony articulations showed as a terrible white in comparison with the dark grime that began an inch or so behind the knuckles. The arms were pretty skimpy – the deeply rumpled folds in the sleeves of the overcoat revealed that plainly enough. His back was slightly humped, but that is normal among Delta degradees.

His face came as a shock. Instead of the dazed mask typical of degradees, I saw the features of an utterly sentient being who could have had nothing whatsoever to do with the Delta; no connection with the pools of glinting electrolytes, the rotting hovels, the rats, the violence of the charity food and clothing drop zones. His face simply did not belong. If that sounds in some way prejudicial, I can only say there is no other way to put it. And I say it again: Freyn's face did not belong. Yet it was not as if his features were in any way unusual: a rather long nose, thin of nostril; a matted grizzle of lank white hair and a thin, wavering glint of pale scalp marking the remains of a parting. His eyebrows were straight and still surprisingly dark and definite.

His eyes were the true mark of his sentience, this knowing of something beyond the immediate – or maybe within the immediate. Freyn's eyes were perfectly clear and calm, the signs of a singular purity (though I say that with trepidation: the remark is wholly unscientific). They glittered, they saw, they harboured something inviolate. Seeing them, I knew instantly that Freyn was non-feral. I knew that he did not hide in refuse and spring out shittily at other degradees; knew that he did not steal children or copulate with dogs or fling hepatic refuse at real or imagined enemies. Even before we spoke I had the immediate sense that Freyn harboured something unusual, from another time and place, and that he held it securely.

Even then, I still might not have spoken to him, for I had been unnerved by those first moments. And I wouldn't have replied if he hadn't said such an odd thing to me, a meaningless thing really. He said: 'You can go in too deep, you know, like Luchenne did.' I thought he meant the Delta. And then he added: 'I doubt very much if Luchenne ever owned another horse, except perhaps in a dream.'

That was all – and it was enough to hook me. I am a scientist, after all, and I can't accept disorder except on my own terms. I felt compelled to ask him who Luchenne was. He considered me for some time, long enough for me to wonder if he was about to retract back into his box like a suspicious crab. I think he was surprised that I had responded at all. He frowned slightly and said: 'Do you know what you're looking for?'

I asked again: 'Who was Luchenne?' I think our contract must have begun at that moment, that contract between the teller and the told. And contracts can be addictive, can't they? Anyway, our conversation continued, rather cautiously on my part I admit. I cannot remember precisely what was said at that point, except that the conversation was general. After a minute or two it began to drizzle and, with a look that suggested he had suddenly remembered a distant fact, he invited me to enter his box. I was startled and it must have shown. He smiled.

I had never done such a thing before, having been taught like everyone else to respect the privacy and inherent dignity of the less fortunate. It is hard to dismiss a form of manners that the Demcorp has inculcated in us all. Freyn began to slip backwards into his box, holding aside the sackcloth and plastic sheeting so that I could enter at a crouch.

The interior was surprisingly clean and it didn't possess that unnervingly sweet-sour odour that issues from most of the boxes.

And there was light too. Freyn had fashioned an large eternal candle from collected gobbets of wax and an old stone mortar. I looked round in the buttery light and noted the contents of his home. The flooring, as is common in the Delta, was carpet laid on linoleum, with another layer of lino between the underside of the box and the wooden pallet on which the whole thing rested. This keeps the bottom of the boxes remarkably dry, though not entirely protected from the occasional flash floods emanating from the Essex Decon-Recon water processing plant. The internal walls of the box were covered with small, tightly wadded bricks of scrap hessian glued to the cardboard to improve warmth. A thin foam rubber oblong took up the width of the back of the box and was covered in a grey rough-weave blanket.

There was little else. There were certainly no clothes apart from a small woolly mound that suggested a bobble hat and gloves, and perhaps a scarf. There were some small boxes, of course. I say that as if it were obvious; it's only that the recollection is important to me now. I noticed a few small artifacts, or souvenirs – personal items. And there was a special box at the head of the pallet. I couldn't see it clearly but sensed it was important to Freyn; a wooden box, it was, and – though hard to tell in that light – it seemed to have a marquetry pattern on it. I remember thinking it was probably a trick of the light.

Everything in the box seemed both mundane and bizarre; and there was a feeling of separation too. Quite suddenly, I realised I had lost touch with things outside the box. I had been absorbed. I was in Freyn's property – or a property of Freyn, I'm not sure which.

His story, when he began to tell it, was steeped in the usual sounds pertaining to the Delta: the juddering whine of security gunships on patrol; the occasional thud of Riot-Kwel cannisters being dropped into a deemed social lesion zone; the yowl of feral pets and children being cornered or punished. Within Freyn's box these things seemed vague, undifferentiated.

Maybe it was his eternal candle that did the trick. The light that rose out of the grubby wax took away the edges of things.

We take things on trust, don't we? Identification, I mean. Everything is what it seems to be, or needs to be. And in that box, in that wavering light, Freyn's eyes and lips were the focal point.

I will always wonder why I should have been so triggered by Freyn's mention of Luchenne. When he began to tell the story I had, at first, almost no idea what he was talking about. He was describing a time and place which, to all intents and purposes, never existed: a tropical colony called Roraima in the late 1930s. I'd never heard of it. Nevertheless I switched on my recorder, an aged but reliable Duino-Wong TaggaFact Mark II. Habit, the tape; the old lecture notes reflex.

And so Freyn began to ramble, and it never irritated me. There was something circular in the manner of his exposition, something ever returning, glancing lightly but unerringly on the story, as if every unlikely detail had a specific role to play. Freyn's story, which I have presumed to call *Horse Latitudes*, was not delivered seamlessly; its telling veered unchronologically and was broken either by his descents into sleep or by my own necessary absences over a period of almost a month. I have mimicked Freyn's chronological waywardness and I think it's appropriate. I would like to imply that this was a matter of choice, but it was not; it is due solely to my chronic clumsiness with the concept of time in the abstract.

Freyn never turned me away or asked why I kept coming back. He expressed polite puzzlement over my professional doings – 'your dear science, Walter' – and would return to his narrative with very little prompting. He behaved immaculately and treated me with a subtle consideration that quickly put me at my ease.

I can only conclude this prologue by emphasising that I am a scientist who has strayed from his specialism. I have dabbled in subject matter that is difficult for me to grasp. The only mitigation I can offer is that I couldn't help myself; and that, having failed to restrain myself, I have done the best I can. I say 'the best' because, as Freyn later pointed out, I have no sense of history. It's foreign to me; to all of us, I guess, because today, in 2021, only the future occupies our thoughts. Freyn said history was anything remembered that was resonant – that 'exposed the soul', as he put it. And he also told me, though not unkindly: 'The trouble is that you're all fascinated only by change, and the faster the better. But be careful, Walter. If you claim to be a man of experience it may just mean that you have the ability to assimilate developments – *any* development, mark you – rapidly and without question. And if so, you might ask yourself how you developed this ability.'

Morphen's telegram

LUCHENNE lived in the interior of the British colony of Roraima and Freyn would not have met him had it not been for a coincidence. Freyn received a cable; it was on a Tuesday and he remembered the day because Spivey, the managing director of the shipping agency where he worked, was at home recovering from jaundice; and so the fateful telegram was placed in Freyn's right hand by his Roraiman factotum, Augusto. Freyn described this slightest of beginnings – nothing more than a dry touch of paper against his fingers – as 'the accident that has not yet reached its conclusion; a fact of the matter in which the fact and the matter have only a tenuous relationship'.

As for Luchenne, he was an oddment – Freyn's description, not mine. Oddments were not particularly welcome in Roraima's capital, Temhari, though they were acceptable in the interior where the ruling society's hierarchy – its seamless processes of social conjunctions or estrangements – did not operate in any significant way. Luchenne was rarely discussed in the long, low white-painted wooden building originally built by the Dutch, and known under British rule as the Temhari Club. If his name came up it did so either in drunken conversation or during ladies' nights when one of the filigreed wives or daughters wanted to cast acceptably risqué aspersions on the character of one or another of the gentlemen present. It was widely held that the initially well-regarded Luchenne had reverted to a type; that he might have been associated with an obscure fragment misplaced by Darwin – 'a shadowy, withheld monograph almost certainly entitled The Origin of the Faeces', as Freyn put it. There was doubt even about Luchenne's nationality. He was thought at various times to be Belgian or French; it was once rumoured that he was a covert German from Alsace. I know now that he was born in Geneva of French parents who had taken Swiss nationality.

If Luchenne had reverted, so too had the majority of the properly classifiable British, and they had made a characteristically thorough job of it. Drink was the liquid grail served by the elderly 'boys' at the club, typically in a concoction involving straw-coloured rum, sugar, bitters, the juice of limes and a stirrer called a swizzle-stick. A man would drink to forget certain things and to remember certain others – 'to forget', according to Freyn, 'the sound of rain on the tin roofs of the servants' quarters, or the colour of their wife's skin, or the fact that they had little chance of an early return to head office in the City. And they drank to remember the smell of cab interiors, the delightful young woman in accounts who agreed to a meeting in the Kardoma tea rooms in Eastcheap and then failed to keep the appointment, the crumble and slightly abrasive melt of icing on the tongue peculiar to Fullers walnut cake. They drank to imagine that they were, after all, thoughtful about the things that mattered but which, in most cases, were paltry issues.'

Freyn was no different. He drank 'for the most painful and undeniable reason of all, the reason that most of them refused to consider. I drank to remember those who were trying to forget me.' He smiled and raised a scabrous finger. 'Now then, Walter, a little local colour for you. Bartop at the club: solid teak and varnished to shine like russet-coloured sheet ice – quite feasible to slide a shot glass the full length of it without spilling a drop. God, what a raddled history this is going to be!'

Freyn said history was nothing more than a nostalgia for space born out of a horror of home, a 'vagabond dream of the peculiar safety of dying far, far away. We are always in a condition of thronged beginnings and yet we are not satisfied; people want to begin from nothing, from a clean slate. You don't want history or continuums. The appetite is for legends without antecedents, debris that goads us on, arbitrary fabrications that can be used to justify arbitrary actions.'

This is hard to take, though it begins to put a faint marker on Luchenne. And it is Freyn's marker, his fingerprint on the forgotten pages of colonial history. I have checked everything. I have roamed the ROM, surfed the Omniweb, delved into the Dotsilt. And this is how I know that what Freyn said must have happened, more or less. I even have a photographic printout of the quayside at Temhari from a photograph taken in 1938, the very year that the crucial telegram passed from Augusto's hand to his. There are three white people in the background, two of whom cannot be much more than twenty-five. I once asked Freyn if he had any wish to see copies of such photographs. 'Burn them,' he said. 'Burn them. They are not the truth, they are degraded myths and they are contagious and addictive – damned viruses, if you ask me.'

Had Freyn been one of those young men in the quayside photo? Was that him looking slightly away from the camera? I shall never know and I shall always wonder about it.

I like to imagine that the photo was taken soon after Freyn's arrival. He was a remittance man – that was still the operative term in the autumn of 1936. 'Know what that means, Walter?' he asked. 'Means a person who, despite a respectable and more than comfortable upbringing – a bit of *background* – did not quite come up to scratch. But no matter; he could be shunted off somewhere pukkah and helped with a regular stipend from well-to-do parents or suitably horrified relatives. The stipend, do you see? He who is remitted by land or sea must of course receive a remittance. You're a remittance man too, Walter, if you don't mind me saying so. You all are. You don't know where you're from or where you're going, and you don't know why you do what you do. All you know is that you're getting paid.'

Freyn's parents were well-connected and moneyed. I have a

copy of the title deeds of the capacious home they owned in Beckenham between March 28, 1916 and February 14, 1956. They owned other properties in Kew, which they rented specifically to retired clergymen. They found Freyn – James Noel Penrose Freyn to be precise – a management position at the Temhari offices of Spivey & Co, which was then the second biggest shipping and freight forwarding agency in the world with a head office in Gracechurch Street. Its address in Temhari must have seemed reassuring to new arrivals: it was simply, Regent House, Bay Prospect – 'dominion laced with the promise of a comfortable, passive expectancy', as Freyn put it.

'In any case,' he said, 'a bank draft from father once a month. A small consideration during my period of development.' Freyn asked me if this remark seemed bitter or small. I wasn't sure what he meant. 'It shouldn't seem bitter,' he hastened to add. 'And I have to admit that I left for Roraima quite hopefully. How else could it have been? I had no idea about the terms of my shipment, so to speak, no inkling of their binding nature. I was simply going to another part of the Empire, a part that needed to be assisted because it was poor but had potential.' Freyn began to laugh at this point, laughed until he started to wheeze dreadfully through those often cyanic lips. 'Potential!' He was gasping by now. 'That's the ultimate factor, you know, the killing joke. If you're poor or downtrodden you're allowed to have potential, but the implications of the potential will be carefully obscured. And should you realise the truth despite that, the response will be an even more exquisitely detailed form of repression, one that will create the ultimate horror – complicity.' And then he began to laugh again. 'But I'm safe,' he wheezed, 'yes, yes, I'm safe because I have potential which is contained in a *box*.'

And then he referred to his mother. He looked hard at me as if he had detected something interesting or odd in my expression. He hadn't, of course; I had mistaken the nature of his look of concentration. But he said this: 'I regretted leaving my mother. There is not much to say about it because there is not much to remember and perhaps that is fortunate. I had asked her if it was strictly necessary for me to go to Roraima. She said she knew very little about the particular advantages but was sure there would be many. And then she said, trying to be flippant: "Perhaps one day when you are older you will explain everything to me." I have often thought about that remark. One remembers it again and again. One worries at it. The passage of time has not helped.'

I too have thought about his mother's remark. Was Freyn finally, in that God-forsaken box in the Delta, explaining everything to me; telling me what he might have told his mother, who died two years after he sailed from Roraima on the *Manahatta* with Luchenne's horses?

Freyn's reference to his mother was a typical digression, which he called, in yet another digression, 'oxbow lakes of reminiscence left behind by new currents and hungry erosions'. I suppose he was trying to make light of the personal erosions of age. 'One doesn't bump up hard against things any more, Walter, and one treats words like a child smudges around with poster paint,' he said. 'Sometimes I wonder if I'm not just part of this mouldy box – an expression of it, you might say. You're interested in mouldy things, Walter, and I suspect that's what you find interesting in me. You and your little spatula and all those plastic phials, eh?'

But I'm digressing too. Back to the main point – the telegram. His factotum Augusto waited quietly while Freyn read the message. It said:

Re Luchenne mare and yearling. Please collect from Luchenne and ship aboard SS Manahatta accompanied. Provisional sailing date July 2 Temhari. As previously arranged deliver in cash sum of dollars two thousand only to Luchenne in situ. Cash wired to Standard Chartered Temhari in favour of quote Luchenne, care of Spivey & Co unquote. Your pre-delivery part commission to be wired upon confirmation that animals have been loaded. Take this message as final instructions and cable me of your receipt of them. Yours etc Morphen.

I have never seen a cable. I associate them with the kind of dramas shown on the Fictiviteez channel. Even the word *docks* sounds strange. I can just about imagine dotted lines etched precisely on a ceramic globe in a nineteenth-century Liverpool magnate's office. From there it is a small jump to think of a similar globe in Morphen's office in New Orleans in the 1930s. It would have been a large, ostentatious globe, I'm sure, perhaps lit from within; the land masses in shades of brown denoting highlands and lowlands, small violet patches indicating notable elevations, green for savannahs and forests. And all of it glowing, warm to the touch. A world at Morphen's fingertips: a slight prod from them and the sphere would revolve soundlessly.

Freyn recalled the telegram's ink, faint and as grey as bone. 'One imagines, usually wrongly, that important developments will present themselves clearly,' he mused. 'Clearly, and with sharply defined outlines. You're a scientist. You're trained to look for or fabricate ideas with a nicely whetted cutting edge. Temporary answers to imagined questions, eh? Questions of the moment, as it were.'

It's true. I wish the delivery of Freyn's story could be as cut and dried as the wording of Morphen's cable. My tapes have spooled his words into tight DAT coils, but they remain a maze. I could leap over the hedging and strike for the centre, but what meaning could the centre have in those circumstances? Freyn has had an effect on me.

At the end of our first session – I was just about to switch off the recorder – there was an impact nearby, an explosion of the muffled kind that is worrying: experience warns of either tear gas or short duration immobilising neuro-toxins, the latter used to prepare sections of the Delta for thorough, unimpeded searches. Freyn's reaction was interesting. He merely smiled and asked in a mild tone: 'Was that a Riot-Kwel tinny, do you think? I rather hope not. They leave one nauseous for hours. But you will have noticed that I've placed the box so that its entrance faces away from the prevailing wind. No point in complicating one's life needlessly, I always say . . . not that I say anything *at all* very often. This isn't exactly a dappled veranda on Main Street, Temhari, in 1938, is it? And if you had known me then – I was, what, in my late twenties? – I wonder what your opinion of me would have been?'

I had no clear opinion of Freyn early on. He was one of our nation's internal diaspora and as far as he was concerned I might as well have been a vaguely acceptable form of visiting dignitary, just another explorer professing objectivity and pretending that he did not really hope to hit paydirt.

A word about Freyn's voice and verbal manner. Though it had the usual chemical rasp typical of Delta degradees, his words flowed seamlessly. He told me that he rarely had cause to speak at all and my presence – 'my hazardous curiosity' as he put it – had simply released his memories in detail. I wondered about that and asked if he had been inert when I met him. 'How can you *not* remember such things?' I asked. 'There are many ways to exist,' he replied. 'I am old and therefore in a state of concentration.'

For the record, his first taped words to me were: 'You say your name is Walter Cowley and you want to know about Luchenne? Well, the point is, Luchenne lived in the interior. You have to go in before you can come out, and when you're out you may forget where you came from in the first place, which can make things difficult. In any case, this is the story of a journey. Consider yourself in the departure lounge, with a return ticket, of course. My only regret –' and here I remember that he glanced round his box in an amused way '– yes, my only regret is that you must travel economy class.' He meant his box, which he also referred to from time to time, and jokingly, as his 'estaminet' or 'station of the damned'. I have no idea what he was on about.

Temhari

IN 1938 Main Street, Temhari, was formed of two broad lanes divided by a narrow canal from the lots that contained the government buildings, the separate precincts of the law courts and the Anglican cathedral (a vast white-painted pitch pine structure which Freyn called 'the whale'). Main Street ran dead straight for three-quarters of a mile until it met the sea wall, passing on the way the Temhari Club, the Masonic Lodge and the palatial residences of the key inhabitants. Those who were extremely poor were kept away from Main Street during the day, but according to Freyn could be glimpsed at night fishing in the canal or gathered on the grey sand beyond the sea wall – though never on the Main Street side which was kept clear of those of notably decrepit or otherwise alarming appearance.

These outcasts could only guess at the life of those who lived behind the twelve-paned Georgian-styled sash windows, the raised balconies, the top-hung shutters constructed in such a way that oblongs of ice – once shipped in sheaves of insulating hay from America – could be slotted into a holder to cool incoming air. On hot still nights in the late nineteenth century they dripped water from the Great Lakes on to the bronze leaves of ornamental cannas and the occasional venomous snake.

The rest of the town's buildings cluttered the alluvium behind the sea wall, then followed the polders lining the Takarani river, whose headwaters had their origin four hundred miles inland,

and whose writhing path through savannah and forest passed forty miles to the west of Luchenne's property.

In the poorer sections of Temhari the whitewashed wooden structures were seared grey by the sun. According to Freyn, their tin roofs 'trembled and ticked with contraction or clattered like those damned festival timbales with heat expansion or an incessance of fat, warm raindrops. Quite a sight from Robert Belchamp's Tiger Moth when you were racketing and side-slipping along at twelve hundred feet.

'From that bloody old crate Temhari looked like nothing more than a tidy gathering of molars crowned with the glints of silvery dental fillings. The pale orange of the laterite earth was like inflamed gum. And there would be Bob Belchamp's hand pointing down as he dropped the wing slightly to reveal the main government buildings and the rest of the establishment. From above, the three government buildings appeared to be shaped, in turn, like an H, an E and an L. Belchamp used to take young ladies up and tell them that Temhari was sheer hell. Passed for wit in those days. The recipients of this wind-whipped drollery would no doubt have smiled back gaily into the prop wash. That's what young ladies did when a man demonstrated both certainty and fatuousness simultaneously. And you can be assured that those bright young smiles were as righteous as they were delightful.'

Temhari's commercial success depended upon Roraima's natural resources and its port, such as it was. According to records it was rather shallow. It was only after the war that a deeper navigation channel to the open sea, which the locals called 'the bluecoat', was cut through the bar and maintained. But by then things had changed in Roraima. A shift to the left in its post-independence politics in 1959 ensured that its inherently valuable resources – gold, diamonds, dense hardwoods, rice and sugar – were suddenly, and strangely, subject to underfunding by international agencies and the negative effects of foreign cartels.

The photograph I mentioned earlier showing the three white men on the quay gives some idea of the sturdy functionality of the port. Freyn remembered the details with gusto. He recalled the solid greenheart pilings and decking, which were virtually indestructible. 'Received the arrival of foreign matter with impunity. Saw a crated Bechstein piano dropped on it once. Bounced. The thing actually *bounced*. Mind you, pianos were rare arrivals. The planking more often felt the tread of uncertain feet – the Morse tip-tap of their uncertain exile, or the dockers' naked soles, as hard and shiny as Bakelite. The decking flexed under the weight of dumped cargo – huge grey blocks and boules of raw latex, sacks of rice and sugar, strongboxes accompanied by blustering men. It even tasted Meddlycot's blood the time he ran amok. More cargo left than came in, of course. You might say it was an example of the Empire's empirical.'

Meddlycot and Belchamp were not significant characters. According to the records, the former left the colony having experienced difficult local circumstances and it can't be ascertained if this was the accepted *lingua obscura* for having behaved in a way that threatened the reputation of the British, or whether it simply meant that Meddlycot had been unable to cope with the physical conditions. The central register of births, marriages, divorce rates and deaths shows that he died in a property in Esher in 1987. As for Belchamp, he returned to England in 1940 and, having joined a paratroop regiment, died during a training jump when his chute candled. I only mention these details because of Freyn's insistence that 'it is the details on the periphery that matter the most, like the cross-hatching of a shadow which emphasises areas of light'.

That thick planking felt Freyn's own weight and Luchenne's; and it must have been marked with the sharp-edged imprint of those presumably well-shod horses. They would have been small marks, I imagine, little broken arcs scuffed randomly into the dense wood as they capered in the salt breeze.

I have six RecceSat photos dated May 13, 2001 which show the remains of Temhari's docks in useful detail. The wharf has gone, its planked surface no longer polished by the magnesium glare of sunlight at midday, its wooden knees and elbows jammed and rooted into the sand and black silt. All that shows is an abstraction of broken spars and sea-worn piles rising from jade water.

'I stepped ashore in 1936,' Freyn recalled. 'For one fleeting, unconsidered moment I had one foot on land, the other connected to the vague movement of the sea.' And he added with some relish: 'One was balanced on the cusp of an ambiguity. A second later, I stepped off the slightly moving gangway and had two thoughts. First, that I had arrived; second, that I hoped my life could become something firm and decisive. I should have known better. I was nothing more than a well-spoken second lead in one of dozens of commercial productions that had played to packed houses in the City of London for more than a century.'

Freyn's baggage was still being landed when he heard a voice say: 'I trust you're fit, Mr Freyn.' He turned and saw a short, slightly bow-legged man wearing a decrepit white linen suit yellowing at the lapels and cuffs. This was Pritkin, the ageing senior administrative clerk at Spivey & Co. He wore braided leather sandals and told Freyn: 'Everything you achieve is through your own efforts. You inherit nothing.' Indicating his considerable belly (he failed to survive a radical colectomy at King's College Hospital, London, in 1957) Pritkin added: 'It is a case of the survival of the bulkiest. Eat well, that's the thing.'

The extent of Freyn's recall of the senior clerk was impressive: 'After saying that, Pritkin's lips stretched in something reminiscent of a smile, revealing gold-capped teeth and one notably fine incisor clasped by a denture-clip. I watched to see if the incisor might catch on the lower lip. It didn't and I reached out to shake his hand. He studied my hand for a few seconds, clicked his heels together at an odd angle and then grasped it. "Quite so," he said, "the particulars are adhered to." '

It was also at that moment – Freyn insisted quite vehemently that it was precisely then – that he first sensed an impending weightlessness, 'that uncertain feeling, that fracture line between meaning and purpose that so quickly became my second shadow.

It still is and I will always wonder about that moment. That distant landfall is like an old rosary in my mind: I fret at the well-worn details compulsively to preserve them. I can't afford to forget. I keep the beads polished so that I can rely on them to slip through my mind familiarly and without hitch. Where was I? Yes, Pritkin. He asked me to follow him; said we hadn't far to go.'

Freyn paused and massaged the skin between his eyebrows. 'Far? Of course it was far to go. All journeys are the same journey and they are all long because the smallest movement casts an infinite shadow. And eternity, as that dear man Augusto pointed out so presciently just before a termite-hollowed floorboard in my office gave way under him, be not the same as slave living.'

And did Freyn still live like a slave, hunched up in his carefully-tended box in the Delta, metamorphosed into a febrile echo of Augusto? If so, he gave no obvious sign and ensured – I re-quote Pritkin – that the particulars were adhered to. For example, at the end of our second session, Freyn apologised for the foam cushion I was perched on. 'I hope the sponge is not over-moist,' he said. 'I find it helps to turn it over every half an hour or so. Evaporation, do you see?' I demurred. 'Ah, kind of you,' he said quickly, 'but you're being too polite. At least I think you are; I'm unsure because politeness is not common coin in the Delta. Yes, please do, Walter. That's it, just turn it over. A fundamental improvement, I trust.'

Freyn's abrupt changes of direction were confusing at first. The way he spoke, his choice of words, his replacement of an immediate past with an equally immediate present took some getting used to. The past, of course, is rarely discussed now and the present is naturally subject to prescriptions. The future is our accepted tense, yet here was somebody I barely knew plunging me in and out of a dead realm like a compulsive baptist. I got used to the water in the end.

Freyn's marginalisation

AS far as its masters were concerned Temhari was a civilised place, not to the extent of a Delhi or a Hong Kong, but it was nevertheless an outpost subject to a shared degree of order which was enough to guarantee Freyn's eventual shunning. It was a process achieved with thoroughness and which, by a well-tested formula of manners, cast the disregarded into an exile of impeccable politesse.

It seems that Freyn behaved in a way that was regarded as normal, at least to begin with. I must now quote him directly, though some of his references are obscure to me. Let's just say that I offer his more anachronistic remarks in the name of historical verisimilitude (one of his words, of course), even though, as a scientist, it is my instinct to reinterpret any hypothesis.

This is how Freyn set the scene for his estrangement. 'It was all right to overdo the rum swizzles now and then and make a thoroughly temporary BF of yourself, provided you remembered to thank your hosts for a wonderful evening and encouraged others to make fun of you,' he said. 'And preferably before you vomited over the shoes of the houseboy helping you to your transport. It was also quite acceptable to make love to another man's wife as long as he had already been marked down as a duffer or a cad of some sort. Or even to take a local mistress on a strictly nine to five basis – that's p.m. to a.m. of course. All very civilised, as I say. There was no difference in this respect between Temhari and Cadogan Place.'

The mention of Cadogan Place threw me momentarily because I happened to recall that it was once a residential bastion of a social class that was referred to as the *haute bourgeoisie* – though it's hard to think of it in that light since the security forces' limited-radius toxic strike during the designer fashion hostage crises of 2006.

Freyn tapped his knee and said: 'But you know what you must never do, Walter? Never let them see doubt in your face. I mean *doubt*, d'you see? Not doubt about whether your collar stud is showing or whether you should or should not do something. No, no, quite irrelevant, all that. One could do almost anything dubious if one just barrelled along in a certain manner. But reveal to them that you doubted them as a whole, that you thought the whole kit and caboodle was rotten – that was quite a different matter. You were branded as an *agent provocateur*; you were no longer worthy of the fullest trust and therefore no longer in the circle. Well, one day I was one of the elect, the next, dropped from the first team. Now, they couldn't remove my membership of the club because I hadn't committed fraud or a crime of violence. Therefore any attempt to cast me out would have inferred that the mistake in originally accepting me had been due to poor judgement on their part. I remained a person there. I could come and go; but most of the important invitations dried up, as did committee work. Not all of it, though – that would have been uncivilised, indiscreet. You look puzzled, Walter. Yes, well, fair enough. But you see, being placed beyond an invisible pale was the method; if it is invisible you're never in a position to dispute it, are you? If you attempt to do so you merely make yourself more ridiculous.'

Freyn was therefore twice remitted, the second time during the summer of 1937. The records of the Temhari Club show that his membership was discontinued on April 7, 1939, almost ten months after his departure on the *Manahatta*, and formally revoked *in absentia* a month later.

The shunning had followed a public argument between Freyn and his mistress, a local girl in her early twenties – a 'blazing row' as he put it, outside a bar in the port quarter. During the contretemps Freyn slapped the girl, Eglantine Marris, at precisely the moment that the governor's secretary, Charles Melhuish, passed in his official car accompanied by a new arrival, the daughter of an industrialist called Seddon. That was at about eight in the evening. 'By the time I had tidied up and put in my usual appearance at the club for a concluding drink or two it was all over for me. I was nominally in – and absolutely out.'

Freyn experienced a difficult night. 'Oh, yes, everybody spoke to me, provided I spoke to them first. All very civil, all very brief, nothing mentioned. But I knew something was up and it could only have been Melhuish's witnessing of that stupid argument. Now, a little fact, a bit of flesh: did you know that Melhuish went on to become the poodle of an African despot in 1956?'

I didn't, but it didn't take me long to get the data. The entry in the insurrection section of the BiogROMa says this:

Melhuish, Charles James Mayfield, b Thame, Oxon, 1894; d Rhodesia 1974; Foreign Office; senior attachments in Trinidad, Ghana and Roraima (pro-Governorship, 1939–40); attached to War Office as Cabinet Adviser (Strategic, Caribbean sector) between 1940–46; resigned 1952; represented British business interests in African countries; personal adviser to Chief Kwabena Wilson-White, leader of the SIMA faction of the Mid African Liberation Movement (*see* Political cells, 20th century; Funding, international; Infiltrators, proxy, on behalf of external powers); fatally wounded in mortar attack on SIMA headquarters, Kotoka, 1974.

Freyn imagined that the sudden coldness to him at official functions was a punishment which would be rescinded after a time; a punitive dissociation which would be removed as discreetly as it had been applied, allowing him, as he put it, to be let back into the fold. This expression was new to me. It refers to a confining fence into which sheep or other farm animals are driven and penned for a period. It seems apt in view of the social methodology employed by the pre-war British. The expression bears no etymological relationship to a modern equivalent, focaling, which refers not to the gathering of farm animals but to low-cost, workforce-rich industrial zones.

The point about his behaviour in the port section was not that he had slapped the girl, but that he had done so publicly in full view of local, non-British people. He had demonstrated that there might be a reason for them to think of the British as not worthy of aspiring to or respecting. And there was an extra factor at play. There were Dutch in Roraima, particularly in Temhari, and they had been present in Roraima for more than two centuries. The country had been a Dutch colony before the British forced them to accede control. By the end of the nineteenth century their presence was tolerated but amounted to little more than a well-set trading community, mainly in the form of better-class shopkeepers. The blacks despised them because they were white but plainly inferior socially and financially to the British, and because they had usurped the blacks (and their women in particular) in the smaller commerce of selling basic food and goods to the workers on the sugar and rice estates. They were also judged to be far less refined than the British. Freyn had therefore behaved in a way that was 'merely Dutch', as he put it.

At first, Freyn carried on as if nothing significant had happened. 'I kept writing to my mother and father. Fortnightly letters; two for every one of theirs, which my father would have regarded as a minor, but in some way decently accountable return on his little investment in the devolution of his son. My mother would send the occasional extra note under separate cover. They were always brief and apparently signed by both of them, but I knew they had not been. I told them nothing of my interesting new social position. I read and re-read their letters, trying to detect any remark that might have signalled that they knew. Nothing, thank goodness.'

And so life went on. Again, I leave you to Freyn's description, this time in a demonstration of what I heard referred to once or twice at my Midlands satellite campus as the 'impressionistic' mode.

'July and August were bad months in Temhari, ninety in the shade most days and as humid as fever. Intense rainfalls, lasting two minutes or two hours, sometimes a whole day or night. Local girls cycling to work down Main Street, slicing through the puddles. The greensward between the carriageways glowing in the peculiar ochre light just after a deluge.'

Freyn paused, distracted by something outside the box. 'Pull back the curtain, would you? Yes, right open, just for a moment. All right, let it down again. Thought as much. Notice that fellow going past, did you? It's a funny thing. In the Delta there are certain things one has learned to take notice of. If you hear running feet you may ignore them nine times out of ten: they will either belong to children or to some villain running away from the scene of a crime. If you hear shuffling it's merely the usual to-ing and fro-ing. But if the footsteps are slow and deliberate, with pauses, you can assume either the approach of an undercover patrol or a rob-and-run. The fellow who just passed might have been the latter and I asked you to lift the curtain so that he could see there were two of us. They avoid pairs if possible.

'Mind you, I do have something – you might call it a discouraging item. Allow me to . . . yes, here it is. Oh, yes, please do. It was called a cutlass in Roraima, but they are more usually known as machetes. Touch the edge of the blade by all means, but do it carefully. At my age I would only have one chance to inflict disabling damage if attacked and, as you see, the cutting edge is very fine indeed. It was bought in Suares General Goods three days before I set out to collect the horses from Luchenne. I had no idea how to use it and my palms bled. After which – well, let's just say I know how to use it.

'Nobody crept around in Temhari; the sound of footsteps rarely advertised a threat. No, it was motors and carriages for the Brits and the better-off Portuguese and East Indians, and shanks's pony for the rest. The successful Indians – they were usually lawyers or doctors or middlemen traders – ran Fords and Austins. The Dutch, too, though they would have preferred to run Benz's. And I can include some of the freelance miners, though their crazed largesse was based on sudden and extraordinary wealth one month and burnt-out poverty, gambling, the clap, scrounging and self-excoriating violence the next. Very few of the big gold or diamond strikes left permanently wealthy men behind. But some of these itinerant miners – pork knockers, they were called – managed to keep their heads and accumulate sizeable capital. It was in the goldfields south of the Kimbala plateau that I ran into Wintle. I thought little of it at the time. This was on the way to Luchenne's place.'

Freyn paused and scratched distractedly at his cheek. This, I later learned, was a sure sign of tiredness. 'I hope I'm not wandering,' he continued. 'Scientists don't, do they? Wander, I mean. I imagine you're always well prepared. I certainly wasn't. Spivey was ill with fever and I had been given only the minimum of advice from others as far as my trip into the interior was concerned. I wonder if Spivey knew Morphen? Spivey'd been manager in Havana before his posting to Temhari; might've known Morphen from then. New Orleans is not so far from Cuba, is it?

'Sorry. Let's see. I mentioned Suares. Oh, incidentally, I must thank you again for the long socks. They are very thick indeed, aren't they? Quite ideal. If one is able to retain a layer of warm air between the foot and the interior lining of the boot it facilitates both ventilation and warming. I wear over-large boots as a matter of course and these stockings suit them to a T. I'm really most grateful to you, Walter.' Freyn was particularly enthusiastic about the double-knitted soles. He fingered the wool and murmured: 'Shameless luxury!' Then he looked up brightly. 'Now we have something absolutely in common, Walter – socks.'

I suggested he put them on but at this he looked at first defensive, then amused. 'Have you ever seen extremely old feet,

Walter? Very, *very* old feet of the type to be found in the Delta? It's a funny thing: the rest of my body is somehow expectable, if I can put it like that. You would expect it to be scrawny, and it is; and pale, pale as the base of a freshly-pulled spring onion. There is also a certain amount of grime, as ingrained as a tattoo, which will accompany me to my hereafter at the burning ghats. And then there are my feet. It's not what you think: I keep them as clean as I can. But age does terrible things to feet. It makes them inexpressive. The functional shape changes into a non-shape. The toes look horribly useless, almost leprous. One thinks of these necessary things.'

The last passage is not relevant but I've included it for a personal reason. I remember that after that particular session with Freyn I found myself plagued by his last remark about thinking only of 'necessary things'; that, and another thought which arose quite spontaneously and whose image remains with me: that the lichens on Freyn's box had the same relation to the box as the box had to the Delta, and that the British had had to Roraima.

No, I've been hasty. Nothing could be that simple. I have succumbed to the innocence of Freyn's throw-away line and tainted it. I'm sure there's something missing or misunderstood in my deduction.

Weightlessness

A FEW days later, in one long session, Freyn covered a great deal of ground which I was not able to 'tidy' as I might have wished. Maybe it's better that way.

I had pressed Freyn to tell me more about his 'fall'. For that is what it was: he called it 'a fall from a false pedestal'. He dealt with my enquiries deftly. He knew that the reasons for his initial degradation were not simple and could not be reduced to tidy links in a neat chain of causes and effects. I think he must have detected my interest in the Water Street incident, the slapping of the girl; detected it and sort of played out his line. He was shrewd and, as you will have gathered by now, a bit playful. He meandered but he knew he had a story to tell and knew that I, not he, was the fish being played.

I naturally wanted to know how he had reacted to his estrangement within the colony. 'Well,' he said, 'I became a little scruffy. Never guess it, would you? Wouldn't cross your mind, sitting here now in my dressing room, eh? Not badly scruffy, of course. Just rather careless about having my things washed and pressed to the pluperfect standards which were common among us — us, as in aliens, Walter. And I had no excuse to be scruffy, actually. Laundry didn't cost more than a couple of shillings a week and it was always done beautifully. But I lost interest, d'you see? Collars lost their meaning. Rucked up a bit at the tips? So what! I was suffering from the sartorial insouciance that is the

hallmark of the very aristocratic or the completely inconsequential. And pale linen . . . everything shows, a grease spot on
the lapel, a smudge of laterite. The word gets round.'

Freyn's condition was noticed quite rapidly. He recalled
hearing his secretary giggle as he walked through his outer
office a few weeks after the Water Street business. 'I glanced at
her to see what had amused her so early in the day,' he said. 'She
glanced up and excused herself. "Pardon, Mr Freyn," she said,
"your collar be turning up like a bird wing." ' Freyn smiled
wistfully. 'And there was Augusto, rather pointedly volunteering
to take my shoes down to Tack Spitim Mabura's cobbling stall at
the corner of Acacia and Flamboyant. Or raising the subject of
laundry in a roundabout way and mentioning that he knew of a
woman who was said to have legendary skills with Wright's
soap. "She so good," he said, "they others tryin put dye in the
water butt." '

Freyn was at pains to point out that his physical condition
had not been a matter of choice. 'I didn't elect scruffiness,' he
said primly. 'I wasn't even aware of it. It didn't register in the
slightest. Yet there must have been some sort of decision on my
part, however obscure. If you've taken care with your appearance
for the best part of thirty years, it can't be accidental if you stop
doing it.'

I suggested that his scruffiness had been a form of protest,
which amused him considerably. 'Well, it might have been,' he
said. 'But it could also have been a case of role playing. In a
structured society, the neo-outcast must quickly learn how to
look and behave like an outcast; he must make it easy on the rest
by differentiating himself with all speed, if not God speed.' Freyn
was again caught up in a bout of the emphysemic gagging that
passed for his laughter. 'My God – *protest*? The word protest was
only ever used in two situations – in jest, or in a business
transaction. As in: "We must protest in the strongest possible
terms to the continued delay in the delivery of the contracted
consignments." Or: "Really, my dear, I must protest at your
description of George as a layabout on the grounds that he lacks

the imagination to be such a thing." But one never protested at one's situation, not in a wide context.' Freyn paused and then added: 'If the shipment of Luchenne's horses had been delayed . . . if only I had received a letter from Morphen protesting at the delayed shipment.'

He paused to scratch the back of his hands. I waited, unsure whether or not to prompt him. And then, still looking down at the rucks of dry skin, he continued. 'To be British among the British was to be essentially passive,' he murmured. 'So my protest, if you want to call it that, was entirely suitable.

'Scruffiness did very well in my case because it conveniently confirmed their worst fears about me. Imagine: from acceptance to worst fears in the space of a month or so. I used the club rather less, naturally. For Mordecai's sake – Mordecai, the barman. I didn't want to embarrass him, get him ticked off for chatting too readily to a dishevelled member. Retained my membership, of course. The club remained the carotid artery of existence in Temhari, even if you weren't quite there – even if you were a weightless person, a ghost, an eccentric.

I wasn't sure what Freyn meant. 'Eccentric?' he said. 'Let me tell you that that is the most complete diminution that can be inflicted. It does not necessarily mean that somebody is a character. It means that they are considered fundamentally useless – or it did in the 1930s.'

Freyn took to wandering the streets at night. He would stop for a drink at two or three favoured rum shops in the poorer parts of Temhari. 'Let's see. There was the Inn Famous on Blantyre Avenue; one had to be alert there because it was frequented by a ropemaker who wore spectacles without lenses who threw bottles around now and then. And there was the Just One Only near da Rosa's timber sheds, and the Sweet Rain between the botanical gardens and Madame Jopahl's place. Always stopped at the Sweet Rain last. And then, as often as not, I'd nip back to my place and drag Eglantine out for a late supper at one of the little restaurants in Camptown – eaties, that's what the locals called them.'

Freyn looked up, assessing me carefully. I know now that his gaze must have contained an element of wryness, as if he knew I couldn't possibly grasp the nature of his meaning. 'Out for a late supper, as I said, under cover of darkness. The air a little softer, tin roofs milky in the moonlight – ah, the preferred memory, Walter! – and having to duck under some low rickety balcony or roof overhang if a sudden downpour clattered out of nowhere. Frogs muttering in the ditches; the unmistakable, lisping *ssshuth* of a snake moving away in the long grass at the corner of one of the allotments along Destiny Street.'

Freyn's tone changed again, becoming more matter of fact. 'Perhaps one's taste for unattached assimilation began there, in those shadows with Eglantine, or in the ochre lamplight of the rum shops. I wonder what Luchenne's diagnosis might have been? Perhaps it was the start of what he called "the crucial surrender". What do you think? Have I come out of the saloon with my hands up? No, the real question is: do you know what you're surrendering to? Don't answer that, Walter – trick question! I know the answer now, but I didn't then. And neither, in retrospect, did Luchenne. He put everything into the release of one arrow, only to have the arrow release him.'

Freyn mimed the motions of an archer: left arm straight out and braced; a two-fingered pull-back on an imaginary string; a rather convincing sighting down the arrow shaft. He recomposed himself, setting his hands on his knees. 'Anyway,' he continued, 'once I realised I was scruffy, things simplified. I might even say that my life improved. The phantom guy-ropes around my ankles didn't feel so tight. Nobody gives a second look to a soiled fiver, do they? Anyway, after a couple of months of increasing dowdiness, they barely looked up when I stumbled into the Inn Famous or wherever it was. And when I took Eglantine to the Ritzy for supper, it was always: "You starvin again for prawns. Do they English eat nothin but?"

'Don't imagine that I was happy. I wasn't. Things became a bit less fraught, that's all. And in the streets at night things seemed less substantial. Darkness can be a true friend, Walter.

I could look at things without suffering their full weight and confusion – the train of connections that turns an unimportant, momentarily glimpsed object into an accelerating rush of associations. Almost physically choking at times, those whirlpools of history and information.'

I asked Freyn to give me an example. His response was interesting. At first – it was only a flicker – he was taken aback. And then he suddenly looked pleased, like a boy given a present. 'An example?' he repeated slowly. 'Right, here's one. I remember once catching sight of a rusty nailhead. I think it was on a bench in Barbuta Street. No, it was at the docks. A rusty nail sticking out of the corner of a crate. Within seconds, and in broad daylight, I found myself caught up in a maelstrom of associations: sweatshops, bacilli, dried blood – God knows what else. Shadows in the cave, eh? Far too simple an idea, that; misleading. Doesn't allow for information, does it? Useless information, I mean. No, I wasn't living in Plato's cave and shadows weren't the issue. The problem isn't shadows, Walter – it's too much damned ersatz *light*.'

Freyn became known as the Ghost of Main Street. One evening Eglantine asked him if he believed in wraiths. Freyn demurred and Eglantine insisted that ghosts existed because she knew one. Freyn asked the identity of the ghost and she replied: 'Only be *you*, thass all!' Freyn chortled at the memory. 'She was thrilled to put one over on me, to know something I didn't. It seems that somebody at her place of work had spotted me out wandering one night.

'So all of a sudden I was the ghost, the pale figure seen passing quietly through the layered shadows. And particularly in the botanical gardens. Got to know the watchman quite well. He let me wander, as long as it was in the western half of the gardens, well away from the manager's lodge, which was equipped with two nervous Kerry blue terriers with those stubby, tumescent tails.

'The watchman was called Vibert and he would insist that I take one of his walking sticks as proof against snakes. "Be tappin it down as you go along, lettin everythin know you comin. They be happy so long as they don't be surprised." And so I would stroll by the lily beds tapping my stick down every couple of steps, skirting the soft halos of light from the lamp posts. Very ornate, those lamps; tulip-shaped glass bowls clasped in wrought iron worked to look like vines. Made by Ormerod and Isaac of Bow – said so on the base of each standard.'

Freyn liked the gardens at night because they were deserted and quiet. He could look south and see the well-lit heart of Temhari: the illuminated face of the clock tower, the topee-shaped cupola of the Occidental Bank, the faint flicker of amber fairy lights from the eaves of the assembly rooms and the acute silhouette of St John's cathedral whose white weather-boarding produced precise shadow lines on moonlit nights.

'It was easy to imagine, standing there like some blind innocent among the cardiocrinums and yuccas, that one had a choice – to remain in the Garden of Eden or elect civilisation. Leaning on Vibert's old stick, I naturally chose Eden – and then tapped my way back to his hut like a blind man to wish him good night. He was charming, you know, and solicitous. He invariably asked if I had by chance noticed a certain plant. "You be seein the new plumbago? Lookin very fine this night." He turned a blind eye when I filched the occasional bloom for Eglantine. She liked gardenias. She would fill one of my tea cups with water and carefully lay the bloom into it. Within minutes, my rooms would be sickly sweet with its scent. She claimed it discouraged bats.'

Freyn raised a finger. 'Now here's something amusing for you, Walter. Those same botanical gardens were the scene of a coup attempt in 1963. After independence the Roraima Progressive Cooperative Party built a presidential palace almost opposite the main gate to the gardens, not more than a furlong from the manager's lodge. The palace lay, in effect, between the gardens and the cricket ground. A fabulous building too; what the Americans call carpenter's gothic, with pilasters and carved classical motifs thrown in for good measure – Demosthenes chewing the fat with Daniel Boone, as it were.

'Well, the insurgents, funded by a syphilitic central American businessman, came ashore in six rubber assault craft. They possessed three mortars, three Bren guns, self-loading rifles and a box of grenades. Two of the squads wore plain clothes and loaded their stuff on to a barrow which sympathisers had hidden in reeds near New Hove Sands. They then toddled off towards the headquarters of the government's Golden Dawn radio station with their synchronised matt green Rolex watches ticking towards the go-point or whatever it's called. One's knowledge of terrorism is based mainly on *Time* magazine's editing protocols.

'At any rate, the other four sections overpowered the brace of guards in the gardens and set up their mortars on admirably flat ground behind the lily beds. The mortars' positions had been precisely marked out by accomplices, using twigs jammed into the ground. The direction and distance to the palace had also been established in advance with large-scale Ordnance Survey maps.

'The Brens and riflemen moved forward to the edge of the palace grounds – three groups in all, in a pincer, all set in less than an hour. Three mortar shells were dropped into the tubes; three curt *pungs* as the shells hurtled upwards; three agreeably loud explosions as they landed, about a hundred yards apart and nowhere near the palace. The first salvo left one of the forward Bren-loaders dead, and confusion ensued. The second salvo's bracketing was even more awry: one shell exploded in the sizeable ornamental lake, concussing a specimen manatee known as Gladly; shrapnel from another mortar round shattered the kitchen window of the garden lodge.

'And it was only then that the commandos realised that the ground on which the mortars were set wasn't quite solid. In fact, as I had learned on my night walks three decades earlier – and with the particular aid of Vibert's walking stick – the ground there was simply a thin crust of lawn which virtually floated on swamp. But there were no baseplates on the mortars. The fools had committed an absurdity. Terrorism only succeeds if the paperwork has been attended to.

'And from one crucial absurdity flowed others. As soon as the first stick of shells had landed, the insurgents were themselves advanced on – but only by an extraordinary chance. An hour earlier, the mother of one of the two coshed guards happened to have cycled to the nearby barracks to harangue him because he was late home. When the duty sergeant failed to reach the soldier by walkie-talkie, two corporals were sent to investigate in a Jeep. Almost simultaneously, a thick pall of acrid, oily smoke was beginning to lift from New Hove Sands – some fishermen had stumbled across the assault dinghies and had decided to burn them to see what sort of flame they produced.

'This was observed and, more important, smelled by two Young Progressive cadets, mere teenagers. They decided that a secret government oil cache had been sabotaged and reported it to the police. Mrs Spango, the irate mother of the senseless guard, and the casual police report about the remains of the dinghies, reached the barracks almost simultaneously and even as the Jeep lurched towards the gardens RPCP troops began to move into various positions around the grounds. They simply waited for the insurgents to reveal themselves.'

Freyn was enjoying recounting the story and I made no attempt to deflect his narrative back to more important issues. 'Paperwork and chance,' he muttered. 'The vital ingredients of revolt.' I found myself wondering if the coup attempt had happened at all, or if he had embellished the truth for my amusement. In fact, he had not. I have checked his account and it is surprisingly accurate, right down to the lack of mortar baseplates and the name Spango. It transpired that the insurgents were rounded up after a brief firefight referred to in the *Roraima Truth* newspaper as a 'glorious battle'. The ignominy of the raiders, known as the Roraima Freedom Collective, was complete. They were manacled and paraded down Main Street the next day, replete in the Arctic camouflage drab which they had selected in preference to tropical battle dress.

The squad that had been sent to storm the government radio station mistakenly overran an illegal Rastafarian broadcasting cell putting out dub music interspersed with the sayings of Haile Selassie. Their attack was accidentally broadcast as it happened and they were arrested minutes later without a fight.

The terrorists' leader was a Miami property developer called Basilio 'Chi-chi' Regardo and he was not with the assault force, preferring to await word in the safety of his lilac-coloured condominium. I managed to source a photograph of Regardo and can offer two remarks: he was pictured wearing pale kid gloves and two-tone footwear; and his smile revealed teeth of varying dimensions and reflective properties. I think Freyn must have seen pictures of Regardo because he too remarked on the man's appearance, noting that 'one had the feeling that he must have been clammily gangrenous everywhere below the collar'.

The RPCP recovered two copies of tape recordings which would have been broadcast over the captured radio station: Regardo's victory message to the oppressed of Roraima. It began with the words: 'Friends, Roraimans, countrymen, I come not to bury the RPCP but to lift up once again the sacred palanquin of your great culture, which has been lost in a wilderness of mediocrity. I, Basilio Regardo, tell you that Roraima will rise again like a palanquin and be carried on high through a rich harvest of trade diversification, profitable land use and exponential growth in overseas support.' The coup attempt made six paragraphs in the *Daily Telegraph*, five in the *Guardian* and gained similar space in the British quality Sunday papers. The tabloid *Daily Mirror* carried a two-paragraph 'funny' headed: 'Carry on, cretins!' In Roraima, the coup attempt ceased to be a subject of conversation within a month and its only tangible result was the development of a new fashion among the moneyed classes: disco clothing based on the cut and patterns of the commandos' Arctic-issue clothing.

'Gardenias,' mused Freyn. 'Very delicate, you know; the petals bruise easily and they don't last long in water. I surprised Eglantine one night at the Ritzy; had a bunch of them delivered to our table in a vase − tin water jug, to be precise. I was particularly cut that night. Old what's her name, old . . . doesn't matter. She popped the jug down and said to Eglantine: "If you be as sweet as they pretties, you be too sweet for this worl." And she was, you know — too sweet for this world. I never met another quite like her. Not that she took any notice of the old woman. The flowers in that tin jug, at that moment, were more important to her than wisdom. She insisted that we eat quickly. She wanted to carry the jug back to my rooms as soon as possible, while the scent of the gardenias was strong.

'I was drunk as usual and insisted we return via Main Street. Her initial horror turned to pleasure as she noticed the amazed, enquiring glances of passers-by and the faces of drivers flicking towards her as their motors trundled past. When, at last, she stepped lightly through the door to my rooms and neatly elbowed it shut, she said: "I must be the only girl carryin a bunch of gardenias down Main Street with an English man." What a progression! Half a bottle of Utrecht gin had addled the sentimental brain that produced the jug of gardenias that had apparently assured Eglantine's place in Temhari's oral history.'

Freyn paused. I wanted him to continue immediately. I had sensed something unravelling in his digression about his walks in the botanical gardens, and again in his recounting of the minor incident involving Eglantine. I looked at him and nodded slowly, trying to egg him on. He looked tired and I wondered if he would excuse himself with his usual elaborate courtesy and ask me to return another day. But then his eyes suddenly narrowed. 'Eglantine would be about a hundred if she were still alive,' he said. There was a tremor in his voice, almost of disbelief. 'I have no idea. I cannot even imagine her at that age. No, there's . . . there is one thing, though: I'm sure her hands would still be graceful; certain of it. Her hands were the last things that I saw of her — saw properly, I mean. I could hardly bear to look at her face. Her eyes were bright and dry and I knew that she would cry only when I had left for good. To look at her eyes at that moment — well, I couldn't manage it for more than a moment. I looked down at her fingers as she handed me a small gift. When

I tried to kiss her she said: "No, it is bad luck. Only when you come back is it good luck."

'And so I left, giving her nothing. I kept the room for her; gave Madame Jopahl three months rent in advance, with instructions to keep an eye on her and pass on five shillings a week. In little buff envelopes with "Eglantine" and a weekly date inscribed on each, the flap stuck down carefully. All very thoughtful and meticulous. No need, though. I was coming back, wasn't I? That was my tawdry arrangement, the deceitful charity of a young Englishman out of his depth.

'Know what I was doing, Walter?' The question surprised me. I replied that I wasn't sure. 'Hedging my bets, Walter. I was doing it carefully and under cover of kindness – and weightlessness, of course, let's not forget that. Why, I was no better than old Tang, who a week or two earlier had waved that filthy old jack of hearts at me with his hooked and palsied hand as the steamer pulled away from the landing, sending me upriver towards my rendezvous with Luchenne.

'Yes, just hedging my bets. Under cover of – did I say kindness? When one was a lush, one preferred to hide in the bushes, so to speak, studying the doings of others from a distance.' I interrupted Freyn to suggest that habitual drinkers tended to prefer noise and people. 'Ah,' he replied quickly, 'but only because those things also provide the distance of immediate distraction. But your bush, your well-established perennial shrub of fantasy, that's the best all-round bet.'

Freyn rolled his shoulders slowly and sighed. 'We get a lot of alcoholic brethren here in the Delta. One has to watch for shattered glass. It's the small shards that cause the problems. I travel about with a little brush. If I see a spray of glass, it's just a quick flick-flick and on I go. You want a brush with nylon bristles rather than natural bristle, incidentally – natural wears out in no time here. It's the surface acids, as you no doubt know. Organic for socks, manmade for soles and bristles, that's the thing.'

I had been right: Freyn was tiring. His speech took on what

I had recognised early on as a trademark tone signifying impending exhaustion; a light, quick tone, the words tripping out almost gaily as he changed the subject again. 'Are you doing any research into mosses, if you don't mind my asking? Algae that thrive on acid solutions? Does that mean they release something into the air that isn't oxygen? I only ask because there's a very odd degradee who passes this way occasionally who wears bells on his cuffs and claims he's of aquatic origin – says he's developing gills, though they look more like rather unpleasantly obsessive mistakes with razors to me.'

He switched the subject back to Roraima. 'Chemicals,' he said decisively. 'The water in Roraima was quite hard. There was a lot of iron in it, must've been all that laterite; gave you diarrhoea when you first arrived.' Freyn smiled. 'It's just occurred to me: in a way you're no different to Wintle, the American. He took samples too. Mind you, you haven't got a hidden motive, have you? You don't scrape and pick for concealed reasons. Expect you're a nine-to-five sort of chap. Mind you, who knows? Nine and five . . . perhaps they're what Augusto would have called criminal numbers. My age, a hundred and tennish I think, might also be a criminal number for all I know. Perhaps the Democratic Corporation which watches over us employs numerologists. They don't miss a trick, Demcorp!'

Freyn rubbed gently at his forehead. 'Haven't touched a drop in a serious way for – oh, must be forty years at least. I don't stand in the bushes any more. I kneel here instead, a grateful host in this cubist Eden. No, no, nonsense, I mean it, Walter. I am truly grateful for your presence.' He yawned and his eyes suddenly looked bleary. 'That red light is showing on your recorder,' he murmured. 'No, it's stopped again.'

He gathered himself, slowly straightening his back and stretching his arms straight up. 'Not sure if that's better or worse. Now then, can I offer you a morsel of Swiss Stylisch? I find myself with a superabundance of this reliable Alpine cheese, which I would like to reduce. And – no, no, don't demur too quickly, often a mistake, that – because I can also offer you a little Algerian port in a crystal glass; let's *pretend* that it's crystal, shall we? I found it fifty years ago in a scree near the permanent basecamp on Kanchenchunga.

'It's an amusing prospect, is it not? Grape fermented by the will of Allah, in a glass imbued with the Zen spirit of a mystic mountain. Beats communion wine hands down, wouldn't you agree? Better infinity than the Trinity, eh? I mean, look where the trinity formed by those mortar supports got Señor Regardo's motley crew. Rule one: know your terrain.'

The prospect of the cheese alarmed me. The new strains of listeria are persistent and can cause significant damage to nerve sheaths. But Freyn's peculiar charm and the empirical proof of his own health prevailed. I think I managed to accept his offer without betraying the effort it took, and he immediately busied himself with the task of serving me. Even in the candlelight I was able to see that his utensils looked clean. And having passed me my helping of cheese and port in the heavy shot glass he looked genuinely pleased. 'Have I given you enough?' he asked. 'You mustn't be polite. Really? Excellent. Please allow me . . .'

Freyn's story took another turn. 'I've just remembered something. Those terrible bothies that I used in Temhari. Out of the way, sweet and sour with the stink of Regal Apostle rum, cracked glazes of dried vomit along the skirting boards. I used to introduce myself as Monsieur Le Remittance. It was rather trying at first because conversation tended to stop when I walked in – they must have thought I was a prying government official, or a desperado. Try ordering a drink in deadly silence in a strange place for the first time and see if you can keep your voice from sounding either cowed or overly brisk! I stuck to the three or four dives that got to know me well enough to ignore me. I'd take a book with me and pretend to read; pass the time of day with the barman or a regular; had a standing joke about being given time off for bad behaviour.

'Which reminds me – just a small point, but you like details, don't you? My money, the remittance, arrived in the third week of every month: London to Liverpool, Liverpool to New York, then to Cuba and Port of Spain and finally Temhari. Money is like Lamb's No. 1 Navy rum – it sloshes around or evaporates, or leaves a stain if you're not careful. Money is sweet and sticky. And I existed as proof of money's essential liquidity.

'I'm sorry to prattle on about this, but you can't have any idea of the effect this arrangement had on me. A remittance is two conflicting things. It is both largesse and condemnation. You might say that I was tethered to a respectable existence by the ghostly braid of regular bank drafts.

'The drafts were drawn up and dispatched by the Holborn branch of the Standard Bank. The envelopes were always addressed by the same typewriter and carried the same typographical flaws every time. The first letter of my surname, the F, always sat slightly lower than it should – top stroke of the F fainter than the rest of the letter; as if its invention, or demise, was in the balance. James Freyn, care of Spivey and Co, Temhari. And just above that, handwritten in a fulsomely cursive application of brown ink, Private and Confidential. As if mere privacy was not enough, as if secrecy was the vital issue. But secrecy from whom, and why?

'When you look at me, you're looking at the remnants of deployed capital, Walter. Just think of the *rhythm* of the process. Didn't Augusto always take the envelope to the bank's scrupulously polished rosewood counter in that musty old building in Rose Street? And didn't he always return an hour or so later with the receipt pincered between thumb and index finger? And, presto, there I was – James Freyn, man of substance – except that the nature of the substance somehow made me insubstantial. My life in Temhari carried no hint of the future and my work made it worse. I was doing something specific and effective in its way, but it had to do with a future that I felt divorced from. Do you know, I envied the burnished callouses on Augusto's hands. They seemed to be – well, *hands*. I would study them surreptitiously and think them quite extraordinary, like accidental extrusions from another physical plane.'

Freyn was losing me again. Then, as usual, he flicked back to solid subject matter when I least expected it. I had begun to suggest that I should come back later in the week when he said: 'When I used Madame Jopahl's so-called coffee shop, I think it was to forget. I would awake next to a girl, a dark, lax shape on the pallet, and sometimes experience an almost physical feeling that that invisible braid of pounds, shillings and pence was utterly taut, about to snap; and that I would be flung outwards, away from everything known. And that there would be a final welter of chaos. One minute, I would be sitting in the Flamingo cinema behind Flamboyant Street watching formations of Busby Berkeley chorus girls opening like flower buds, the next I would find myself among the rat people in Fritz Lang's film, *M*.'

Freyn studied me with a look that seemed to say: you don't really know what I'm talking about, do you? But he persisted anyway. 'Those terrible bars! Saw a few fights. Sudden affairs, flurries of accusations and fists; once a knife, and blood being staunched with a rummy cloth.' He cleared his throat. 'Could've done with a rummy cloth yesterday – right here, outside. Plain clothes chaps surrounded three degradees and there was a vicious little set-to. Two of the degradees were killed immediately with those nasty close-quarter weapons. A stray dum–dum took off the foot of a girl asleep on blankets nearby.' Freyn's cracked lips appeared to form into a smirk. 'You're not plain clothes, are you, Walter? Or forensic? After all, you do possess spatula and plastic bags. I haven't made a fatal verbal slip, have I? Condemned myself to a life –' and he began to chortle phlegmily at this point '– to a life of bondage?'

I laughed with him and said that I would arrest him only after the tape had run out. 'And on what grounds?' he asked, still wheezing alarmingly. I suggested the theft of a glass from holy ground. He began to laugh again, with that unsettling crackling issuing from his lungs, then caught himself. 'Do you know?' he said urgently, 'I think the chief of police must have been in on it.' I was baffled by this side-step but let him go on. 'I'd always pegged Wesson as fundamentally reliable; and there certainly wasn't much significant crime in Roraima. The occasional

44

shooting in the interior, of course, usually over gold or diamonds; but the incidents were hermetic, over and done with quickly and the perpetrators mostly gave themselves up.

'No, the only crime I can recall was the theft of Lady Phail's emerald brooch. I was at the party where it was taken. And I was questioned by Wesson, like everybody else. That's how I met him. Reliable man, as I said; no side to him. Knew what he was about too; worked fast. He immediately let it be known that a local girl was under suspicion. Didn't name her, though, which was the clever bit. He had it put about that she was a cert. But it was a ruse. He had worked through people's statements very carefully and discovered two things: the local girl, the supposed cert, was a cook at the Phails'. But she was also Sir Philip Phail's mistress. Second thing: Phail had snubbed Thurmand, who wanted his son to join Phail's chambers. Wesson had the idea that Thurmand wanted to embarrass the man and that he had duly lifted the brooch. Knowing about the maid, Thurmand would have secreted it somewhere in the kitchen. And according to the various statements, Thurmand had indeed been both upstairs and downstairs during the party. But he had also been seen coming out of the kitchen, which was most unusual.

'And that was that. Exit Thurmand and son aboard the mail packet by discreet mutual agreement. I saw him go myself. It was a surprisingly cold day and he was wearing an overcoat with sleeves that were slightly too long. And just as he stepped on to the deck one of the black dockers piped up with: "Don't fear bout the coat, suh, be plenty of time for growing into." Thurmand heard, all right; hesitated and then stepped away up the ramp, ignoring the laughter.'

Freyn detected my impatience and shrugged in a kind of mute apology. 'Sorry, Walter. There *is* a point to this. Because I wonder if Wesson knew what was going on with Wintle? Knew what he was up to, I mean. Wintle is crucial to my story. Wintle was there, in the forest and on the *Manahatta*. Wesson knew everything that was going on in Roraima. Surely . . . or am I just foolishly looking for proof that there does exist a great, all-seeing narrator in the sky. No! If God existed he would be a plain clothes officer. And if he wanted to imbue faith he'd need a pump-action weapon to stigmatise those who cowered before his terrifying ordinariness. First Spivey, then Wesson, now an undercover God. I seem to be implicating everybody, don't I? I suppose I'm side-stepping the real subject matter.'

There was a long pause. Freyn looked down and began to wheeze again. 'Talking to you . . . well, it's as if I'm playing out line into deep water; a last chance to catch something important. What if my line breaks or can't run deep enough? What if I lose the fish that I have already lost once all those years ago?'

Without warning, a tear dropped on to his cheek and stuck there for several seconds like a velcroed pearl. I was embarrassed. But he only smiled. 'Sorry,' he said. 'A mixture of emotion and less than efficient kidneys. Don't be alarmed, Walter. At my age, irritation, sadness, physical pain – it's all the same thing; they come and go and I ignore them as if they were no more than the reflection of weather passing in a mirror.

'However, I am prone to side-stepping things. People who are born fully alive, alert and completely connected with their environment rarely get into tangles, unless they're born evil. Others just barrel ahead so that things don't stick to them too easily. The doing's the thing, as long as it makes sense. I think I have been implicated in my own life, but it took me a very long time to get the drift of it. Now, *drift*. There's a word that Lawton liked to use. He was a poet. He used to say that words were useless if one regarded them as precision instruments. Lawton said that it was the drift, the current that drove words along like shoals of fish – it's the drift under the complexities of the waves that does the trick.'

Freyn asked if the tape was about to run out, so I checked the counter and assured him that time was not a problem. I risked a little aside. I said: 'I have nothing against detours.' At this, Freyn delivered an instant riposte. 'Precisely,' he said vehemently. '*Precisely*. This whole story is about detours. Luchenne, the horses, the *Manahatta*, this box we're sitting in. Detours, all of them. We look for signs and waymarkers and never ask who put them there, or wonder who told us what to look for. You look for lichens and safety and I . . . I look for nothingness because I know that it will finally cleanse me.'

His outburst, which was delivered in the thready, wavering tones of a muttered prayer, ceased as suddenly as it had begun. And then he became jocular again. 'Forgive me,' he said. 'Particularly my assumption that you seek detours that will lead you to safety. I hope I haven't insulted you.' I insisted that he had not.

'Ah, well,' he continued. 'Yes, well . . . one leads a crustacean life. I've given quite a bit of consideration to the question of shellfish, Walter. Tried to work out which of the crustacea most suitably parallels my own situation and existence. Now, a crab has a carapace and you might say that I have too. Crabs scuttle around scavenging; they scrape around prying things up, leaving stitchy tracks in the sand. Zippers that vanish. And they can dig into the sand, of course. Busy-busy! So, apart from possessing a cardboard carapace, I cannot compare myself to a crab, can I, as I'm hardly busy? Well, then: a mussel, perhaps? Mussels stick to rocks around the high tidemark; they form a crust like a tenacious tidemark in a bath. They live together in great numbers, packed tight, shell to shell. That certainly applies, doesn't it? And if mussels are not actually wet, they're always about to become wet. And they look so very alike, those shiny black rashes of shells. The roar of the surf around them – a sound surprisingly reminiscent of the observation drones that growl and hiss over the Delta. But, no, I don't associate myself with mussels, either.'

Freyn looked at me expectantly. 'You don't mind my mentioning crustaceans do you? Try to guess which one I feel akin to. You must know the names of quite a few. Well, I can see you're just being polite. You don't want to accuse me of being a whelk – admit it. Quite understandable. But I'll put you out of your misery. The creature I feel linked to is the limpet. An odd choice, at first glance, I'll grant you. A limpet doesn't have the sheer range of particulars-that a crab does; it's not articulate in any sense; they're rum, taciturn coves, and drearily conical, fixed like cement to the hull of a ship.

'Try to picture it, Walter! Submerged, the sea surging past at a steady twenty knots, the cradle movement of the dark hull as it pitches and rolls. And on the shell of the limpet, other, tinier creatures infesting the layer of slime. I can feel the vibration of the engines trembling into me through the rusting steel plate. Paying passengers above me, darkness and plummeting depth beneath.

'Now, you might have thought the mussel provided the best paradigm for living in the Delta – and the crab has a strong case too, if you judge it on the basis of its scuttle factor. But I insist upon the limpet. Know why?' Freyn paused to give me time to guess. I made a couple of guesses. 'No, no,' he interrupted briskly, 'that's not it. It's the *hull*. That's the whole point.' He paused a beat and whispered: 'The Delta's on a hull too, a concrete hull.'

The image startled me, doubly so because I had assumed he was rambling. And then my feeling of surprise gave way to a strange sense of tension. I knew, without knowing how I knew, that he was talking indirectly about the Luchenne business and of other events that were crucial to the tale that was being gathered by my pop-up microphone. My condescending patience over his 'detours' had been shamefully arrogant. I realised at that moment that his discourse was coming at me from two delicately poised positions. He had certainly volunteered to tell me about Luchenne and the horses. Even as he spoke, it was as if he feared his words were wasted on me, yet felt compelled to finish the story anyway. The other tension was simpler. I guessed that he was afraid, though I had no inkling what of. His detours were a way of preparing himself for – what, exactly? I remember that the phrase 'critical mass' occurred to me as I mulled over this revelation and hoped that it didn't show in my face. Having gathered myself, I said: 'Why the hull?'

Freyn's words came briskly again. 'Because of the water sliding past. But for water, substitute events outside the Delta that we – and there are a lot of us – know nothing of. As for the smaller creatures on the outside of the limpet's shell, think of the jobs we degradees provide: health inspectors, chemists, medical researchers, building materials testers, garbage disposal teams. The Delta, the hull, must be the single biggest employer in Essex. I mean, if you're going to abandon people, do it properly, eh?'

Freyn paused and took several slow breaths. 'Oh, yes, let Demcorp barrel ahead! And there's another item, a nice paradox. An individual can recognise and be recognised, can be seen and heard, can demand specific things. But a large group is identified as such. The communications and remedies directed towards groups are groupish. If the group grows too large and demanding it can be deemed unmanageable – or subject to forms of management that are not applied to individuals or small groups. Ultimately, the scale of responses and remedies is reduced until large groups don't expect them at all.'

It was unusual to hear him speculate in such a logical way. I was about to take him up on his reasoning, which I felt was rather general, but he continued without pause.

'I know about things being jettisoned,' he said slowly. 'And you never know how precious, or disgusting, something is until you've left it behind. I hate . . . I hate to think of certain things. One doesn't really lose one's memory, you know. One has mistakenly tried to lose it – or part of it anyway. There's a difference.' Freyn produced a handkerchief, tightly scrunched, a grey lump of cloth. He dabbed at his nose with it, then began to knead it absentmindedly.

'I think Eglantine sensed the change in me even before my social repositioning. She took to asking for presents from me – nothing grand, trinkets and shoes, that sort of thing. She wanted my cast-offs too: shirts, trousers, collar studs – even my battered canvas tennis shoes covered in Meltonian whitener, as cracked as paint on a backstreet windowsill in Temhari.

'She became tearful once when I balked at letting her have my hairbrush. It was silver-backed, Jermyn Street, a gift from my mother.' Freyn gave the handkerchief a final squeeze and stuffed it into the sleeve of his sweater at the wrist. 'The tears on Eglantine's cheeks were of a far purer silver. They were not to be weighed against rows of bristle.'

Freyn looked down and said quietly: 'I'm afraid I'm running out of steam. I'll have to retire now – the hull's rocking me to sleep. Please come again as soon as you like.' He glanced up and added: 'I've started this damned story so, obviously, I must finish it.' A constrained, low rumble of laughter made his shoulders shake for several seconds. I had no idea what was so amusing in his remark, but smiled back at him anyway. He stopped and coughed three times, rather painfully. 'Sorry,' he wheezed, 'sorry about that, dear boy; pay no heed.'

And then: 'No, wait. I've really must make an effort for you, mustn't I? To explain things properly.' Freyn waved a hand at me to stop me saying anything. 'If only to satisfy your whirring little *aide memoire*. Please forgive my French accent, incidentally.

'Now, Madame Jopahl's French wasn't bad at all and she claimed to have French blood in her. I'm sure she had, if only on a temporary basis, and for money – if you follow my drift. Your machine could have picked up an interesting tale or two in the coffee shop. Most of the Brits, the younger types like me, used the place in a relatively decent way – except Franklin, of course. I say *of course* as if you'd known the man yourself. Franklin was crude – no, not crude, he was raw matter. Bloody man's irrelevant to all this, can't think why I mentioned him.

'No. Now, Madame J. When one entered the coffee shop, there were certain pleasantries to be attended to. Madame Jopahl would appear with a tray on which was your preferred tipple; mine was rum and ginger. And there would be a spot of good-natured banter. Finally, she would ask, by way of a little tradition, if one would prefer *une petite café noire* or a delicious *café crème* . . . her little double entendres. Some of the chaps replied in a pretty disgusting vein. I don't condemn them and I used to wonder if I wasn't secretly envious of them – of their super-ficiality, I mean. A superficial life might only be half a life, but it's a damn sight less trouble.

'The Delta's a superficial place. Not much weight on it, is there? There was no weight on me in Temhari, yet the cracks appeared all the same. Every person experiences dilemmas, or at least some confusion that later turns out to have been crucial.

'That particular feeling invaded me without my knowing it and I was only able to piece it together later. I remember the day quite well. Massie, the notary public, came into my office to get the name of the captain of a coaster that had just docked. I gave him the information civilly enough, though I disliked him intensely. Massie was a middle man, you see; lent money to local traders — money that was supplied by a barrister who dipped into trust funds. Massie would lend money on difficult terms and if the trader or enterprise later went broke, his contract always gave him first claim on what was left. If the business improved, he would find ways to lend more on apparently irresistible terms, in exchange for a portion of the equity. He couldn't lose, you see, and nobody could lay a glove on him: he was doing his dreadful trade in his spare time, with private funds and impeccable legality.

'Anyway, the captain he wanted to see was landing cocoa from Ghana. Massie wanted to get aboard before the goods were landed to make sure the consignment, which was for one of his pals, would come from the middle layer of the load: no risk of damage from deck leaks, or from anything sloshing around underneath. The captain would oblige, of course, as he didn't want his rather amateur diamond-smuggling antics to be disturbed.

'So that was Massie, who left my office. And in came Augusto, as always, to see if anything needed attending to as a result of a visit. Now, Walter —' and here Freyn raised a finger '— you must understand the normality of the scene. Papers on the desk, faint voices drifting in from the other offices, the slow tick of the Remington next door, perhaps the purring wing-beat of a flycatcher under the eaves. And let's not forget the solitary bead of sweat that always seemed to loiter on the bridge of my nose. And there you have it: the scene, no different in its essentials to any other moment I had spent in that office for the previous two years. And that is precisely what strikes me as remarkable – but only in retrospect.

'Augusto handed me a bill of lading to approve. I can specifically recall the dry sound that the slim sheaf of papers made against my palm as I took it, and the treacly whup-whup of the blades of the overhead fan. Outside in the yard, young Warburton Worricks was taunting a drunk who was trying to put a spell on the mangy mutt that frequented the space under the steps up to the building.

'Was it the fan that instigated the confusion? For it was then, quite suddenly, that I was overcome by a tortuous idea: that it might be possible, and desirable, to feel a profoundly powerful contact with ordinary things – a painful contact, even, but worthwhile and meaningful. Instead, my existence at that moment was like ... well, it was like a hand holding a ten-pound weight that it couldn't actually feel. I could almost see the weight right there: brass, shaped like a bell, well handled, polished to brightness by the touch of a million ordinary fingers. I could even imagine my own fingers closing round it and hefting it. But no actual sensation of its weight. The bare fact of it, yes, and even the details. But no weight, no gravity.

'That might seem a small thing to mention and it must be hard for you to understand what it meant to me – me, Walter, sitting here and now in my box in the Delta. You must wonder at the remorseless grip of certain memories. Well, as Augusto made his usual quiet exit, something came over me: a truly terrible feeling of physical and spiritual weightlessness. I actually grabbed at the edge of my desk. The feeling only lasted an instant and then it was gone. I never felt it with such intensity ever again. And yet, from that moment, I had changed and knew that the change was irrevocable. I sat there, sweating and afraid.'

Freyn paused and I asked if he had been suffering from any ailments at the time. He smiled, 'Do you mean an ear infection? Or tense muscles in the neck or shoulders?' He shook his head and smirked. 'Fit as a flea.' I wanted to pursue this line of questioning, but thought I'd better not derail his commentary.

'Ever been trapped by a dilemma?' he asked. 'The sort that mimics your every move? That wretched brass weight, that damned image, was actually to do with how to live, how to remain in contact. But the very act of wishing for it immediately tainted it; it's the doom of the weightlessly aware. And there was another little trap. If I ignored my wish then dissolution beckoned. Dissolution! "Are you dissolute, Mr Freyn?" Those were the first words Bobby said to me. He was no more than ten years old, and I couldn't help laughing. What prescience! Of course, Bobby came later; you'll hear about him in due course.

'Where was I? Now . . . yes, I took my hands off the desk quite gingerly, as you might imagine, ready to make a fresh grab in case I was suddenly heliumised again. I suppose it was around that time, now I come to think of it, that I really applied myself to drinking. It was an inverted form of self-preservation. It was safer to be on the verge of falling down than of floating away. Such is the logic of the newly hollow man.

'Thank heavens Eglantine didn't apply logic to the details of my behaviour after that. I got angry over little things; pure desperate confusion – and fear that I might become too dependent on her. Or perhaps I was trying in my clumsy way to make a fuller contact with her. I certainly didn't succeed – not in the terms that I sometimes dreamed might be possible. She had beautiful skin, you know.'

Freyn tapped a finger against his cheek. He looked a shade distracted. After twenty seconds I began to wonder if that was it for the day. He seemed to be weighing something up. But when he spoke I knew for sure he had more or less signed off.

'If you don't mind my trading on your specialism,' he said, 'this plastic stuff, the stuff on the outside of the Delta boxes – does it breathe? I mean, does it let air and moisture out, is it a one-way process? Impermeable unless damaged? I see. I must say, I don't like the thought of things being impermeable – such an unnatural idea. What can be the sense of something so humiliatingly containing in an endless, uncontained universe?

Take the common or garden lightbulb: a white hot tungsten filament in a vacuum, giving out light and a certain amount of heat. But there's glass around it — there has to be or it wouldn't function. But the meaning of things isn't always in their function, is it? In Temhari I dealt with shipping matters, but was not myself a shipping matter. You might say the horses were a shipping matter. But they damn well weren't.'

I didn't understand Freyn's reference to the horses, but interrupted him to suggest that he had merely been doing a job like anybody else. 'Not as simple as that,' he replied. 'There must be *contact*. One needs to know beyond doubt that not only are things apparently outside you fully alive, but that you too are fully alive — and that the two states are interdependent. Lightbulbs are switched on and off: their existence is arbitrary. When the filament glows, that glow has no meaning in terms of what it illuminates. There's no fundamental purpose to it, except what the finger on the switch decrees. It's like the genii and the bottle. My goodness, Walter, was there ever a more dangerous idea? That you can stopper up something extraordinary and call it into existence at a whim. I know what I'm talking about. Eglantine was my temporary genii, but in reverse: I was the bottle and she filled me — or I thought she did. She didn't, of course. She simply put a gloss over my emptiness.

'Dear me, that's far too morose. It's hardly worth magnetising what I'm saying on to that tape. The tape is magnetic, isn't it? Look —' Freyn paused and gave me a steady look '— about these digressions. It's just that I can't explain about Luchenne and the horses without building up to it. I mean, I'll give you the bare bones if you prefer, if you're in a hurry. I daresay I'm keeping you from your research as it is.'

Freyn's gaze suddenly went strange. I reassured him that there was no hurry and added, not for the first time, that even apparently irrelevant details could prove highly useful. I said scientists often depended on such details for making final sense of things. I knew that I had to keep his trust and that part of my job was to make sure he was comfortable with me. Freyn looked reassured, but I thought there was still uncertainty in his eyes.

'About this plastic coating on my box,' he said, yawning. 'I'm still not convinced it's so very good. I mean, even cardboard has to breathe, surely. You see what happens –' he pointed out a spot near one of the box's corners '– just there, for example. It's just a small patch of rot but it'll spread. After that, the rot bubbles through the plastic layer on the outside.' Freyn smiled unexpectedly. 'You quite sure it's not part of a conspiracy? The government supplying the Delta with boxes that promote the growth of fungus? Fungi that could be marketed as a health food? Genuine Delta ginseng, perhaps. What? Oh – could've sworn ginseng was a fungus. But anyway, another point: could you advise me on ventilation? If you've no objection, I hope we can have a conversation about it at a later date. There's probably a simple formula for working out how best to ventilate these boxes: volume of box multiplied by the size of the opening, divided by the average prevailing wind speed – that sort of thing. Can't be too complicated, can it?'

Interjection concerning a dream

THAT night I had an unusual dream. I report it here because it seemed, quite clearly, to have been provoked by that last session with Freyn. The dream may be worthless. I include it because it occurs to me that I can count it as part of the diaspora of Freyn's recollections: the begetting of image by image. Another reason for its inclusion is that it was the first dream I had which was provoked by Freyn – the first of many, most of which were equally inexplicable. I like to think of these dreams as an echo of Freyn's weightlessness.

In that first dream, I found myself in Temhari's botanical gardens, standing before a mausoleum. I'm not sure when. I like to think it might have been in 1938, thought it could have been yesterday, or tomorrow. I guess it doesn't matter.

The mausoleum was moonlit, a low, glistening marble oblong. I was barely aware of the shrubs and trees because my attention was focused on the centrally-positioned entrance to the building. There were three wide steps up to the double bronze doors. On each step was a pair of short columns in the ionic style, except that the pediments carried sculptures of tropical birds.

I was fascinated by the doors. They were slightly ajar and I made my way across the grass and up the steps. I pushed the doors open and found myself in a room filled with junk. There was no discernible lighting but, nevertheless, I could make things out. The range of junk was extraordinary and I was excited by it.

I am inquisitive. I like ferreting through things. Classification is meat and drink to me. I was in my element. I found myself wondering where Vibert was. I even called out his name, intent on borrowing the same walking stick he'd lent to Freyn so I could poke around more efficiently.

I began to pick my way through the detritus and as I did so the extent of it seemed to increase. It seemed infinite. Then the walls vanished and were replaced with a greyness which diminished into a final, dense black horizon.

I seemed to be in the room for a considerable time, poring over bits and pieces: boxes of tinned produce, busts, dental equipment, lavishly illustrated coffee-table books, a teach-yourself Chinese audio course. There were one or two things that stuck in my mind: a thick report from the UN's Food and Agriculture Organization with the title: 'Eating Well in Developing Countries'. When I opened it a revolting smell of stale sweat and shit jabbed up my nostrils. Another strange find was a red flag wrapped tightly round a small pole. When I touched the flag's cloth it exploded without warning into a storm of moths which whirled away into the blackness.

The atmosphere of the dream changed when I came across a fat bundle of banknotes. I bent to pick them up and as I touched them my hand recoiled: the wad felt hairy to the touch, as if the notes had a pelt or hide of some sort. Quite suddenly I was afraid. Backing up, I bumped into something and turned. There, in front of me, was a large horizontal glass case about eight feet long and three feet wide. It was thick with dust, but a dim light emanated from within it. I reached out and wiped a swathe of the dust off the glass top with my sleeve – and flinched. Inside the case were the remains of a man. The corpse was superbly dressed. Most of the skin had gone and there was nothing more to see than dry, frayed muscle and contorted ligaments at the wrist and ankle. The gloves and socks were rotten. The face of the corpse was unrecognisable.

The glass casket was full of gold and precious stones. The body lay in them as if floating on a gentle swell of glittering brine. As I began to try to identify the gems, which for some reason seemed a crucial issue at that point, they started to glow. The light from them slowly became unbearably bright. The remains of the corpse began to smoke and after a few moments burst into flames. The glass case shattered with a loud echoing crack and just before I awoke I heard the sound of waves – and voices too, some way off, but insistent. They sounded excited or frightened about something.

I woke and looked at my bedside dataglow. The hologram digits poised above it read 3.27 a.m. I felt hot and unsettled. I got up and, after preparing a pot of tea, I did a few gentle stretching exercises. I then decided to look through my transcripts of the Freyn tapes to date. It was pretty pointless. I think I was only trying to ensure that when I returned to bed I would be in a different frame of mind. After shuffling through the papers, I ritualistically checked my computer files of associated research material pulled off the DupeLoop web. My eyes ran down the headings for Temhari – sewage conduit layouts, Masonic membership lists, high resolution aerial photographs, architectural drawings for the Roraima Anglo Occidental Bank, dated 1912. I found the lists soothing. Reassured by the detail at my fingertips, I took half a tab of Etherdan and got back into bed.

I resolved to resume my taping the very next day. I felt newly focused. The dream had given me the feeling that I had, at last, locked on to Freyn's narrative. I felt involved in a new way. I was both unnerved and amused by the prospect. Unnerved because of a new duality which put me in a delicate position: should I question him more rigorously or just go with the flow. And amused because, whichever way I intended to play it from now on, Freyn's little jibe pinged around my head as I lay there: 'You're not plainclothes, Walter? Or forensic?'

His image of the hull came back to me, but with an extra ingredient. I pictured the hull in cross-section: half an inch of riveted steel plates dividing two worlds. On one side, containment and order; on the other, thousands of tons of displaced water streaming past in infinitely complex vortices. That second world seemed pretty wild compared to my own existence. There I was, lying in my bed and hearing, faintly through the quadruple glazing, the usual late-night outbreaks of sect-on-sect violence or the frenzied chanting of the children in the barracks – yet I experienced all this in the complete safety afforded by the block's communal privacy systems.

The fetish priest

SHORTLY before Freyn left for the interior to collect Luchenne's horses, a fetish priest — they were also called 'obeah' men — appeared in the neatly tended gateyard of Spivey & Co. From his first-floor office, Freyn heard him 'jabbering and cooing and whinnying' and ignored him.

'My secretary's Remington stopped its ticking and tacking and Augusto appeared in the open corridor outside my open door to get a better look at what was going on below in the yard.' (I had, incidentally, managed to return to Freyn's box two days after my previous visit. It was a relief to see him looking rested. And he actually seemed pleased to see me. I confess that I felt honoured. He continued his recollection in a businesslike manner and, for the first time, I found that after playback I could pull out a large unbroken chunk of it, confident that the material was relevant.)

'The fetish priest seemed to be proclaiming the same thing over and over again and punctuating his diatribe with hoots and barks and other animal noises. Augusto turned to me and said: "He an old congo fetish." Congo being the term that Roraimans gave to old Africans who lived deep in the forest, avoiding contact even with the native tribes. Augusto could understand him, though, and said: "He be tellin bout gold at the bottom of the sea." He paused to see if I was interested and decided I was. "Tellin bout gold, Mr Freyn. Shinin like stars at the bottom of the sea. Be near the bottom, he keep sayin. Not havin to dig for it, he sayin. The gold be floatin in the water all round, he say."

'I got up – with a sigh, probably. These obeah priests were a daily sight in Temhari. However, I obviously wasn't going to get any work done, not with that racket going on. When I stepped out into the passageway, I saw that Augusto was not alone. All the secretaries were lined up along the banister, hands side by side on the hardwood rail, their painted nails as shiny as a row of Smarties. They were terrified, and therefore fascinated.

'I don't think the fetish man noticed me straight away, though I might be wrong about that. I could see him plainly enough over Augusto's right shoulder. He was indescribably frail and wore only a dirty loincloth. He was covered in ashes and streaks of blue dye, which was fairly typical. But he was not quite the usual obeah man. If his lips hadn't been moving – if one hadn't been able to see those livid, toothless gums – it would have been difficult to judge his features at all. You see, he had eyes painted all over his shaven head and neck, and skilfully painted too. Compared to that the rest of him seemed as hazy and insubstantial as a spider's web.

'I could barely understand him. He spoke a mixture of pidgin and what I took to be a West African dialect. I recognised bits of his story about the gold and, later, followed him quite well when he began his recitation of the Lord's Prayer and selections from Revelations. But he jumbled everything up and punctuated the mixture with words that didn't belong. It was eerie. Augusto was certainly nervous. He turned to me and whispered: "The fetish be receivin a visit from the Jesuit fo sure. A man can only be takin so much missry because how you tellin where one start and the other be beginnin?" Augusto's fears were not singular. Several of the secretaries had evidently decided that at least one of life's mysteries should end and had begun to finger their charms or rosaries.

'There was no question of anybody removing the fetish man forcibly. Not even Spivey, even if he'd been there. None of the staff would have dared to lay a finger on the obeah. If I had got it into my head to move him along, he would have cursed the ground on which the building stood, and that would have lost us staff immediately. And that's how it would have stayed until the spirits had been neutralised by Mystic Clover, the tame obeah man who had a juju booth in Camptown – a booth paid for, incidentally, by the Anglican diocese on the understanding that he stayed in it when not performing cleansings.

'The mutt under the front step began to whine and yap, whereupon the fetish priest started plucking out handfuls of grass from the lawn. He stuffed them in his mouth and chewed slowly and deliberately. I leaned forward to ask Augusto how long he thought the performance would last. As soon as I spoke, the fetish priest stopped what he was doing and spat the wad of grass out. His head and limbs were suddenly perfectly still.

'For a moment – I don't really remember how long, it might have been a few seconds or a minute – everything seemed frozen. Temhari seemed to have been turned to stone. And then the bush priest let out a scream, snapped out his right arm and pointed a rigid index finger directly at me. Augusto started back in shock and bumped into me. A warm feeling thrilled across my shoulders. And then Augusto, whispering: "He be puttin a curse on you, Mr Freyn. You got to be doin everythin he doin fo stoppin it!" I said he needn't worry because I was already damned, and you couldn't condemn a condemned man.

'The fetish man kept staring at me and began to utter a peculiar high-pitched wheedling sound. Then he started to dance on the spot, kicking his legs up and arching his back. "You bess do that also, Mr Freyn, juss like he doin it." Dear Augusto! "I'm tellin you a true thing."

'The dance degenerated as the old boy grew tired and increasingly entranced. He fell several times and finally lay on the ground, panting, his back arching in flurries of spasms. When he had calmed down a little he began to try to pick off bits of grass with his lips.

'After a few more minutes – he'd been at it for half an hour and it was a hot, close day – the obeah lay still for a while. Then he seemed to gather himself and stood up rather shakily. He fixed his eyes on me again and waited, as if . . . anyway, the girls began to whisper among themselves and I sensed that the priest had singled me out. I asked Augusto if I was expected to give money. "No money," he replied firmly, "or he be makin big business out of cursin you." '

At this point Freyn paused. It startled me: he had never delivered such a clear-cut narrative and I thought for a moment he had lost the thread. I was about to encourage him to continue when he began again, almost as if I weren't there; as if he were giving evidence in a court. His voice was firm, as before. There were no musing inflections. The words − to use one of his expressions − 'flowed like hot wax'.

'Despite Augusto's warning I resolved to give the obeah something. It seemed right to provide some sort of conclusion − a way to give the man a decent exit line, as it were. I decided to offer the glass paperweight on my desk, which contained a model of St Paul's and Ludgate Hill. It wasn't solid glass: it contained water. If one shook it, tiny flakes of white quartz whirled around in a mock snowstorm. God knows what made me think of it, but I took it off the desk, made my way along the corridor, down the internal steps to the lobby and finally to the entrance porch.

'I certainly had an audience, Walter. The drivers were craning out of the window of the gatehouse; the girls leaned over the banister above me. I also saw, quite clearly, the look of horror on poor Augusto's face. I heard the mutt scratching around beneath the floorboards. And the obeah man, this cobweb of a fellow, was already waiting at the bottom of the steps. His stare was steady, unbreakable. I remember thinking at that moment: this man is very, very old. He had cataracts and the whites of his eyes had been replaced with a curdled amber glaze which wept on to his cheeks like pine sap. Blades of grass were stuck to his chin. I stepped forward slowly, placed the paperweight on the top step, pointed at it and then at him, and stepped back into the doorway. For some reason, I reached out to touch the doorframe. It felt purposeful and reassuring. The fetish priest glared at me, but it was a look of simple concentration rather than anger. I pointed at the paperweight again and nodded.

'One of the girls along the rail began to sing a hymn softly. Her voice was barely audible, wavering, and the melody was uncertain. Well, to cut a long story short –' and here Freyn managed a self-deprecating smile '– the old congo man took a step up, reached forward and grasped the wretched thing. Then he stepped back, turning the paperweight in his filthy fingers. He held it up and the sun seemed to flash through it and he yelped and began to rub it vigorously on the grass. After which, with considerable wailing, he raised it high again and shook it at everyone he could see, one by one. Augusto promptly ducked away into my office and several of the girls fled with a mixture of squeals and giggles. Finally, the paperweight was waved specifically at me. I simply stood and waited – there was nothing else for it.

'Then, in mid-shake, the old man stopped cold. He sniffed and yawned, as if he were waking up. He bent down quite normally – no jerking about – pulled up a handful of grass and laid it gently on the top step. And then he turned and positively sauntered off, holding the paperweight against his stomach. When he had passed through the gates into Dankwa Avenue, Augusto reappeared and called down to me: "He mystified, Mr Freyn. You stir him up." '

Freyn yawned and took a long, slow breath. I heard, quite clearly, a slight bubbling sound at the end of his exhalation. I immediately thought: pneumonia. But Freyn was oblivious to the state of his lungs and just rattled ahead. 'That dusty old dervish knew more than he or I realised. Makes one wonder about time. Do savants look into the future, or do they simply recognise every expanding iota of the present?'

Freyn scratched at his cheek and coughed painfully. He was sweating. 'I never saw that congo man again. And here's a thing. As I turned to re-enter the office I happened to put my hand on the doorframe. For some reason I paused to glance at it. And I thought: what an arbitrary thing a doorframe is. It seemed – well, it actually seemed ridiculous at that moment. Yet only moments earlier I had found it completely reassuring. It had meant something, and now it had the same clear form but meant nothing.

'Anyway, I chivvied everyone back to their work, with instructions to do things that were probably unnecessary. And, after listening patiently to Augusto rehearse the whole episode twice – and taking great care to agree with his theories – I settled down to catch up on my work.' Freyn looked at me. I had the distinct feeling I was being assessed. 'Am I making sense, Walter? Do tell me if I'm being a bore.'

He took some convincing that he wasn't. It was only when I insisted that I found the details of his story interesting that he continued, though in a rather subdued way.

'I tried to get back to work,' he said. 'Couldn't concentrate. Fiddled with my papers, got things out of order. Called for some tea. No improvement. Know what it was? The wretched paperweight – *damned* thing. My desk wasn't right, d'you see? There was something missing, something apparently inconsequential, but missing nevertheless. It was as if I had looked up into the night sky and found that the North Star had been erased; or woken to find that a tooth was suddenly missing. Identifying the problem helped, but I cleared off down to the dock anyway. A spurious exit, quite unnecessary, but I needed to distance myself from that place for a while.'

Freyn had run out of steam again. The strange thing was that I felt tired too. There had been a tension in the air when he spoke of the obeah man and the feeling hadn't been resolved. I decided not to press him for more. Perhaps he needed to gather himself again. As it turned out, there were a few drops left in his tank, though they weren't much use. I include them anyway.

'Is it true that they narcotised one of the northern sections of the Delta a couple of days back?' he asked. I told him that I had no idea. 'I don't suppose you hear about everything that goes on here. Why should you? We're a psycho-social rash that's been covered in a thick obliterating mulch of international aid agency reports. However, I'm sure I picked up just a hint of that sweet, tangy smell yesterday. I thought it might be a degraded, downwind whiff of narcotemp.

'Now then, this might interest you –' he reached behind him as he spoke and produced a small cylinder '– I keep it on standby.' He had begun to wheeze. 'Just a . . . just . . . yes, better. Now, *this*. Made it myself. Yes, do examine it; it's perfectly solid, you won't break it. It's a large baked bean tin, open at one end as you can see, with small holes punched in the other. Inside, there's a layer of packed charcoal granules – not too fine, of course, otherwise I wouldn't be able to draw air through – then a thin layer of wadding. I simply wrap a thick cloth round the edge of the open end and stick my nose and mouth in. It works very well as far as breathing is concerned; not that I've ever had to use it.

'I read that charcoal is a great purifier. Perhaps I should add some garlic. Not very apt, I expect – it's anaesthetic gas one is watching out for, not bloodsuckers. Which reminds me: saw a leech the other day. A leech, on a child's ankle. God knows where it came from. I told the girl to put salt on it, but she had no idea what I was talking about. I tried to explain, but she was demented. As soon as I mentioned the sea she said: "My mother's been to the sea," over and over again – made a little song of it. Then somebody threw a rock at her.'

Freyn shook his head. 'I feel old today, Walter, very bloody *old*.' I began to assure him, probably too hastily, that he seemed hale and hearty, when he interrupted me. 'Gold at the bottom of the ocean!' he exclaimed, spreading his arms wide. 'I wonder what that ashen old congo would have made of all of this! And another thing, do they sell paperweights containing representations of the Delta in London?'

The answer to this was obviously no. But I recalled something that I thought might amuse Freyn. 'No paperweights,' I said. 'But you can buy computer-generated aerial analyses of the Delta as large decorative prints to frame or pin on walls. There are all sorts: heat scans, ultraviolet scans, moisture density scans. They're accurate but they've been tarted up – fractalised at the margins of the prints.'

Freyn's momentary puzzlement snapped into keen attention. 'Fractalised?' he asked. 'What's that?' I explained, as simply as possible, about the computer-generated patterns. 'Signifying what?' he asked. When I told him that fractals were seen as a representation of patterns of order in chaos, he nodded. 'Pretty, are they, these fractals?' I replied that they were often beautiful and were popular with both mathematicians and artists.

Freyn fell silent for about half a minute. I assumed he'd lost interest and began to reach down to switch off my recorder. 'No, wait a moment,' he said gently. 'I was just thinking about something that has to do with the Luchenne business.' I withdrew my hand discreetly.

'Some fellows came round here the other day. They had visitors kitted out with video cameras and sound equipment. I listened carefully to what they were saying and deduced they were making a programme about folk music. It seems there's some sort of music that is indigenous to the Delta. You may have come across it in your algae scraping tours. It's mainly percussive, with flutes and pipes thrown in – quite a bit of rhythmic clapping too. These chaps were doing interviews. They talked to the crone in the box to our left and then tapped on my box and peeked in carefully. I pretended to be unconscious and put on my best death rattle.

'I mention this because after they'd gone I found myself thinking about the trek from Caribat to Luchenne's farm. About ten miles south-east of Caribat – no, make that fifteen – we stopped at a shelter left by loggers; it was just a few walaba poles strung together and loosely thatched with palm. We had lunch, a bush turkey that one of the boys had got with the 303 – pure luck in that thick bush. Then we settled down to rest. I dozed but couldn't sleep. I kept hearing a sort of pulse. After a time, I realised that the pulse was the sound of drumming, but quite some way off. Now, this is my point: at first the drumming seemed quite simple. Yet the more I listened the more delicate and intricate the rhythm and the accents became. What do you think of that?'

Actually, I didn't think *anything* of it, but I considered it for a moment to be polite and said: 'Probably a case of getting used to the sound – an effect of it.' Freyn waved my suggestion away impatiently. 'No, you've missed my point. The question is: did I create the intricacies or were they there in the first place?' I wondered if it mattered. 'Of course it matters!' he insisted.

I couldn't let this pass and asked him how he could ever know whether he had created them or not. 'You're behaving like a sidewalk sophist, ten drachmas for ten minutes' worth of dispute,' he replied rather heatedly. 'The point is that the question has been posed, and that an answer might exist.' Again, I felt bound to query his line of thought and asked whether know-ledge was gained by accident. He looked at me as if I was deranged. 'Well, of course you gain it by accident. Things happen. You'll see how things happen. You'll see how I came to be in this box. You'll see that everything is driven by accident and amnesia!'

I apologised for irritating him and said – though it was untrue – that I had only been playing devil's advocate. Quite honestly, I was terrified that he was about to tell me not to come again. I had barely got into my placatory stride when Freyn cut in. 'You're a thoughtful young fellow,' he said, 'and it is I who should apologise to you. Why should you agree with everything I say? Why should I think everything I say is sacrosanct? Perhaps it's the curse, or blessing, of having so little. One hoards one's ideas, one mulls them over. In the end – and the end has been more than a hundred years coming in my case – there is very little difference between one's spiritual and physical existence. Which means that memories that have been reduced and refined become very important.

'I can't help thinking that there is only one will – the will to meaning. And that it has nothing to do with getting used to things, as you put it, or with decorative chaos. Fractals? That what you called them? I said everything was driven by accident and amnesia. Well, it is. Look around you. But that doesn't mean it shouldn't be fought against!'

Freyn looked a little shaky; perhaps he was coming down with pneumonia after all. He closed his eyes and took several slow breaths and I realised he was trying to calm himself. I thought I would try a compliment. I said: 'You seem to have kicked against it pretty well.' He appeared not to have heard. Unsure what to do or say, I waited. After ten or fifteen seconds his eyes flicked open.

'You're right, Walter, I have,' he said. 'I'm rare. I'm part of a –' and here he spluttered into a mixture of laughter and hacking coughs '– part of a boxed set!' This was pretty funny and I joined in. Freyn's hands went to his chest as the tears ran down his cheeks. He gradually got his breathing under control and his laughter petered out in the usual gluey gasps. He produced the handkerchief from his sleeve and dabbed at his eyes and cheeks.

'The thing you must grasp,' he said, 'is that the Luchenne business and what happened later are the way-markers in my life. Everything I tell you is fundamentally about damage and destruction, and they beget more of the same. You must also understand that I owe my advanced age to an obsession that has so far outlasted my decay. And there's something else, Walter. Since meeting you I've had the idea that if I explain what happened in Roraima in a certain way, the events will, after all these years, carry enough meaning to allow me to rest. And when you come again I'll tell you how the damage began to manifest itself.'

A note on our relationship

FREYN'S closing remarks on that day marked another shift of emphasis in our relationship and the realisation had an immediate and potentially dangerous effect. As I left the Delta that afternoon, I was barely aware of my surroundings or the petty violence going on around me. It was only after I had passed through the cannula at the end of Causeway 3 that I realised I had forgotten to key in the Ready-Max setting on the butt of my stun-baton. Anything could have happened to me and I would have been completely unprepared.

That thought – that anything could have happened – began to dig in. Not in terms of me but in terms of Freyn. I began to speculate about our relationship in the light of his comment about being intent on explaining things to me correctly. Was he talking about his redemption? If so, where did that leave me? I suddenly felt exposed – but to what? I confess that I made my way home that day in a pretty frazzled state of mind. I even made a mess of operating my pathfinder handset. It took me three goes to access the low-risk route update. For a moment I thought I'd accidentally wiped the receiver sensor chip.

To make matters worse, I was unable to return to Freyn's section of the Delta for four days. The research bureau had, in its wisdom, decided that some lichen samples brought in from zone nine, at the other end of the Delta, looked interesting. The researcher working nine, Miriski, was arguing that the sub-species he'd found were more sensitive to infrared than ultraviolet light. His theory was based on one or two unusual mutations in the plants. He had been given leave to prepare his notes for consideration by the lichens directorate. I, meanwhile, was sent to collect a range of normal samples from the same area to establish basal variations in form, acid content, colour and adhesive properties.

It was infuriating to be deep in a part of the Delta that was unfamiliar to me (I am a recognised authority on zone three sub-types) and doing the legwork for somebody else's dubious proposal. Miriski was clearly desperate for recognition, but I was pretty sure those mutations had nothing to do with light wavelengths. My money was on pollutants within the boxes.

I glanced through Miriski's proposal, which happened to be lying on the mediator's desk. And guess what? There was no cross-referencing of box types or box contents. These listings are a requirement of ISO666, the research quality control standard. It occurred to me that Miriski might attempt to fudge the listings, so I bit the bullet and not only collected the samples but took a full survey of boxes in the designated area. It was a depressing business. Unlike Freyn's box, most of them were poorly maintained, with a strong stench. Quite a high proportion of the degradees were drugged, which made several of the interviews difficult. There was also the usual quota of trouble – I had to stun two of them. I got the information, though, and decided to hold it back until I knew for sure that Miriski hadn't done his homework on the capillary factors.

I am not normally an aggressive, scheming type. But I was being unnecessarily held back from both my normal research and my discreet sessions with Freyn. I should admit that, at the time, I was far more interested in Freyn than in my own work, let alone that cretin Miriski's.

Three days later I was back in my own research zone. Anxious to reach Freyn as soon as possible, I had begun my work shortly after dawn – the idea being to get a long session with him. I worked fast and by the time I began to pack up the day's lichen samples it was raining steadily. Once I had taken the bearing and noted it on the back of my hand (Freyn's box was north-west of me on a heading of zero four niner) I had to force myself to walk slowly.

Damage

IF FREYN detected any tension on my part he did not reveal it. We exchanged pleasantries and he said that I looked tired. I laughed it off while busying myself with the recorder. 'Just a bit of accident and amnesia,' I ventured.

This pleased him. 'Ah, yes,' he said. 'Quite so.' And then he just launched back into his story, the next section of which I deliver more or less intact.

'I mentioned damage, Walter, did I not?' he said. 'In my case, the primary damage was achieved via alcohol. My consumption of this, that and the other increased remorselessly. Sometimes, lashed by a hangover, I would arrive a little late at Spivey's. And there would be Augusto waiting with his usual nervous diffidence by my door, trying to judge the extent of my condition. I think he feared getting sacked – being thrown out with the dirty dishwater, as it were. Dismissal by association.

'Had I understood his worried looks I would have reassured him. The truth is that I didn't give his nervous behaviour a second thought. I just looked down at the polished toecaps of his second- or third-hand Oxfords and said: "Very smart." Those toecaps were among the few constants in my private world of inconsistencies.

'Drinking. The difficulty is that it tends to reinforce one's preoccupations. My preoccupation was weightlessness, therefore I found myself becoming more and more insubstantial. I had lost my sense of boundary. I had no shape, no form in the world. People usually ignore drunks, do they not? It's because they don't really register. There they are – shapeless, leaking out their anxieties in slurred monologues of both the internal and external variety.

'But if I was experiencing what I call weightlessness, why was I drinking in the first place? After all, it was solid ordinary things which confused me, which induced my feeling of dissociation. The more solid, mundane and certain something was – the copperplate lettering on a dance programme, a window latch seen out of the corner of my eye, a bill of lading – the more I felt threatened and repelled.

'Could I have tackled this thing head on? Work hard, play hard? Sweated the damn thing out like a fever? Forced myself to participate? I don't know the answer, Walter. The theory is all very well. But the point is that once one thing seems insubstantial, it's like a house of cards. If one, then all. And if all – then nothing.

'It was bad sometimes,' he continued. 'Really, it was most dreadfully unnerving. Sometimes I felt that objects were giving off an electric charge, or that I might be magnetic. Anti-magnetic actually, in the sense that I suspected I repelled things – veered away from people and events, bouncing off their charges . . . my hand refusing to move when my brain told it to turn a door handle, or failing to reply to a direct question. Fear, do you think, Walter? Fear of thanking somebody for their kind invitation to something or other, only to get sucked into space for my pains?

'Fear is obstructive, d'you see?' Freyn paused to see if his remark had struck home. It hadn't because I hadn't grasped his point, but I nodded anyway. He smiled slightly. 'It is obstructive, Walter,' he said. 'Rather a lot of people don't realise that. They stuff it away, pretend it isn't there; which is when the situation gets difficult and truly gripping.

'And just in case you might be tempted to classify me as paranoid let me say that I don't for a second imagine, sitting here on my offcut of recycled Amtico, that I was the world's first human magnet; or that one false move, one polite handshake too many, would have consigned me to the void. Yet I believed it at the time. And it was a fear that governed my life far more than Spivey and his irritated asides; more than the rules of the club; more than the eddies of social movement in Temhari.

'Drinking! Alcohol gives the copious imbiber a taste not for hops or malt but manic depression, or so I read in one of those dumped magazines before I made it into a briquette for the brazier. There was a piece about a European princess known for her vivacity and gaiety. Depression did for her. There were photographs of her in a hospital room, a paparazzi shot taken with a telephoto lens; terrible dark shadows under her eyes and a vacant look, her famous lips cracked and lifeless.

'Alcohol pulls a similar rabbit out of the hat, but on a smaller scale and in quicker cycles. One used to behave like Fred Astaire for three hours, a stunned bear for two, sleep for five, get up, behave like a snail on ground glass for two, and work until it was time to reach for Mr Astaire's silver-headed cane again. It's a cycle that's perfect for industrialised civilisation: predictable and — let's not forget to tip our caps to manufacturing — a nice analogy for repeatable processes.'

Freyn rubbed his hands together and said jovially: 'What do you think, Walter?' By now I could tell when he was pulling my leg. I deliberately replied in an even tone. 'I'm not in a position to comment yet,' I said. 'I reckon you know that.'

'Right,' he said. 'Quite right. So that was the bare scenario. What else can I say? That a person usually has a reason to drink, a problem that can't quite be resolved? The strange thing was that I didn't behave like Fred Astaire or Jack Buchanan when I was "up". In fact, I tended to be troublesome at the very phase in drinking when most people were extraordinarily jolly and hail-fellow. Give you an example — Snowcroft. He ran the agency for automotive spare parts; had it all locked up in Roraima, undercutting all comers until they withered away. Snowcroft was always holding forth about *service*. One night in the club he was going on as usual, talking to one of the district officers and a couple of Cambridge undergrads who were spending a holiday studying tree growth rates. "Service is a necessity," said Snowcroft. "In any society, no matter how efficient the government, one needs to put back, one needs to find a way to serve the community. I myself serve on three committees and do so gladly. And it's also –" by this time Snowcroft is peering in a lordly manner at the boys "– and it's also a way of understanding the thinking of the local people, which is most important."

'At which point I butted in disgracefully from my bar stool: "Yes, Snowcroft, but the real advantage of being chairman of your precious committees is that you can give sound advice, teach the locals a spot of refined behaviour – and make very damned sure that you hear of commercial opportunities first." And I wasn't even satisfied with that. "Put *back*, you said? Surely you mean, take more out."

'Well, Snowcroft's face turned to stone. "Hardly an appropriate remark," said the district officer, stiff of tongue. One of the boys compressed his lips, the other blushed excruciatingly. Snowcroft said absolutely nothing, of course. He was cunning and rolled with my powderpuff verbal assault. After allowing several seconds of silence to intervene, he turned to others and said in measured tones: "I think we might be more comfortable on the veranda, gentlemen."

'I was still leaning against the bar an hour and a half later. Mordecai – such a graceful, subtle fellow – was deliberately not noticing my raised finger, trying as usual to slow my intake. The screen door leading to the veranda critched open and the four of them – Snowcroft's party – proceeded to the main door and disappeared down the steps. Snowcroft didn't give me a glance, but the other three looked at me hard enough.

'Which meant that he'd told them all about me. Revenge for the truth of my remark. I could just imagine him waiting for one of the undergrads to say, "Who on earth was that fellow?", thereby giving him the excuse to sink me without trace, beginning with the words: "Freyn? Well, of course, it is important to judge his outburst with a certain perspective." The perspective being every known rumour about me, delivered in parsimonious tones as if they were fact, the same tones that would have been employed to squash some wretched East Indian who'd had the effrontery to import a batch of carburettors from Panama. Snowcroft had manners, you see, and manners maketh manna.

'And that's the advantage of being a soak: no need for manners. Indeed, one's behaviour was sometimes regarded with a kind of affection. A few of the chaps treated me like the club mascot. No, not mascot, straight man – as in slightly angular man. As in leaning precariously. Especially if they had a decent-looking girl in tow. "Wakey-wakey, Freyn," one of them might say, "like you to meet somebody." That sort of thing.

'Some of the wives took pity on me, but in a discreet way. There is a necessary limit to casual kindness in a British colony. One of these pitiers seemed to think I was a roué – always expected me to make a pass at her. She asked me about my secret friend, meaning Eglantine. She asked if I liked doing things on the quiet. I told her nothing about Eglantine and declared that my life was an open bottle. I remember her reply. "Bottles usually have caps on," she said. "It's unusual to find one that's always ready to pour."

'Dreadful B-picture stuff, Walter, quite stunningly awful! I remember her: her name was Charlotte Granville and she was not unattractive. Good eyes, fairly young and married to a cattle man in the savannah. I remember noticing minute beads of sweat on her top lip and thinking that she had been excited by her own innuendoes – thrilled by the coded euphemisms of imagined passion and excess.

'But I was already drunk, so she could indulge herself quite safely; take a chance, knowing that in the event that I suddenly objected, or actually made a messy pass, she only had to broadcast a laugh and and an arch look for the rest to laugh me out of whoever's drawing room I was in. I told her that my life was, in fact, an empty bottle. I was skilled at this chat. "Goodness," she said, "what a terribly active young man you must be."

'I put up with this sort of thing all the time. And I had no grounds for complaint because, after all, I hadn't been completely ostracised. No need, because I had gradually ostracised myself, as I'm sure everybody knew I would. I was all too ready to admit that I hardly existed.

'Not like I exist now! I'm well aware of myself now. One feels assimilated, almost like a participant, a being in the world. I quite understand that difficulty. It's all to do with the weight of things. Too much weight dulls the senses.

'I'm saying that here and now – I, who suffered severe weightlessness in nineteen thirty-something, before space travel was invented. A very delicate matter, the weight of things. Some things go down when you expect them to go up, and vice versa. And some things – some things come up when you want them to stay down. One remembers it all . . . all of it, as if it were yesterday. And as if it were going to happen again tomorrow. There are constants, Walter, but only if you think in terms of movement.'

I had noticed a distinct change in Freyn's voice when he spoke about 'remembering it all'. But instead of persisting, he dried up after his little paradox about constants and movement. He had clearly distracted himself with those last remarks. I tried to get him back on track but his face had taken on an unsettled look.

'Your machine is making an odd noise,' he said, rather curtly. I had a listen but it sounded fine to me. 'I expect it's objecting to irrelevancies,' he said. 'Is it true there are machines that think? Cognitive – that the right word? But surely the point is that there's no real sense of weight or movement in computers. It's no good being able to think if you're simply designed to come up with practical solutions to questions. I mean, the Delta's a solution; Roraima in 1938 was another kind of solution. But they don't last, do they? There's always another solution waiting. Mind you, I'm out of date. I've survived too many solutions, that's the trouble – far too many course corrections.'

I asked Freyn if he was tired, which was pretty obvious to me.

But he fought back with a quip. 'No, no, not tired,' he insisted, 'just pausing for thought ... having a quiet word with the sponsors, otherwise known as one's autonomic nervous system.'

I thought that was all and reached out to hit the stop button when he spoke again. 'But I was just thinking,' he mused. 'Thinking that one has developed a horror of the static. Now, I'm *sure* I heard something that time. I really do think your machine could do with a drop of oil.'

The latex incident

FREYN reached his low point in January 1938, when he was involved in an incident at the docks which was both dramatic and public.

He and Augusto had walked to the docks to 'do the usual', as he put it. Augusto was carrying copies of a particular ship's manifests. Freyn was filling in for a clerk who was ill. His task – and it was, strictly speaking, far beneath him – was to make sure that the cargoes tallied with the documentation.

'The docks were busy that day,' he recalled. 'A considerable quantity of rice had been carted down there, as had several lorry-loads of raw latex from Ramasi. The rubber was in two forms, sheet balata and massive boules. A fresh inshore breeze whipped in off the bluecoat and the peculiar smell of raw grey rubber was everywhere.'

Freyn shrugged, looking blank for a moment. 'Within minutes, I was bored. And for no reason at all,' he said, 'I began to wonder where the rubber would end up. At the vast Dunlop works near Birmingham which, fifteen years earlier, I passed four times a term on my way to and from boarding school? To be reworked into tyres or gaskets or God knows what – the rubber, not me. Standing there amidst all that activity it seemed difficult to equate the two ends of the thing: the natural substance and the unnatural artifact; nature versus a separate final function. I imagined a continuous haemorrhage of latex trickling from the plantations straight on to the shiny rims of a million whirling wheels. You can see that my mind was, shall we say, prone to obscurity by then. When one is partially weightless the connections go awry. No, wrong. Not awry – thick and fast, that's how they come.

'Balata sheets, all from one producer, were being weighed when a particularly ramshackle lorry juddered to a halt nearby. I glanced at it but took no notice. I was keeping one eye on the scales, the other on the docket which Augusto had handed me. I scribbled the weights in the margin of the docket, ready for a final reckoning before the sheets were strapped and tagged by one of Morton's chaps. Morton was the dock manager, incidentally. The final load was hauled off and, as usual, the foreman said: "End of load, Mr Freyn." And I nodded and began to tally up my weights. They agreed with the figure submitted by the producer within the allowed variation.

'I looked around for Augusto and was surprised not to see him. I noticed that boules of rubber were being taken from the back of the rattletrap lorry and pulled on large bogeys to the weighing station. It was quite a sizeable load and I made nothing of it at the time. There was something about the shape of the boules that seemed different. But, as I say, nothing registered and I gave it no further thought. I even turned away as the rest of the boules were trundled up, preferring to gaze out at the bluecoat.

'Here's a little fact for you, Walter. The reason why Roraima never became a major colony was the harbour. It was small and shallow, no more than thirty feet deep to the bar, though it rapidly shelved away to more than a thousand beyond it. Well, there I stood, staring out at that thin strip of deeper water, as crisp as a ruled line of royal blue ink. And I thought: how odd that such a thin line could indicate real depth – an entirely futile speculation which had nothing to do with the practicalities of my situation.

'Consider it. My stout soles on the hardstand, the sudden burst of ululating chant from the stevedores as they combined to shift something heavy, the clang of metal somewhere in the bilges of the small freighter that had slipped in on the tide the day before; and the cry of the black women chivvying through the press to sell their rice patties and grilled meat and slices of sunlit pineapple carried in glass boxes balanced on their heads.

'And there was Augusto, dodging between the boules with a worried look on his face – and a flash of excitement too. "Excuse me, Mr Freyn," he said, "but these boules is something funny happenin. A man behind the lorry bringin them. He wearin a gun. It say Smithson on the lorry but I don't know about that."

'I took a look at the shipping details. The export of the boules was an agency arrangement, a part-load to make up a cargo that was being shipped to Manaos. The rubber had been delivered by Smithsons for cash to be paid dockside by a man called Tragger from Kingley Spraque. So I sent Augusto to find Tragger. But nothing: nobody in Morton's crowd had seen him that morning. I thought Augusto's gun story rather fanciful and began my dreary noting as the boules began to be weighed.'

Freyn stopped. 'Boring you, Walter? Do say.' The question took me by surprise. 'No,' I said. 'You know I like details.' That seemed to amuse him. He shrugged in a comical manner and cleared his throat.

'How does one deduce something without being aware of having done so?' he asked. 'I am given to understand by the *Scientific American* – first rate, Walter, burns beautifully – that one is not really aware of very much at all. Our physical sense of the world is apparently woefully incomplete. We take in less than one-hundredth of all typically available stimuli. We're geared to respond to anomalies in particular. And I think that must be true. Normally, if things don't add up, you know it pretty quickly. But there at the dock that morning it didn't work like that. Things hadn't added up, something was out of true but I failed to twig it straight away. I must have mulled it over for half an hour without realising it.

'I was right about the gun, though. There wasn't one. Augusto had merely seen the handle of a machete sticking out of some wretched fellow's shirt. And yet truth arose from an initial untruth because I'm certain I wouldn't have become suspicious unless the false report about the gun hadn't somehow conditioned me or sparked a train of thought. And a tenuous run of connections they were too. Was it the slightly different size and shape of the boules? Probably not: there were always variations. In the end, it was Tragger's non-appearance that rankled, the point being that the boules would not normally have been taken off the lorry unless the money man was there – and Tragger was that man.

'But they had been taken off, pretty sharpish too. And by now the three East Indian loaders were nowhere to be seen. The weighing master was uneasy. He asked if I wanted to delay the tallying, which the driver and Tragger should have been watching. But I was irritated and told them to carry on.

'It took the best part of an hour. Near the start of the weighing one of the boules didn't settle properly on the scales. The weighing master gave Augusto a steady look. And Augusto said: "Somethin be wrong with the boule." I got him to roll it aside and let the rest of the weighing continue. In all, four of the boules proved peculiarly unsteady on the weighing table. I had given no sign of my suspicion. I kept my running tally, and when I noted an unsteady boule I asked in an unconcerned voice for it to be pushed aside – low key, no excitement.

'I added up my tally, ignoring the fact that the weighing master and Augusto were staring at me, obviously waiting for me to speak. The tally was very nicely within the variation limit. I announced the total weight and handed the sheets to Augusto rather than to the weighing master. At which the grizzled old fellow – I seem to think his name was Ranks – picked up my cue. He puffed out his cheeks, reached down and handed me a machete with an unusually long thin blade, tapered at the tip, very sharp. I thanked him and hefted it as I stepped across to the boules which had been set aside. I ran the blade into the centre of the first boule and felt it glance off something hard. I did the same to the next and the machete jarred and turned slightly in my hand. I turned to Augusto and told him to get the dock manager to collar the driver and bring him to the scales.

'A couple of stevedores dragged him out of the cab of the lorry just as one of the loaders was beginning to crank the engine and yanked him along to the scales. There was the most terrible sound of shallow gasping coming from him: he was too frightened to speak. I asked him if he knew anything about the boules. He squinted at me for a few seconds and then – I've no idea how – suddenly twisted and leapt away from the stevedores and was haring away up Quay Street towards . . .'

Freyn stopped in mid-sentence and looked at me quizzically, his eyes squeezed almost shut. 'Well, Walter,' he asked, 'what would *you* have done?' It didn't, for once, seem like a trick question so I replied that I would have told the stevedores to catch him and bring him back. And that I would have sent Augusto to collect whoever was in charge of security at the port. Then I would have waited.

Freyn's eyes closed entirely, vanishing behind crabbed tracks of horizontal wrinkles. His eyebrows knuckled down beneath the corrugated skin of his forehead. He nodded. Then his eyes popped open again.

'I had absolutely no reason to go after the driver,' he agreed. 'None. The evidence wasn't going anywhere. It was sitting right there, grey and smelling slightly rancid, a small boulder rolled into the core of each to increase their weights. But, you see, I *did* go after him.'

This surprised me and Freyn picked up on it straight away. 'I did go after him,' he repeated. 'I saw him cut through the fruit stall that led to the entrance of Endurance Market. I followed, skidding through the rotten pulp underfoot. And then he was clear and sprinting off towards the cut that led to Camptown. I knew that if he reached that part of Temhari I'd lose him in the roaring twilight of the timber mills.'

Freyn's actions were beyond understanding. I actually inter- rupted him and pointed out that it couldn't have mattered where the driver disappeared to. He must have been known and would have been found quickly in a place as small as Temhari.

Freyn agreed. 'Quite right, Walter. He would have been tracked down in an hour or two, and might even have given himself up. But the truth is that I had focused my own concealed desperation into this chase . . . this utter folly. And when I tripped, just as I was reaching out to grab his filthy collar with my left hand, my right arm swung forward. I think it was a balance reflex. Whatever it was, it failed and I fell in a heap. The awful thing is that he trotted on for a good twenty yards before I saw what I'd done. I'd caught his hand with the machete blade.

'He suddenly stopped and knelt on the cobbles and doubled over, wailing terribly. I got up and headed for him. My shoe skidded on something. I looked down and saw it: a single finger, bloodied and curled like a raw, half-eaten prawn. When I reached him he looked up and flinched. Then, with a high-pitched shout, he thrust his right hand up at me. I'd sheared off two fingers at the knuckle. His fist was glazed with blood. His trousers were spattered and there were small, gleaming smears on the cobbles. "No more work!" he wailed. "No work!" Over and over again. And then he began to cry, uttering an awful growling sound. There was blood on his skinny forearm. Flies settled on his shirt.

'Within half a minute we were surrounded by a crowd. At first none of them realised what had happened and they were rather cowed by this odd spectacle: a black man kneeling and a white man holding a machete. Then the penny dropped. A woman said: "Somethin bad wrong with his hand." I explained that he was trying to escape and that there had been an accident with the machete. The driver was still grizzling and I watched a fat tear roll down the end of his nose and fall on to a bloodstain on his trousers.

'I had just asked someone to fetch a horse and cart when a scream cut the air behind me. Then consternation and voices, proclamations: "Is a dead finger!" . . . "Dead finger pointin up to the sky" . . . "Soul finger go to He Jehovah!" The crowd moved towards exhibit A. Then one of them, a youngster, scurried back and took a close look at the driver's hand. "Thass one finger!" he

called. "He got two fingers loss! Nother dead finger be missin!"
This information induced a kind of hysteria. The women lifted
their skirts and began to scan the ground. The men and street
urchins began to fan out, heads down in a gruesome form of
study, fingers pointing as they pirouetted this way and that,
searching the cobbles for the missing finger. And then, finally:
"Be th'other dead finger! Be right here, pointin at the clock
tower!"

'I waited for the cart, saw the driver lifted on safely and paid
the carter to take him to Mercy Hospital and tell them to send
the bill to Spivey & Co; gave him half the fare and told him he
could collect the balance from me at Spivey's provided he came
with a note from the hospital confirming the driver's admission.
The cart rattled away with the driver curled up in the back on
a pile of empty sacks. I noticed that his head bounced as the
cartwheels bucked over the ruts. The fingers of my right hand
felt hot. I looked down. There, unremarkably, was my wrist,
my knuckles, the polished handle of the machete. There was a
thin trace of my sweat on the blade, which had run down the
knurled indentation and merged with a tiny smudge of blood
near the tip.

'There was nothing else for it. I simply walked back, feeling
nauseous and faint. Everything looked unusually pale and the
light seemed to skewer off things unpleasantly. The pink awning
above Farouk's Selectorium fluffed in the breeze on the other
side of the street, and the pinkness seemed to flare for a moment
and become riddled with acid green stripes. I felt blank with the
horror of what I'd done to this pathetic man, this nobody caught
up in somebody else's scam. It was absurd – and utterly real.

'And yet, do you know what disturbed me most profoundly
on that walk back to the dock? That nobody took any notice of
me. My crime, my moment of idiocy, had left no mark; as if
water had closed over a drowned body. By the time I got back to
the dock everything and everybody seemed not only tenuous
but positively glowing with falsehood.'

Freyn sighed. 'Better make you a cup of tea – a meagre

reward for your patience, I grant you. We'll take five, shall we?' I hadn't a clue what he meant by that, but accepted his offer. My mouth and throat were dry. I think my breathing had shallowed; but not exactly because of the drama of the machete incident. That was peanuts compared to any of the dozens of violent episodes in the Delta daily, if not in London's financial securi-zone. It was Freyn's tone of voice, which had grown increasingly tense during the telling of the tale, that had disturbed me. His normal easy cadence had gone. And as he had become less fluent, so I had become tenser, as if I myself were being sucked into the scene. Freyn's description left me feeling threatened. I watched him pour the green tea.

'Not too much salt in your tea, I trust?' he asked, holding the mug out to me. I noticed the trembling surface of the tea. 'Talking dries the throat, Walter. I put a little salt in everything, even boiled water. One never knows, does one, about organisms? When I first came to the Delta I suffered terribly below the belt. I think the salt helps. I chew orange peel regularly, of course, to balance the sodium. Water retention's the last thing a chap needs in the Delta. Why don't you scientists direct your attention to developing an atmospheric diuretic so that we can turn this perpetual acid fog into a good dose of rain. If there's too much salt in your tea I can add some orange peel. Here, I can just pop a bit in if you — no? Well, as you wish, Walter, as you wish.

'Let's see. The poor man's name was Murti. His name springs to mind very readily. He survived my idiocy, of course. It was as if either I didn't quite exist, or that I did exist but had imagined the whole palaver. When I got back to the docks I was in a state of shock. This sense of being separated from everything — the fingers on the cobbles, Murti doubled over, the weight of the machete in my hand — had overwhelmed me.

'The first thing I did was tell Augusto exactly what had happened. Augusto's only comment was: "Be two fingers less be cheatin with." When I took a drink at the club later, I forced myself to tell a fellow — Candace, was it? — what had happened. He grunted and suggested airily that Murti had probably bowled his last leg break. I couldn't accept these responses. I wanted the event to be substantial, instead of which it became increasingly transparent.

'I don't know how I managed to complete the morning's work. But I did, and when I re-checked copies of that day's paperwork later I found everything in order. I hadn't missed a thing – even down to spotting a small error in a bill of lading. When I got back to the office it was lunchtime. Spivey, as I had hoped, was still at his usual haunt, the Kensington Chop House, and wouldn't be back until half two. I told Augusto I was going to have a sleep on the settee in my office and that he should wake me at two-fifteen. I wanted a little time to prepare my report of the incident for Spivey. I wanted him to . . . to respond. I'd sliced two fingers from the hand of a complete stranger and somebody had to tell me that this was a bloody awful thing to have done. I knew I could rely on Spivey.

'I dozed fitfully under the fat cream-coloured blades of the overhead fan, watching its rhythmic draught flick up the edge of the same bit of paper on my desk again and again, moving the sheet sideways very slightly every minute or two. Just the fan stroking the air and the dry rustle of the paper. Perhaps I became mesmerised. I was fascinated by the motion of the fan's three blades, a milky blur which at two points produced the effect of shiny, radiating streaks – daylight reflecting off them at a certain angle. The blur was circular, of course. It was easy to see where the blades joined the centre, but very difficult to see their outer edges with any precision.

'And I lay there wondering fatuously: where do the blades end and the air begin. It was rather like that time a few months earlier, when I grabbed the edge of my desk because I thought I would float away or evaporate. I felt that same acute feeling of something stretching, trying to pull clear, a taut rope whose strands were on the point of snapping.

'I closed my eyes and must have slept for a while. When I woke I thought . . . I thought for a moment that everything was on fire. There was a tremendous sound of flames and air being sucked through something collapsing. Only a trick of the senses: the fan and the crackle of the paper had been magnified by my disorientation. And then I remembered the bleeding hand and the spattered trousers and the man's repeated cry: "No job, no job!"

'I glanced at my watch, a rather good Bensons given me by one of my uncles. It was twenty past one. I heard a couple of the girls pass along the corridor, and a screen door slamming and bouncing twice against the jamb before coming to rest. It wasn't outstandingly hot – I remember that quite well – yet I seemed to be sweating a bit. I was unconcerned. The steady whup-whup of the fan lulled me and I dozed off again.'

Freyn stopped to sip at his cold tea. 'Do stop me if I'm wandering above and beyond the call of duty.' I reassured him, saying that I had again been impressed by his recall of detail. He was ready for that. 'Yes,' he replied quickly. 'Some files never get lost, no matter how hard you try.' He offered to make fresh tea but I declined. And then he was off again.

'My eyes flicked open just as that bit of paper on the desk was pushed a crucial millimetre too far by the fan's draught and as it skipped sideways off the desk and side-slipped I tried to catch it. A pointless reflex as the desk was six feet away. My grab caused me to roll off the settee on to the floor. "Be like tryin to sleep on a ship, Mr Freyn. Cept this a land ship." It was Augusto, in the doorway at the appointed time. "It be comin upon ten minutes after two o'clock, Mr Freyn." I thanked him from the floor with an all too literal gravitas and asked him to tell the boy to bring up some tea and a couple of slices of lime.

'I reached over and picked up the sheet of paper. It was a cargo declaration: coffins bound for Caracas via Port of Spain. I got up, stuffed it into the relevant folder and waited for the tea. And it was only then, sitting there trying to rub some feeling into my face, that it occurred to me that I might have committed a criminal act: Englishman, twenty something, runs amok with machete, sued by native, beats hasty retreat to Guadalcanal. But, my God, was there a *bank* in Guadalcanal, or a postal service?

Would I be able to receive my remittance? Or would that be that? For a minute or two things seemed very real.

'But the moment passed quickly enough. Warburton Worricks padded in with the tea and put the cup and saucer down with an elaborate two-handed swooping movement. He glanced at me as he was doing it and said: "Buzzard comin in to land, Mr Freyn!" The saucer made contact with the inlaid leather pad on the desktop. There was barely a ripple on the surface of the tea. Master Worricks must have noted my surprise. "Juss be slow at the lass and turnin up and gettin on so the branch be hardly movin at all," he said. I thanked him and complimented him on his dexterity. He took it coolly, studying me with the steady, appraising eye of the lawyer he later became. "Any time, Mr Freyn," he said with a big grin. "Juss be callin for Worricks's air mail service, special delivry suitin you to a T, like tea, Mr Freyn. Be a T like tea. That be my advertising, like on Mr Chinero's shop the sign that sayin you never be shoppin another place if once you be choosin at Mr Chinero's. But Mr Freyn, mine better than Mr Chinero's because it be shorter." I gave him yet another box of matches for his model of the offices and he skipped out at a rate of knots. I think that boy had a far greater aptitude for colonial life than I did. I finished my tea and gathered myself.

'Spivey looked liverish and winced slightly as I entered; could have been his gallstones playing him up. He began to reach for his lapels and then dropped his hands to the desk, having thought better of showing any sign of his irritation at my presence. He stared at me, which was usual. He never spoke first when I confronted him in his own office – the silence was a little method of his. Neither did he offer me a chair and that too was normal. I explained what had happened and when I told him the worst, in some detail, he simply said: 'Dead?' Not dead, I replied, just the two fingers. I began to finish off my account but he interrupted again. "Sent him to hospital?" I nodded. "Just make sure you get a note from the place, that's the only thing to worry about. In fact, send your man down there now, get him to collect it. Give him a covering letter to take so there's no confusion. Headed notepaper."

'Spivey was dealing with the mess with his usual briskness, and I braced myself for an equally brisk critique of my actions, or even the sack. I began to ask about the possibility of complications but he brushed it away. "Insured," he said. "All contracts pertaining to the carriage of goods are covered by personal insurance and certain disclaimers, one of which clearly eliminates payment of compensation for injuries sustained during security measures."

'Spivey paused and frowned, tapping his finger on a file. It was the general agency agreement with Smithsons. "Full marks for your balata sleuthing," he said. "Draft a letter to them. Tell them, concisely, what happened at the weighing machine. Give the tally details and say we feel that one or more of their staff may have let them down. Say that we have received warning shots from other balata dealers who have objected to the weight trickery. Say that the reputation of the trade may have been damaged."

'That made me blink. Just couldn't accept his reaction. "News travels faster than you think," said Spivey. He'd just had lunch with Porgress, the balata man from New Kent and had already roped him into the idea of pressuring Smithsons on another matter. And now he'd spotted a fresh opportunity. He told me to conclude the letter by saying that after careful consideration, and at some risk to the reputation of Spivey & Co, we would continue our shipping services to Smithsons but at increased rates – say, eight per cent net. "Get a draft done in the next day or two," he said. "Clear it through me. There are one or two more balata wholesalers I'd like to chat to before the note reaches Smithson. One must be thorough." I waited. Spivey tapped on his desk – my cue to leave. End of story!

'My brush with reality was over and I was again invisible. The truth was that in Roraima certain crimes did not exist if you were British. One did not have to go on the run at all; one didn't have to throw the stained, implicated machete into the beige waters of the bay; one didn't have to hide; one merely had to carry on being weightless.

'Which didn't stop me reliving the incident many times in the next few weeks. I think I drank a bit less — at least for a while — and spent a good deal of time out walking or tucked away in my room above Madame Jopahl's. I was working at it, you see, trying to get a purchase on my guilt and the giddy horror of the memory. But . . . *nothing*. The whole incident seemed to evaporate. Oh, I still felt squeamish when I thought of the blood and the blade slicing through those fingers. But that sharp feeling of horrified guilt faded to nothing, as did the sense of farce that pervaded the memory. The shambles slowly tidied itself, like a film run in reverse or a collapsed house of cards reassembling itself, until I might as well have been standing on the polished tiles of an empty room, listening to voices offstage.

'After a while, they even stopped calling me d'Artagnan at the club and in the drawing rooms, and went back to avoiding me as my drinking resumed its normal pattern and volume. As for me, I reverted to established type. I bought Eglantine new shoes once a fortnight, and rings set with semi-precious stones — once, a silver Virgin with tiny zircon eyes. You could get zircon for next to nothing in those days. She always kept the Virgin in its little veloured box, which had two opening flaps. She liked to hold the box close to her face and open the flaps slightly, letting in just enough light to make the eyes sparkle. Then she'd whisper to it and shut the flaps again. Eglantine had to have her mysteries. We both did. Unfortunately, mine were not padded with velour; neither could I conceal them behind two cardboard flaps embossed in gold leaf with a legend.'

Freyn yawned and pointed at my mug. 'You didn't finish your tea, Walter. Expect you thought I hadn't noticed! No, good Lord, leave it, leave it, otherwise you really will taste the salt. It's fine when it's hot — and pretty damn devilish when it's cold. Mind you, I could have done with some of this tea in Temhari. Might have jarred me awake sooner, given me my weight back. Oh, yes, don't fret, Walter, I did awake in the end because there was a cure for weightlessness after all. There always is. The light on your machine has just started showing red. Does that mean anything?'

Irritating interruptions

FREYN had delivered the last stretch of his story rapidly, practically like a businessman dictating a report – and so vigorously that I had to remind myself of his age. To be blunt, it was at times hard to connect the powerful currents of his recollection with his marginal physical condition. If I wanted to be cruel I could refer to him as a bag of bones. I only say that to make it clear that I was finding him increasingly remarkable. Maybe I mean fascinating – fascinating enough to dump me into an embarrassing episode.

I might as well mention it, as Freyn was the cause. It concerns my partner. She has disengaged herself from me. Two days after that session with Freyn she informed me by intra-mail that she was unable to continue seeing me because of the state of my securispace. For the record, her name is Viola Kremmler. She said she was not prepared to continue our interpersonal physical pursuits amid 'all that morbid junk'.

This means it's over. I admit that her physical skills were exceptional, but I can't understand why she was unable to separate our relationship from the condition of my securispace. It's true that I'd overdone it on the research front. I don't mean lichens – I mean Freyn. In the previous two weeks I'd really gone overboard: maps, digipix, reports, all kinds of stuff. I'd been pretty indiscriminate; the place was awash with the parallel story of Freyn in Roraima, the extra details I had assembled. Example:

one day I got out of bed and stepped on a blow-up digipic of the Spivey & Co logo. For a split-second I imagined I was in Freyn's room above Madame Jopahl's.

I suppose Viola had a point. Things had got a little out of hand. We had been stepping on or around stuff all the time. Not that I'd planned to say anything to Freyn about this mess. If he thought I'd been second-guessing him or checking on his details, it might have killed the whole thing.

On the other hand, second-guessing paid off in another way. I might have screwed up with the Viola fiasco, but not over that Miriski business. I had been right in my suspicions. As I expected, the control specimens that I had been told to collect on his behalf were inconclusive. I waited right to the end of the meeting – Miriski, I and a particularly unpleasant assessor, Swinton – to make sure Miriski wasn't going to table other mutation factors. By then I could see that Swinton was not overly impressed with Miriski's theory. So I said, casually: 'I nearly forgot. I thought you'd like the chance to rule out capillary action through the boxes. Here's a list of internal conditions. The list includes the boxes from which both the control samples and the mutant samples were taken.'

Swinton didn't say anything right away. He just stared at Miriski and said in that nasty, wheedling voice of his: 'No harm in comparing Cowley's content listings with yours. What do you think?' Miriski couldn't think of a get-out quick enough and Swinton was in for the kill. 'Do you have your list with you?' He knew he had Miriski, and Miriski knew it too. He was like a specimen insect, pinned to a board. He tried to get out of it by saying that mutations of that degree of grossness had never been associated with box capillary actions. Swinton reminded him condescendingly that gross discoloration had not been associated with capillary action until Vikram Chandra's discovery of the relationship between certain capillary products and the effects of cordite concentrations in the air.

'The best solution,' he said, 'would be for you to make your own list of box contents, just as a back-up to Cowley's. But you can put the project on the back burner if you like, as I'd be very keen to get your help on something else that's come up that's almost certain to pull in big numbers from the Koreans.' That was Swinton's way of getting Miriski to dump the mutation project: any mention of really heavy money for commercial spin-off research usually stops any time-wasting academic waffle stone dead.

I was pleased at the time, pleased that I'd put Miriski in his place. There's no doubt he deserved what he got. He's now working on a digital colour rating system, office based – plainly a demotion. But now I feel rather guilty about my subterfuge. When I went back to my securispace after the meeting with Swinton I felt like an intruder. I looked around at all that stuff about Roraima spread on the floor and over the furniture and pinned to the walls. And I thought: I am not worthy of Freyn's confidence.

I stayed away from him for two more days than I needed to. It was a case of disciplining myself. When I eventually tapped on the top of his box with the usual four-tap signal, he called out straight away: 'That you, Walter?'

The assignment

FREYN was ready for me and wanted to get on with it. I know this because he not only forgot to ask if I was well, but even forgot to brew up some tea. This was unheard of. I only just managed to hit the recorder's start button when he got straight into it. At first I wasn't sure what he was talking about. After a bit I worked out he must have been talking about a time shortly after the Murti incident.

'I awoke from a dream which had something to do with water,' he said. 'My skin felt piping hot and bone dry. It was early. I could tell that easily enough. The resident lizard, a small lime-green fellow, was still asleep on top of the mirror frame. Old Bonnie McCloud, who was Madame Jopahl's do-this woman, was at the standpipe under my room's back window, the water drumming tunefully into her bucket. Which meant that it must have been about half past six in the morning. Through the window I glimpsed a pale blue haze. It was going to be very hot and dry. The quay would be dusty and Augusto would soon be carrying out "ventilations" in my office and arranging my papers into piles according to size rather than subject matter.

'Eglantine was uncovered, as usual. I think her skin relished its intimacy with the night and the early morning air. It was thirsty skin, thirsty for life. Her hands were drawn up to her forehead and her crucifix lay on one of her breasts. Its silver chain left a delicate track like a snail's trail. She wasn't a Catholic, not even a Protestant. It was simply that she had taken a shine to the image of Christ – that, and the fact that this one on the crucifix glowed in the dark. She woke me up sometimes to tease me with its faint green glimmer. In the dark, there was just the glow, but no form to it. She took the representation of Christ on trust – well, you do, don't you, when darkness rules and the great architect's travelling representative lies crucified on a warm breast?

'I probably yawned and did some calculating: present time, office schedule for the day. And I would, as usual, consider them against the foreign landscape of her body. The bagatelle of duties, the whole business of being British in Roraima, weighed against an innocently sleeping Eglantine. And the strangeness of my always wanting her despite my evaporating soul.

'Anyway, on that day I remembered about a shipment of bauxite – some question about the documentation which needed amending before Morton's lackeys got sight of them. I reached across and gently prodded Eglantine just below her navel, her most ticklish spot. As usual, her eyes opened immediately. I had a fleeting impulse to introduce myself, just to be flippant. I suppose I *was* a stranger; hardly mattered at that moment. She got up and made tea, did it meticulously; boiled the water on a small wood-burning stove in the corner; sluiced the pot before adding the Jacksons; filled the pot; put the lid on with a soft scrape and ting. And then she put the pot and cups and saucers on to a small square of plywood on which she had painted a gaudy rendition of Buckingham Palace by way of the Tower of London. She brought the tray to the bed, set it down at the foot end and filled the cups with great deliberation. We didn't take milk.

'She was always so intent when she poured. The very opposite of her casual nakedness as she went about making the tea. She put the tea down and covered it with the corner of the sheet. Outside, old McCloud began her daily moan: "Ho, the *punishmen* of it." A pause and then: "Why this pipe water stoppin when it only juss start – ho, the punishmen, I'm sayin, the punishmen. Always punishmen comin too fass."

'At about this point – mother McCloud's complaints arrived to the minute on most mornings – I would take in a deep breath, trying to fill myself with everything in that room: the bed, the mustiness, the mirror, the lizard, the wisps of steam rising from the willow-pattern cups. And Eglantine's body, too. I was like a bottle, had to stopper everything up, keep it safe while I got on with my British things, which would commence the moment I stepped into the alley and waved a thoroughly decent good morning to old McCloud who, by then, would be cursing the punishment meted out by the spigot, which was hard to close.

'Does it surprise you that I remember this particular morning so clearly, Walter? Perhaps I don't remember it at all – it could be an amalgamation of many similar mornings in Temhari, I grant you that. Events overlapping, one consuming another. Do you think memory has a future as the gift-wrapped product of a multi-national company, a licensed recreational hallucinogen? They could bleed me for mine. I'm a continental shelf of memory, littered with half-remembered wreckage.

'Even so, I must ask you to accept what I've said about this particular morning. I genuinely do remember, even if one or two of the details might be slightly off. I remember that morning because five hours later, just before lunch, Morphen's telegram arrived. It was obviously important – and equally obvious that it concerned matters that Spivey already knew about.

'Spivey was ill, as I think I mentioned. I decided to take the unusual course of calling on him at his home and showing him the telegram: judging by the wording time appeared to be of the essence. I needed to know if he would collect the horses from Luchenne himself, or whether he might want me to do it. The thought of getting away into the bush for a while was attractive to me and I thought that if I showed some interest and keenness he might let me do it.

'Spivey lived at Fairhampton, a pleasant and well-protected

residential cantonment for upper echelon Brits. He had a large house. That day, the watchman and dog were asleep under the balcony next to a tethered hound, out for the count. I struck the gate bell with its ornate chained hammer and waited. There was no sign of movement from either the watchman or the dog.

'Then I heard a swing door creak and clatter shut, and here was the reclusive Mrs Spivey coming slowly down the veranda steps, cheeks ashen with powder, flecks of it on her sunburned neck and hair, which was a tired fawn colour – thick, though, and marcelled into stiff waves. She was wearing expensive-looking shoes. Her nails were perfectly painted and set into fingers cluttered with liver spots.

'Spivey was in a steamer chair in the deep shade of the back veranda. He looked tired and irritable, as per normal, but not particularly ill. I noticed two or three half-dried rings on the lacquer of the wide wooden armrest on which his right arm lay. Flies were dipping around the rings – therefore something sweet, therefore rum.

'He was obviously surprised to see me though he tried to cover it. He kept me standing until he noticed the telegram I was holding. He told me to take a seat. His voice was sharp, down to business straight away. He scanned the sheet and handed it back to me. "You will have to deal with this yourself," he said. "As you can see, I am out of sorts and even if I recover quickly, I'm not going to risk a relapse in the interior – and certainly not in the vicinity of that bloody man Luchenne."

Spivey may have been ill, but from the neck up he remained as sharp as a tack, rapping out the orders without a pause: 'Allow five days to get to Luchenne. Go by road as far as Samuni. Pick up the river steamer there and carry on to Caribat. Sort out your mules and supplies at Caribat. Then go by bateau to the penal colony and ask Fanshawe to let you have one of his trusties, who can look after things when you go across country to Luchenne. Then do the whole thing in reverse. Time the whole journey so that the horses can have at least a week of stabling in Temhari before joining ship. You'll need to travel with them to New Orleans, where you'll deliver them personally to Morphen. Having done that, take the first decent boat back. I'll leave you to sort that out. I hope that's all quite clear. Let me have your detailed itinerary, including shipping arrangements, by the day after tomorrow. Another thing: have a word with Scable. He knows the ropes. Let's face it, bloody man's gone bush already.'

'Mrs Spivey – christian name, Dorothea – appeared with chilled glasses, ice and pawpaw juice, which clearly infuriated her husband. She ignored him and set to, engaged me in conversation; wanted to know where my family was from, school – the usual nonsense. Spivey began to fidget, scratching on the edge of his armrest. I noticed that Mrs Spivey blinked hard two or three times as if trying to ward off the sight of his fidgeting. Spivey pointedly ignored his fruit punch despite the heat of the afternoon.

'When it was polite to do so, I claimed a pressing appointment and took my leave. Mrs Spivey accompanied me to the gate. I could think of nothing better to say than to thank her for the cooling drink. She smiled and a fine vertical crack appeared in the talc just above her left eye.

'And as I began to turn away she said something odd. She said: "If you run into an American called Wintle, in the bush I mean, be careful." As Spivey hadn't mentioned him, I was taken aback. I asked her what she meant. "They say he's mixed up in something," she replied. I thanked her and left. I had the idea she was trying to get at Spivey in some way I couldn't possibly understand. I thought nothing more of her remark.

'I spent the rest of the day dispatching messages. For a while it was like being normal again, surrounded by details that seemed to matter: the cost of a guide and mules, shipping schedules, maps. I was excited, without at first knowing why. I thought I had lanced my own feckless boil. For a while, as the details proliferated, I thought I had stumbled on to the road to Damascus and that from now on my life would radiate purpose.

'That evening I went, as Spivey suggested, to seek out Scable at the club – more specifically, the bar. Scable was a tough nut and drank with a steely professionalism. He was often soused but never incapable, and he had that skill that only truly gifted drinkers have of being able to switch from buffoonery to cold, detailed alertness in a second. He agreed to cast an eye over my itinerary and then got down to business. "Like you to try my latest concoction."

'He talked like that, Scable, as if language had to be kept in check. He pollarded sentences, treated them like rogue oaks. In any case, he became rather maudlin about a mule he'd seen in Port Said; one of those mules that perform with women. It's extraordinary that people would pay to watch such a spectacle – but it's the fee that's the real lure, isn't it? If you pay for something you are both the possessor and the absolved.

'One always ends up paying for culture, doesn't one? And the components of culture are not so very different from an hour with one of Madame Jopahl's petits noirs or the bunched muscles in the flanks of a performing mule, or the ankle of a bored-looking girl behind the perfume counter of a department store in Oxford Street. And gratification . . . rather a mythological business, wouldn't you agree, Walter? In those days gratification was a singular matter: nobody knew what it meant to anybody else.

'Scable rattled on about myths that night. "The god Horus," he said. "God of time. No – wait one. Not sure about that, Freyn. But he probably looks like your Augusto. Add a bit of dust and gold leaf and turquoise. Do the trick, eh?"

'Horus or not, how strange to be a god of time; in charge of something that ticks away remorselessly in all directions and dimensions. Measured out, endless, like an assembly line of Scable's precise, deadly cocktails and each one delivered in a glittering cut-glass tumbler.

'Scable got quite drunk and took a particular shine to Mordecai, to whom he began to explain the virtue of travelling light and keeping on the move. As Mordecai looked on impassively, his hands folded demurely on the bartop, Scable commended the idea of breaking the law. "Break the law and then go on the run," he said. "Better still, don't break the law – but go on the run anyway. Pretend you're an outlaw. Pretend you've pulled off a real shocker. Pretend you mustn't be seen. Death if you're identified! Keep moving, that's the thing. Then you'll be all right, believe me."

'And then Scable leaned back on his padded bar stool and winked. "But first, bring me a refill, Mordecai. And when you've done that ask that young lady in the kitchen with the emphatic euphemisms if she would do me the honour of consenting to be my lady wife."

'I thought Scable might dry up at this point, but he lurched forward and tapped his lapel. "See this jacket? Chamberlain and Jones, Regent Street. Chap who sold it to me – big sort of chap. Hair on the back of his hands. Tried to sell me a blazer I didn't want. That I *did not want*, d'you see? Did *not*. He had a slight limp. Left leg. The left one, no question. Excellent material, don't you think? Horus tweed. As worn in Temhari!"

'Fifteen minutes later, with Mordecai to lean on, Scable made his usual mock-scandalous exit. "That man in Chamberlain and Jones!" he yelled from the veranda. "That's a lie. Can't remember a damn thing. Invented the lot." He then asked Mordecai to tip him into the drainage ditch. "I cannot, Mr Scable, on account of the snakes be frighten." Scable was a classic colonial type. I imagine he's exceedingly dusty now. But Spivey was right: Scable was round to my office bright and early the next morning and went through my itinerary like a dose of salts; tremendous attention to detail. I hope this information . . . my god, Walter, is that a *sandwich*? Is that for *me*?'

It had seemed a good moment to offer him the sandwich I had bought at the Causeway 3 kiosk. I hoped it might keep his strength up. His colour had not been very pleasant during the previous two visits. Freyn seemed both excited and a little embarrassed. 'Well, I must say,' he said, 'it's hardly necessary, but thank you. I see there's a touch of Mordecai about you, Walter, except that instead of a bartop we're separated by your shiny little machine. I will consume this with the greatest pleasure. I'll do it now, if you don't mind.'

Freyn got to work on it. 'Well, I must say, this is very nice indeed,' he said. The effort of eating – it was a pretty thick sandwich – was causing him to gasp slightly for air between mouthfuls. 'It has a faintly familiar taste. I can't quite – smoked salmon, you say? Really? It's quite delicious. But that's interesting, isn't it? I can remember certain events and scenes perfectly well, yet I failed to identify the taste of smoked salmon, which is so definite and substantial a taste – sharp and oily on the tongue. Do you think taste buds have a limited recall? If so, this would be the first salmon sandwich I've ever tasted, but for the second time.

'Well, there you are, Walter: even in a state of advanced decay, a person's prospects are endless provided they have suffered enough. No, but you're too kind, Walter. Really, a *second*! I think I'd better squirrel it away if you don't mind. I'll just find my wax paper. If I ate the second one straight away you'd be carrying me out, just like Mordecai carried out Scable that night.'

Travelling upriver

FREYN, accompanied by Augusto, travelled to Samuni where they boarded the shallow draught steamer *Alafos* – 'nice old thing with covered fore and aft decks and four small cabins under the bridge and the luxury of wicker seating along the sides'. The captain of the *Alafos* was a half-blind old man called Darnok who'd been operating the steamer for more than twenty years. According to Freyn, Darnok was proud of his blindness: 'Never gave a clue about it, but you could tell he took pride in his extreme alertness to even the most subtle changes in light or sound or vibration.' Darnok spent most of his time in the little raised cabin that passed for a bridge, sitting in a battered old chair.

'He had a young Chinaman up there with him, at the wheel,' said Freyn. 'They would converse quietly and almost continuously, a litany of the river. For example, Darnok would ask the boy what he saw upriver and the boy might say: "Coming to slip by Rannoch jetty." Then Darnok would ask how the boy intended to steer, and he would reply: "Litoo starboar, pass sandbar on lef." The two of them kept this up most of the way to Caribat, old Darnok muttering away as he rehearsed the details in his memory, the foibles of a river that he almost seemed to invent lovingly as he went along.'

Freyn described the steamer's progress as slow going. His supplies, such as they were, were stacked and sheeted in the stern and Augusto had insisted on standing permanent watch over them. 'A party of gold prospectors had colonised the bows and were drinking olive oil and Eldorado, a particularly fiery rum. They were getting used to the olive oil before reaching their claims, where it was sipped to dislodge the quartz dust from their throats.

'One of the miners had been carried aboard at the Samuni landing and laid on a straw pallet –' Freyn patted his own bedroll '– not unlike this in terms of discomfort I'd guess. The man had fever and complained that he didn't want to return to the interior. His colleagues jollied him along to start with, then grew tired of his misery. "Don't worry," said a wiry fellow with veiny hands, "you won't have to go back at this rate because you'll be as stiff as a dried squid before we reach Indomitable and even less to behold, I'll wager."

'There was much hilarity at this and the grizzled old card was rewarded with a great deal of back-slapping. The sufferer managed a smirk and squeezed his eyes shut. His forehead was lobster red and, even from where I was standing at the corner of the deck-house, I could see he was streaming with sweat.

'It was mostly smooth running that afternoon, though very slow against the current. The regular slosh of the propeller was positively soothing, as was the thumping of the pistons somewhere under the afterdeck. On the other hand, Augusto's face remained a rigid, determined mask.

'Half an hour before we made Tang's landing to tie up for the night, the aft deck hatch slid open with a bang and a sweating head appeared, followed by a stout neck and naked shoulders. The fellow gave me a friendly nod and produced the stub of a Navy Twist cigarette and some matches and lit the thing with evident pleasure. Blue smoke wafted from the stub over to Augusto. I asked the engineer if all was well below and he replied, sharp as a tack in a clutter of wrenched vowels: "The lodge meetn's goin dahn a treat. It's the worship of vat boiluh, see? Moochl respect, mayn to boiluh, boiluh t'mayn."

'Captain Darnok appeared at the aft bridge rail and enquired after my well-being. I suspect he sensed the engineer rather than saw him in detail; he'd probably heard the skid of the hatch or caught a pungent whiff of that Navy Twist. He peered down and called: "Is that you, Bentlers?" The engineer replied in the affirmative and Darnok told him that we'd be making Tang's landing – and here I noticed the engineer's lips moving in a silent and precise mimicry of Darnok's words – "in twenty minutes by my reckoning." The Navy Twist was promptly flicked overboard and with a final wink to me Bentlers grabbed the hatch and, in one tidy movement, ducked down and slammed it shut. I think I heard singing from below.

'Darnok said he'd have one of Tang's men prepare my cabin as soon as we'd tied up. He said he usually went ashore for an hour or two before retiring, for a bit of poker – threepence, top stake – and asked if I'd care to join him. I must have paused a moment too long because he then said: "In case you're wondering how I can bid I assure you I have a method." I said I'd be delighted to make up the numbers.'

Freyn recalled that the *Alafos* docked with precision at Tang's landing. The mysterious dialogue between Darnok and the Chinaman continued as the steamer deliberately overshot the landing stage and was allowed to drift back twenty yards on the stream. At that point in the river a natural arc in the current pushed the boat towards the shore at a convenient angle. 'It was masterly,' said Freyn. 'Hardly a bump as we touched the stage pilings. Ropes were thrown and we were still. There was some shouting from below deck and then a shrill release of steam from the rusty funnel. It was just before dusk and the sky above the trees was flecked with bats.'

Freyn stayed put until the prospectors had disembarked, to wait for Darnok. Augusto apparently refused to leave the baggage because he had decided that the engineer was a freemason: 'A freemase, Mr Freyn, so I sit here makin sure he don't cass a spell on the goods.'

Tang's landing was a huddle of small buildings set in a sizeable clearing which contained a kitchen garden and livestock penned in a picket corral. There were two open-sided benabs – simple lashed-frame shelters roofed with palm leaves and slung with hammocks. There was also Tang's provision store and according to a streakily painted board nailed to the lintel of its side door something called 'Tang's Restore Rant'. Darnok, accompanied by the Chinaman, showed Freyn the way.

Freyn took up the story again. 'After disposing of the fufu and spicy soup the table was cleared and old Tang appeared with a pack of cards so worn that the pattern side of them was mostly a dirty grey. The card corners were frayed. Three of the prospectors sat in with us. Darnok had his Chinaman next to him on a stool. When the cards were dealt, Darnok held them up close to the Chinaman, who would then lean forward, cup his right hand in front of Darnok's ear and dispense the facts soundlessly. Darnok would then rearrange the cards, fan them, and study them a while longer, squinting ferociously. When it was his turn to call he'd snap out a bid, or throw in.

'Tang had a different manner. He said very little, though he maintained a steady humming which would occasionally turn into an explosive hiss delivered through pursed lips. The miners played poorly because, faced with two months digging, they were more interested in calling for their beloved Eldorado and lime cordials. The paraffin lamps cast a pretty dismal glow over the proceedings. A few villagers leaned in through the window and watched intently. The talk didn't amount to much. The miners rattled on about a place called Molly's at Caribat. Darnok told me a little of the history of the *Alafos*. And Tang was well ahead when I decided to throw my cards in and return to the steamer.'

Freyn stopped to put a question to me. He asked me if I believed in knowledge. I was about to ask him what he meant when he said: 'No, not knowledge. I mean warnings.' Well, I had no idea what he was getting at. I said the idea of warnings seemed a bit too general to tackle. He gave me a look, the kind that makes you suspect you've missed the point.

'No matter,' he said. 'No matter at all. Now, let's see. As I stepped up the ramp on to the deck — it was amidships — I happened to glance towards the foredeck. I noticed the dim shape of the feverish miner still on his pallet. I glanced aft and saw Augusto asleep on the tarpaulin covering our bits and pieces. And then — I've no idea why, because a surprisingly comfortable bed was waiting for me — I turned and stepped quietly onto the foredeck.

'The miner's cigarette tip glowed in the dark. After a moment's adjustment I could make out the man's head and the tangle of an old blanket which had been thrown over him. "That you, captain?" he said. I introduced myself. "Gold, is it, or are you trying for the hard stuff?" I explained the purpose of my journey. The cigarette tip pinked a couple of times and the man coughed. "I prefer it like this," he said, "dark and quiet is best. Trouble with the fever is you lose track, see? Worst of it is you get jammed up between sleeping and waking. You dunno if you're dead or living. Everything around you looks fake, like. Cardboard . . . nothing solid, that's what you think. Nasty, I can tell you, real nasty." I asked him if it was wise for him to smoke in his condition. Well, that got a snigger. "Wisdom don't come into it, guvnor," he said. "If this fever decides to take lodgings in what's left of my brain I'm a goner in any case. I don't worry about a smoke. It's right satisfactory when the sweats let off a bit, stretched out quiet like this in the dark with a smoke." He sniggered again. "Yes," he said, "you got to take the philosophical view of these things."

'His name was Suttree. He'd jumped ship in Cartagena some years before, only to be hauled drunk aboard a tramper bound for Port of Spain. Once there, he decamped again and learned about the gold finds in Roraima. The dingier the rum shops, the bigger the finds that were being discussed. He stowed away aboard a mail packet boat and was duly arrested at Temhari by Morton's predecessor. "Worth a go in clink to get at it, like," he said.

'After a month or two he managed to inveigle himself to Caribat and joined a party of pork knockers — freelance black miners, tough as teak, who dug and sluiced on other people's concessions for fifty per cent of whatever they could find. Suttree told them he expected nothing except food because he wanted to learn the ropes; and within a couple of months he'd done just that.

'He went back to Temhari and convinced two Dutchmen, the Houten brothers, to stake him. They made their way upriver past Caribat and footslogged it to some small ridges beyond the Borapurta swamp. And they struck lucky. Four months later they cashed their gold and bought the hotel in Caribat outright. A bit later the Houtens took Suttree's share after a two-day poker session which left one man dead in a ditch and Suttree owing thousands. And here he was, having plied the creeks and hills ever since, picking up here and there with old hands willing to put their shovels and picks into untried greensand and almost inaccessible ridges.

'Suttree was interesting. "Funny thing, gold," he said, and his words seemed almost to have been issued by the darkness. "It's the *seeing* of it that does for you. The sight of it gets into you even more than the hope of money. You clear away and there you are – quartz stringer in the rock slap before your eyes. And you really go at it then, I can tell you. Why, you can't help yourself. You're scrabbling like a dog, see? Ripping away at the loose stuff. Your eyes, mind, are fixed steady on that run of quartz. You're scrabbling and breathing heavy because you're waiting for that first streaky little flicker that means gold. Hungry for the glint, you get. And when you see it – well, you think this is the strike to end all strikes. You see that gold, especially if there's no green in the shine of it and you think it's the wrinkle over the motherload."

'The cigarette tip flared and that dreadful little snigger came again from the darkness. "And for all that, look at me. Floating in the dark, I am. Wondering if I'm talking to a flesh and blood gent or a ghost made of cardboard and kiddie's paint." Suttree was breathing heavily and seemed to be shaking again. "It's the seeing of it, like I say. Why, I can see it now, lying here, see it plain as day." I waited until Suttree fell into a doze and went to my sleeping berth.

'My bunk was comfortable and I fell asleep almost immediately. I seem to think that it was that night I dreamed of Spivey walking into the sea with a sheaf of documents. Augusto was standing on the shore scooping handfuls of tiny, glittering numerals from a bucket and throwing them like confetti.

'I awoke just before dawn to a rumbling sound that I thought must be the boiler getting up steam. But it was the howler monkeys that Tang had mentioned during the poker session. I had a quick wash and went on deck. Looking ashore I could see Tang's servant asleep on the veranda of his stores and smoke rising from the mud brick chimney. I had with me an anthology of poetry and made for the wicker deck chair I'd used the previous afternoon.

'I was just about to settle into it when I heard voices murmuring. I thought it might be the miners on the foredeck. But they were all dead to the world. Then I remembered: the voices could only have belonged to Darnok and the Chinaman. I heard the floorboards of the deck-house creak and then Darnok's deliberate tread on the stairs. A few moments later, he walked past my chair and said: "An early bird are you, Mr Freyn? Or was the bunk too much for you? Well, you're up now and I think I can promise you a pleasant day on the water. There's no rain moving down from the interior ranges. We should make the stage at Houten's Hotel by mid-afternoon."

'He excused himself and, reaching ahead with his left hand, moved towards the stern with a measured step. After half a dozen small paces he stopped, slid his right foot forward across the deck, identified the deck hatch and stamped on it twice. The hatch clattered aside and the engineer's head bobbed up. "Just finished cleanin er up, Mr Darnok," said the engineer. And Darnok said: "In which case, see if you can coax some steam out of her." The hatch slapped shut and Darnok turned slowly in a shuffling sort of pirouette, very precise, and then paused. The Chinaman cleared his throat very distinctly. I glanced up and saw him leaning over the rail, watching Darnok intently. The captain turned slightly to his right. The Chinaman cleared his throat again, at which Darnok set off, retracing his steps to the side rail.

'Augusto appeared, frowning towards the huddle of buildings on the shore. I chided him on his apparent surprise at his surroundings. He said nothing, just eyed the river and the trees. The deck trembled and I heard the dull slosh of the propeller beginning to turn.

'A couple of minutes later the *Alafos* was pulling clear of Tang's landing. Old Tang stood and waved us off with a playing card in the curled fingers of his right hand. Though it was a little misty my eyes were excellent and I could have sworn it was the jack of hearts. Augusto was immediately suspicious. "Why he be wavin that," he said. I told him it was an ancient Chinese custom, very esoteric and powerful. Augusto was unconvinced. "I be thinkin the Chinese man be runnin out of this worl," he said.

'As we slid upstream, I looked back down the river. The propeller, which was only just below the surface, cut the dark water into slices of mahogany foam. A trail of dove-grey smoke hung in the air above the spreading wake until, first Tang and his metronomically waved card, and then the clearing, were lost in a strange temporary dusk surmounted by the silvery wash of light from the morning sun.

'The remainder of the journey to Caribat was uneventful. The propeller churned. Bentlers popped up periodically from his underworld for a breath of air and a smoke. And in the background, I could hear the steady litany of Darnok's meticulous reinvention of the river and journey that was his addiction.'

Freyn was looking a shade haggard by now. He had stuck pretty well to the story and I guessed the concentration had drained him. And, sure enough, he changed the subject.

'Caribat was like the Delta, you know.' He scratched at his bottom lip.'They share the same contradiction: impossible messes, yet able to hang on somehow or other. But I do think this box is preferable to Houten's Hotel – cleaner too. And here's an extraordinary thing, Walter. When I was talking about the sun rising above the river just now I suddenly felt I was making the whole thing up. Stone juju, as Augusto used to say!'

Freyn smiled and flexed his shoulders. The smile twisted into a wince and he paused to resettle himself. 'If you don't mind my asking,' he said, 'what does the Delta look like from, say, Highgate?' I told him I had no idea. 'No? Well, I just wondered if the mist of the Delta obscured the sunrise in Shepherd's Hill or changed its colour. One is quite used to the mist here, of course. We'd probably be blinded if we got a real look at the sun. We're druids here, in a certain way. When the mist thins and the sun is at a particular angle it . . . one might almost say that it breaks through, though only in terms of relative brightness. And I can always tell when it's about to happen. Know how? Everything goes quiet. And then you hear a great shuffling of feet; no talking, though perhaps the odd cry of a baby; even the curs are silenced. We all appear from our boxes and peer at the . . . well, let's call it the increased radiance. Then we retreat into our dwellings and wait for normal disservice to be resumed. Or do I mean exhumed?' Freyn's lips compressed into a tight smile.

His face wrinkled into what I think is called a quizzical look. 'Perhaps to grow old beyond a certain point is to begin to see a film run backwards, sprocket by remorseless sprocket,' he said. 'Perhaps I'm returning to Tang's landing, except in extra-ordinarily slow motion. Perhaps I have a fever and I'm really in Caribat in 1938 after all. Not carrying a jack of hearts are you, Walter, by any chance? And about to grow a wispy beard and suffer an attack of yellow jaundice? I trust not. That would mean the *Manahatta* all over again, wouldn't it?

'About the view from Highgate. I wonder what the Delta would look like through an excellent pair of binoculars – Zeiss or Leitz, preferably. Perfect definition and corrected distortion. You have to pay for clarity, of course; you always do. I expect you're more familiar with microscopes. Mind you, the trouble with making small things big is that you invariably find even smaller things which need to be clarified. Seek and ye shall never quite find, eh?'

Freyn lands at Caribat

CARIBAT was a term of disparagement in Temhari. It was the Coventry of Roraima, according to Freyn, though I had to check his reference. I couldn't make the connection. What could Coventry, a city administrating Polish industrial production in that part of the Midlands, possibly have to do with Freyn's world? I was too embarrassed to ask him; I usually am, which must be a fault in me considering my scientific background. For the record, my research has established that, up until the late 1990s (though I have never come across the expression myself) to be 'sent to Coventry' meant to be ostracised. I must say that I find the expression incredibly specific, almost like a curse. I mean, nobody would bother to 'send' anybody to Coventry now. That would imply a strong enough reaction to somebody's words or actions to want to brand them and make sure that everybody else knew they'd been branded. Who takes words or actions seriously now, unless heavy money is involved?

That was a digression in the Freyn mould. But I have re-read it and, on balance, it is not completely irrelevant.

In any case, I'll let his description stand: Caribat was the Coventry of Roraima. It was sizeable as far as upriver settlements in Roraima went. Its transient population usually numbered about two thousand and a high proportion were prospectors, who flowed around the place 'like an abrasive, scummy tide' according to Freyn. He said the town was like a leech, the first of many which faced the miners returning from the bush with their tightly strapped, unnaturally heavy bedrolls. Their mules stumbled into town bleeding from the rubbing of drunkenly set loads, or the whippings of disappointed pork knockers.

I managed to source three photographs of Caribat taken in 1929. There's not much to describe: dusty shopfronts with dark, barred windows, alleys heaped with refuse, men wearing wide-brimmed hats whose slashing black shade obscured their faces. The impression I got was of nothing more than scorching heat. Survival is the only other word that comes to mind.

Freyn's descriptions are more worthy. And when he began to speak of Caribat it was with the first signs of the overt tension that became an increasingly noticeable feature of his story from this point on. Here's his account of Caribat, more or less as he delivered it.

'From the *Alafos*, under a brassy mid-afternoon sun, the place looked quite big: a long frieze of wooden buildings mostly built on stilts covered in orange dust. The town's river frontage stretched along the shore for a quarter of a mile – and that was it, more or less. There was activity at the quay and two strident toots of recognition issued pointlessly from a steam contraption on the wharf. The *Alafos* answered and began its arc of approach through an almost flat calm. The stream was rather wide at this point, which is why Caribat was where it was: the breadth of the river and its slow current made it ideal for shallow-draught boats of all types and for floating tethered scrums of hardwood logs down to Samuni.

'Not that Augusto seemed interested. He was fidgeting with our luggage. The hatch banged aside and Bentlers popped up and gazed shorewards. Then he dipped down again, closing the hatch with that neat flick of his hand. The miners had gathered on the port rail, supporting Suttree, livid-cheeked and wrapped in a blanket. Darnok looked over the rail and called down to me: "That's your *pied à terre*," he said. "Houtens. Look there, next to the church mission building. Once your baggage is landed Bentlers will secure its storage. You'll be safe anywhere in the town before dark." I thanked him for the information and he accepted my invitation to join me for a drink before dinner. And then the old boy ducked away from the rail to get on with other things. I went aft to put Augusto in the picture.

'One smelled Caribat about fifty yards from shore and, mind you, that was on a still day. It was a sharp, sweet smell that I hadn't come across before – an *active* smell, Walter. It comprised the various stages of things rotting, mixed with the metallic whiff of sunbaked dust and the musty green smells of the forest pressing against the place.

'The vibration of the *Alafos*'s engine decreased and a few moments later the sideplates thumped and squeaked along the cork buffers which hung in verdigris-covered bunches from the pilings.

'The miners were the first off, jumping with their bundles before the ramp was lowered. They jeered as Suttree stumbled off with the blanket over his head. Once our baggage had been landed Bentlers appeared. He was without a shirt and seemed to have transformed himself into a creature of oil. He positively gleamed with the stuff. He grinned, revealing a shortage of teeth, and announced that he'd come to "sort" my goods. Whereupon he nodded and strode off across the quay.

'The very *strangeness* of Caribat, Walter! We spent two days and nights there, leaving early on the third morning. Places have a rhythm, don't they? Cities, towns, villages; changes of pace, so there are times when there seems to be quite a lot going on – and other times, dead times. But Caribat was truly strange. I really don't think it had any underlying pulse whatsoever. Oh, yes, things happened. Brawls, simmering hard-bitten talk. There was a fight in the hotel itself and another in the alley beside the Bide A Wee guest house.

'The place seemed quite ordinary in other ways. The traders certainly did a brisk business, especially the mineral assayers. Spivey told me there wasn't one of them without at least ten hundredweight's worth of Krupps safe set into a concrete slab. And that's how you could spot the assayers straight off: their places were on the ground, not raised on stilts.

'Life seemed abundant. Urchins racketed around, people came and went. Things happened, sweat fell. And yet . . . as I said, I really don't think there was anything under it all. Caribat might as well have been a rock hanging in space where there was only endless night. There was a somnambulistic air to it. Day or night, it felt the same – static, no change, and we were wraiths passing through a place that seemed to exist only by a complicity of greed.

'Once our baggage was safe, Augusto and I made for Houtens – a rickety bloody shambles and no mistake. One's present address may have more to commend it than Houtens did. The hotel must have been about forty years old at that point; two storeys, twenty-two rooms, smoking room, bar, dining room, kitchen, and the staff quarters crouched under the stilts – and the whole contraption bulging out at all sorts of angles. The dishevelled iroko weather-boarding had been bleached to silver, the grain of the wood so raddled by the sun and rain that it had become raised. It was like bleached bone in the process of shattering in slow motion.

'The interior wasn't much better. Nothing fitted any more. Result: continuous creaking at all times. You could hear a chap crossing his room at the other end of the building. The movement of the food trolley in the dining room was transmitted to the floor of the veranda, and the surface of one's rum punch would riffle very slightly. At Houtens, one was involved with the architecture.

'The lobby was littered with women asleep or dozing in chairs, or slouching up against the walls. They all wore brightly coloured shifts and gaudy shoes. Their wrists were cluttered with bangles and trinkets. And around them, what I took to be the normal scene simply carried on: miners haggling with Portuguese and Chinese assayers or merchants about prices; short, sharp discussions about the accuracy of scales on one side, and about the purity of gold on the other; raised voices and guffaws from the shade of the back veranda; the rhythmic claps of children chanting out some game or other in the alley between the hotel and the Regality Saloon.

'And there was this old burned-out cove camped at the end of the reception counter saying: "Now I'm telling you that my sand is purely auriferous." Whereupon he prodded the burly creole opposite him on the lapel of his besmirched linen jacket. "Auriferous, like. Means pure, as you heathens wouldn't know. Soft, got that warm orange look to it, see? And I know where there's plenty more. A greensand reef, tucked away tidy."

'The creole scratched the side of his nose and began to examine the backs of his hands. Then he began to rub at one of his fingers with a look of cool concentration on his face. It was a really masterly display of feigned disinterest. "G'wahn," said the knobbly old prospector, "lookit up if you can read. It's A, U, R —" At which point the creole cleared his throat and said: "Eighty-three dole-are." The old sweat's eyes narrowed below his seared grey brows. "Don't you get it? I'm tellin you there's more of it!" he shouted. "That's the whole point. Nobody else is bringing in much quality sand and they haven't been for a while, neither, and you know it, Rosario, you scoundrel. Which means you're going to sell it on for at least twenty more greens than your usual take. I'm damned if I'm going to take your regglah price. And I say you should be damned for offering it – specially to me who's always offered to you first!"

'Rosario scratched at his nose and pursed his lips slightly. He seemed uninhabited by emotion. There was no impulse, no sign of a reaction to the miner's outburst; he might not have existed. As for Rosario, his demeanour suggested that he might just as well have been at Haywards Heath station, waiting for the 8.29 to Victoria, the taste of smoked bacon and poached egg persisting on his satisfied tongue.'

Freyn stopped for a beat and then blinked. 'I gather the trains don't much run on time any more,' he said. 'Is that true, Walter? I can hear them sometimes when the mist is in a certain condition. First, a distant tick-ticking, then a hard whirring sound; and after it's passed, rattling echoes. The fast train between Norwich and Liverpool Street, I imagine.'

Freyn smirked. 'I shouldn't have mentioned the bacon and eggs, Walter. A serious mistake. I used to think that one needed to see and smell something savoury to get the juices going. But it's absolutely not true. In fact, the actual smell of cooking does very little for me nowadays. There's a constant smell of cooking in the Delta, as you know – mostly vegetables and those peculiar beans they parachute into the charity drop zones; a bit of meat now and then, and fermenting fruit. But you're better off with potatoes and greens. No, I can sit here and not think of food at all. One eats rather automatically: potato and a little dubious butter in the morning; potato and cheese or vegetables in mid-afternoon. And a little supper before retiring. All food washed down with tea only, otherwise your stomach's a gonner – cramps, you know.

'No, but as I was saying about that catatonic creole . . . I felt such a tremendous pang. It's extraordinary – one casually fabricates the image of a woollen-suited banker on the platform and there he is, as plain as a pikestaff, smelling of his own breakfast and thoroughly satisfied with the particulars of his life. The distant chuffa of the approaching 8.29, the chitter of the rails that tells him his train will arrive within the minute; magpies on the station roof – two for joy, no doubt. Good lord, Walter – *words*! Words into pictures, pictures into excess saliva, excess saliva into stomach spasms. Words into the first scene of a weepie starring Trevor Howard. Words from this man in this box. How many worlds are we each responsible for? Gods, the lot of us! Except that our six days of toil create only ersatz things. Perhaps God is like that creole, Rosario, scratching his nose and thinking of something else because he knows we'll always take the eighty-three dole-are. And knows that we invariably lie about that secret reef of the pure stuff.

'But imagine that, Walter. Words into saliva, I mean. Would that be considered progress in evolutionary terms, or the early sign of some fatal pathology?'

Freyn looked at me expectantly. I made some remark about the difficulty of drawing a line between threatening physical change and the development of tougher, surviving organisms. Freyn listened alertly. 'Well,' he said, 'here's another idea for you: life is just a condition of vibration, and words too. Given that, would it be feasible for one species of vibration to develop into another type of vibration? Might one, if one had the refined skill to do it, create bacon and poached eggs on a warm clean plate just by speaking those words? Well, what do you think?' He didn't wait for an answer. Frowning slightly, he added: 'Luchenne might have thought it possible. Yes, he just might've.'

The finding of London Dry

FREYN took one small detour before setting off for Luchenne's ranch. Scable had told him that two good mules must be secured. Freyn duly organised this in Caribat. It couldn't have been difficult: there was a corral full of the animals on the edge of town and a Scotsman at Houtens helped Freyn pick them. Freyn then organised to travel to Fort Burroughs, a small penal colony a short distance upriver from Caribat, and select a trusty to act as his trail boss. Two mules carrying baggage would have been too much for Freyn to handle, even with Augusto's help.

Fort Burroughs was a model institution run by an Englishman, George Fanshawe, 'a Quaker built like the Forth Bridge', according to Freyn. I managed to track down a small piece about Burroughs in the then-and-now section of the academic disciplinary quarterly, *Panopticon*. Fanshawe had developed the colony using the relatively unusual approach that most offenders could be returned to society effectively if they could be shown how to regain self-respect, or develop it if it had never existed in them before.

His methods were based on two requirements: that the men should understand and accept the need for an orderly, disciplined life; and that they should work hard, be challenged in their work, and think carefully about what they were doing. To that end the colonists' days were divided into two segments. Firstly, exercise, in the form of land clearance and general duties, and after lunch the emphasis was on construction activities – dam- or bridge-building, roofing, repairs. And he made them think it out for themselves. Design, choice of materials, it was all left to them. Prisoners in their last year were allowed out on special leave to work for miners or loggers.

Freyn had cabled ahead to Fanshawe about the possibility of taking on a trusty for his trek and Fanshawe had replied saying there were three suitable candidates. Freyn referred to this part of his journey as 'the finding of the marvellous London Dry, esquire'.

The penal colony was about ten miles up a wide creek which branched off the river just south of Caribat. Freyn left Augusto at Houtens with instructions to rest in preparation for the journey to Luchenne, and set off in a skiff with two Indian pole men. He was pleased to be on his own again.

'After half a day and a night in Caribat, I was anxious to get away to anywhere I could,' said Freyn. 'Sleep had been impossible at the hotel – arguments, singing and the interminable sound of the timbers moving. I might have been in an eighteenth-century slave ship for all I knew. I got up at dawn that first morning and took a stroll to the quay and back. Nobody noticed my coming and going. The hotel lobby was devoid of life. The receptionist was asleep in his chair. I noticed the barrel of his shotgun glinting in the corner behind him and heard somebody retching upstairs. That was about it.

'The river was quiet. And there was the *Alafos* lying on the smooth surface of the water. Darnok was on the bridge with the Chinaman. The engine room hatch was fully open. It was almost a still life . . . no, not a still life, more a quaint mezzotint. The early morning light had given a platinum patina to the old deck and rails, obscuring the rust and flaking varnish and occasional splits in the teak. She looked almost as good as new in that light, ready for a maiden voyage.

'I was fifty yards off when I heard the two of them – Darnok and the Chinaman – muttering away. I was coming up to the stern and stepped quietly so that I could get a bit closer without disturbing them. "And the sun is what colour?" Darnok was asking. "Sun like mango, water is small yellow." "And the clouds?" "Clouds like smoke far away over north-west." "Is the water above the stump at McPhee's path?" "See stump number two root." Darnok stopped to have a think and then said: "I agree. A clear run, in my opinion, but possibly some rain after clearing the mission."

'There was a clang from below deck followed by a shout of pain and considerable swearing. The engineer's head popped up above deck for a moment, then disappeared. The man was like a seal! Bentlers appeared again and reported that a cylinder casing had cracked and that there was a chance the crankshaft bearings would go. So there wasn't going to be a clear run after all.

'Darnok apologised; claimed he was at the end of his tether, which I didn't for a moment believe. But I realised immediately that I'd have to improvise another way back to Temhari. I sent a cable to Spivey's assistant to organise for two lorries to meet us at a certain rest station on the Ramasi turnpike, which lay a fair trek north-east of Luchenne's place.

'When I walked into Houten's lobby – Darnok had insisted I take coffee with him – there were at least a dozen dishevelled girls slumped against the walls. Most of them were half asleep and snoring in a jerky, stop-start way. The one or two who were awake were smoking rather amateurishly. Raised voices. "I want a bloody poached egg, not a ball bloody bearing!" That came from the dining room. There was a murmured reply, the timorous case for the defence. Then the sound of a chair being scraped back and heavy, clumping feet.

'A miner appeared in the doorway connecting the dining room to the lobby. He was wearing striped pyjamas, over which he'd draped himself in a rather fine, but utterly filthy smoking jacket. He walked to the counter, clattered through the hatch and grabbed the shotgun. The receptionist awoke and gave the fellow an extraordinarily charming smile but said nothing – just sat there.

'The miner stumped off into the dining room. We had no difficulty following the scene. "Now, either you bring me a poached egg to perfection, firm at the edges, soft yolk, or you won't need to take your trousers off to shit? Get me?" This prompted a quavering yelp from the unseen waiter followed by running footsteps and the creak of the swing doors into the kitchen. There was a further clunk – the shotgun being laid on the floor, presumably. I elected to eat breakfast on the veranda.

'But you can see why I was pleased to be in that slim bateau, the smoke from the pole men's chubby cigarillos trailing a thin gauze of violet. It was the last bit of peace and simplicity I was to experience. What I wouldn't give to be sitting back in that rickety cane chair again, watching the forest slip by and imagining that an Eden like that could go on for ever.'

Freyn stopped to rub at his swollen, blotchy knuckles. 'You think I'm just being picturesque, don't you? Or that I'm gilding the lily.' I wasn't sure what he meant. I began to reply, but he interrupted me. His tone was unusually impatient. 'I mean it literally, Walter! There was Eden. Why couldn't it swamp everything else, instead of being itself swamped by irrelevancies? How could something so hugely complex become little more than a passing interest to logical minds? I think of that two-hour journey in the bateau up to Fort Burroughs quite frequently.

'I still speculate about the forest and the water that morning and I try to reconcile them with me, here and now in the Delta. It's not an exercise in self-pity. It would be simpler if it was. My difficulty in trying to make connections between the two states is that I cannot accept that my surroundings are natural. The soul of the forest pervades everything in it and it's a complex elemental soul that demands adaptation and survival. And within it all life has a clear purpose; no self-consciousness, no doubt caused by imagined futures. Information – light, shade, sound, smell, vibration – is everything.

'And there's the difference. Eden may be red of tooth and

claw, but the blood is pure and vibrant, the tooth or claw sharp and purposeful. By comparison the soul of the Delta is a shattered thing – of no more significance than a road-kill ignored by passing motorists, snug behind their wheels, laughing at a joke on a radio quiz, or being told of a plague that is sweeping a far-off country.

'You might argue that the Delta is part of a meaningful spiritual evolutionary process. If it is then God cannot exist. The Delta is not a rich but innocent primeval silt; it's an outflow of outcasts and its fertility will only breed mutations. The Delta isn't an example of life creating life, it's the shunned by-product of vicious minds and commercial complicity. You're looking at sludge, Walter. Waste matter.'

Freyn held up his hands in a gesture which I now recognised well: he was apologising for 'rattling on about things', as he put it. 'Let's see,' he said. 'I was saying that it was the last bit of peace I was to experience. Well, in many ways, it was true. From that point on things changed, got more complicated. Of course, I get plenty of peace now, relatively speaking. One's senses have become increasingly selective. Do you find the same thing, outside the Delta? I would guess that, sitting here, chez Freyn, you would hear everything going on outside my box: children, dogs, wind tossing some sheeting around, a spot of early morning percussion. Well, I don't because my ears are selective. It's like hearing the sea in a conch shell; it's there, but it's not. On the other hand, I hear certain sounds immediately – but only if they're out of the ordinary.

'The other night I heard the following: a slight, irregular scraping, very quietly done; nothing much to it, barely audible. Then I caught a whiff – only the slightest scent, mind – of petrol. I became restive and finally lifted the outer flap discreetly to take a look around. Know what it was? A degradee was very gently pushing some wooden laths through a hole in the bottom corner of a box about twenty feet away. Don't forget that we of the Delta see better in the dark than we do in the light. Anyway, the degradee had an old thermos flask by him. I still couldn't work out what he was up to. I decided he was doing some repairs and I was just about to duck back into the box when I saw him pour something from the thermos on to the laths. Then he crouched and a match flared. Well, I did the usual: ducked back into my box – anonymity is imperative at certain times – and shouted fire three times, loud as I could. Then I grabbed my pan and began to beat it with the blunt edge of my machete. Ten or fifteen seconds later, I heard a shout and raised voices. It was safe to look again so I raised the flap and saw half a dozen people beating out the flames.

'It was just a slight scraping, d'you see? Otherwise, I might as well be deaf as a post. I was certainly neither deaf nor blind on the bateau to Fort Burroughs. Blue morpho butterflies skipping through the air, as brilliant as the flash from a welder's arc, a drizzle of tiny caterpillars falling from low branches disturbed by the bateau's canopy, and the thrash of fish snapping them up as soon as they hit the water. Splays of bamboo forty feet high, old tree roots against the bank, like knuckles and dead grey fingers clawing down into the the dark tea-coloured stream.

'And greenness. Green smells too, changing all the time – musty, then a tang of something citric, then something dead and sweet. All this invisible cargo carried to me on a cool breeze. And me feeling that rare thing: a relaxed alertness, taking it all in; the bow man sitting on the prow, now and then raising a hand, signalling to slow or change direction slightly, watching the patterns of current in the water ahead for signs of submerged objects, reading the little eddies and the shapes of the flows with astute calm – for all the world like a Brighton palmist about to collect two shillings and sixpence from a jilted shop-girl smelling of talc and pear drops.

'Funny how one always says *like* when describing things. When, of course, nothing is actually like anything else. They're only like themselves, aren't they? Even two ball bearings cannot be considered identical, though they might be compared. No, but I was thinking of the use of one quite different thing to describe another and give it some sort of weight. Her lips were like cherries; legs like tree trunks; his eyes were like chips of blue ice. We just can't seem to . . . well, it's as if reality was not satisfactory. Reality: beta minus, can be improved.

'Let's see. London Dry. No, the creek, the creek. I fell asleep in the bateau, though probably not for more than about half an hour – wasn't used to Eden I suppose. I woke and sat bolt upright at almost precisely the moment that the bow slid into the sand. And there was Fanshawe standing there grinning at me, holding the hand of his eleven-year-old daughter. Guess what she said. She said: "Is Mr Freyn going to be a prisoner, father?" Demure as you like! And as Fanshawe reached out to give me a hand ashore, he replied: "Only of his own dreams, like the rest of us."

'Fort Burroughs. Tidy isn't the word. Labelled shrubs, specimen trees, long low wooden buildings, very well kept. The colony even had small cocoa and fruit farms run by the convicts, who were allowed to use profits from the sales to Caribat to buy tobacco and other extras. There's no question that the place was an achievement. It covered less than fifty acres of land, which lay in a tight, wide loop in the tributary.

'The whole show was controlled from Fanshawe's home, which was at the narrow landward end of the loop. Just beyond the house was a high-gated causeway across a vertical-sided canal about ten feet deep. Extending outwards from the canal on both sides, and into the tributary for more than a hundred feet, were half-sunken palisades. The felons could have tried to swim round it or clamber through it, but Fanshawe's advisers had planned carefully. The water was known to harbour both alligators and electric eels – the latter were particularly fond of loitering around rotting wooden pilings. Only two prisoners had tried to swim for it in the eight years Fanshawe had superintended the place; neither got away. One drowned, the other was taken by an alligator.

'I'm not saying the prisoners walked around singing hymns and slapping each other on the back, but it was immediately noticeable that they were calm. Fanshawe showed me some of their building work. Each item carried a placard noting the names of the prisoners who had built it. And his daughter – was her name Hettie? – showed me a puppet theatre built by one of them. It was rather a subversive piece, I think. It was remarkably reminiscent of the courthouse balcony in Temhari. All the picture frames in Fanshawe's lodge, the furniture too, had been made by the men.

'We sat at table for lunch flanked by polished brass jardinieres. There was a whiff of port and polish and the young lady showed me her collection of cards carrying the tinted images of famous ballerinas. "And this is Karsavina in The Firebird, Mr Freyn. Not actually in it, Mr Freyn. She's posing. And this one is Markova . . ." And all the while, from outside, one could hear the swish of grass being cut with machetes, the chink of bricks being stacked, the wheezy flop of palm leaves against the tin roof.

'I took in these details quite profoundly – took them in like blotting paper absorbing a dose of Watermans indelible. The scene was strange and new to me. You might think it was merely an extension of my spell on the *Alafos*, or the nights in Caribat. But no, not at all: that was civilisation with the manners scraped away and one was still part of the usual. The creek was a separate matter, as was Fort Burroughs because Fanshawe had made it so. It was impossible to be deaf or blind in a place like that – certainly no question of being selectively deaf.

'To think, Walter, that in my case it's come to not hearing things except peculiar little scraping noises. One might as well be moribund. Mind you, that fellow with the laths and the thermos; one can't help wondering why he didn't just pour the petrol straight on to the box and light it. Why did he fiddle around with the laths? I can't see any reason to it. Do you think cretinism is necessarily a hereditary issue, or might it be induced by one's situation in life? Over the longer term, I mean.

'Perhaps we have no choice in certain circumstances but to imitate the doings of the majority. Perhaps one's environment occasionally insists on one acting cretinous, or vicious. Acting! In which case, it's an appalling play, this. Wonder who's running the theatre, eh?'

Special forces and tourism

FREYN didn't tell me anything about 'the marvellous London Dry, esquire' at that stage. He had been going along quite well up until his cryptic remarks about inherited traits and, although it was hard to follow his little twists and turns, I kept my interruptions to a minimum.

Freyn was always fascinated by ideas connected with transformation. Words into bacon and eggs, environment into fast-forward cretinism. It's almost as if he'd given up on the recognised processes of change and evolution. And what had been the point of trying to draw conclusions by comparing a two-hour drift in a skiff in 1938 with conditions in the Delta? I mean, why invoke the image of Eden? I don't get it. I mean, that stuff is only for professional media stylists.

Suffice it to say that London Dry was the name of the trusty chosen by Freyn at the penal colony. He chose him because, as he put it, 'he had an interesting gaze. He looked at you as if he was privately debating whether or not to tell you something important.' That was enough for Freyn. And there was something else he said: 'It felt strange taking London Dry away from Fort Burroughs, as if I had some inkling I was taking him from an ordered garden into some sort of chaos.'

The article in *Panopticon* I've already referred to contained three pictures: a mug shot of Fanshawe, a shot of one of the prisoners' huts taken in 1946, when the place was still in use, and an aerial view of the colony taken in 1989. The last provided a scene of devastation. By then the place had been taken over by drug-runners who ran it as a staging point in the cocaine trade. It was destroyed by American special forces, ostensibly as part of an operation designed to cut a major narcotics conduit to Florida.

The truth came out later. The US had gradually built up its presence in Roraima by piggy-backing teams of 'technical' advisers to major development loan packages. By 1980, small groups of special forces had been given permission to use sectors of Roraima's interior for what was described as jungle training. According to documented records, the special forces had two fundamental tasks: to learn enough about the land to draw up a map of potential defensive and offensive networks throughout the interior; and to discreetly track and liquidate any freelance drug-running organisations whose profits were found to be trickling back to left-wing organisations or governments.

The old penal colony had for many years been used as a staging post by drug-runners linked to a right-wing political party in Ecuador. In 1987, Fort Burroughs had been overrun by gunmen from another cartel which supported left-wing insurgents in central America. US special forces, who by now knew their way around the interior very well indeed, attacked the colony at 3 a.m. on a moonlit night and slaughtered the drug-runners within ten minutes. All native Roraimans on the site – mostly innocent servants, cooks and drivers – were never heard of again. It can be deduced that the involvement of US troops ensured that they too were killed to stop news of the operation getting out.

There were two anomalies associated with Operation Sinus, as it was codenamed: first, though it was generally known that the Ecuadorians had local helpers, the bodies of the locals were never found; second, six members of a British REME attachment to the Roraiman security forces were in central Roraima at the time of the assault. I have established that the British forces were troopers seconded from from the signals element of the Special Air Service.

I have digressed, but not as much as Freyn did at the beginning of his next session. I had expected him to carry on as before. Maybe he'd kept up too much of a pace and needed a break. At any rate, he was in a state of some excitement when I reached him – but not about Luchenne or the *Manahatta* or the horses.

'Leaflets everywhere, like a leaf storm,' he began, before I'd even switched the recorder on. 'You must have waded through hundreds to get here. They dumped them last night. I've got one here. Take a look, Walter, take a look. It seems that it has been decided that the Delta has some merit, after all. It's going to be declared a conservation zone. The Essex Delta, a Moist Cellulose Environment of Outstanding Scientific Interest. Isn't that droll, Walter! It means that Demcorp can now ensure that nothing is done about conditions here on the grounds of – it says so right there! – on the grounds of unique biological and social diversities.'

He tapped the side of his nose. 'I had my suspicions some time ago. The increase in scientific activity for one thing. No offence, by the way – your job's a job and all that. But I had noticed other things: a greater number of helicopters flying over the Delta, usually at night, sweeping the place with searchlights. A bit of market research, do you think? Show the Delta to groups of volunteers by air, with running commentary, then ask them to fill in detailed questionnaires afterwards. User profiles – that what you call them? The phrase social tourism springs to mind, eh?

'That'll be the next thing, Walter, mark my words. There's even a little hint of it in the leaflet. It's just, let me . . . here, right here where it says: "The Delta's uniqueness as a MCE has generated considerable interest all over Britain and northern Europe." A bit further down it says, apparently in passing, that it may be possible to pass on a portion of any benefits derived from MCE conservation status to the population of the Delta – quote unquote. Which means they will give us some cash handouts from the profits of tourism and research, provided we don't shoot down anybody wealthy. Imagine a helicopter load of Singaporeans going down in a ball of flaming Gucci leatherware.

'I shouldn't criticise people from Singapore. It's not helpful, is it? It must be purgatory travelling all over the world looking so neat and tidy and never saying boo to a goose and having to restrain yourself from buying everything that isn't dead or bolted down.

'You look surprised, Walter. Or is that shock I detect on your face. I keep myself informed, you see. It's a sport, information, nothing else. In any case, I can tell you that the Delta isn't called a moist cellulose environment for nothing. They drop tons and tons of old newspapers and magazines every week – Mondays usually, near the old terminal building. I do know what's going on. If my knees aren't too bad I go and spend an hour sifting through the heaps and come back with an armful – good degradable mulchy stuff. I read them, then I burn them in my brazier.'

Freyn's reference to a brazier surprised me. He noticed my reaction immediately. 'One must take extra measures to keep warm sometimes. Look there, behind you.' I turned and saw a metal object, cylindrical and punched with a pattern of holes. I didn't recognise it. 'It's the inner drum from a washing machine – makes the perfect brazier because it lets in just the right amount of air. It produces a nice, slow rate of burn and gets almost red hot into the bargain. One quite covets it.

'But I don't burn books. I've only come across seven and I've kept the lot. Three westerns, a book on French cuisine in the nineteenth century, mysteries of the occult, and a dreary thing concerning interior decoration. How many's that? No, I've missed one: it's a novel about a novelist who dreams he's murdered another novelist by extracting all his teeth – except that the other novelist turns out to be himself, disguised as a dentist, in the first place. Rather complex, I seem to remember – but oddly empty. Maybe life's like that outside the Delta. I'll never know.

'How did I get on to that? Mind must be going. Though . . . oddly empty. That's what I was when I set out for the interior – lacking any sense of purpose yet being drawn to it; knowing that I could do nothing except learn to float before I drowned. On the other hand, I like the westerns and re-read them from time to time. The chap in the black hat with thin lips. One simply waits for him to get plugged – it's irresistible, like a mantra. Most comforting.

'But what do you think they'll do about the smell of the Delta, tourism-wise? We had some crop sprayers through the other week; three of them flying a very tidy pattern, putting down a fine spray which smelled of roses – Albertines, I think. Wonderful rose, the Albertine. How can such a robust, brutishly thorned thing produce such an abundance of delicate blooms, and with such an exquisite scent? And, do you know, the unopened buds are even more delightful than the blooms, just like unused lipsticks – cerise, very much like the colour of Catherine's lips.'

Freyn blinked and even looked a bit angry for a moment. 'No,' he murmured, 'I'm just maundering on. I'm not ready for that yet. You'll have to forgive me. I've been trying hard to keep to the story properly. I can't talk about that until I've explained everything that happened before I met her – before the *Manahatta*, I mean.

'I hope you'll be patient, Walter. One is trying to blunder ahead with this. One doesn't like to put a guest under the cosh. So . . . if you're quite sure. Really? Well, you're a Mordecai reborn.'

I sensed pretty clearly that Freyn had unsettled himself by his accidental mention of Catherine. I didn't press him to explain who she was. I suspected he might 'blunder' on for a bit. I was right – and I found the accuracy of my guess pleasing. I was beginning to pick up on his shifts of mood and rhythm.

'No, but this spray,' he said. 'I thought it might be disinfectant, except that the smell lasted for the best part of twenty-four hours. A few droplets must have got into my saucepan because I found myself dining on pommes de terre Albertine that evening. Three days later the same aircraft buzzed over in formation; next thing we knew, everything was dripping with something very like strawberry extract. If it'd been raining a bit harder one might have imagined one was at Wimbledon.

'You see what I'm getting at, do you? Delta tourism. A pleasant Scandinavian family would not wish to leave their London hotel clean and buffed of cheek and get back from an air tour over the Delta smelling of whatever this place smells like . . . the grave, I imagine. What's that? Fruit that's gone off a bit? Really? You're just being kind, Walter, I'm sure of it. But that wouldn't be too bad. A bit acidic, then? Or a sweet mushiness? Thank goodness for our sluices is all I can say. Though one does suffer for one's fart. It's the chemical cleanser they use on the sluice-run seats. We all suffer from it, you know: Delta buttock, a broad horseshoe of inflamed skin, always tender and slightly warm feeling. I suppose that means the chemical continues to react with the skin. Not that I would complain. It's better than dysentery or cholera. Yes, thank God for the sluices — or bang goes the tourism, strawberry extract or not.

'The fog's pretty bad today. I'm surprised you were so prompt. It's been worse, mind, the fog. I remember waking up one morning — two or three years ago, this was — and thought I'd developed galloping glaucoma. It was dark in the box, as usual. So I poked my head out . . . but nothing, no detail, just a thick dove greyness; couldn't even make out the other boxes properly — had a job even seeing the details of my own hands. Eventually, I began to pick up sounds, blurred sounds, as if I had water trapped in my ears. And then the coughing started, a tremendous racket, even in that thick, almost spongy mist.

'Later, when the fog dissipated, the Sannie teams began to comb the area. They took away an old woman who called herself Genesis. Her box was near the bottle dump. I saw them take her. Just a shape in a black pop-seal vinyl bag strapped to one of those PortaMort barrows. The vinyl made a crackling sound as the load jiggled past. Genesis was tubercular and that freak fog must have been too dense for her bronicals, as she called them. She used to sit in a chalked triangle in front of her box putting the curses of the ancient Egyptians on anybody who passed.

'God, that body bag. Made a very distinct crackling sound. One remembers that sort of detail. I suppose it helps one brace oneself for . . . except that it is galling in the extreme to think that the inevitable is made of vinyl that crackles. It will be hard to be dignified in death if one is making a noise like a bag of potato crisps being torn open. Are you partial to crisps? I used to be. With the salt separate, in a twist of blue paper.

'I seem to have got off the subject. It's a good thing you don't have to pay for your tapes. And that you've the patience of Mordecai, as I've said. Have you by any chance worked in a bar? No? I used to work in a bar. Notice that I say bar, rather than pub. It was quite a few years ago, in Spain, when criminals and publicans were leaving the country in droves after the tax explosion. I had been in North Africa before that, where I became enmeshed in certain rather trying complications. I pitched up in Alicante and found myself talking to a pleasant enough Lebanese chap who owned a bar called the Garotte.

'Now . . . where was I? Yes, right. First night out of Caribat. So we'd tethered the mules and prepared a meal of corned beef and tea. After we'd eaten we climbed into our hammocks, which were slung from tripods made of bound staves. I slept almost immediately and woke an hour before dawn. I looked across the clearing to see if the fire was still burning, and very nearly fell out of my sling. Patches of the ground were glowing as if they'd been sprinkled with green embers! A pale green light, delicate, wavering here and there into creamy yellows. I had the idea that we must have spilled something reactive on to the ground. Once I'd got used to the glowing I dozed fitfully until I was awoken by the rumble of howler monkeys. I looked down again, but the green embers had gone.

'I asked London Dry about them. "Be the soft rottin on leafs. Be callin them moon duss." Augusto raised the subject after we'd set out on the second morning. "I see the leafs," he said in a whisper. "Be not moon duss. Be evidence." Evidence of what, I asked. "Pork knockers be stealin gold. Special clay on they boots, leavin behind and shinin at night, bringin revenge on they fat heads."

'Augusto and his revenge! But I wonder if you've noticed something, vis–à–vis stereotypes? In westerns revenge is obligatory. Yet revenge destroys the revenger. Why do people say that revenge is sweet, or that it is palliative, or that it can be just? It can't be any of those things, can it? It can only confirm its own necessity. Luchenne, for example – surely he was just taking an unceasing and remorseless revenge on his own corrosive dissatisfactions.

'I suppose I might have found a way to take revenge on my – well, my circumstances, particularly after the *Manahatta*. I don't suppose I would be here in the Delta if I had revenged myself. But revenge can't alter the facts. It only produces new facts. I have found it's best to simplify my reactions to events.

'Good Lord, what a waste of your tape, even if it is free, gratis and for nothing! Look, just tip me the wink when I abscond from my narrative. It's Luchenne you're here for, after all. And the *Manahatta*. I apologise sincerely for all this ranting, Walter. I shan't be offended if you elect not to turn up again. I'm lucky to have such attentive company. What about a codeword if I go seriously ga-ga on you? You know, just a word or phrase that you could slip in to remind me to keep on track. What about . . . I know. How about *dementia alert*!'

Freyn and I had a bit of a laugh about that. Like I said, I'd got his drift. And another thing: I just liked to hear him talk – about anything, really. I was beginning to be able to imagine what he was describing. For example, even before tracking down that stuff in *Panopticon* I found I had formed a pretty amazing image of the penal colony. The weird thing is that my version bore a passing resemblance to the main photo in the article which related to the penal colony before it was trashed by special forces.

My decision to go with Freyn's flow paid off more and more. Though the story became steadily stranger and more uncomfortable, I was at this point really relaxed with him. I even began to imagine that I was myself being steered quietly up that creek. But instead of poles splashing, it was his words that were pushing me along, deeper into the green shadows that he had talked about. Sometimes I'd lose the sound of his voice entirely and just be fascinated by watching his lips move and the way his eyes studied me. The candle's flame would waver in a certain way as if I was seeing him in a trance – as if he was something I had made up. It was seriously weird. Then his voice would come back and I would always seem to know more or less what he was on about. And I would also know that it was him that was real – and somehow more real than me in a way that I still can't explain.

The K trance

THREE days later I found Freyn in a bad way. The hallucinogens had softened him up and, for a minute or two, I missed my cue.

That's a scientist talking, isn't it? The old one-two: everything is potentially discernible because everything is evidence. Except that by this point in our relationship Freyn already had me trying to second-guess myself. And I didn't mind a bit. The idea of doubt had begun to intrigue me. I was even wondering if I might be able to get a grant to study it – doubt, I mean. Only one snag: I'd need to find a commercial hook to hang it on. *The role of doubt as a metaphysical proxy agent in positive multiple-purchase decisions in Papua New Guinea.* Something along those lines.

A breeze had been blowing from the north-east when I entered the Delta that afternoon. A few minutes in, I passed a couple of degradees who were completely wiped out and gibbering. They weren't walking very well and their limbs were jerking with small spasms. I began to notice quite a few more of them and they were obviously spaced out. My tox-badge began to bleep. I unclipped it and tapped the liquid crystal display. The readout indicated trace levels of ketamine hydrochloride. I clipped the badge back on to my jacket and reached into one of my inside pockets for the neutraliser pack. I found a plastic blister containing an anti-ketamine tab, popped it and headed in deeper.

The rest of the way to Freyn's box was your typical Delta post-strike freak show: degradees tripping out, having pretty well lost the ability to move. It was easy to deduce that there had been a Special Kay strike within the last two hours. Ketamine-release canisters are a particularly favoured preparatory item when search squads are choppered in. The drug, which is both psychotropic and immobilising, is less physically damaging than, say, CS gas.

There were no signs of search squaddies, so I reckoned it was safe to carry on. These guys can get pretty feral, whatever your status. By the time I reached Freyn's box twenty minutes later things seemed to have returned to normal. A few degradees looked out of it; others seemed to be behaving relatively normally. But when I tapped on the top of his box there was no reply; at least, I didn't hear one. I tapped again, a bit harder. Still nothing. I glanced around to see if any of the degradees shuffling around nearby had been watching me. Apparently not. A few were working on old bits of machinery, one or two were sprawled, drunk or still kayed out and arguing in the slow motion, repetitive way they have. A little boy was whispering to a filthy doll whose head poked out above the neck of his matted sweater.

I crouched and pulled the flap aside slightly. Freyn was inside, all right, but I saw straight away that something was up. He was lying on his pallet, on his side in a foetal posture, facing the flap. His eyes were open but I got the immediate impression that he couldn't see me or was seeing something else. I began to back out of the box.

He blinked. 'I know why you've come,' he said. 'I know – and it won't make any difference.' Freyn was staring at me dreamily. I crawled into the box and squatted, watching him closely. He still seemed not to have registered my presence – not precisely anyway. 'Are you all right, Mr Freyn?' I asked. 'Shall I come back–'

'Can't do it,' he said. 'I can't do it. Not afraid of death. Not that, absolutely not that. It's more than death. More than you know. Can't navigate any more. Refuse to fly again. It's just maps in the dark. Dresden burning like a sunset. Put down what you like, indict my soul if it helps. Couldn't care less. Lack of moral fibre – don't give a damn. Nerves shot – don't give a damn. Enemy of the people – do not *give* a damn. Just put down anything, get me out of here.'

Freyn's tone of voice didn't match his words. It was a gentle, thin alto; a young man's voice. By then I knew he'd been pretty badly whacked by the ketamine and was still tripped out. I should have left straight away, yet there I was, with my recorder on, watching him as if he were a patient and I was an icy clinician looking for new and interesting variations on psychotropic symptoms to collate into a research paper.

Freyn stopped and blinked. And, very suddenly, his face was slick with sweat, a grey sheen in the candlelight. 'That you, Walter?' he said in a different, much weaker voice. I nodded. A frightened look flashed across his face. His breath began to come in thin, hoarse gasps. 'Were you there?'

I thought I'd better play it simple and go along with him for a bit. 'It's Walter,' I said. 'Walter Cowley.'

Freyn looked at me for a long time; more than two minutes, to be precise. He tried to stretch but it only made him wince and he shrank back into his original scrunched-up position. He looked pathetic. He managed to wipe his nose, but it was hard work and he began to wheeze again. A thin line of spittle slid from the corner of his lips, which were as dry and shiny as old prawn scales.

'Walter?'

'Yes?'

'What are you doing here?'

'What do you mean? Shall I leave?'

'Where? Can't walk out of the forest just like that.'

'No, I mean go back home through the Delta, as usual. I'll come back tomorrow when you're better.'

Freyn frowned and then, very slowly, closed his eyes and worked to steady his breathing. 'Sorry, Walter. Feel a bit nauseous. Bit confusing for you. I'm not bats.'

'There was a ketamine strike, that's all. You're a bit zonked. I can let you have an anti-K tab if you like; got plenty.'

He nodded. His eyelids trembled but remained clamped shut. 'Thank you, no,' he said. 'Very kind. Better leave me be, Walter. I seem to be a long way from home. Have to concentrate, find my way back. Tomorrow? What about that?'

'OK, I'll come in the afternoon.'

'Yes.'

'It should wear off in about half an hour.'

Freyn began to sigh; deeps gasps with a reedy moan at the end of the exhale.

'It's all right here,' he whispered. 'I feel quite safe. Such beauty. I wonder what she sees? I see my face in her eye. Huge, soft, reflecting eye. The *smell* of her. Safe here in the deep water. Don't care about the surface – up *there*, the surface. Way up above the tree tops. Absolute beauty right here. Weightless, we are. She's leading me out. Perfectly safe. London Dry . . . Mr Dry, *at your service*. Thinks I've lost my head. Don't you? Don't you? Eh?'

'It's Walter, Mr Freyn. I'll see you tomorrow.'

'Walter. Yes.'

'Tomorrow afternoon. That all right?'

'Yes,' whispered Freyn. He blinked and then closed his eyes very slowly. 'Sorry.'

As I began to back out of the box, Freyn started to whisper something. I stopped and listened hard. It took a moment or two before I picked up what he was saying.

'No more compasses,' he murmured. And then after a short silence: 'Beautiful. I see them there, still. Smell them. Safe, you see. Perfection.'

Just as I was about to back out of the box, he sniffed once, loudly, and cleared his throat. 'Got a bit mixed up,' he said. 'Got jumbled up. It was something in the war. I was remembering something. Got mixed up with the horses.'

I made my way home without giving the incident much more thought. I just felt sorry for him. When you get to know a man like Freyn it's not very pleasant to see them in such a state. And nothing he said meant a damned thing to me. Maybe it would have made more sense if I'd been tripping out on K, too. Maybe. But, like he said, he was a long way away – and I was not qualified to navigate in that strange land that had flickered into life somewhere in his brain.

A vision at the Look No Further

FREYN was in good nick when I saw him the next day. He unrolled his story pretty briskly – 'like a spivvy carpet salesman, eh, Walter?' – as if he were trying to make up for his confused state the day before. Neither of us mentioned the K strike or his subsequent condition.

He apologised for having earlier jumped ahead to the first day in the forest, said he should have set the scene first.

Freyn equipped his party for the expedition and the five of them – London Dry had convinced him to include two young boys to take care of the loads and camp-making – set out on one of the main trails out of Caribat with two loaded mules. They moved south-west and soon took to a smaller trail which had been recommended to them. To begin with, Freyn checked their direction with a compass but became less interested in doing so the further into the forest they went. 'The compass needle seemed so definite,' he said. 'So definite and so comic in that welter of light and shade. It felt funny in my hand – a dead thing, a magnetic turd.' In places the path was severely overgrown and London Dry, followed by Freyn, would cut a line through the vegetation. The rain that had fallen the night before they set out was steaming up from the leaf litter in places.

After three hours the party forded a small stream and paused to examine its bed. 'London Dry took off a shoe and worked his foot into the sand,' said Freyn. 'Then he began to jab his heel deeper until, with a smug grunt, he worked up some gravel with his toes. He showed me a handful and said there must be good workings nearby. I nodded with as much sagacity as I could. I knew bugger all, of course.

'The sweat ran off us and despite the humidity my tongue might have been crusted leather. And for the next two hours – nothing. Just the sound of our breathing, the swish of our machetes and the stumbling, uncertain beat of the mules' hooves and, once or twice, the klaxon of their strangled braying.

'Boyone and Boytwo began to argue about something foolish – whether manatees had developed from birds, or vice versa – when I happened to look up and see a slight break in the trees ahead.

'The trunks and secondary vegetation gradually thinned and we stepped out into a shambles of abandoned mine workings. The sun hammered down and we stood there, eyes squeezed almost shut. The workings rose away from us in a shallow shelf until it met a small cliff scored with vertical gulleys. The cliff wasn't more than thirty feet high. All around us sun-bleached stumps of felled trees rose from greysand soil which lay thinly over darker clay. The stumps reminded me of deranged grid markers. The whole area – it couldn't have been more than about three acres – was either compacted or heaped with weathered spoil from the workings. There must have been a spring-line in the cliff because running across it all was a small stream which passed us no more than twenty feet away and ran off into the forest. The stream bed was perfectly flat and smoothly glazed with turquoise and green deposits. A thin flow of water trickled noiselessly over this bizarre enamel.

'I asked London Dry if the miners had finished there, or were likely to come back. "The place dead," he said. The boys were bored and had begun to tease the mules. I suppose we should have pushed straight on towards the Neptune Mine, which was en route to Luchenne. There was certainly no reason to loiter. And yet the strangeness of the place lulled me into a state of inaction.

'I ordered a short break and while London Dry and the boys tethered and settled the mules, I walked along the stream to the base of the cliff. I could hear Augusto wheezing along behind me. "Is ghosts here, Mr Freyn," he said. But I knew he preferred to risk ghosts with me than be in the vicinity of London Dry, whose vigour and burliness worried him. "Be ghosts," he kept muttering. "What be the good of lookin roun here?"

'And he was quite right: there was no worth. But I ignored him and stopped for a moment to look down a crumbling vertical shaft. I told Augusto I would drop a stone down to see how deep it was. He looked affronted. "And be wakin up *what*?" I suggested that the devil preferred to operate in the light so that he could identify cowards better. I tossed a sizeable rock into the shaft's musty throat. It took at least three seconds to hit bottom. "There you are, Augusto," I said. "It's about eighty feet deep. Eighty feet nearer to perdition." Which caused him to click his tongue and walk off muttering his general-purpose protective incantation: "One-two-three, time be wake up."

'I looked up and saw the stringers of quartz in the rock bands of the cliff face that must have lured miners to the spot in the first place. They weren't much, just thin wavering lines, a glittering here and there of quartz or pyrites. Suttree and his fascination – the seeing of it, like! The wordless message in a glint, the craving for it. The sterility of the place was deeply unsettling: the dead, scraped-out cliff, shafts heaped with earth braised by ten or twenty years of sun. Who knows how long that place had been abandoned, how much sweat and shit and urine and blood had been absorbed and obliterated by it? Augusto had been right, of course. The place was ghostly. But it was as if the ghosts had been locked into an amber too pale to see under that killing sunlight. The ghosts, too, were dead.

'My flesh did not prickle with fear and there wasn't exactly an atmosphere of premonition . . . no, that's not quite right. There was, but it was more complicated than a premonition. There was something else in the air, another feeling, much more powerful. Can a vacuum radiate power? Can it radiate its own emptiness? Standing there, ducked down a little bit to get some shade from an overhang, it was as if the place didn't exist. It had been worked and stripped of whatever was of value to the diggers and scrapers, the men who operated the hoppers and stampers that broke down the rock and fined out the gold.

'They say the moon is sterile. Well, the Look No Further – I'd found the name painted on a board which had been nailed to a post set under a tree near a group of tumbled-down benabs – was also dead. And I had the distinct impression that I was being given a taste of the kind of hereafter that was to be avoided at all costs. Walking back to the tethered mules, past the rotting buckets and the bleached axe handles, I noticed that even London Dry looked pensive. Augusto was pretending to adjust one of the loads.'

Freyn smiled. Then his eyes practically lit up. 'But, Walter, the stream bed!' he said, in some excitement. 'It was quite extraordinary. I have often dreamed about it. The first time was the very night I started the fever. But I'll come to that. It was the sheer colour – that bright turquoise and the utter smoothness of the deposit. It was so stark, so perfect, so unnatural, running through the chaos of those abandoned workings. There was something warning about the colour, poisonous; something revealed that shouldn't have been revealed. Hardly worth mentioning, I expect. You'd have taken a scraping of the stuff, no doubt. Anyway, I bent down and put my hand into the stream and touched a finger against that coating. Know what it felt like? Felt like skin.

'Anyway, we got the animals moving again and headed off into those enfolding shadows. I can't remember how far we managed to get that first day. I trudged along trying to imagine what the scene at the workings had been like when the diggers were there. My thoughts were often interrupted by muttering from Augusto who, as always, trailed five or six steps behind me, just ahead of the boys and the mules. His subject was London Dry, as in: "Be noticin that London Dry havin a clef in his chin like a split pea."

'I had no idea what he was grousing about. The dear man's cosmology and webs of meaning were beyond me. It was as if he thought that discomforts of the mind could be assuaged by reference to something quite other. It occurred to me that I might have to give some thought to the riddle of the split pea to try and defuse Augusto's opinion of London Dry, who was clearly an excellent man.

'Wintle, on the other hand, was not an excellent man. I must tell you everything I can remember about Wintle, for reasons which will become obvious later. How to begin? Well, let me try to describe him. He was an American; tall, rangy fellow, fair-haired with a pretty poor wisp of a moustache. He was what you might call an entrepreneur, the kind of fellow whose background remains obscure and whose intentions are never clear – a kind of third-rate Luchenne, now I come to think of it; but more of a ducker and diver than a man of means and strategy.

'I had heard Wintle's name mentioned in Temhari, though it was never accompanied with much talk or speculation, which meant he wasn't what I think is now known as a player of any consequence. The only time his name came up directly, before Mrs Spivey had mentioned him, was when the governor's administrative secretary asked me to point Wintle in his direction if he turned up at Spivey's with any freight forwarding requests – something to do with his papers, some clarification or other.

'And that was the point about Wintle. Just when you had him in focus, he blurred; or if one got him talking about one thing, the subject would change seamlessly into something else. Even his clothes were indefinite. He blinked a great deal, as if he were astigmatic. In fact, that's what he was, an astigmatism on legs, a curiosity. It wasn't surprising that I couldn't get a handle on him. Sometimes I think I should have been able to, but on balance . . . why, even the canny London Dry was baffled. Wintle tried to give him an order once and London Dry feigned stupidity and cleared off. He came to me later with an unusual pleading in his voice: "Boss, please be askin Mr Wintle to leave me be, on account he try speakin to me and his face in front of me but his voice coming from the other side of his head." All very comical – or so I thought at the time.

'Well, we reached Neptune Mine shortly before midday on the second day out of Caribat. Augusto bucked up immediately at the sight of so many people, so much activity. The trees on the site had mostly been cleared, though one or two grand old bouras with split boles and huge buttresses had been left standing to give a bit of shade. And the benabs had deep eaves so the men could sit out and play cards. There was a strong smell of freshly turned earth mingled with petrol fumes, wood smoke and cooking. From that point of view one might have closed one's eyes and imagined standing in a suburban lane in Surrey on a Sunday afternoon – except that I was sweating like a stuck pig and doing my best to wave away mosquitoes, and failing to discourage the one which left its mark: a small red weal which I later paid for dearly.

'I introduced myself to the foreman, a Welshman called Gwynan. Augusto bustled off to enquire about the possibility of a meal and, finding the camp was short of meat, sent the boys off into the bush with the .303 rifle. No ghosts in *this* camp. There must've been twenty or thirty men, not counting the native Indians brought in to work the hoppers and stampers and cook and keep the camp tidy. Even so, the place was riddled with potholes full of water which ran off from the sluices – hence the density of mosquitoes. Gwynan said I'd be wanting to speak to Wintle, as if it was *de rigueur*. Gwynan described him simply as an American who was carrying out research. He soon pointed him out.

'Wintle didn't notice me straight away – or if he did, he wasn't letting on. He was doing something to a generator motor, a battered French machine with two fat cylinder casings and a skeletal blur of connecting rods in the open crankcase. There was a dark mist rising from the oil in the crankcase bath and Wintle was fiddling with the motor.

'He finally glanced at me and stopped to stretch. There was a Colt pistol holstered on his right hip. His eyes were matt grey.

No highlights, no variation in the corneas – just like cement dust cored with a small obsidian circle. His eyebrows were blond and hardly noticeable against the faintly tanned skin. The nose was slightly snubbed, the mouth wide, with a peculiar overbite. Gawky, as I said. And vast hands, by the way, the kind that fidget, have to keep busy. There was always a slight tremble to them, though his health was, as he put it, "perfectly outstanding, thanks be".

'Wintle said definite things but in an indefinite way. He spoke as if delivering a school essay. For example, when I asked him about the motor, he said: "Why, yes. This is a Rhone Poulenc Boule de Feu four stroke," and then proceeded to explain the whole workings of it as if reading from its manual. He spoke in short sentences that started firmly and then tailed off in a mumble, as if he was beginning to forget what he was talking about, or expected to be interrupted. But he kept talking, you see, kept going once he'd started and never took his eyes off your face. Blinking, concentrating, possibly not fully aware of what he was saying – but trying to read your reactions all the time. Another thing: Wintle never quite asked you about anything.

'He was the sort of man who waited for others to speak. He'd listen for mention of something familiar to him that he could elaborate on – then proceed in that monotonous voice of his to do just that until he either drove his listeners away or forced somebody to interrupt. Talking to Wintle was a form of barter. I bartered information about my commission concerning Luchenne's horses, just the sketchiest details. It was interesting that as soon as I mentioned Luchenne's name he immediately drawled: "Well, Luchenne's dead, you know." Just as several people had replied in Temhari when I mentioned my expedition.

'And Wintle was adamant: "I think you've been handed a three-dollar bill, Mr Freyn." Then he laughed and said: "Maybe he *isn't* dead, though. Horses, you say?" I asked Wintle if he'd ever met Luchenne. He stared at me for several seconds, thinking. "I guess everybody's met Luchenne at one time or another." Then I asked if he'd ever been to Luchenne's ranch, El Arroyo.

"El Arroyo?" he replied. "Not very familiar with that stretch of country."

'It seemed an odd answer and I had the immediate impression that he knew Luchenne quite well, but I didn't want to make an issue of it. I just held his gaze, smiled and changed the subject. I mentioned my delivery schedule and my sailing date. He made no comment – which in retrospect was interesting because he must have known he would be travelling with me! It could only have been the *Manahatta* that he was booked to sail on.

'I asked him what had brought him into the interior of a British colony. It was soil research – different types of alluvia, and ferrous clays in particular. He showed me a neat stack of sandbags, twenty or so, each about the size of a small neck pillow. He'd stashed them under his hammock – must've been a two or three hundredweight's worth. And they were all carefully labelled: dates, depths, grid numbers.

'He said the samples hadn't been taken from the mine site, but further away, deeper in the forest. He was assisted by a couple of native porters. One would slip away at dawn to help him for a couple of hours, and he'd go back with a second an hour or two before dusk. The natives did the digging. And then every two or three days – this was according to Gwynan – Wintle would stride out of the trees with one or two of his little sandbags. Then he would retire to his benab and write out the labels. I saw him do it that night, head bent over, candlelight gleaming off the ebonite barrel of his fountain pen.'

Freyn broke off suddenly to ask about my transcriptions of the tapes. When I told him about my Verbator DAT-to-disk software he was amazed: 'What, straight from playback? You mean your computer can turn my voice straight into printed words? My God, do you even *own* a pen?' He was only slightly reassured when I told him that I did. 'What sort?' he asked quickly, as if trying to catch me out. I told him I owned an electric pump-action Sheeny, which only made the corrugations of his frown deeper. 'A Verbator, you say?' I thought it best to keep him on track and said that he'd made Wintle sound an interesting character.

'Interesting? Well, in the same way as something peculiar in a laboratory Petri dish. No, I'm not being fair. He did interest me at that point. His whole demeanour intrigued me. Before setting out on the third day, I got up very early to stretch my legs. It was just before dawn and one could see enough to walk. I took the rifle and slipped away into the trees. I had my pretext ready: I was looking to kill a bush pig, and I took Augusto with me to prove it.

'We duly found Wintle's digging site after about forty minutes. And we were lucky to find it because he hadn't cleared the way properly. But we found sheared off lianas and secondary vegetation that had felt the blade of a machete and we followed the line as best we could, then stumbled, almost literally, across a squarely dug pit about five feet deep and six feet square. There was an iroko thinning pegged into the ground next to the pit and on it was a waxed label. Written on the label in smudged blue Chinagraph pencil was: A14. I remember that clearly – A14. We poked around a bit and found two more similar pits, sticked and tagged with references. Augusto became jumpy. "Bad numbers," he said. "They sticks a spider net be trappin folk in they holes."

'We cut a straight path back towards the camp. It was just getting light and a few minutes later I hacked through a mesh of aerial roots and there, in front of us, was Wintle. We hadn't heard him at all. He blinked several times and said: "Any luck?" I told him that that particular lady had failed to smile on us. Wintle scratched at one of his eyebrows and said: "I think you must have forgotten your cartridge magazine. Good thing you didn't come across a peccary with her young, or a mamba."

'He was right. I had forgotten it completely – the rifle was unloaded and useless. Wintle just stood and stared at me. Quite rapidly, I realised that he had deduced that we'd found his pits, or at least been near them. So in my blithest voice I said: "No danger from peccaries, but I can't say the same for your holes because I damn near fell into one of them." He nodded and said: "Too bad you didn't have more time. I could've showed you the layout." His voice trailed away as usual. I wished him luck and we shook hands. He turned away and vanished into the shadows.

'When we'd been walking for five minutes Augusto panted up to my shoulder and said that he'd noticed that when I'd shaken hands with Wintle, I'd only done two "shakins", as he put it. "Excuse me, Mr Freyn, but I advisin you do three shakins or seven shakins if you be holin on long enough. Two is bad. Two mean things splittin in haff an conflictions." I thanked him for his advice but I was hardly listening. The meeting with Wintle had unnerved me.

'When we reached the camp, there was London Dry cuffing Boytwo vigorously and threatening him rather theatrically with his machete. He saw me coming and said: "Don't you be frettin, boss. I teachin this fool boy a lesson fo saying black be white ceptin on how you be lookin at it. See, he goin whiter all the time. He muss be right after all!" At which he was seized with mirth and dropped the machete. The boy, who had been whimpering pathetically, wiped his eyes and began to giggle. London Dry armlocked him round the neck and rubbed his horny knuckles hard across the boy's head several times, then released him with a cheerful kick which propelled the urchin towards the mules.

'I suppose I should have been enlivened by London Dry's comical discipline. But as we set off, and for some time afterwards, I was bothered by an image that kept coming back. It was of Wintle rubbing at his eyebrow. I couldn't rid myself of the idea that he was trying to erase himself. It wasn't an amusing thought, Walter, it wasn't cartoonish at all – wish it had been. I kept seeing him rubbing at his face, harder and harder, until bits of skin began to come away, dobs of it sticking to his fingers like bloody clay.

'I was thoroughly unsettled. The thing is, the evidence was right there in front of me, Walter. Damn it, I knew there was something wrong about the fellow. Why didn't I see it all coming?

I had even been warned in advance. My God, Walter, I'd had the whole thing spelled out for me by that sick miner, Suttree, on the *Alafos*. All these men, the diggers, the pork knockers, the whole population of Caribat, the men in well-appointed offices in Temhari — the whole damned lot were shot through with twenty-two carat greed. And here was Wintle, whose very flesh was riddled with stringers of deceit.' Freyn shook his head. 'And the stream, Walter! The blue stream bed! I touched it and it felt like skin! Strange days had found me.'

Pollution from the Neptune Mine

FREYN got pretty confused after that, just when I thought he'd got on to a really good roll. Things were beginning to happen and I sat there thinking – go ahead, cut to the chase, tell me about this damned person whose name drew me into the box in the first place. Tell me about Luchenne, and about going in too deep. I really thought this was it, we're getting to the heart of the thing. Then, as I said, Freyn got confused. Actually, he began to cry. I didn't really want to mention that. But then I thought the reverse – that I had to do him justice.

He didn't cry, exactly. It was more like a wheezy sighing, with tears. I didn't know what to do. What can a twenty-eight-year-old say to a man of over a hundred? I mean, I wasn't even sure how he had got himself into that state. I just sat there, running through what he had said during that session. I guess I had been too startled by his emotion to think straight because, suddenly, it was obvious. All that stuff about him missing the clues and the warning and the greed. It meant that he and Wintle got involved in something else later, something that Freyn should've stopped.

Freyn grizzled on for about five minutes. He kept on about the abandoned camp, little details about the Look No Further. He seemed almost desperate to recall it. He'd been agitated before – never like this, though. It was odd that he should get so worked up about such an essentially unimportant part of his story: the abandoned workings didn't amount to anything.

They had just sat under the sun, white as a bone, just like he said. They couldn't have stopped there for more than half an hour. And yet something must've happened to him there. Maybe something turned in his head. Or he'd got to the point in the story where stuff was going to start happening. That's a stupid thing to put down: of course he knew.

Anyway, he gradually got himself together again – enough to offer me tea. I didn't want any but I thought I'd better accept. He was OK again by the time I'd finished my cup. I told him I wouldn't be back for four days as I had some reports to write up. And he said, jokingly: 'Just don't dig any pits, Walter, promise me that.'

Except that I did, in a way. When Freyn spoke of the mines, I couldn't help thinking of Dr Jeremy Crattman. He's quite a well-known academic now, and he'd been one of my tutors.

When Freyn mentioned the Neptune Mine I knew I'd be able to get some specific low-down on it from Crattman. I took care of my lichen reports straight away, which gave me the best part of two days to contact Dr Crattman and do the necessary research.

Though I was unable to track down any old photographs of the mine, I did source a small amount of data on pollution caused by mining activities there. I have a report prepared by World Bank consultants in 1979 covering pollutants emanating from the Neptune Mine between 1976 and 1978. A study of the relevant watercourse sediment profiles suggested that pollution had begun decades earlier.

The pollution surveying techniques included the use of a Secchi disc to establish the photic zone in various waters downstream from the mine. The Secchi disc is white, and attached to a calibrated pole. The pole is lowered vertically into the stream or river and held steady once it hits bottom. Then the disc is lowered on a slider. When it can't be seen any more, the pole is raised and the position of the disc is noted from the calibrated depth indicator. At only two downstream points in the Conmado river, which passed the western boundary of the mine, was the water classified as transparent. The other four measuring points recorded the following: 'water opaque'; 'mustard yellow'; 'opaque, yellowish-brown'; and 'sediment plumes visible'. In one opacity reading, the Secchi disc vanished at a depth of only eleven centimetres.

The report also noted that gold mining carried out at the Neptune site after the war used suction dredges which ripped up clay and gravel from the bottom of streams and rivers and separated it from most of the sediment tailings. To this day the 'de-sliming' and separation process involves the use of mercury, which draws out the gold particles.

The amount of downstream mercury pollution can be reliably estimated as a factor of the amount of sediment released by dredging. For example, the estimated sediment discharge in the Conmado river, downstream from the Neptune, in 1976 was just over one million tons – and significant mercury contamination was found in every sample. The concentrations found in sediments ranged from 61 parts per billion to more than 500,000 parts per billion. The general average was 1,500 parts per billion. Which translates to more than 100 kg of mercury solids in the water annually. The report notes in its conclusions that mercury emanating from dredging at the Neptune Mine had entered Roraima's considerable commercial fish stocks, much of which used to be exported to the US and northern European countries.

I realise that this information may not be of particular interest. I include it for personal reasons. Freyn's emotional outburst had given that particular part of his story an edge. And when Dr Crattman was able to send me data relating to the Neptune I admit that I felt a twinge of excitement. As in the case of the penal colony, only more so, I got the strong feeling that I was following in Freyn's footsteps. I pored over that World Bank stuff almost expecting to find a reference to Wintle's soil research.

And I'd better come clean about something else. When I called Dr Crattman to thank him for his assistance (I didn't refer to Freyn, of course) he mentioned that he'd been appointed by the EuroFund to lead a multi-disciplinary environmental study in the south-west quadrant of the Delta – and he offered me a four-year contract as a team leader, bracket, fungal growths, bracket! The money's excellent and he said I didn't have to decide until September, which gives me three months.

I wondered if I should mention it to Freyn. When I thought about Crattman's offer, I began to feel some guilt because it occurred to me that I had received a first-rate job offer partly on the strength of an old man's recollections and emotions.

What had Freyn said? Something about words mutating into bacon and eggs? Right. Which means that in my case, his words have mutated into a research post worth the equivalent of 76,000 Unees a year.

Approaching El Arroyo

IT took Freyn and his party another two days to reach El Arroyo, Luchenne's property. On the first afternoon out of Neptune Mine, one of the mules was swept two hundred yards downstream before managing to right itself in the shallows. Two small packs were lost in the incident. The mules were roped after that, and passed through any fast water only after London Dry had crossed first. Twice more, the mules lost their footing in the torrents, but came to no harm. No more baggage was lost.

The walking was just as tough, though there were remnants of trails and the land was gently undulating. This allowed Freyn to take compass bearings to the so-called Blue Plug, one of Roraima's high points, which lay south-east of Luchenne's spread. The bearings were probably unnecessary. Freyn said they often sighted Blue Plug from the clearings of abandoned timber and mining camps. The boys, who were proving to be natural pathfinders, sweated on ahead, cutting a line with their blades, followed by London Dry who led the mules. Freyn and Augusto brought up the rear.

'One can lose track of time and distance in the forest,' said Freyn. He was, incidentally, back to his usual self when we met again — quite perky, in fact. I got the impression that he had gathered himself, sorted things. 'Buckskin boots awash with sweat, breathing that thick wet air in and out until it seems that you exist only as a barley-twist of vapour, the steady shush of leaves underfoot, sudden glimmers of colour . . . butterflies, the flick and scrabble of unseen things, the boys arguing about something or other . . . times when you think you might not be moving at all. No clear view of the ground ahead or behind, up to your waist in vegetation, no sense of having covered any ground.

'And now and then, an acute awareness of how simple it must be to become irredeemably lost in those dunny shadows and leopard spots of light. You see a rotten stump or a group of saplings, even a single liana trailing down from an iroko like a fallen telephone line, and you think: been here before. You think: if I don't take action now we may walk into difficulties. You're just about to call ahead to stop when you notice something novel – something you've definitely not seen before. And the call dries in your throat and you plough on.

'But by now I trusted London Dry and the boys completely. London Dry had earlier suggested we turn almost seventy degrees off our heading to the west. I asked him why. "Trees gettin different and be water in the groun. We be comin to a rock hill." I could see nothing ahead and asked if there was any harm in carrying on for a bit. He was politely insistent: "Groun gettin wet."

'We duly turned west and forty minutes later I noticed that the vegetation had changed – and quite distinctly so. A few minutes more and we crested a rise and glimpsed the outline of Blue Plug in the distance. I took a bearing. London Dry hallooed the boys, gave them the new line and shooed them into action. It was after this demonstration of prescience – the wisdom of an instinctive naturalist – that I decided to accept any suggestion from him concerning the route.

'Those two days after the Neptune were hard, by any standard. Thank God it was two and not twenty or two hundred – though I sometimes imagine that I am, in a sense, still out there taking bearings and hoping for a comforting sight of Blue Plug.

'They use the word stress now, don't they? I suppose I must have been under considerable pressure on that expedition. I hadn't touched a drop of the hard stuff since Caribat. And there I was, in charge of collecting two horses from a man who was alleged to be dead. I watched London Dry tippling from his bottle of rum with a pang of envy. And he knew I was watching too. The man had a way of appraising situations – subtle displays of inattention, as if the best way to see something properly, in its very essence, was not to look at it directly.

'I'm not surprised you look so blank, Walter. I'll give you an example. We'd pulled up to take a drink and check the pack straps. London Dry was yanking away at something or other, facing me. And then, without turning around to look at the boys, he yelled out to them: "Be keepin the sun off they machete less you want to feel a bite of snake." The boys' amusement at this suggestion chittered back to us down the trail they'd just stopped cutting.

'London Dry finished adjusting the pack with a grunt and ambled ahead to where Boyone and Boytwo were standing. They were a couple of feet away from the buttress root of an old boura tree. The buttresses had partly sheared away from the huge trunk in one or two places and there were pockets of rotting debris around the shadowed base. I heard an excited yelp from one of the boys. I trotted ahead to the three of them. They'd moved away from the buttressing. "Pit viper!" said Boyone. "Be right here, is gone quick." London Dry smirked and pinched his ear. "You be gone quick if you be flashin the machete foolish all the time."

'I talked to London Dry about the incident later, asked him why he'd alerted the boys at that point in particular. He gave me a blank look and then nodded. "Be two snakes," he said. "Maybe the small green ones. I thinkin I see them." I reminded him that he had been facing me when he called out to warn the boys. "Yeh, boss," he said, with a big grin, "But seein be not the same as knowin what you lookin at. They *there* all right, thass all."

'For some reason, the feeling of physical struggle lifted after that – for a short while, anyway. London Dry's acute senses weren't going to remove every danger, of course. But after the stream crossings and that almost psychic awareness of the viper I realised that only profound stupidity or an accident would prevent our getting back to Temhari.

'I began to feel oddly carefree —' Freyn's eyebrows shot up rather comically '— though not in an immediately improving way. It may have been a feeling connected with the fever that arrived soon after. Whatever the reason I was surprised to find that I had accepted my new surroundings and situation; the insistent nature of the forest seemed an excellent form of reality. I remember thinking what a vast and simplified improvement it was on standing in the dark alongside the drift of lilies in the botanical gardens in Temhari. And how pleasing it was to be far from the fairy lights of the central market. How much better was my immersion and careful movement through all that extra-ordinarily detailed growth and life! Towards . . . what? An experimental ranch cut from the forest less than thirty miles further on.

'I wish I could say that the change in me was dramatic; that something known as the truth came to me at the foot of that rotting boura tree; that my weightlessness flaked off then and there like the skin of a viper. But that would be a lie, Walter, an outright deceit. And let me tell you why: doubt is adhesive and colourless. One doesn't quite know where to begin to remove it. It won't peel or scrape away like one of your precious lichens. In those four days in the forest I hardly thought of Temhari. My office, my room, even Eglantine, seemed wafer-thin visions. Yet when I did, I was momentarily rattled and for a second or two the forest would become stark and strange.

'I asked London Dry if he liked being in the forest but he just doubled over with a volley of grunting laughter and took a puff on one his foul Black Fat cigarillos. "Not matta about that, boss," he said, wreathed in blue smoke, "it be if the foress be likin *me*." I asked him if it did. "Yes, boss, juss so long as I be seein it right. If you juss waitin careful, you seein the foress good. Be a busy place, things movin roun over here, over there, busy-busy. We juss on top of the foress, boss, movin careful." Just as I, James

Freyn esquire, was skating carefully along the surface of my own life without London Dry's ability to move careful.

'We broke camp early on the fourth morning and within an hour I noticed that London Dry had wandered into the bush, well off the cut line, and reappeared two or three minutes later. He did this half a dozen times, saying nothing. Around mid-morning there was a shout from one of the boys ahead on the trail. London Dry immediately drew the pistol I'd issued him with in Caribat. He asked us to keep back with the mules. Three minutes later he was back with a terse message: "Your fren been roun here."

'I went up the trail with him and, just off it, he showed me two square pits. There were several others according to the boys. London Dry gave me a rather accusing look as if I had committed some obscure breach of etiquette. I looked down at the marker stick that had been firmly driven into the ground by the nearest pit. A tattered waxed label hung limply from it. It was damp and all I could make out on it was a scrawled blue seven.

'Augusto announced the obvious. "It be Mr Wintle," he said. "Same holes like before." I could feel London Dry's eyes on me. I agreed that it was Wintle's work. One of the boys asked if the pits were animal traps and London Dry finally broke silence. "What Mr Wintle doin takin the groun away, boss?" I tried to convey the idea of soil research, but that only made London Dry rub hard at his nose and look away. "Man dig a hole like that, mean he got plans," was his verdict. Which caused Augusto to deliver his own appraisal. "Be a trap," he said firmly. London Dry was not impressed with that diagnosis and capped Augusto with the comment that Wintle must've been a tidy fellow, "cep he be putting his heat round here". We moved on.

'That was the second thing Wintle had omitted to tell me. First, no mention of his having booked to travel on the *Manahatta*; and now he'd failed to mention that he'd been working near El Arroyo despite knowing that I had been on my way there. Scable had been right: you meet some strange fellows in the bush.'

Freyn stopped for a moment to take a stretch and re-gather himself. And then, briskly: 'You're bored with all this – I can tell. So let me deliver you to my destination on that day. Luchenne's spread looked like an orderly, well-tilled crater. There was an almost lunar feel to it; the Sea of Tranquillity clothed in crops, fruit trees and, of all things, patches of well-tended fescue. It must've covered the best part of fifty acres.

'We came on it almost without warning in the late afternoon. The trail had been rising imperceptibly for the previous hour. London Dry had gone off wandering again. For my part, I had noticed a slight thinning of the forest and more sunlight, and just the hint of a breeze. And then, a whoop from up ahead. One of the mules took this as a signal to bolt and hobbled away, chased by the boys. London Dry materialised with the crucial news: "This be the place comin. The foress stoppin."

'El Arroyo was lunar, as I said. We stood for quite a time in the shade of the perimeter trees, just taking Luchenne's place in. From what passed for its rim, the ranch spread down and away into a declivity which might have been a hundred feet deep at its lowest point. Luchenne's house was set half way up the south-facing slope, a large one-level wooden structure raised on thick stilts. Its layout was based on a deep, covered veranda from which ran raised walkways to a semi-circle of four stilted chalets.

'The veranda was in deep shadow, the walaba-shingled roof silvery in the late afternoon sun. Set a little apart from the house were the servants' quarters and the cook house. And round about, rising up the slopes of the depression, were stepped crop-growing areas and an orderly arrangement of ditches and sluices. About a third of the north-facing slope was given over to pasture planted with small groups of shade trees. From where we stood – and I can tell you, we stood and marvelled – there was no obvious sign of a stables.

'But the cause of my journey, in every possible sense, was there: a chestnut mare and a yearling together near a trough. The mare's head was ducking to crop the grass. The yearling was standing by her, all legs. Time will never erase that first sight of the horses. I was electrified. I remember thinking: my God, they're perfect, like sharply cut reliefs in a legendary frieze. Even from the best part of three hundred yards their grace was remarkable, Walter! I knew very little about horses but understood immediately that they were very special indeed.

'They held the eye, I can tell you. The mare looked up towards us and the yearling followed her gaze. Their pale chestnut coats were brilliant in the fading light, almost metallic. They were exquisite – and I couldn't imagine why anyone would have brought them so deep into the interior. We stood like heathens on the perimeter, sweating in the shadows, getting our breath back.

'I noticed that London Dry was staring off to the left, peering along the curving edge of the forest. And then I saw her: a native woman wearing little more than a shoulder cloth was making for us. Just as she reached us, a naked boy – he couldn't have been more than ten – skipped soundlessly out of the trees and took her hand. The woman studied us coolly for five or ten seconds and then said something. London Dry replied and she promptly turned away and began to retrace her steps. London Dry said she'd been sent to fetch us by Luchenne and we followed her down the incline, chivvying the mules. When we approached the house, she turned and gave London Dry and the boys a look. She cut away towards the servants' quarters and they followed her, with the mules. Augusto began to follow them.

'And then a voice: "Mr Freyn, if your factotum is interested in administrative systems, perhaps he would be happier in the company of Raleigh, who keeps records of all my work here." Luchenne's voice was extraordinary in effect, though perhaps not in its particulars. It was a rather high tenor in tone, delivered with utter calm and a flat, unhurried articulation that heralded a man to whom control was important; the kind of voice that you did not interrupt without good cause.

'I heard the creak of a chair and there he was, stepping out of the shadow and coming slowly down the steps of the veranda. He was tall, his thick dark hair brushed straight back from the brow and temples, a brow of such smoothness and evenness of colour that it was almost childish. He had pale brown eyes, almost amber in that light. What else? Smoking jacket, mono-grammed leather slippers. There was a certain hollowness to the cheeks, perhaps, accentuated by a thin, carefully trimmed moustache. Augusto had, of course, stopped in his tracks at Luchenne's appearance, immobile with indecision.

'Luchenne offered his hand to me and produced a small but neutral smile. "Three men, two boys and two mules, just to collect a pair of rare horses," he said. "Nothing wrong with that, of course." He welcomed me and hoped that my passage through the forest had been more interesting than my stay in Caribat. I assured him that it had, and told him about the change of plan caused by the *Alafos*'s engine failure. "Darnok'll get it going again," Luchenne said. "I think his life depends on it in every sense." He turned to Augusto and told him to settle himself in the servants' quarters and then ask to be taken to Raleigh in the morning. Raleigh would show him the records room. Luchenne asked me if I had any objection to the plan. Naturally, I had none.

'I suppose Luchenne was a kind of perfection. Alert, courtly, unflustered: a precisely-wound filament in a vacuum that he himself had devised with extraordinary precision. Oh, I didn't think that then, of course, as I followed him up the steps on to the veranda. No, I knew nothing. We settled on to the steamer chairs just as the fruit punch was delivered silently on a silver tray. And I thought: well, this is a civilised fellow. One can get one's bearings in a place like this, I thought; one can gather one's strength for the return journey.

'And Luchenne put me at my ease deftly. "I don't propose to force you to make conversation for more than a few minutes, James — if I may call you by your Christian name? But if you don't mind I would like to hear your first impressions of El Arroyo while we take our drinks. And then I shall let you retire to your room until the gong is sounded, ten minutes before dinner at eight." See what I mean, Walter? He just had this way of keeping things orderly, without making an issue of it – courtly, as I said. I told him what I had thought when I saw the place. "It's not quite a lunar landscape," he said, "but there is some sense to your image."

'He rose from the lie-back and, without a word, receded down one of the walkways, returning a minute later with a lump of smooth, shiny rock which he handed to me. He asked me what I made of it. It was like obsidian, except that, here and there, patches of the surface had bubbled. But the thing about this fragment was that it had no sharp edges. I wondered if it was an agate. Luchenne smiled and produced another piece of rock. "And this, James? What do you make of this?" It was metallic, rusty-looking and covered in small black pits. I suggested it was some sort of ironstone. Luchenne nodded. "The first rock," he said, "is local. It has been vitrified by a sudden and extreme heat." He picked the reddish rock off the wide arm of my lie-back and began to turn it in his fingers. "But *this* rock is not of this world."

'And then he explained. It seemed that El Arroyo lay in the remains of a shallow crater formed by the impact of a sizeable meteorite. He suggested I set aside an hour the next morning to walk around the rim of the farm to the south-west side. From there, he said that I would see that the depression was not round but roughly oval, narrowing slightly towards the north-east. Luchenne had worked out that the meteorite had struck at an angle of about fifty degrees, travelling south-west. Its impact had blasted earth, trees and rock before it, and this had formed the slightly raised south-west rampart. "One thinks of the heat generated by the impact," he said, "the mindless velocity and the shock." He became quite engrossed by the shard of meteorite, turning it over in his hands compulsively. And he said something odd, something I still don't understand: "Everything is a cipher of the unknown. It's unavoidable."

'The remark was a bit odd, but he had a way of inducing doubt. In any case, I was too tired to take him up on it. Luchenne had noticed this, of course. He asked casually about the route I'd taken to El Arroyo. When I mentioned the Neptune Mine he looked interested. And when I mentioned Wintle he laughed. "Ah, Mr Wintle," he said. "People say he's an odd fish." I let that go and Luchenne asked if Wintle had mentioned him. When I told him that Wintle said he'd not been to El Arroyo, Luchenne looked momentarily puzzled. He patted the arm of my chair and announced that he had things to attend to and looked forward to seeing me at dinner. I thanked him and began to haul myself out of the chair, but he was striding away before I'd even got to my feet.

'A servant appeared a second or two later and gestured for me to follow her. She led me along one of the walkways and, at its end, pushed open the sprung door of a small stilted chalet which projected away from the end of the walkway into the shade of a clump of trooli palms.

'And what a wonderful room, Walter! The angled slats of the window shutters threw stripes of light on to a dazzlingly white sheet covering a thin mattress, which lay on a stout hardwood bed frame. There was a wooden cubicle which contained a small washbasin, night bucket and a rudimentary shower. Quite a clever arrangement – a well supported water tank with a shower rose fitted to its descending spigot. The servant reached up to turn on the tap for a moment to show that the tank was full. The floor of the cubicle had been formed with a solid grid of hardwood cross-pieces which allowed the water to fall through. She showed me the rug that was to be thrown across the grid to keep insects out at night.

'As soon as the servant left me I undressed, showered and fell gratefully across the bed. I think I must've fallen asleep in seconds. When I woke the room was in shadow. It must have been a bit before sunset – there was some light, but not much. I was surprised to hear voices below me: some of Luchenne's people up to something or other; sounded as if they were breaking up wood. Well, it took me a minute to get my bearings. Then I found that my washing kit had been delivered while I'd been asleep. And that decent clothes – obviously from Luchenne –

had been laid out for me. There was an old black blazer, double-breasted, a white shirt, detached collar, a rather nice set of onyx and silver studs, cream flannels, sandals, socks and a tie which, many, many years later, I discovered was the members' tie of the Royal Hong Kong Yacht Club. And there was a note, of course: "I hope you find these suitable." It was signed, "Roland".

'So there was nothing else for it. I splashed some water on my face, brushed my hair and dressed. Everything fitted reasonably well, except, for some reason, the shirt. The gong sizzled out a short discordant tone just as I stepped out into the walkway.

'I found Luchenne standing by the veranda rail, near the chairs. He gave me the once-over and I could sense that he was faintly amused, though his face remained serious. He was similarly attired but to a higher degree of refinement. Diamond instead of onyx, Shantung instead of cotton and a beautifully cut blazer which hung without a crease.

'Luchenne gestured with an open hand to the darkening land which at first fell away, then rose gradually to surround us. At its edges was the thin, decisively darker band where the forest waited beneath the early evening sky. Apart from the sound of servants splitting up wood nearby, El Arroyo was at rest. A dog whimpered somewhere and there was a thin sound of chanting from some of the men. Otherwise, nothing but the natural sounds of the forest.

'As Luchenne put it, El Arroyo was a question, firstly, of intention and, secondly, of organisation. Without organisation, he said, there could only be itinerancy, random movement from one bit of land to another, clearing ground, planting, hunting until the useful game was either killed off or driven into strange habitats – "the killing places", as Luchenne said several times. On the other hand, there could be intelligent crop selection, systematic gathering of fallen or rotting wood and the maintenance of soil fertility by application of night soil and animal manure. Which sounded pretty kosher.

'The dinner table was a marvel, button polished so deeply that the grain appeared to lie under a layer of thick glass; no texture to the wood, just a perfect smoothness. Cuban mahogany, I seem to recall him mentioning. The table was set for two: silver, crystal tallboy glasses, napkins – worn a bit thin in places, but spotless. We sat on wicker chairs whose cushions were covered in the kind of material one used to see in those chi-chi places off Sloane Square or Old Bond Street.

'But above us, Walter, *above* us! There it was – Luchenne's homely masterpiece, his decree of light. I might describe it as a chandelier, but I say it was a decree of light because it was so very deliberate. He had had built a strong but elegant wooden frame, circular and bordered by a vertical rim about three inches deep. The tray was perhaps two feet across and carried, to a perfectly measured fit, eight oil lamps whose flues had been made to bend inwards to direct the fumes up through a hole in the wider circular mirror that was fixed on finely turned columns two feet above the tray.

'The whole thing was suspended from the rafters. The light reflected down, struck the thick layer of shellac on the mahogany and sheered off, gilding everything within six feet with a wavering magnolia patina. Luchenne's decree of light, Walter! And on the first day Lucifer said: "Let there be Luchenne."

'And so we ate and I listened to Luchenne expound on this and that. He didn't speak eagerly or excitedly and there was absolutely no hint that he had not been to Caribat, let alone Temhari, for at least three months. He talked in such an unruffled manner that I became fascinated. When he asked me a direct question I would answer simply. I preferred to listen to him. I was out of my depth – let's face it, what could I have said that would possibly have interested him?

'The chicken was excellent and I was ravenous. I think I must've relaxed quite a bit; enough to tell him that he had recently been alleged to have died. Luchenne blinked and put his fork down. And then he blinked again and smiled. "I will refrain from the usual rejoinder," he said. "In any case, death is not so much a physical fact as a point of view, wouldn't you agree?"

'Not that he wanted my opinion. "By that," he said, "I mean that it's quite possible to cause the death of a person by wishing it in the correct way. I have seen it done in Africa, for example, and some of the obeah men in Roraima undoubtedly have similar psychic powers. It may be that certain persons in Temhari find my self-imposed secretion here at El Arroyo an affront of some sort. It may be that they expect the forest to consume me sooner or later. And in the meantime, it may comfort them to draw the wrong conclusions from inaccurate information from this part of the country. The word might go out that one of Luchenne's farm hands was seen on the Falundi road wailing and gnashing his teeth. Therefore, it must be almost certain that his master is either dead or dying – and if dying, then to all intents and purposes dead."

'I asked – and, Walter, I cringe to think how gauche my question must have appeared – I asked why some might wish to imagine him dead. He was ready for my impolite enquiry. "Lay preachers who revile the established church are not forgotten," he said.

'And it was with this remark that Luchenne opened the door to himself. What came out was not so much a decree of light, but an impression of cold incandescence as glassy as the polish on which my forearms rested. He talked, Walter, and I can't remember it all; it was too flowing, too brilliant to retain. His words were delivered lightly and precisely, his thoughts laid out like a collection of perfect yet utterly strange specimens pinned to a board.

'And the more he seemed to reveal, the less I could grasp. I simply wasn't equipped to understand him fully; not I, not a standard issue pukkah Englishman who already had the makings of an outsider, and who already found it difficult to accept the minutiae of ordinary, decent existence.

'But I'll tell you what I *can* remember. Luchenne had pitched up in Temhari eight years before, an engineer with an unusually wide interest in subjects ranging from geology to paganism. And he was also a lay preacher. At first he was called to pantheism –

to a confluence of religious experience. Or as he put it, "different skins, same pulse". But he was mainly rather good at engineering and made a great deal of money quite rapidly – anything from dock cranes to bridges to steam-driven sugar cane pulpers.

'He was talented, no question; managed to secure two quick patents, one on sugar-processing equipment, the other on a piece of mining equipment, the Luchenne rotary dredge. And as if that wasn't enough, he had been left a considerable private income by an aunt in Amsterdam. Then, slightly bored by the demands of his professional life, he began to spend more and more time preaching. At first, his change of direction was accepted; after all, here was a cultivated European educated in England and France delivering sermons on what he called the confraternity of religions.

'When he had told me that much, he changed tack. He said that one day, looking down at the enervated faces in the pews at St Anselm's church in Temhari, it occurred to him that they would never experience the greater force. That was his expression: the greater force. And it was at that moment, in St Anselm's, that his great idea came to him. He called it "the crucial surrender". He said to me: "Blood flows where it will. Blood is not aware of the subtleties of the veins and arteries through which it travels. Blood is driven by a pulse of which it knows nothing."

'He said enervation was the condition required to achieve the greatest faith and grace – but only if it was the servant of the greater force. Those dreadful faces that peered up at him that day in St Anselm's had surrendered, but only to the gnat of righteous civilisation. That was how he put it. He said their passivity was the result of centuries of ridiculous stage management; said it had nothing to do with genuine supplication or the crucial surrender.

'Luchenne duly became a scandal after a sermon which he delivered in the cathedral. At first the congregation thought they were listening to the normal sort of evangelical exhortation to faith. But they became restive when he began to speak in unusual terms about the blood of Christ. As he said to me: "The blood of a *ghost*, James, always remember that." Well, the congregation didn't like it. One or two walked out on the turn.

'Luchenne then called for an exodus of will, a complete surrender to that greater force without a name. And, then and there in the pulpit, he produced a cut-throat razor and slashed the ball of his left thumb. He held his hand up and as the blood ran down his wrist he told them: "This is what faith is like. It flows with a simple perfection of purpose that is beyond understanding. How can you deny the very force that informs every moment of your lives." Those were Luchenne's infamous words, though when he repeated them to me he did so quietly and with no histrionics.

'The sermon made Luchenne into a pariah. The diocese banned him from preaching on any consecrated ground. His professional services were, very soon, not required by any significant individuals or organisations. And the governors of the Temhari Club attempted to rescind his membership, though Luchenne proved too clever for them. He examined the club rules minutely, found a loophole, took the club to court and won. Having made his point, he resigned.

'And so there we sat, eating fruit at the end of the meal. Luchenne asked me if I had found his story a strange one. I said I thought it was simply another curious colonial tale. "Quite right," he said. "But it is also more than that. Remember that the British, or the Dutch, or the French for that matter, are simply rashes on darker skin – a temporary condition. They wish to bleed their hosts without cutting too deep, not unlike the tin cup quietly receiving droplets of latex; tin cups to be collected and replaced by the hands of servants." Which Luchenne thought was a perfect allegory of the colonial dynamic.

'One didn't hear this sort of talk in Temhari, needless to say. I avoided agreeing or disagreeing with what he said. It was difficult not to be swayed by him: he was a communicator. Dime a dozen now, of course! We even get them in the Delta. You've heard of Christ's Delta Army, I expect. No? Well, they're rather hush-

hush. The authorities keep an eye on them, mainly to ensure that they don't join forces with evangelical groups beyond the perimeter.

'Sorry. Where was . . . yes, that's right. Luchenne and I had finished the fruit and green tea was served. I was a bit fuddled with alcohol. And I said, apropos of nothing: "The horses. Why have you sold them?" He gave this question considerable thought. And then he said, rather curtly: "A small sacrifice. One must go deeper." '

Freyn glanced at me. 'Ring a bell, Walter? No? Well anyway, Luchenne changed the subject; started talking about crop rotation, drainage systems, hereditary factors in plants and humans. The talk, mostly his, must've gone on for another half an hour. Then one of the lamps in the chandelier went out. A swathe of shadow fell across his left shoulder and part of his mouth and chin, accentuating his frank, enquiring look and the almost translucent skin of his forehead.

'I asked again about the horses – about their value, I mean – and his mood changed; not instantly, but quite inexorably. At first he spoke of them as if they were precious and inviolate. He asked if I'd heard of the Akhal Teke breed. Naturally, I hadn't. The mare and yearling were indeed valuable. The mare and a stallion had been shipped from Turkey after an extraordinary trek from Ashkhabad in the Karakum desert – northern Iran, I seem to think.

'Luchenne called the breed the "mystery horse" of the world because after three thousand years in existence it had contributed to many other breeds but had been influenced by none. The nearest thing to the Akhal Teke is the Arab munahgi racing strain – but even that seemed to be debatable. Luchenne said I'd find the mare and yearling very fine coated. "Desert horses," he said, "thin skinned, incredible stamina, pure blood-line. Darius's 30,000 horsemen rode them and so did the Bactrians who encountered Alexander." He said Akhal Tekes were known to have trekked from Ashkhabad to Moscow – that's more than two thousand miles – in less than ninety days on minimal feed.

'But when I asked Luchenne why he'd shipped them to Roraima and then into the forest, his mood changed. "It hardly matters. I've grown to hate them," he said. "Their beauty and their virtues have become repellent. I despise myself for seeking to own them in the first place. They have nothing to do with El Arroyo. They are too fine. They disgust me. When the stallion was bitten by a mamba nine months ago, I was pleased. It died in the dust, drained of all grace, in a series of spasms." I asked Luchenne if he had attempted to treat the horse. "Treat it?" he replied. "No, I watched it die; I watched closely to see exactly how its elegance and lineage was stripped away by the effects of the poison."

'And then he stared hard at me. "I care nothing for grace or beauty," he said. "Where is the surrender in those things? Where is the enervation, the blood? Where is the truth? Those animals are ridiculous here: they came from a dry place – let them return to one."

'If you were Luchenne, Walter, telling me this right now in my rank little box, I might have the wit to reply that beauty or grace, or even evil, were specific expressions of individual natures – and that their expression was only possible because of blood, as Luchenne would have it; of blood and of a surrender to nature. Of course, sitting at his table, trying to read the expression on his shadowed face, the only thought in my head was: don't provoke him.

'But it was already too late. "I'm selling those horses because I owe Morphen a favour," he said. "If I have to look at them for much longer I'll take a long-bladed machete to them and let my people roast their flesh." Something moved in the dark behind Luchenne. I said nothing, hoping he would change the subject. "I tell you, those animals are evil," he said. "They are proof that I am being tested and I will not be beaten by them. And when you take them away my last connection with the systems of civilisation will be severed. You will deliver them back to Temhari, where their good breeding will be of endless fascination to those mealy-mouthed curs whose own physical and social conformation is a subject of daily speculation on the verandas that matter."

'I laughed politely, trying to turn his remark into a joke. But his eyes were as hard and cold as marble. "You don't know very much, do you?" he said. I replied that I knew about cricket and shipping – still trying to make light of the situation, d'you see? He ignored my remark. "You're like the rest of them," he said. "You have no purpose and you are a slave. You are no better than those you command – and like them you are damned."

'There was nothing I could say. But just as I was about to excuse myself, he produced a silver cigarette case and offered it to me. He saw my hesitation. "Take one," he said. "If you're damned, you should be attracted to smoke." His mood had switched in a split-second. I took one and his servant appeared from somewhere behind him to light our cigarettes.

'And then, as if everything he'd said before was of no consequence, he asked about Wintle. The same question – what had Wintle said about him? I repeated what I'd told him earlier and mentioned that we'd found evidence of his soil surveying quite near El Arroyo. Luchenne said nothing. So I decided to be direct; asked if Wintle was working for him. "For me?" he replied. "I think Wintle must have lost his bearings. A pit, you say? Harmless enough. He *has* done assessments for me, though that was some time ago."

'We finished our cigarettes and he wished me good night. Then he said something odd. His exact words were: "I trust you will take full advantage of your room's facilities. Breakfast is at half past eight."

'I began to undress the moment I entered my room – and stopped cold, one leg out of my trousers. There in the dark, in my bed inside the two layers of mosquito netting, was a young woman; a native, but with East Indian blood. She was naked, hands crossed demurely over her navel, her face quite expressionless. I was startled and lurched against the shower partition. I pulled my trousers back up and stood there. I had no idea what to do or say. After ten or twenty seconds, I shook my head and gestured for her to go. That made her sit up with a jerk and she began to whisper. At first, I couldn't make out what she was saying; then I realised she was murmuring Luchenne's name over and over again. When I persisted in gesturing towards the door, she began to whimper. She repeated Luchenne's name and made a beating action with her right arm.

'Words are not always necessary, are they? By the time she had stopped her desperate little pantomime I understood that she faced punishment unless she accommodated me. Luchenne had set me a vicious ethical dilemma – either I accepted his cadeau, or the cadeau would be punished. I undressed. A few moments after I settled in the bed I heard a door creak shut very quietly. One of the servants had clearly been eaves-dropping. The only thing I can say about that night is that I was weak.

'When I awoke, she'd gone. I was aware of bird calls and there was a deliciously cool breeze drifting through the shutters. But I was sweating, which puzzled me. I got up, feeling slightly muzzy, and showered. And when I'd finished I happened to glance out of one of the windows and I saw a fellow hammering at something set on a stump below – something grey. After one or two blows it shattered, throwing up a little puff of pale dust. He brushed the fragments forward off the stump with his hand and reached down to a heap of what looked to be pieces of sun-bleached offcuts. Another piece was laid on the stump and broken up. I couldn't work out what he was doing so I finished dressing.

'It was just after seven and, attired in my khakis and boots, which had been cleaned overnight, I decided to explore – I'd had a sudden and strong desire to see the horses. The house was quiet but the rest of El Arroyo had certainly woken to the day even though the sun was barely up. The sky was pale above the forest to the east but still murky to the west. I found the horses stabled in a large benab which had been encircled by two cordons of picket fencing. The ten-foot gap between the fences had been filled with dead thorn bushes. Luchenne had thought out the corral very well: it was proof against the leopards which were the chief danger in Roraima's forests.

'God, but they were beautiful, Walter! And they came to me, just like that; came to me as if I were something substantial rather than weightless. They came and I stroked their necks and withers and thought I'd never felt such a delicious blurring of strength and tenderness. They were warm . . . smelled like musk and roasted nuts. They considered me carefully: huge eyes glistening like gelatine, nostrils tubed out and opened wide to suck me in, sample the condition of my soul.

'I don't remember how long I stayed with them, but it was certainly long enough to decide that Luchenne's outburst had been something akin to madness. In fact, as soon as I began to fret about his comments, I left the horses. It seemed tainting to stroke them while thinking of Luchenne coming at them with a machete.

'I made off towards a pool that Luchenne had mentioned at dinner. That took fifteen or twenty minutes and led me south through the terraced vegetable plots. Ditches were being cleared and one or two small groups were threading their way towards the trees, presumably to check traps and collect wood. I kept going and after another ten minutes of easy walking – the incline was very gradual – I stopped and looked back.

'And there it was, Luchenne's kingdom, lit by the rays of the sun, the house centre stage and the orchestra spread out around it: the patterns of tillage, the tidy drainage cuts, the figures moving unhurriedly to their ordained tasks. And there I stood – please feel free to picture me, Walter! – in the gods, so to speak, with the chatter of the forest at my back, the very sounds of my deep unconscious; the great unwashed fidgeting in the one and nines.

'Taken a bit of licence there, haven't I, Walter? I mean, that's how I can recall it now. The idea of Luchenne having a kingdom didn't occur to me then and there on that slope. The image of the theatre came later too. One can't escape the past but memory has more to do with the present than the past, don't you find? I wonder if Luchenne ever imagined he had escaped his?

'At breakfast I said I had taken a stroll and had been impressed with his agricultural system. "Simple enough," he said. "It's only a case of analysing the physical factors and manipulating them correctly." I could find no fault in what he'd said. Still, I wondered about the almost robotic way his dozens of servants went about their jobs.

'Perhaps it showed in my face because he held up his left thumb and said that if I cared to examine it I would find the scar which had resulted from his bloody demonstration in St Anselm's. And it was there, all right: a thin grey line of scar tissue running diagonally across the pad of his thumb. "You might say that I've made an incision in the forest," he said, "in preparation for a profounder surrender to faith."

'He stopped to take a mouthful of scrambled egg and said, with a eerily charming smile: "The fools think I came from the *sky*." He pointed upwards. He said the supposition was hardly satisfactory, but that his origins were not a significant issue. "The *issue* is surrender," he said. "My people are primitives who think they want to be saved. I, who have been routinely saved by baptism, seek instead a savage faith that will scorch the font water off my forehead for ever. They're too stupid to understand that. Intelligence doesn't matter here, not out here on the perimeter. Out here, we may become immaculate. And that depends on one thing only – my leadership."

'But surrender to what, exactly, I asked. Luchenne put down his knife and fork. And then he tried to explain. His idea was that the greater force, or the invisible truth as he also called it, only manifested itself to those who gave themselves to the environment – as in "the final surrender" and "one must go deeper". But he gave no detail about what might be finally involved. And what did he mean by the environment? Whose environment? I asked if the natives were his congregation. He replied that they were students waiting to graduate. "Everything you see here is part of an elaborate ceremony," was how he described it. "It's part of a ritual of rebirth."

'I tried to change the subject; asked how he'd become connected with Morphen. He claimed it was pure chance. Before the St Anselm's incident, one of Luchenne's privately printed religious tracts had found its way to New Orleans and then into Morphen's hands. A correspondence was struck up between the two men and when Morphen learned of Luchenne's slightly straitened financial situation – one of his sisters had apparently obtained part of his inheritance by legal chicanery – he offered to buy the horses for a considerable sum. Morphen also knew of a party who might in due course be interested in buying El Arroyo, should Luchenne decide to take his congregation elsewhere.

'It occurred to me at that point that he might actually be dangerous. I'm sure he detected something in my look; scepticism at the very least. He said his students had learned enough to be orderly – "orderly in the process of a correct surrender to the true pulse". And then he almost showed emotion. "Inland," he said. "One must journey inland, away from incense and purple cassocks and righteous dullards."

'The remark, which was delivered with an uncharacteristic raising of the voice, bucked him up considerably. He changed the subject completely; asked me if I knew anything about phrenology. Obviously, I didn't. Whereupon he smiled and said: "Let me show you my little ossuary – my scullery, as it were." I followed him to a walk-in cupboard which had been built under the steps of the veranda. He pulled the double doors open to reveal six or seven shelves laden with craniums.

'Well, I can tell you, I caught my breath. Luchenne reached in, picked a skull off the nearest shelf and held it out to me. "Don't be squeamish," he said. "It's perfectly clean and happens to be a classic example of Matthey's frontal formation." I took the thing and did my best to look calm and interested. I wondered immediately what could be the connection between those revolting things and Luchenne's path to the final surrender. And what's more I asked him. He said it was obvious that one had to identify reasons for one's actions. Which was a simple enough remark. And yet it also seemed vague.

'Telling you about it now, Walter, the remark has a deadly ring to it – absolutely deadly. Because one doesn't always act on reason, does one? Or not consciously. Sometimes, one is left reasoning about the acts. We take certain actions and worry about the justifications later. Example: a degradee was set upon outside my box the other day and there was a terrible to-do. The attacker was pulled off, which only made him wilder. "I've got no fucking alternative except to make some other fucker starve," he yelled over and over again. I took a discreet look: he was a filthy old boy caked in God knows what. A few of the other degradees had lassoed him rather than lay hands on him. Make somebody else starve? A justification of sorts, eh? They tied him to the totem pole along the way and punished him by burning his feet on the top of a paraffin heater. Shocking noise, he made.'

Never had Freyn managed such a long spurt. He looked ashen with tiredness. He rubbed his eyes and maundered on about the mare, but his words were too slurred to register properly on the recorder. I suppose I should have thanked him and cleared off immediately. But I think I was a bit stunned: he'd kind of reeled me into El Arroyo with him. So I just sat there like a lump until he got going again. He was certainly game that day.

'They should ban paraffin heaters in the Delta,' he said irritably. 'No question. We have flash fires. They haul these damned heaters into the boxes with them and wonder why they develop tuberculosis or chronic bronchitis. They never seem to understand how much water vapour is released by the burners; never wonder why their boxes begin to dissolve from the inside like a rotten lung. You can crawl past some boxes on a cold day and see the steam issuing from them and smell the stench of infected sputum and accelerated foot rot. You'll appreciate that at my age the slightest intimation of a chill or numbness around the toes, the slightest malfunction at the extremity of one's legs in particular – well, one immediately thinks of kaput circulation, ulcers, swelling, gangrene, spongy necrotic tissue.

'One hopes to freeze to death, incidentally, preferably under a freak snowfall, increase one's chance of being recovered from the ice sheet a thousand years hence as an object of scientific interest: *homo Deltans*, curled up neatly like a grinning prawn or a dreaming foetus. I've been toying with the idea of secreting myself somewhere when my time approaches and attaching a message in a plastic wallet; a set of symbols to convey a message concerning the early years of the twenty-first century. I'd fix it to my lapel – how about a blue seven like the one on the post by Wintle's pit? – and make sure it was baffling, something that could lie dormant with me and cause confusion later. I'm rather keen on the idea of leaving a false trail.

'Not unlike the malaria parasite, as it happens. The symptoms don't show immediately; might take two days, or two weeks or two months. I was sweating badly on that second morning at El Arroyo and feeling slightly nauseous; my right side felt tender too. Luchenne was just about to take me to the paddies to show me how the drainage worked when he looked at me carefully. Then he announced crisply: "The trouble with staying at Houtens is that it's full of malarial riff-raff. I see that you've paid more than the usual price for your bed bugs." He walked me back to the house and – you may picture me sitting on my bed with my hands on my knees, trembling – snapped out orders like a martinet. I was undressed and showered and put to bed. A servant girl sat alongside wafting fumes from smouldering twigs in a censer which she waved absentmindedly like a drugged priestess.

'That was my first go of fever and it lasted for a couple of hours. When I'd settled down a bit a thin soup was produced, which I managed to eat. Then I was helped into my clothes and led to one of the steamer chairs, which had been pushed into the darkest part of the veranda. A split-cane rain screen was lowered from the eaves to reduce the glare. A fruit juice was waiting for me. I settled on to the towels that had been spread over the cushions and, right on cue – everything happened on cue at El Arroyo – a small boy appeared, a chubby little buddha of a lad, and he began to cool me with a heart-shaped fan – red, as it happens.'

Freyn paused and repeated the last sentence rather dreamily. 'A heart-shaped fan, Walter! A *connection*!' I hadn't a clue what he was on about. Freyn nodded vigorously. 'The curse of Tang!' he said with a smile. 'That mouldy old jack of hearts in his filthy claw as the *Alafos* drew away from the landing. Or maybe it wasn't a curse. Because the truth is that at that moment I felt perfectly happy – but not because I was being fanned and tended to. It was because I was beyond responsibility. Things could happen around me and they would be irrelevant because I was not in a condition to influence them. Looking out through the cane screen at the land rising away from me, Luchenne's kingdom seemed beguiling. And as I lay there I had no sense of the future. I was neither weightless nor substantial, just pleasurably weak, and completely fearless for the first time since arriving in Roraima. I dozed and thought of the horses. I had the crazy idea that they could see me and were watching me.

'How easy it is to misconstrue a situation, Walter. All glory is fleeting. That's Marcus Aurelius by the way . . . or is it? Though it could just as easily have been Scable, eh? Not that I know the classics very well. In fact, I learned that saying from a tap-dancing astrologer whom I picked up hitch-hiking near the Eselen Institute at Big Sur. That must've been in sixty-eight or nine. Do you know California, Walter?'

Luchenne's 'perfect population'

FOUR days passed before I was able to return to Freyn's box. He appeared to be quite ill. I noticed, for the first time, a distinct and almost continuous tremor in his hands. It must have been more than tiredness because, instead of the usual ashy whiteness that accompanied his exhaustion, he looked a little hot. I asked if he was up to carrying on, or whether he'd prefer a bit more of a break. He just laughed it off. 'No, I'm not too bad,' he said. 'Though I suppose that if one becomes significantly ill in the Delta it must follow that one becomes significantly dead – and much more completely than Luchenne's idea of death being simply a point of view. Imagine that: death as a bijou item, a philosophical luxury.'

I still wasn't sure about Freyn's condition so I tried to change the subject. He ignored me and rattled on. 'One fears a blockage,' he said. 'An obstruction, followed by intestinal fissure, followed by peritonitis. Deep breathing's the thing – keep the diaphragm moving. Half an hour a day, various positions. Of course, one must be careful. I don't want to be removed to one of the medical bunkers. I have seen successful treatments, but I've also noticed that degradees who survive their treatments come out of the bunkers in a strange form of shock. I've seen it.

'There's a chap round the corner – lives in that box next to the heap of hub-caps – who was taken in for a hernia op. He was out two days later and has been a zombie ever since. No, as I say, one must pray for hypothermia when one's time cometh. I'll leave you a note: *may be gone some time.* D'you know, Walter, I've always wondered what Oates really said. I mean, there he was, lips ulcerated by frostbite, delirious with hunger. Perhaps he said something quite different, such as: "I must go and prune the roses. Kindly stop your whining."

'I knew nothing about horses. None of us did, though London Dry had worked with a carter in Brightown before running amok with a broken bottle of Destiny stout. Boyone and Boytwo were fascinated, of course, and by the yearling in particular. They were terribly disappointed when he wouldn't eat the flowers they offered him.

'Sorry. Jumping the gun a bit. Now let me see if I can get back on track. We were talking about . . . yes, I remember now. That first day of fever passed as if in a dream. I noticed Augusto flitting around with Raleigh. I remember taking a bit more soup and Luchenne brought some paperwork to do on his lie-back – I suspect to give me a bit of silent company. The papers were a hotch-potch to do with his phrenology; diagrams of skulls, columns of type and numbers and lists of names. He caught my eye once and said, tapping his papers: "The perfect population."

'He suggested I take an early night. He thought my attack had not been too violent and would probably come and go for a while. He'd put the quinine by my bed and thought the herbal fumigation would help me to sleep. The air in my room was hazy with pale smoke rising from a hardwood bowl. The same girl who had wafted the censer was tending to the smouldering twigs and leaves. As soon as I came in, she rose to leave the room. There was nobody in the bed, thank God, and Luchenne proved right: I slept reasonably well. Only one bout of feeling unpleasantly piping hot, which passed quickly.

'It was still dark when I awoke. I lay and watched the fireflies, feeling perfectly at ease. I dozed off again and when I woke again I felt fine. When I appeared at breakfast Luchenne took one look and said: "Remission, but probably deceitful." When I insisted that I felt tip-top he waved my remark away. He said there was no question of my leaving that day, rest was the thing. And he watched me closely throughout breakfast, assessing my condition. He must have been satisfied with it because, after insisting that I take a little more lime cordial than I actually wanted, he began to talk about my journey through the forest to the Ramasi turnpike. Earlier, I'd rather overplayed London Dry's experience. Luchenne had already assessed the rigours of the return journey and knew the kind of forest we would be passing through to get to the road.

'When I asked about the care of the horses he waved my concern away. They needed little or no water, he insisted, had hooves like iron and he'd already had their meal prepared — carefully packeted daily rations of mutton fat, cassava and maize. He said the trip to the turnpike would take three and a half days at the most. The lorry run to Temhari would take between ten and twelve hours. And the damned fellow was spot on: it took just under three days to reach Hernandez Station on the turnpike and just over eleven hours more to reach Temhari.

When he'd dealt with that subject he gave me a guided tour of the place. Luchenne's congregation must've numbered at least two hundred, of which a dozen or so worked around the house to serve him personally. There couldn't have been any shortages. Apart from the terraced growing plots there were pens containing chickens, bush turkeys and even peccaries. The forest was worked too, and in a highly organised way. Small groups of men were sent to hunt or gather wild fruit and honey, or fallen wood.

'Luchenne had a thing about wood. He said: "If I find anyone carrying green wood, I punish them." I asked how. "I shut them in the ossuary for three hours after dark and have a selection of 78s played on a Victrola just outside the door. I tell the culprit that the spirits of the dead will spring from the bones if he moves or makes a noise." This seemed so bizarrely cruel that I couldn't think of a sensible remark to make. So I asked, rather absurdly, what 78s were played. "Raleigh operates it. He plays Cole Porter 78s. I find that 'Just One of Those Things' instils the greatest fear. Raleigh, fortunately, is deaf and is therefore immune. Sometimes I dance with one of the girls while the punishment is being conducted. I have taught two of them to waltz and quickstep. They tremble with fear. They expose their breasts in a pathetic attempt to turn my mind to the physical. And then I beat them; they prefer that to Cole Porter.'

'And that was all it took for Luchenne to control them, Walter. He had found the fulcrum: a musty closet under the veranda steps and – to the natives – freakish music. As for the wood I thought was being broken up under my room, it wasn't wood at all . . . it was bone. "I have it broken up finely and spread on the allotments," was what Luchenne said. "I tell them it's the way the souls of the dead rise again from the earth. The dead being my phrenological collection." I didn't have the nerve to ask Luchenne where he'd got the skulls from.

'He controlled them by this simple device. And he confided in me at lunch that day that it was the only way to make them follow him. He had it planned. At a certain point he would tell them that he had received a portent that the dead were about to rise. "They are not unimaginative, these people," he said. "They are perfectly capable of visualising skeletons rising from their orderly rows of greens." And then they would all up stakes and head south into the forest, and he would take a small selection of skulls and the Victrola with him for protection. He'd already put the idea of what he called "the bone people" into the minds of his flock – told them that if the bone people were angered they would strip away the flesh of others in order to live again. Luchenne couldn't stop himself smiling, which unnerved me. "I've told them they have nothing to fear," he said. "I am not a pious fellow. I believe that faith should be like an overcharged, smoking battery. It should be hazardous."

'After lunch I excused myself and went to check on the others. London Dry was sitting in the shade by the corral, dozing with his hat over his eyes. Boyone and Boytwo were chasing each other through the servants' quarters, pretending to dual with their machetes.

'At that moment everything seemed reasonably satisfactory. True, I appeared to have malaria, though it didn't seem too important. I think Luchenne was the key factor in my attitude. Looking back, it's obvious that he was purely evil. But, above all, there was an air of unreality about him. The details were clear enough – Luchenne's cogs hummed and meshed perfectly. But the whole caboodle . . . I mean, what was one to make of this human contraption of faith?

'Talking to Augusto, feeling the sun on my neck, listening to his gleefully conspiratorial information, that feeling of satisfaction must really have been a feeling of disconnection, even from my previous malaise. The question of weightlessness had suddenly become irrelevant. Why? Because there was nothing around me that possessed any weight of its own – therefore nothing tangible for me to doubt, nothing to rankle me.

'What's that? Luchenne's obsession? Yes, a perfectly fair question, Walter. But it didn't signify then, not at that moment. Why should it? I was leaving the next morning. There is something rococo about horror. If you're right up close to it you can't always feel its power. Stand back a bit, give yourself some room . . . that's when the detail strikes home. Luchenne was one of those people whose full horror only seems to exist properly in retrospect.

'Just like me, Walter! You're sitting there, listening with your usual politeness to the retrospective Freyn – the once and future Freyn, the eternal Freyn! – provided you look after your little tapes. Mind you, why should you look after them? You should take care of number one, Walter.

'But I was just wondering the other night: do the . . . those particles on the tape? Are they capable of anarchy? Wouldn't they rather produce a random hissing sound? A roar of static? Fearfully clever, all this technology. The art of darkness, eh? You must find these questions terribly irritating. Erase away if you feel like it. Rub out the bits you don't need. Feel free to do a Wintle.'

As soon as his last words were out, Freyn's eyes closed and his head dropped. He murmured something indistinct. And then he said, a bit louder: 'Sorry, Walter. That was unfair. You can't be anything like Wintle.' I told him not to worry about it. To which he replied: 'Well, you don't really understand what I mean and I hope you will accept my apologies.' He seemed to be making an issue of it, so I said: 'OK, no problem.'

'Right,' he said. 'I'll try to concentrate on the matter to hand, which is Luchenne. As we were leaving the next morning, Luchenne insisted on giving me a small fragment of the meteorite; smaller and flatter than the shard he'd shown me earlier. "Please take it," he said. "Consider it a memento of your visit to the point of impact." And then he stood on the steps of the veranda as we trailed off. He watched us all the way until we reached the edge of the forest. Just as we were about to strike ahead into the trees I turned to take a last look back at El Arroyo. He was still standing on the steps, not much more than a tiny wavering shadow. I raised my hand and I'm certain I saw him do the same. And then he was gone.

'The trail was good and the machetes began their work, trimming back the sprays of growth. London Dry led the mare and I took the yearling, which skipped ahead eagerly into the watery murk, long elegant ears cocked forward. I could hear Augusto behind me, panting already, and behind him Boyone and Boytwo chivvying the mules and arguing about something, as usual. And that was Luchenne. I never saw him again, though I read about him now and then in later years.'

I had been waiting for Freyn to reach this point in his story because I had already completed my own research on Luchenne and was pretty keen to chip in my bit. So I interrupted to tell him what I knew. I wondered if, for once, I could tell him something he didn't already know. I spilled the beans as casually as I could because I didn't want him to think I was trying to be clever. And I didn't want to deflect him from his story, either. So I told him that, according to various sources, I had established that Luchenne had been sighted in both Vienna and Berlin just after the war and had been described as a powerful entrepreneur. Later, however, his name cropped up in connection with Branchata, for whom he had acted as an adviser after a Central American coup attempt in 1958. After that, no useful information, except that his name was mentioned in the manifesto of the so-called 'Emerald Beyond' Hindu terrorist cell which destroyed the Sony tower in Bangalore in 2006.

Freyn found the info interesting and didn't seem surprised by it. As I expected, my interjection brought on one of his speculations. 'Men like Luchenne play tricks with time,' he said. 'They are sighted. They are referred to. But information about them is often incomplete or contradictory. Their names crop up on the edge of turmoil and even after they die, even after some peculiar funeral attended by withered flunkeys and deodorised magnates and chauffeurs in dove-grey suits carrying cellphones. Even then the sightings continue. It's as if people need vileness to be personified rather than vague; it's a form of therapy; a case of the devil you know.

'Perhaps I exaggerate. After all, Luchenne was not a Mengele. Or perhaps he was, but managed to conceal his work in a diaspora of fear. But I doubt if anybody knows what really happened. I imagine he took his congregation deeper into virgin forest. And either abandoned them there or destroyed them during some ghastly rite to achieve their enlightenment. He might've had the money for El Arroyo transferred in advance to, say, Caracas or Beirut, and simply continued his life in another guise, never alluding to Roraima if he could help it, well stocked with bundles of his tracts and his patents. Perhaps he changed his name slightly and went into public relations for a while, or became a consultant for the World Bank or Unesco – gave sound advice to Marcos or Somoza. Or perhaps your research is flawed after all, Walter. Luchenne might have died in the forest in 1939, torn to pieces by his followers and thrown into a grave along with his skulls and that deadly Victrola.

'Men like Luchenne leave a wake of speculation. Ultimately, there's only one interesting question to ask about such people, and it's this: did he ever experience doubt? And even if he did, did he recognise it as doubt? What's that? No, no, Walter, I beg your pardon, but you really cannot just say that doubt is doubt. I can assure you that true doubt can only be suffered by those who see themselves as a small part of the greater whole. And doubt is not affected by intelligence or stupidity. A person like Luchenne – I'd call him a singularity rather than an individual – cannot be attacked or corroded by doubt as we might be; though I must own that from the vantage point of genuine decrepitude I'm beginning to see it as a luxury.

'No, but *singularity*, Walter: Luchenne examined everything minutely, atomised it. And whether he would admit it or not, he must have seen himself as a specimen of sorts. Phrenology, irrigation, theories about faith, meteorite shards – these were specimens too. Even if he had suffered a flicker of doubt he would have dealt with it as meticulously as he overcame an irrigation failure. People who deal with doubt in this way always require supplicants of one sort or another. They can't exist as true visionaries because they need their obsessions to be recognised. Anyway, bugger Luchenne! You say he was Swiss? Interesting. But who knows: maybe he was really a runaway Polish aristo with a false name and a chameleon gift for languages.

'Well, Walter, what do you think? About Luchenne, I mean? Was it worth the wait? I suppose – what's your expression? – I suppose you had to be there. I shan't take offence if you say Luchenne sounded a boring old cove or . . . the *Manahatta*? That was a couple of weeks later. I'll come to that. But remember that Luchenne was at the heart of all this. He had the horses and he sold them. And it was he whose soul carried a fatal flaw from which only bad could flow. Luchenne was the pulse, but not the only pulse.

'Now, if you don't mind, Walter, I must have a break. I'm pleased to report that I managed to salvage a crumpled box of Marks & Spencer extra-strong tea bags. I say salvage, but actually there was rather an unseemly struggle. One of those young ferals thought it was a box of chocolates and tried to tear it out of my hands. I held on to it, which surprised him for long enough for me to take a tea bag from the box to show him it wasn't chocolate. He took it and ate it and began whimpering about chocolate. We stared each other out and after a bit something else caught his eye and he loped off.

'And so here we are. More tea, vicar? Oh, yes, I insist, Walter! Think of yourself as a kind of minister doing the rounds in your bio-parish, calling on an aged sinner in his box. We get them around here, you know: men of the cloth wearing tracksuits and trainers, with shoulder bags chock full of Bible extract – Marmite for the faithless, rich in vitamin Believe – and emergency packets of sterile host. I'll just get the kettle going. All this talk of worship! You mustn't think that I'm religious, because I'm not. Which reminds me of what Mrs Slocumber called Captain McCandless: called him a muscular agnostic! McCandless nearly split his sides laughing. This was on the second morning at sea. McCandless replied, quite maliciously, that he worshipped flying fish and said it wouldn't be long before loaves developed wings.'

The midway air

AS soon as Freyn began the tramp to the rest station on the Ramasi turnpike he sensed there would be difficulties.

'I couldn't put my finger on it,' he said, 'though it should have been obvious. At first, I worried about the horses. Then I was overcome by a strange feeling, as if I was about to lose control. I tried to reason it out and concluded that I was simply nervous because, once again, I was responsible for ensuring that I fulfilled my task. Maybe that was it: the weight of things returning.

'The horses were skittish at first. They didn't like wearing the leather gaiters that Luchenne had insisted on. But London Dry was superb. He walked by the mare's head, stroking her neck and murmuring to her for most of that first day out of El Arroyo. I led the yearling on a short rein, and he followed his mother obediently, but all of a twitch – too much energy, I suppose. I kept my mind occupied by rehearsing the details: the extent of our supplies, feeding arrangements for the horses, how best to tether them at night, whether the transport would turn up at the rest station on time, how difficult it would be to get the horses aboard. I didn't really need to think about these things. I was just stopping myself thinking of Temhari and my room and my office and my desk – my little world. I just fixed my concentration on the silky head and that frank eye bobbing along beside me, and on the repetitive ripple of muscle passing through the mare's flanks four or five yards ahead. I was trying to concentrate; didn't want to let my mind wander.

'I pictured the *Manahatta*, for example. I visualised a stout ramp and London Dry coaxing the mare up it and glaring at the dockers, waving to them to keep quiet. And there would be people standing along the rail of the boat deck, with parasols, looking down. The sun would be sheering off the ship's white-painted bridge.

'And then, all of a sudden, there was London Dry, slap in front of me, staring hard into my face. "Stopping to ress, boss?" he asked. To which I replied that the horses needed grooming. I turned to the yearling and began to stroke his neck. London Dry rubbed at his nose. "Be stoppin fo ress, Mr Freyn?" Well, we did take a break. I sat hunched over my knees, trying to imagine the details of the *Manahatta*: the patterns of the rivets on the hull and superstructure; the foaming ribs of wake seething away from the stern; faces half glimpsed on the edge of my increasingly feverish vision, and always in the process of turning away from me.

'I began to fret about where, exactly, the horses would be kept. In my vision, I roamed the ship looking for them. But they weren't in the holds, which were full of rice sacks and crates. And I couldn't find them on deck. I felt a terrible panic rising in me. And then London Dry's voice again, polite, from a distance: "Time be going, Mr Freyn?"

'The moment I stood I realised what had been happening. There was an immediate wave of dizziness and nausea and I began to sweat; throat was as dry as one of Luchenne's skulls. I felt a flash of fear: I was going to fail to deliver the horses. Was that image an exchange for the fear of dying? I wondered about that later. But I think not. One does not deliver life into the hands of the fateful freight forwarder. No . . . it's that shrouded version of Spivey, the irritable reaper, who invariably delivers the goods. And remember, padre Walter, a shipping agent never makes a mistake – even when he makes a mistake!

'At any rate, London Dry had known something was up well before I did. During the rest of that day's walking, he suggested two additional stops after lunch. He was very subtle about it. "Be special hot day, boss," he said, "an they horses not use to it." I was too weak to quibble and he was too polite to raise the subject of my condition directly. But he was worried, all right. I remember at one of the stops watching him fiddling with a stick. I became almost mesmerised by the rhythmic tap-tap of it on his knee. He was, as he told me later in Temhari, plotting how to get me home "if fever be fallin you down bad".

'I can't remember much more about that first day. Just the feel of the yearling's rein in my hand; the steady tug of his head. And the sound of everything seemed to get increasingly blurred, as if I'd trapped water in my ears.

'And in a way, I had.' Freyn put his hands over his ears and frowned. After a moment or two he lowered them to his lap. 'I was floating and the only thing that made sense were the horses. I gradually became less aware of the details of the forest. My vision and my thoughts became filled with the horses instead. *Filled*, d'you see? Wherever I looked I seemed to see only their beautiful coats and the complex, flowing movement of their muscles. If I glanced down I saw only their long elegant legs. If I raised my head, there were the mare's eyes and long ears pricked forward; or it was the nodding and wickering of the yearling. I think that what developed en route to the turnpike – my relationship with the horses, I mean, the extraordinary power of their presence – defined me; defined me then, defines me now.

'I was barely aware of my actions. Sometimes I was leading the mare; then I was talking to the yearling. They were indivisible, flowing together like water that was the same dunny colour as their coats. And shimmering with light, Walter – the mare's eyes, in particular, flaming like the burning bush. I was transfixed; didn't look where I was putting my feet; stumbled alongside her, linked by a halter lead that might as well have been an umbilical cord.

'When I looked into her eye I swear it expanded like water running away to the horizon; and then I was swimming in it.

And I saw myself through that same eye – saw my hands and my face, my staring eyes. I *saw* myself, Walter. Weak but loving, you see, and innocent. I saw the truth in the eye of the mare and I hung on to the halter lead because it was the connection. It was the truth.

'It was as if I had dissolved into the horses or into a new environment: hot, wet, blurred – and we were moving like a current in deep water. I remember seeing myself again, this time as a boy in a garden which I didn't quite recognise. Very beautiful, that garden, impossibly so; seemed to know it, but just as I felt I was about to remember it properly – *gone*. And you needn't think I was alarmed by all this, Walter. Never felt safer in my life.

'Augusto tried to talk to me from time to time, but I was barely able to respond and he gave up after a while. Boyone and Boytwo stuck to things rather well. I heard, occasionally, a very distant *shink* of their machetes and the faint quaver of their disputations. I was getting weaker.

'When we stopped to make camp for the night, I remember discussing the tethering and night-watch arrangements with London Dry and then stringing up my hammock so badly that Augusto had to give me a hand. At that point I couldn't ignore my condition any more. I went to London Dry, told him what he already knew about my fever, and said it was imperative that we reach the turnpike by the appointed time; that I must be kept going. After which, I collapsed into my hammock without even taking off my boots – a huge mistake, given what I now know about the relationship between footwear and humidity. One of the boys woke me an hour or so later to give me something to eat. I ate it in the dark with a buzzing in my head.

'And then I slept, dreaming of the *Manahatta*, the ship I'd never seen, and of a dark room which was suddenly riddled with lightning. I kept seeing the horses, but not on board. They seemed to be floating above the ship, lit by stars.'

Freyn tapped the glass of the eternal candle. The flame trembled. He looked up. 'One dreams very little here – in the

Delta, I mean. I think it's because of the lack of B vitamins and the damp. Anyway, there was another dream that night in the forest. I dreamed I was under water, tied up in a hemp sack . . . didn't seem a desperate situation, and for some reason I was able to breathe. I was hunched up in this sack and the water was pleasantly warm.

'But the confusing thing, the part that gave the dream its edge, was that I couldn't get the mouth of the sack open wide enough to get myself out. And then I found myself half waking in the dark in my hammock, only to be pulled back into this dreamed sack and into that warm comforting water.

'They had a job getting me up the next morning. There was Augusto peering down at me, shaking one of my shoulders. The poor man certainly looked worried. There was something wrong with my hearing and I had no desire to move. London Dry's face appeared. He gave it a brisk rubbing – part of his usual cognitive routine – and promptly disappeared again. He returned with a wadge of smouldering green leaves and wafted the acrid, milky smoke in my face. That woke me up in a trice, coughing, eyes watering. London Dry reminded me of my request to be kept going at all costs.

'My feet were throbbing. I looked down and was surprised to see that I had my boots on. I managed to unstring my hammock. I was still weak, but better than I'd been the previous afternoon. I swallowed some tea and corned beef and took a little of the quinine that Luchenne had given me. Things were being packed up, ready for the off. Augusto helped me pack up my hammock and I changed my socks. But when I stood I wobbled, and London Dry called out: "Thass what mister *rum* be doin for *me*, Mr Freyn!" He patted his baggy hip pocket, which showed the vague outline of his remaining quarter bottle. "Be takin time to get use to the worl bein flat, is all." Boytwo sniggered and immediately found his ear pincered between London Dry's thumb and index finger.

'His squeal frightened the yearling who danced sideways, yanking his tether taut. I went to him and managed to calm him.

He seemed fine once he'd fixed my dubious image in those glistening eyes . . . stood quietly while I released the tether from a walaba sapling and there was hardly a fidget as I slipped on the halter.

'London Dry suggested we get moving. By then I'd become engrossed in the mare's neck . . . put my cheek against it. When I glanced around, they were all staring at me. London Dry adjusted his hat and began to lead the mare on. I think of London Dry to this day, Walter. He was like Lawton, you know – a sort of metaphysical midwife. Rare fellow, London Dry; midwife of the soul.

'That was a terrible day. I don't know how many times I tripped on things or blundered through growth that I hadn't even noticed. The normal ration of four rest stops was increased to six by London Dry, whose quiet suggestions I agreed to without giving them a second thought. I don't think he was particularly concerned about the horses. I think he knew I was the cargo he had to preserve at all costs and I suppose he was right, bearing in mind his status in the colony.

'We crossed stream after stream and I drank a great deal of water which sweated out straight away, leaving me drier and drier throated. I think it was the mare's nodding head and that wonderful ocean of an eye, dancing like a hypnotist's dangled watch, that kept me going: always there, always ogling me, reflecting fragments of my face back at me. One sometimes grasps at the simplest things. That eye was my comforter . . . the eye, the humid, heavy smell of her coat, her dainty steps over the roots and leaf mould, the toss of her head in those russet and green shadows.

'As we sweated on I began to feel weightless. And then the horses, too, seemed to become weightless. Solid in themselves, Walter, but weightless in relation to their surroundings – a new kind of weightlessness which was about acceptance and connection rather than objection and disconnection. And then, floating through the forest as if we were under the waves, it came to me: if we were so weightless, so subtle in our senses, then we must be free. Our actions had become the simple functions of our natures. It didn't matter what I did.

'But what did I want to do? I wanted to be like the horses! I wanted the beauty of their movement, the flashing enquiry of their eyes, their pure blood-lines – but not in any qualified or religious way. I wanted it raw: beauty from the desert, a flower growing out of the crack in a hot, dry rock; something springing alive from the void or hurling itself from the cliff face like the choughs of the midway air that Lear couldn't see; or like the stair-tread in the dark that you miss. Roaring, infinite, the expanding moment when you jump from a fuselage hatch with your fingers fretting on a rip cord that turns out to be a rosary.'

Freyn's face suddenly scrunched up oddly. I think he was trying to wink. 'Lost you, have I, Walter? Well, I wasn't lost *then*; not there in the forest with the horses. I was *found*, d'you see? Those beautiful creatures had absorbed what was left of me. They were the delicate hunters who showed me where to look and what to look for. I found them, and they found me.

'By late afternoon I was in poor shape. I'd had two or three attacks of diarrhoea and, despite taking more water and the juice of a couple of limes, I began to feel very hot again. I stumbled along feeling warm imaginary water slopping around me. The sounds of the forest became vague. The last thing I can remember at that point was that all-seeing eye floating along beside me.'

Freyn glanced down at the candle and frowned. 'Need some more wax and a fresh wick,' he murmured. 'The flame's getting a bit nervy.' He bent closer to the candle bowl and began to poke at the wax tentatively. He shook his head. 'Best left alone,' he said. 'It'll see me out, I expect.' He stretched his arms wide and smiled. 'Where was I?'

'The all-seeing eye.'

'Right. Well, it was a secret between us.'

'What secret?'

'Between me and the horses – the mare in particular. I don't care what caused it: fever, the dull ache of a privileged life in a colonial anthill. I may well have been hallucinating, yet the vision was complete as far as I'm concerned. I don't know how but on the trail to the turnpike it came to me that I *knew* those creatures, and that they had redeemed me. And I could become like them – innocent.'

Freyn stopped to give his knees a rub. 'Yes,' he repeated, 'innocent. I was sure of it. And –' he raised a finger in emphasis '– and that night when we made camp the mare wouldn't settle straight away. Not even London Dry could work it out. He thought there might be a leopard in the area. But when I went to her she pulled towards me on her tether and put her head down to be stroked. Her withers felt as smooth as satin.

'I slept on the ground near her that night. She made no more fuss. I woke only once and felt her breath on my face. Her head could only have been two or three feet away, yet I couldn't see her because the fire had died. There was only darkness. I decided not to reach out to try and touch her in case I frightened her. So I lay and drew her breath in through my nostrils like a master of wine, eyes closed, nosing out the complexities of a rare Bordeaux.' Freyn stopped and smiled. He raised his finger in a sudden, jerky motion. 'Nothing has ever been truer or better than that night.'

Beauty, hope and memory

FREYN didn't remember much about the next day's walk, which took them to the Ramasi turnpike. When he began to talk about it – this was two days after our previous session – he went vague on me. There was a lot of stuff about the mare: that her coat smelled of incense, that her gaze seemed to soothe his eyes; that kind of thing. I let him go on a bit, studying him carefully. I decided he was in pretty bad shape. He became edgy and evasive, starting sentences then fizzling out.

At first I thought some underlying senility was showing through. Then I noticed that he wasn't looking me in the eye as much as he normally did. He was usually a great one for that. His face always seemed to float above the bowl of that eternal candle and I'd feel skewered by his gaze. That look wasn't there this time. Like I said, he kept looking away. It occurred to me that he wasn't going to tell me the rest of the story. Which rattled me. Clearly, whatever this Luchenne business was about, it didn't end at El Arroyo.

I kept on at him, but softly-softly. When he'd dried up in the past I'd always do the courteous thing and make arrangements to come back in a day or two. And he was always pretty chipper about it. I never had the sense that things were about to grind to a halt. But now I did. After three-quarters of an hour of distracted talk Freyn looked at me and said in an almost pleading tone: 'What is it you *want*, Walter?'

For some reason, I froze – wasn't sure what to say. I decided to keep it simple. So I said: 'The rest of the story. I feel as though I've been taken into a room blindfolded and left there.'

Freyn looked down at the candle. I began to say that I hoped he had taken my remark in good spirit, but he waved it away. 'What if I can't tell you the rest?' he said. And I thought: right, his mind's gone, it's all over. I said to him in as neutral a voice as possible: 'Can't tell, or won't tell?'

That got to him. 'I'm not sure I have the strength to finish it,' he said. 'You have no idea how much these sessions have cost me. I'm old and I've had to prepare myself each time to tell you as much as I have. When you're not here I spend a great deal of time trying to extract the details from my memory – it's a bloody dredging operation, Walter. Sometimes the details are almost too sharp and jagged and I could swear I'm back in Roraima as a young man. Other times the whole thing seems like the hallucination of a degradee poisoned by the acid fogs of the Delta.'

There was an uncomfortably long pause, during which Freyn just stared at me – not a blink, not a flicker. 'I know the story contains the truth about me, but I'm finding it harder and harder to reconcile myself to it,' he said. 'What you must remember, Walter, is that I have never ever rehearsed my life in this way, never as a story. For more than seventy years since leaving Roraima my life has been backlit by memories that flickered only randomly. That's the way I prefer it. It has seemed more and more incredible that I'm telling you everything I can remember about that time.

'I keep wondering at the sheer chance that brought you and your wretched spatula to my box in particular, and made me speak to you, and made you intrigued by my mention of Luchenne and the horses. I'm plagued by that, you know. Why you, why now?

'And now I seem to be afraid – rather late in the game, I admit. Afraid of reconciling myself with the truth. Because, you see, this story really *is* my own truth, a truth tempered by time.

While you've been away these last two days the question that threatens to undo me is this: if I tell you the rest of the story, what will it do to me? Will it prove conclusively that my descent over the decades was justified? Or will it prove that I have wasted my life? In unravelling it all I may also be unravelling my values. Don't think for a minute that I have lived in increasing poverty for more than half a century by accident, or because I happen to be unusually hardy. You must understand that I took a decision in 1938, a decision to reject the courses open to me.

'I've tried to explain the beginnings of that decision, the pre-*Manahatta* part. But two more things happened which turned the key in the lock, so to speak. And now I find that I'm afraid. What if, in remembering and relating every detail that's left, I realise that I was mistaken? What if beauty always exists as part of hope and memory, regardless of what is around you? I just don't know, Walter. I'm very sorry . . . I just don't know if I can manage the rest.'

I sat there, numb. Freyn had explained himself in such a way that I couldn't see immediately how to get round him. My shock was balled up with a sudden anger – and emotion. Part of me couldn't handle the idea of loose ends. Another, less scientific, slice of me had simply become fascinated with an old man's story – a story which seemed to be familiar, though I couldn't work out why. And I wanted the rest of the story regardless of what it might do to Freyn.

I decided to fight to get it. My mind was racing and within ten or fifteen seconds, I was pretty sure I could corner him with two lines of argument in particular. I sensed something else: Freyn was not, naturally, a quitter. I needed to lay out good reasons why he should finish his story, reasons that would put his fears in a proper perspective. I was certain that was the key and I decided to set about my task as concisely as possible.

For the first and last time, I'm in a position to quote myself at length from the tape. I realise that this is probably an excessive intrusion into somebody else's story, but the circumstances were unique. Freyn listened without comment. This is what I said:

'OK, I get what you're saying and I can see it's tricky for you. But, look, if you start to take a watch to bits, maybe you can't put it together without dismantling it completely in the first place. Particularly if you want to know how it works. The worst thing you can do is stop half way through. Because then you haven't got a watch and the loose parts can't make any sense. If you don't finish the story, it'll be like being left with a watch that doesn't work and a load of parts that are meaningless. I don't know if I completely got what you were saying about beauty and hope and memory but I think it's about making mistakes, right? Or at least that you fear that you might have got things wrong. And that if you did, then you may have got this far because of a set of values that doesn't . . . that just doesn't hold water. That's scary; I definitely agree with you on that. But you couldn't have lived this long by mistake – you know, by getting things seriously wrong.

'You say you're not especially tough, physically. Well, then, you must be right about *something*. Whatever it is that you've based your beliefs on must have kept you going. And another thing: after all these years, are you telling me that you wouldn't have spotted major flaws in your decisions before now? When I met you, you weren't down. That's what really surprised me, made me think you were different. Could you have made a big mistake and got this far without becoming just like the rest of the degradees?

'You said you kept wondering how I happened to come to your box in particular and how I happened to pick up on your mention of Luchenne? I came to your box sort of like you arrived at El Arroyo: in a way I was sent, just like you. I thought right off that there was something unusual about you; unusual enough to make me want to hear what you had to say; unusual enough to make me go into a box – which I've never done before.

'I need to hear the rest, I really do. You've almost taken the watch to bits and suddenly you're afraid to finish the job because you realise you may never be able to put it together again. I can see that – pretty normal reaction. But it's got to be wrong to stop. If you stop, you've got a useless watch. If you carry on maybe you'll be able to put it together, maybe not – but at least you'll be in a clear-cut situation. At worst, you'll be able to see every last part, even the duff ones.

'You say you're afraid to continue with the story, but maybe you're kidding yourself. I hope you don't mind me saying that. If you're afraid it can't really be of the known. You know how the story goes and you know exactly how it ends. You haven't just dragged all this up from your memory after seventy something years.

'I think you're afraid that by telling it in one go, in a sort of package deal like this, that you'll break the watch for good. But I seriously doubt that. And like I said: what's worse – taking something to bits or putting something broken in a drawer and knowing it's always going to be there waiting to be fixed?

'You've got me into your story and it's – well, it's become a need-to-know situation for me. I don't know what else . . . well, I guess that's about it, Mr Freyn. I don't know what else I can say. I just really hope I've said enough to convince you.'

So that was what I said, word for word. I suppose it makes pretty poor reading; I don't have a way with words. But I said my stuff and he listened. I tried my best to look him right in the eye while I was speaking. It wasn't too difficult – he wasn't sending out any weird vibes. When I'd finished I expected him to say something in return pretty pronto. I braced myself for bad news. Something like: 'Walter, thank you for your kind words, but I'm afraid the watch must remain in the drawer.'

Freyn sighed and rubbed his chin. For some reason I got a quick flash of London Dry as he did it. And then he said: 'All right, Walter. I'll think about it. You'll have to give me two or three days' grace.' He frowned and shook his head slowly. '*Grace*,' he murmured. 'If you could only have seen the horses, Walter, you'd know what grace can be and how much it matters and how . . . and how terrible it can be.'

I thanked him and packed up my tape player quickly. I didn't want to irritate him in any way. I said I'd see him soon and backed out, lowering the flap. He was already looking down into the candle flame. I'm pretty sure his eyes were shut.

I was shattered. I managed to get myself across to section nine to take my quota of samples, but it wasn't easy. My hands were shaking and I felt cold and clammy. I thought: right, don't panic, I've just got some virus thing. Even so, if a feral degradee had gone for me I'm not sure I could have whipped out the stun-baton quickly enough to blank him. I made a serious hash of the samples. I just wanted to get back to my securispace fast. I hustled towards the cannula, feeling increasingly bad, and hyperventilating.

Once I'd got clear I managed to get myself to a personal needs cubicle and just sat there trying to get myself together. I found myself thinking of the mess in my room; all that info about Roraima. I began to feel comforted and after ten or fifteen minutes I seemed to calm down. My breathing regularised, the sweating stopped, I began to feel warm. And I thought: cancel the virus, it's Freyn I'm suffering from.

By the time I walked through the multi-lam entrance door at my block I was feeling pretty good – seriously up, actually. But that changed. I got in, stripped off, took a needle-jet shower, checked for messages. There were two. One was an illustrated fact sheet and health profile submitted by the Demcorp Pret-a-Partner agency. A female, Zembla Van Veen, had filed a formal but non-binding interest in my details and was willing to undertake a seven-day introductory contract with a single sexual episode terminal point – the usual 7-Up scenario. I high-rezzed her key body parts and skipped through the medical history. Looked OK. I tapped in my agreement and hit send.

The second message wasn't so hot. It was from my research cell leader. He informed me that I'd been the subject of an SRA – that's a standard random assessment, as per the ISO666 research quality standard. He said there had been some 'irregularities' in my work; something to do with sample purity. My first reaction was anger. I couldn't believe my work was being questioned.

Then my anger evaporated. I suddenly became scared. It was possible that the time I was spending with Freyn, the intensity of it, had affected my concentration. Had I made one or two small mistakes? It was possible. And I thought: well, screw them.

I began to feel weird again – and desperate. I just knew I had to see Freyn through. I looked round at all the printouts and stuff and thought: I'm going to get to the end of this. I'd just have to deal with the SRA and make sure there were no more screw-ups. I took a two-hour nap. I dreamed I was running, naked, in a desert. I was made of some sort of glowing wax, and the wax was melting. Bits of my fingers and toes were dripping off. At first I tried to re-attach them, pressing the warm gobbets back into place. When it didn't work I lost interest, didn't seem to care. I kept running, watching the wax dribble off me.

On the road to Temhari

HE'D said two or three days: 'You'll have to give me two or three days' grace.'

I wanted to go back after two days, reduce Freyn's opportunity to stew any longer than necessary. Then I became unsure. What if I went back two days later and he hadn't quite made up his mind? What if I turned up at the critical moment and, because of that, pressured him into saying no? I lay in bed examining the problem from every angle. What if I went on the third day to give him more time to settle things in his mind and then he said something like: 'Yesterday, I thought you were right and I had no alternative but to finish the story – but since then I've changed my mind absolutely.' In the end I just had to get back to him on the second day. I couldn't handle the suspense.

I tapped on the top of his box three times as usual and said: 'It's me, Walter.' I heard him say to come in and as I bent down I was hit by a wave of dizziness. Tension, I guess. I began to ask if he was well but he cut me short. 'All right, Walter, I'd better tell you straight away that I've decided to try to complete this . . . business.' I said I was really pleased and began to check the position of my recorder. My hands were shaking.

'You're a meticulous fellow,' he said. 'For example, you always put that thing in exactly the same spot. About eight inches to the right of your left knee and at a forty-five degree angle. Who's got whom taped, eh?' Freyn smiled and I must say I suddenly felt relaxed, or maybe relieved. I told him he seemed good at noticing details and that he would have made an excellent scientist. 'You're showing excessive courtesy and buttering-upness, Walter,' he said. 'I am sincerely grateful for your non-violent company. But are you sure you won't get blackballed if anybody's seen you consorting with me?

'Which reminds me: I gather the Athenaeum was bombed by terrorists last week. I mean, how *could* they have mistaken it for the Liberian Embassy? We don't get terrorists in the Delta, as you know; only the mafia and those damned deputations. We had a Pan American study group through here only yesterday. They distributed leaflets explaining their visit. They're updating their databases on the relative densities of self-help populations and infrastructures. Self-help infrastructures! I think they must mean rotting shanties and paths scraped through refuse.

'Very two-edged, that term, self-help, and extremely useful to the authorities. If one is in a position to *choose* to help oneself and do it effectively, all well and good. In the Delta we degradees have no choice but to help ourselves. And as soon as we do, we confirm that we are a self-help population; not individuals, mind you, but a population. After a certain time – an indecent period, you might say – those in power can announce that we chose this situation and that, therefore, everything is under control. And if it isn't, then it must obviously be our fault. Solution: tighter controls. Anyway, I don't care. I prefer it here because it isn't really under control, whatever they might imagine in the corridors of the Demcorp complex. It'll never be under control – they haven't really grasped that.

'You can erase that if you like, Walter. I'll try and get on properly now. Point one: I didn't remember much about that last day's walk to the rest station on the turnpike. It was just a blur of shadows and creeks. I myself was pretty rank by the time we reached the road. I stank, no two ways about it . . . the diarrhoea. But what a sight the road was! It was properly graded and most of the potholes were filled with crushed stone; a firm, decisive orange ribbon of laterite running dead straight due north-west

– the road that would take us back to Temhari.

'We were still about five miles south of the rest station, but it didn't take long to get there. The yearling became frisky in all that shattering light. By the time the rest station came into view I was feverish and sweating badly again. The reins slipped from my hand without my realising it and I wandered off beam and stumbled back into the trees. Somehow, it felt safer in there. Augusto said later that the yearling had followed me.

'There were three drunken German miners already ensconced at the station. The place didn't amount to much: three benabs, newly thatched, and about an acre of cleared ground. There was a little pyramid of rocks into which a post had been fixed. It carried two direction signs. One said Temhari, sixty-three miles, the other, Hernandez Station, forty-seven.

'The miners appeared to be out for the count, asleep on bedrolls laid across their goods. That meant they were returning from a dig and almost certainly had gold with them. They stank, too, and we slung our hammocks in the benab furthest from them. And as I wallowed into my sling I began to tremble and thought: just let the horses get to Temhari. And let me get into my room above Madame Jopahl's. Let me lie in my bed, cool and clean, with the smell of her coffee rising through the floorboards. Let me hear old McCloud wail about life's punishments and let her words be punctuated by the rattle of the water into her pail. I was delirious, of course. My room had never been cool.

'Dying, Walter? No, it didn't occur to me – or at least not in a way that seemed threatening. Malaria's strange: you become dissociated, fatalistic. It came back only once many years later, in Oslo of all places. This was after a spell in the Middle East – but that's another story, I'm afraid. And the effect was the same. I knew I was ill but I simply didn't care about my condition. Well, at any rate, there I lay in that hammock, half awake, disinterested in my fate, except for that little flicker of a thought – the need to deliver the horses. I don't remember eating and I don't remember that night at all. Yet when I woke the next morning I had the feeling that something crucial had happened: death or, at the very least, a terminal delirium. Why? Because there was a cricket match going on; a middle-aged white man trotting up to bowl; a final stride past a plank of wood jammed upright into the ground; the ball lobbing through the air and a dishevelled miner whaling away at it with a length of two-by-four. The ball, an ancient thing with seams re-stitched with hemp twine, bumbled along the ground with Boyone and Boytwo scampering after it. And there was an Englishman bellowing with laughter.

'It wasn't an hallucination. And I'd better tell you about the Englishman, name of Roker. Picture a fellow of about fifty, broad in the beam but not exactly corpulent. He was wearing sun-yellowed cotton twill trousers held up with a knotted tie through the belt loops. White shirt, sleeves rolled up and wrists . . . the wrists were extraordinary. They looked almost square: the wrists of a wrestler or a Smithfield meat porter, and hands that radiated strength, the kind that are offered with deliberate care in a handshake.

'And that face, that beaming, almost hairless head as tanned and mottled as the walnut burr dashboard of an Alvis coupé. There was a gold pince-nez and a smile that revealed strong teeth of a uniform pale grey which looked as if they could grind quartz to powder. And there was the overall effect of the man. He was one of those who seemed to confront the challenge of existence with relish, as if it were a pleasurable and endless luncheon, regardless of the circumstances; the kind of man, in short, who was capable of rousing three hungover strangers in the middle of the bush and making them play cricket.

'Roker was the government inspector for Roraima's central district and he and his men, two Bengalis, were reputed to clock up about a thousand miles a year on foot, by bateau and by motor. The natives had nicknamed him Ironwood and the traders in the interior feared him as children would fear a strict, no-nonsense uncle.

'Out of the blue an extremely large car pulled up, driven by a chauffeur in livery; a Daimler. The miner dropped his bat. Two more appeared – Germans. They became very excited and began to pile their belongings into the boot and the front seat. The chauffeur was barely given enough time to take a drink and have a stretch before they jumped in and demanded that haste be made back to Temhari.

'Those miners! Rich as Croesus one minute, broke the next. The limousines were the amusement of those who made the bigger strikes. They would invariably make for Caribat, having wired ahead for a chauffeured limousine to collect them up country – a limo with a big bell which could be clanged, and champagne to drink on the run back to the coast. They used to arrive in Temhari and pass up and down Main Street several times to let everybody know that money was about to be spent. There'd always be trouble in the Excelsior.

'The Germans vanished in clouds of biscuit-coloured dust and then there was Roker's face peering down at me. I was still in my hammock, remember. "John Roker," he said, "district officer. You're a fool to have walked that distance so soon after a go of fever. Dig out Dr Masuri when you get back. He knows more about malaria than Whiteley, and Whiteley's a prig in any case."

'By late afternoon the fever had reduced slightly, but I was still too weak to stand for long. Roker chatted easily to me. And London Dry looked relaxed for the first time in two days. The lorries arrived just before dusk with a great gargling of gears. The horses were led up planking lashed to the tailgate of one of the lorries which, as I had requested, was fitted with high sides and a canopy. The horses were tethered and that was that. Augusto and the boys sat in the cab with the driver, and London Dry cobbled together a box seat which he wedged between the cab and the wooden rails of the lorry bed. He reasoned that the horses were more likely to settle if he was always in view. He was right, as usual.

'Well, Walter, as you know, the first time I arrived in Temhari it was by sea. I was neat and tidy, the ship smelled of paint, oil, wax, salt and gin. I had looked out over the ship's rail as we slipped over the bar into the shallow water of the harbour. And I'd thought: no white cliffs, but never mind.

'My second arrival in Temhari in that wallowing Ford lorry was rather different. Dawn was coming up and twenty miles from the coast we broke clear of the forest and hit the flats; ramshackle villages along verges laced with rancid gullies, islands of reeds, vegetable plots; and all the stranger because we had driven into the thinning remains of a dust storm and the light was that peculiar pinky cream colour, like evaporated milk. We had walked through the gloss and filigreed shadow of the forest and now here we were moving through a blurred, indefinite landscape where even the villagers had been chalked pale by the dust.

'And everything seemed still, muted by a sense of expectant pause. One imagined clocks winding down, jammed with the whipped-up silt of a desert deep in the interior. I kept looking ahead for a sight of the horses but they were invisible in the billowing dust.

'The villages slipped by, one after the other. And then a light breeze came up out of nowhere, riffling through the cane fields – vast expanses of it, Walter, and dim figures walking up the paths into the cane blocks with their machetes; others scuffing along portaging their bits and pieces; two skinny East Indian tykes rolling an old tyre along the verge; women with water buckets balanced on their heads; open-sided shacks with bartops supported on stacks of tyres, dead batteries; the loll of a baby's head as it swung along on its mother's ambling hip; sparkles from the wheel of a knife grinder; a fellow squatting among a shambles of cut-off drums and tins lashing out a rhythm with handfuls of bunched-up bicycle spokes. Cane and more cane, more sweet blood destined for the quay at Temhari, and then away, far out past the bluecoat's horizon.

'The first smell of the sea prickled up my nose as we passed Shand airfield. And then we were clacking across the boards of the suspension bridge at Kenley. The breeze freshened and I could hear the chants of the fishermen. We ran parallel to the beach and the shallows were full of black bodies and skiffs, dragging the curtain nets out into a loop, then hauling them in.

'These were lives beyond my comprehension, lives that had been reduced to a two-dimensional tableau rather than an experience of substance. Wicker baskets glittered with fish . . . explosions of flies rising like puffs of smoke as they were lifted on to barrows. All bound for Temhari like the cane – and like us. We were all headed to market; they with their cane and fish, and me with my freight, the shipping papers already prepared. I glanced back at the horses. They were calm; mother and son, shipping items bound for the shiny cobbles at the King Street stables.

'The road got better. The packed laterite gave way to potholed macadam. Then we were on the smooth stuff and I was lulled by the grizzle of the engine and the drum of the tyres. Kerbstones flicked past, brilliant with whitewash. People . . . eddies of them, like human confetti, and the shops and offices which began on the edge of the central district of Temhari. The Cash Store – Chin-Chin Crepes a Speciality. The lorry swerving suddenly to avoid a carter and the driver, Sikander, swearing. Sikander saying: "Civilisation, man. Fine thin, eksep too many peoples going all over the place to where?" The Demerara Life building, fronted by a plantation of specimen palms; the Star Butchery, motto: "Supplied with prompt"; Pradasco's Superior Bicycles, old Pradasco himself sitting on a chair on the veranda, as bronzed and doubtful as Rodin's thinker, compulsively ringing a bicycle bell.

'This was one's return – but to what? The future? There was Gennett's Record Emporium, motto: "We sell Starr Phonograph, the Difference is in the Tone"; and the Roraima Integrity Pawnbrokers. And then into Floribunda Street. The Wizard Agency, which sold everything from piston rings to what they referred to in their advertisements as girdle requisites. A few shops along was da Souza's Imported Lisbon Goods; and the Millord tyre depot – "We Salute this Tyre, You Will Too'.

'And then we were grinding past the first government

buildings: the public records office; then past the lands commission where the better timber concession leases were bought
with back-handers; then Legall's tailoring establishment where,
according to the subscript on the sign, a new suit would ensure
that its wearer would achieve greater prominence. What else?
Another cycle shop called Hack's, with a poster which, if I
remember correctly, implored the populace to "Lighten Your
Darkness with a Quicklite Lamp".

'All very quaint in retrospect, Walter. James Freyn's optimistic
return to Temhari? You might think that, mightn't you? The dust
had cleared a few miles earlier as we reached the tidier sections
of St Leonards Road. There were the carefully tended gardens,
spotless verandas, the whitewashed stone of the gateposts; the
wrought-iron numbers or house names: Sea View, Palm Crest,
The Lookout, Highlands House, that sort of thing. And the
more I saw, the more desperate I felt. It was a desperation shot
through with impotence. Each tidy lawn, each name plate, each
glimpse of a black hand on a yard broom or a garden fork. Each
familiar detail had become part of a tumbler lock clicking into
place.

'I looked ahead. I could see the horses in the back of the
leading lorry, but only just. They were ghostly. I began to feel
physically crushed, as if gravity had run amok. I looked out as
Temhari unravelled past me and wondered why everything
wasn't partially flattened or bulging with pressure. I distinctly
remember glancing at my arm on the sill of the cab door and
being shocked by its normality. And, finally, a roar and clatter of
gears and Sikander cursing as he wrestled with the gear stick to
bring us to a jerking stop in the stable yard – King Street, did I
mention that? – just below a beautifully painted sign that said:
"Stylish Turnouts, Civil and Reliable Coachmen, Prompt
Attention. A Trial will Convince You."

'I suppose I had suffered a further change, without realising it.
The fever had stripped away my reserves and I felt empty;
wanted to be back in the forest with the horses. I had again
fallen prey to my old malaise: I felt the gravities of organisation

around me once more. You needn't look puzzled, Walter. I can assure you that organisation produces its own gravity; a gravity which sucks people in and distorts them. Not quite like the Delta, incidentally. Notice how the charity drop zones are in the centre of the Delta. That's because Demcorp's population department hopes the zones will become a necessity – that charity will develop enough gravity to bind this landscape of boxes together as tightly as patterns of iron filings round the head of a magnet. But it won't work, Walter. It will *not*, because the Delta is like a tricky rash. If you leave it alone, it spreads; scratch it, it becomes inflamed and spreads even faster.'

Freyn paused to have a stretch. 'I call this pretty fancy footwork on my part,' he murmured. 'You're letting me get away with it again, Walter. Those of my generation and class were never in the habit of discussing their inner lives, their most personal thoughts. And you must remember my state of mind at that time. I mean, just imagine for a moment that you're in the cab of that lorry. Here's Sikander leaning out of the window putting the curse of the three-headed hamadryad on some innocent pine-apple seller who's blocked our passage for a moment or two in Electricity Street; and there's Roker's huge head stippled with a silver mesh of perspiration. And as we pass through the flashing colours and shouts of Karantine Market he's saying: "I recommend that you practise systematic exercise. You can reach me at the Magenta Guest House. I'd be happy to introduce you to Sgt Keeps. He'll give you a regime." And you listen, half asleep and half fascinated, as he grinds the words out between those indestructible teeth.

'Ignore me, Walter. You weren't there and nothing I can say would take you there. I'll try to stick to the facts. So . . . while the horses were being unloaded I sent for a cab. And that was the last I ever saw of Roker, who, incidentally, was blackballed by the club membership committee for excessive courtesy to the natives, though that wasn't the reason given. One may be interested in natives, but not *too* interested.

'I was talking about the horses. I saw that they were properly stabled, though I felt at that moment that I'd betrayed them. There was nothing I could do now except ensure their safety. I was going to deliver them to the new world – these creatures that flowed like water and flame. I took a last look at the yearling and there he was, goggling the yard, ears sharply forward, nostrils distended, absorbing civilisation.

'I told Augusto to take a couple of days off. Then I said my goodbyes to London Dry; gave him a little spending money and told him to collect his pay at Spivey's the following day. I wrote him a note to give to the proprietor of a guest house in Camptown, getting him and the boys free bed and board until the *Alafos* was able to carry them back to Caribat. His last words to me still resonate: "If you go back, Mr Freyn, the foress be rememberin you. The foress always know how to wait."

'And then I pitched into the back of a cab. The driver said: "Be goin where?" I slumped against the tatty leather seatback and closed my eyes. It wasn't a question that interested me. I was thinking about London Dry's remark and the horses – trying to fix them in a block of crystal. Couldn't, though . . . the crystal kept melting at the edges.'

The flood

JUST when I least expected it, Freyn dried up. He had exhausted himself to such an extent that it seemed to bring on an attack of asthma, or something like it. His colour went from its usual talcy look to a shade of grey that alarmed me. I told him my tape was on the verge of running out, which was a lie. I got the impression that the story was getting to him again. It occurred to me for the first time that he might be endangering himself by telling it.

I packed up and left. To make matters worse I was unable to get back to the Delta for six days. Tremendous storms had devastated sections of it. I watched it on television. Rioting broke out among certain factions of degradees. I had the television programmed to newstag, with the sound down, so I could just look up from my work to see if I recognised any parts of the Delta as being near Freyn's box. I was pretty sure none of the rioting had been near him because there was no sign of the totem pole which stands about one hundred metres south-east of his box.

I got the jitters again, just like the time before. My condition wasn't helped by a seriously irritating relational development. My new trial partner, Zembla Van Veen, was pressing to go into stage two arrangements. As you know, this requires an expanded range of neutral general activities and intermediate-level sexual routines. I wasn't up to any of this, to be honest. In fact, I didn't seem to care about this side of my life at all. My securispace and all my Freyn stuff seemed good enough – as if I'd made a box to live in too, and that was OK by me. I was just about keeping on top of my sample collection and technical reports but all that seemed more like a hobby now – something to fill in the time until I saw Freyn again.

When I eventually passed through the cannula at Causeway 3 again, I was shocked. The Delta looked as if it had gone into partial meltdown. All the flimsier boxes had collapsed, or had had fresh sheets of plastic lashed to them. And the smell was truly foul. I was used to the rank fug, but this was something else. It was slippery underfoot because of the shit and cellulose slush.

I immediately got into a sweat about Freyn. I moved as quickly as I could, imagining all sorts of things. I needn't have bothered. When I tapped on the box top, he called my name out right away. When I entered I could see straight away that his colour was better, back to the familiar chalky look. He congratulated me on my 'intrepid persistence' and began to brew up some tea. And then, off he went, almost before I'd hit the start button on the Duino-Wong.

'You heard about the storm, I expect,' he said, grinning. 'The sheer flow of water was extraordinary. I sat and watched during the height of it. Wasn't too worried about the box leaking or breaking down because I'd smelled the storm coming late that morning. So I was out collecting any bits of loose sheeting and lashings that I could. That, and the fact that the box is covered in a plasticised coating, did the trick. I just sat, leaning slightly against the windward side to keep the whole thing from deforming. And, as I say, the water simply swirled past.

'One's box is better than most. When I first came here seven years ago I took great care to bring a good box and, much more important, a really good base. Most of the pallets used as bases are no more than four inches deep. But mine is eight – that's three inches deeper than a ISO394 pallet. And that made all the difference the other night. When the floodwaters came through they were running between two and five inches deep.

'And here I sat, at least three inches clear of it, perched comfortably on my offcut of Amtico Etruria. All I had to do was keep an eye on the clots of debris that washed up against the side and poke them away with a stick. I'd tell you more, but you're beginning to glaze over, Walter, I can see that.

'Now, I've done the stables – that right? The taxi, wasn't it? Yes, the taxi. I decided while en route to make a detour to my offices. Spivey was out and I left a message saying I'd be in the next morning at the usual time, and mentioned that I'd come down with malaria. And then, off to my flat. The driver delivered me and I thought I'd be able to slink up the back stairs without being spotted, but there was Madame Jopahl, calling me into her sitting room, insisting that a bath be run for me, and that I take coffee with her. An irresistible creature!

'I sat there, dazed, and listened to her harangue about this and that, about how foolish I'd been to travel so far away from "the sphericals of civilisation". She insisted on reading me some poetry, which I managed to praise. I escaped to my bath and then, wearing a borrowed dressing gown, cut up the back stairs to my room. It was empty. I thought it would be, but was still surprised. I got into bed and it was like sliding into a lukewarm bath. Sleep came like water closing over my face.

'And then this extraordinary dream. Dreamed I was an imposter – or at least somebody in disguise. I wanted to find a mirror so that I could see what I looked like, but every time I found one, it blurred, wouldn't show my face. People came and went, seemed to recognise me. I didn't know them, though. I hoped somebody would say my name, but they didn't. And then I was running through Temhari, trying to get somewhere fast. But there was something heavy in my hand too; wondered what it was but couldn't bring myself to look down. I was tearing down alleys; startled faces, pots and pans clattering aside, fruit baskets. Then I saw the horses ahead of me, cantering through the market stalls . . . the mare and the yearling. I was desperately trying to reach them for some reason. I caught sight of the mare's head turning towards me for a moment. It was wild-eyed and I felt a surge of horror quiver through me like voltage.

'I woke up in the dark, sweating. Eglantine was sitting on the rattan chair by the chest of drawers. A slash of light from the street lamp lit her shoulder and her neck. She was holding her crucifix. I told her I had malaria and she sprang up and lit a candle; held it over my face to get a better look. It was rather comic – she, looking down at my face for signs of mortality, while I gazed up at her childish frown of worry, wondering if there was anything capable of transgressing her beautiful simplicity. Cross purposes, wouldn't you say? I asked her to fetch Dr Masuri and mention Roker's recommendation, and out she clattered.

'And Roker was right. As soon as Masuri appeared it was plain that he was a cut above. Very elegant fellow, spotless linen suit, the warm glow of gold edging two of his front teeth; cool hands, immaculate nails – polished and almost pearly. And very precise, the classic East Indian intellectual. He went on to become Roraima's chief medical officer – knighthood, the lot. Masuri knew how to wait, you see; knew how to dole out interested smiles over drinks. After the knighthood he took to politics. Had to leave Roraima somewhat hurriedly in 1970, after which he slotted into one of those big funding agencies. He was forced to bail out of Roraima for political reasons, which means he was on the verge of being banged up for life by some transient thug wearing a customised uniform made in Savile Row who had half of Roraima's gross domestic product secreted in some bombproof catacomb in Zurich. His name was Rolinga, I think, and his final contribution to Roraima was a bullet-riddled desk, incinerated filing cabinets and gross national poverty.

'After Masuri left, Eglantine undressed and got into bed. Now I'll tell you something, Walter. *I didn't want her.* Quite suddenly and quite definitely, didn't want to see her – didn't want even to touch her. I remember this particular day very sharply simply because my reaction to her at that moment surprised me so much. But it wasn't the fever talking. As soon as she began to undress I knew it was over. Not only that, I knew just how much I'd used her. Well, fine . . . men and women have always used each other, either unwittingly because they're too stupid to know what they're doing, or in the usual dance. I think the complicity of it must have hit me at that moment. There was no emotion on my part. I was calm. I decided to try to lead her to the same conclusion.

'I used the fever as an excuse to stop our sleeping together. Three days later I said that I wanted to end it. She cried and then after a couple of minutes said she didn't care after all. It was only then that I felt the guilt and emotion. There's no point in pretending that she hadn't been delightful in many ways. Or that I'd used her more than she had used me, for the simple reason that I was in a position of power. Perhaps I was casting myself adrift from the remains of my own childhood. I'm past guilt about it. Demcorp expunges that when they hand you the pension book. "Any guilt to declare, Mr Freyn?" "Nothing above the permissible limit, inspector." On balance I think Eglantine was non-declarable. I was intrinsically faulty and she was very young. God knows what she did with all those shoes!

'I can't work out why or how I came to that decision about Eglantine so suddenly – without thinking at all, if I'm honest. I used to think that the fever, or my encounter with Luchenne, had substituted a new form of derangement for the one that already existed in me. I'm not so sure any more . . . the horses had triggered something else in me.

'The fever produced one happy result. I was excused work in the afternoons until Masuri said otherwise. Until Catherine appeared, I spent a good deal of time sitting with Madame Jopahl on a lie-back which she had brought into her inner sanctum. She would take up station on a wicker *chaise-longue* and we would converse quietly behind the chinoiserie screen through which she kept an eye on her girls. And I would listen as she expounded her theories of literature. Iago was a mentally defective homosexual who taunted Othello for his preference for what Madame Jopahl screechingly referred to as "comin in the back door with a steamin baguetty". Jane Austen, she said, would have run her coffee shop superbly. And she made me read to her, which I did, sometimes against the noise of an overstressed iron bedstead in one of the bedrooms. "Pay no heed, Mr Freyn. That is my Syreeta with Señor Dias from the Banco do Espirito Santo – Señor Dias with the unfortunate beatin of the heart."

'I was hiding away, I suppose, just as I am now. Oh, yes, Walter, I am certainly hiding – even from you. However . . . after a week in Temhari, and a week to go before sailing, I developed a strong sense that I was waiting for something. I can say this quite objectively. I am emphatically not gilding memory's lily, not saying it to add lustre to Catherine's appearance. In fact, there was nothing mysterious about that, beyond the actions of chance. She was on her way back to America from Buenos Aires – her husband had died nine months earlier of typhus – and our lives simply intersected at random. And that's everything, isn't it? Arcs and intersections.

'But, Walter, this feeling I'm telling you about was almost palpable. I found myself taking walks to the sea wall and studying the horizon, examining the form and drift of the clouds. A suspicion of thunder in the air, yet not a hint of it in the sky. The weather was particularly fine. Sunny, with rather plumped-up English-looking clouds and a nice breeze coming off the water. I'd be walking along or climbing the stairs to my office or turning the handle of my door and I'd think: something's about to happen. Or I'd imagine I'd forgotten an important appointment. I'd riffle through my diary – nothing, of course. Just the sleepy pecking of the typewriter in the next room, or Warburton Worricks poking his knowing little face round the door . . . or the sound of Spivey's voice meandering dolefully up from the courtyard. Get the picture? But I insist: these feelings had nothing to do with Catherine. I know that now. They were to do with something else entirely. They were a glimpse . . . an echo from the future.'

Lawton throws his hat into the wind

FREYN said he wanted to stop for the time being. He was pretty brisk about it too. 'I'm getting to the end of this,' he said. 'I think I'll have to do it in shorthand if you don't mind. It's hard for me. I've agreed to finish, and I will. But you'll have to let me do it in my own way.'

He claimed he wasn't quite sure how to explain the rest. 'Everything you've heard so far has been history, plain and simple. But there comes a point, sometimes, when events stop flowing. Something else takes a hand, something that makes all that has gone before irrelevant. I mean that certain events seem to arrive out of the blue, yet it's only later that you realise that nothing arrives out of the blue.'

Freyn insisted he wanted to 'get the thing done' and we arranged that I would come back on a daily basis until he'd finished. He said it might take a day, or it might take three. He had no idea. He looked, to me, to be in a hurry, which was totally unlike him. So I went back the next day in an excited mood. I'd got used to his long 'takes' and wondered what was in store. I soon found out.

'To occupy myself in Temhari,' Freyn said as soon as I'd settled, 'I made a private sport: looking for Wintle. It turned out that he'd got back to Temhari two days before me. He had been seen in the Club once. And he had certainly been present at a Lodge meeting according to Blenty, an obsequious oaf who used to creep around looking for his cronies. Wintle was seen twice on the quay, both times by Augusto. But could *I* spot him? Absolutely not, or not yet. And I thought: he's erased himself at last; nothing left but a mysterious spoor of pencil rubbers!

'The *Manahatta* docked three days after my return. A nice-looking ship: 23,000 tons; hardly a giant, but well turned out; split-level first-class dining room, two bars, twenty-two first-class cabins, and about another ninety cabins in the other classes. The cargo hold was forward, and there was a small aft half deck which had been fitted with heavy netting and a partial awning to contain the horses. This arrangement had been specified by Morphen.

'I took a look around the ship soon after it docked. As I left it I caught sight of a striking old fellow. He had a weather-beaten but soft-looking face, an unkempt white beard and large, alert eyes – very pale blue, they were. He carried with him an aura of repose and welcome, if that doesn't sound contradictory. Looking at Clarendon Lawton was like coming upon an old oak in a cleft of Sussex on a baking July afternoon. He was rooted, calm, almost inviting you to pause. He seemed tremendously old – probably as old as I must seem to you, Walter.

'Lawton's face was shaded by a fawn broad-rimmed hat. The brim was crooked and the peak battered and well fingered. He saw me and raised a hand. His other hand rested on the knob of an old hickory cane. A book bulged in one of the pockets of his cotton coat. "Clarendon Lawton," he said. He drawled the words out slowly and comfortably. He was American and obviously from the south. "And if you are James Freyn, I believe you may be able to advise me. Your office, which has so far orchestrated my freight forwarding immaculately, said you might be down here – said you could help me find a reliable carpenter." '

Freyn did not supply much information about the man. Maybe he had been too deferential to Lawton, in view of his age, to ask many questions. But as Lawton figures in the most significant part of Freyn's story, I thought a few biographical details would be appropriate.

Lawton is referred to in most histories of North American literature, and there is even a small entry in the *Infotannica*:

Lawton, Clarendon (1872–1938): American poet and literary commentator; introduced universalist critical methods (a form of mystical reductionism) with limited success; he is referred to by Kerouac in a letter to Neal Cassady, and is believed to be the model for the crucial ghost figure in Edwina Machen's epic cycle of haikus, *Connect-Etudes*; also noted as a traveller, cultural essayist and collector of folk songs.

The only thing Freyn could add to his picture of Lawton was that the writer's name had cropped up in the mid-1970s. 'I was in a tatty little art house cinema in Seattle and when the lights went up I realised I was sitting next to a rather delightful creature; late twenties, short blonde hair, wonderfully engaging eyes. She glanced at me and I noticed the book in her lap. Damn me if it wasn't a collection of essays by Lawton! Without thinking, I blurted out that I'd known him; at which she became quite animated. I suggested we adjourn for a coffee and we spent the best part of two hours talking about this and that. She was from Munich, obviously very bright, doing a PhD on the philosophy of film – wanted to know if it was true that Lawton had a violet aura. I confess, Walter, that my thoughts were on other possibilities. She was an angel straight out of Rilke, and far too good for a battered wanderer like me.

'No matter. Now, Lawton . . . I did find him a carpenter in Shelley Road, in a shed behind Moulis the printer. I remember that when the carpenter asked what was required, Lawton replied: "It will be straightforward because your skill is all around you. I shall return in three hours to discuss it." He looked at the fellow over his shoulder as we left and said: "A simple matter, I assure you." I can see that carpenter now, standing there barefooted in scented pale pink eddies of hardwood shavings.

'And then Lawton made for the sea wall, insisting that I

accompany him. He selected a place to sit on the sand in the shade of palms and drew a book out of his coat pocket. He said he was never without it and was going to repay me for my help by reading me a poem. All I can remember is the opening: "Out of the cradle, endlessly rocking." I recall it as a meandering piece, lulling and hypnotic. Lawton enjoyed intoning the words, stretching out the emphases. And when he finished he snapped the volume shut and gazed out, squinting towards the horizon. "Such poetry reminds us that life is movement," he said. "People are creatures of motion and marvellous chance. Nationalism is a constipated vileness, don't you agree, Mr Freyn?" And then: "I wonder if I could convince the wind to return my hat to me?"

'There was a brisk onshore breeze blowing cool and stiff into our faces. He pulled off his hat, held up his left hand to judge its strength and then flicked the hat, side-handed, up and away from him. It travelled three or four yards, rising steeply, then fell back in an arc. Lawton reached out and made a grab for it, but missed the brim. The hat flopped on to his knee and skidded on to the sand between us. "Hats in motion!" he shouted.

'I must've spent an hour with him, sitting there on the sand – highly unpukkah! He'd travelled up from Montevideo on the *Manahatta*. He'd been collecting native songs and tales. His theory was that the songs of indigents were the expressions of the rhythms of landscapes. He also said that Mr Henry Ford would have it otherwise. I asked him if he objected to progress and he said – I can hear him saying it *now*, Walter! – he said progress couldn't be manufactured, progress wasn't a string of die-stamped cultural artifacts. "Machines cannot become men, Mr Freyn, but Mr Ford knows that men may become wretched machines! After which, sir, there is only greed and desecration in an endless Fordlandia."

'Lawton was a delight. The two of us might indeed have been sitting under that Sussex oak eating cheese and pickles. He carried just that sort of atmosphere with him. Today, I'd call Lawton a mystic. I didn't see much more of him before we sailed

– though there was one moment that sticks. I saw him appear out of the cut to the carpenter's shop, positively striding out into the thoroughfare with a broad smile on his face, the cane flicked forward at a jaunty angle. I remembered that smile eleven days later. I'll always remember it. It was the smile of a man who had mastered himself by opening himself completely to people and events. He was fearless.

'The days before boarding almost passed muster. I still had a sense of something impending, though that's hardly surprising, is it? I was about to take ship to New Orleans and get clear of Temhari – and clear of *myself* with any luck. But luck doesn't always come into it. I was deluding myself. I was simply waiting, and not as keenly and alertly as I thought I was.

'Since then, one has learned to be rather more alert, learned to *receive*; one has become adept at this and the more adept one becomes the more one is removed from things. A box or a fire or the sounds of a fight – why, they seem almost arbitrary. I don't think I'm unique. There must be more than a few like me in the Delta, people whose within is the same as their without. I can recognise them but I don't bother them, or even talk to them. Perhaps you'll be able to spot them yourself, now that you've studied me so carefully. What do you think? Let's see: do I have any distinguishing marks? Am I to be believed?

'Or do you think old people naturally prepare themselves for extinction by weaving a shroud of fantasy? Or that it would be impossible for a horse to float among the stars? Or that Roraima never existed, that it was just a Georgian version of the Delta in an old man's sepia hallucination?

'Ah, my patient friend! I shouldn't goad you, should I? Now then . . . I spent the rest of that day at the office and on my way home I called in at the King Street stables to check on my beauties. The yearling was being exercised on a leading rein on a small patch of ground behind the stables. The mare looked on impassively. It seemed a privilege to watch the unselfconscious spirit of the yearling as it moved. I hold that image close for obvious reasons, or at least –'

Freyn broke off and raised a finger. His eyes narrowed. 'Can you hear that, Walter? That whispering sound. Hear it? No? It's very faint, a sort of hissing. *There* . . . just then! Right, good. Now, forgive me, but I'm going to insist that you clear off fairly immediately. That sound means the Luminians are massing in the vicinity of Causeway 5. They may sound like they're hissing but they're actually ululating prior to one of their attacks. You'd better cut along to your exit cannula before the Paraquell teams are dropped in to subdue them.'

Freyn made a kind of shooing motion with his hands and gave me an impatient look. I asked if he might prefer me to stay with him, but that only made him sigh. 'You needn't spare me the slightest thought,' he said. 'Seen it all before, Walter. I'm perfectly capable of minding the shop until tomorrow. So, off you go and I'll carry on where I – oh, look, I think you've forgotten to switch your thing off. The button's still down.'

I packed up my things, checked that my stun-baton was in Ready-Max mode and began to turn myself round to crawl out through the flap. Then I heard a tinny rattling sound and Freyn clearing his throat. 'No, wait,' he said. 'Wait a moment, Walter.' I turned to face him. He had a shallow A4-size tin box open on his bedroll. 'Look,' he said, 'I think I'd prefer it if you took this. Transcribe it and bring it back to me when you've done, if you don't mind. You don't mind helping me along with this, do you? It's the diary I kept aboard the *Manahatta*. It . . . explains everything you need to know. It's all there, more or less. Come back later and I'll tie up any loose ends. Please look after it. Right, you'd better cut along.'

I took the diary and stowed it carefully in my rucksack. As I headed for Causeway 3 I felt so sharply vigilant that I was almost lightheaded with tension. And as I finally left the Delta via the exit cannula I experienced a strange moment. For what seemed to be several seconds, I blanked. As if I didn't know where I'd been, or where I was going. I stood there, looking down at my route adviser handset, wondering what the hell it was. Then I had a flash of Freyn sitting back in that boat, heading up the creek to the penal colony.

Catherine Bourne

THE *Manahatta* diary sat in my securispace for two or three days, unread. The way Freyn passed it to me, his haste, made it obvious that his story hinged on it in some way. And that had an odd effect: I couldn't bring myself to read it straight away. I was wary, found myself looking at it, touching it carefully, hefting it, putting it down again.

I'll get to the diary in a moment. I have to backtrack first, tidy up one or two things.

Freyn's previous references to a woman called 'Catherine' hadn't until now triggered much interest on my part. But it turned out that Catherine Bourne – then aged thirty-one, of New Orleans – was important to Freyn's story. I shouldn't say 'to his story'; I should say 'to his life'. I have no doubt now that her role heightened what happened aboard the *Manahatta* and its long-term effect on him. I'm also pretty sure that Catherine Bourne was an ingredient in what Freyn had earlier said about beauty, hope and memory.

Yet he had hardly discussed her. It was as if he was afraid to open that particular filing cabinet. I had tried two or three times to get him cranked up on the subject of Catherine but it was no go. There was one interesting moment, though. He was talking about Wintle; something about spotting him talking to Spivey at the club – this was before he sailed on the *Manahatta*. 'They were holed up in a corner of the strangers' bar,' he said. 'Wintle caught my eye and looked away quickly. Then Spivey turned and looked over at me before turning back to resume their conversation. I could tell from Wintle's face that Spivey was telling him something about me because Wintle grinned and looked at me again.'

Freyn yawned. I assumed he'd dropped the subject. But his yawn slurred into a coughing fit. When he'd got his breathing together he said: 'I took Catherine to the club early one evening when I knew it would be fairly quiet. I thought she might be amused by the scene and she was − until Wintle appeared. We were sitting in the inner veranda, looking out across the gardens towards Main Street. I was asking her about New Orleans − anything, really, so that I could watch her face, her eyes, the way her mouth moved when she spoke.

'Then Catherine touched me on my hand and looked over her shoulder. I turned. Wintle was standing a few feet away. He had been waiting to catch our attention. I didn't particularly want to be interrupted but had no alternative: I introduced him to Catherine. After a few pleasantries he turned to me and said: "So, Freyn, what is this? Time off for good behaviour?" And he gave me the same steady provoking look he'd given me when talking to Spivey.

'I managed to get rid of him. Of course, by now Catherine and I seemed to understand each other − well enough for me to explain the reasons for Wintle's little jab. When I finished my résumé, Catherine was superb. She said that nothing I'd said had condemned me in her eyes. She said people like Wintle had nothing to offer. They were happy to swim in the dark feeding off scraps.'

Freyn had got himself a bit worked up. I waited for him to say more about Catherine. When he didn't I asked him what she had been like. Freyn looked away immediately and began to dab at the wax around the wick of the eternal candle. The flame wobbled and pale brown shadows wavered across his brow. He changed the subject.

So there is very little info about Catherine Bourne from

Freyn's lips. I therefore have no alternative but to offer a slab of material from the diary kept by Freyn aboard the *Manahatta*. It's not the only material about her in the diary, but is the only focused chunk.

Here's the entry:

July 4, 11pm I have not mentioned Catherine for two days. This has been deliberate. I do not like to associate my feelings for her with these other events. I have decided to devote one entry to her alone, without mentioning anything else that may be happening. My reason is that I, like Catherine, have become increasingly worried about our situation. I think I should admit that I am afraid. But I cannot restrain myself from writing about Catherine alone. This will be my only entry for the day, regardless of what else may occur. I want to set down, as precisely as possible, the details of our first meeting.

We met at Spivey's office, where she, accompanied by Mrs Slocumber and her son, Bobby (he is ten years old) had come to make arrangements for the forwarding of locally-made chests and carvings. Augusto tapped on the door jamb and said: 'Mrs Bourne and Mrs Slocumber to see you.' He showed them into my office, and passed me a note from Spivey concerning their requirements.

Catherine and Bobby, chaperoned by her aunt, were returning to New Orleans following the death of Catherine's husband nine months earlier in Buenos Aires. She looked frail, and still does. I found that I was immediately rattled. It had nothing to do with the fact that they are Americans. I had to force myself to look away from Catherine. I cannot think what she thought of my staring at her like that. I knew that I had been struck by her and felt both afraid and elated.

I knew immediately that I must see her again as soon as possible, find any excuse to speak to her. Catherine's effect on me is less to do with her physical beauty, which is all in her eyes and the set of her mouth and the way she holds herself, than in her radiance. I have considered her effect and am at a loss to grasp its workings. Perhaps I am being absurd, but I insist that from that first instant I sensed something about her nature that was at once steadfast and, yet, child-like. I don't mean childish. I mean that her radiance seems to come from a clear place. I wonder if my reaction to the horses has something to do with it.

Does that 'clear place' remind me of my extraordinary intimacy with the mare and yearling as we made for the turnpike? These thoughts of her became mixed with memories of my own childhood, inconsequential recollections – the sharp scent of the pines at Angmering at dusk on hot summer days, and the glitter of the droplets of resin weeping from pine bark. Stealing silently to the door of the morning room to watch my mother reading. Or bending down to watch a bee hovering over a pot full of wall-flowers. Or my fingers running over the silky face of a new cricket bat.

These recollections are trifles, I suppose! Yet Catherine's presence caused them to arise in profusion. She animated me the moment she appeared. I felt a stranger to myself, as if I had suddenly been inhabited by another person. And I had the hair-brained idea that if I took her to the King Street stables, she too would feel a deep connection with the horses.

Attending to her shipping requirements was extremely difficult. A task which I would normally have dealt with in twenty minutes at the most was carefully extended to half an hour while I thought of a way to see her again. When the business was concluded I insisted that I be allowed to take them to tea at the Planter's Room. I was aware that Catherine watched me closely as I made the proposal, also that she replied quickly that they would be pleased to if Mrs Slocumber had no objection. Mrs Slocumber had none.

Later, the taxi put us down at the Planter's and we spent an hour and a half there, in the shade of the veranda, looking through the palms to the sharp line of the horizon. Though Mrs Slocumber and Bobby were charming, I only wanted to hear Catherine's voice. When we really could not drink any more tea, Catherine asked how best the three of them could see the sights of Temhari. It seemed a calculated remark on her part. Concealing the thrill that coursed through me, I insisted that they allow me to take them on a tour, by taxi, and we arranged to meet the next day, which was Saturday.

I was certain then that Catherine had experienced some feeling for me. I would say that I, that *we*, had experienced an attraction to each other, and an understanding. The taxi tour was in style, with old Mr Plimpton at the wheel of his Humber. I had arranged the route in advance with him and was thus able to turn round in my seat in the front to explain what they were seeing. Catherine, I noticed, looked mostly at me, rather than the sights I was describing.

When, at midday, I returned them to their hotel, Catherine asked me to join them for a cordial, which I did. I felt terrifically tense, could hardly speak. Bobby demanded to get something from their rooms, and Mrs Slocumber took him up. As soon as they had gone, I looked straight at Catherine and said I was very happy that we would be travelling together on the *Manahatta*. And then, God help me, I told her that I couldn't help saying that I found her remarkable, and had done so the moment she had stepped into my office. I began to apologise for these sudden and rather clumsy remarks, but she only said, in a very quiet voice: 'I understand.' Just when I wanted to speak, to say everything, no matter how badly, I could not utter. We simply looked at each other and when we heard Bobby's voice in the lobby, I said again, and quickly, that to be able to travel to New Orleans with her had made me very happy. She smiled.

I had been able, on the pretext of going through the completed shipping papers with her, to invite her to my office two days before sailing. Having not seen her for three days, I waited at my desk in a highly nervous condition. Would she have thought better of her feelings, or have decided that I had, after all, been too forward? Would there then be a coolness between us, and a certain embarrassment once aboard the *Manahatta*? But as soon as she walked in, I could see that she was pleased to see me, and nervous at the same time. I said that I had missed her very much and that she seemed even more radiant. How dull these words seem – and so they are!

Yet they were not dull to her. I could see a reaction in her frank, grey eyes.

Once alone, we were able to look at each other without interference. I think we were not sure how we should behave towards one another. We said very little. I gave her an envelope containing a copy of the shipping details. After which, we were not sure what to do! I walked her downstairs and called for a car. I held out my hand and she took it momentarily. The touch of her skin, the warmth of it, left me mute. And as she made to get into the back of the motor, I spoke her name – only that, her name, softly. Catherine turned and studied my face for a moment, a searching look (what a marvellously steady gaze it was!) and then stepped into the back of the motor.

I watched it pull away and when I could see it no longer, I waited until the dust it had made settled. At that moment, it seemed to me that everything that I had thought to be insubstantial was, in fact, crammed with possibilities. I could not let the world abandon me, nor could I choose to abandon the world. I had felt a response, a sharp recognition that was unmistakable.

As soon as I finished work, I walked to King Street and commandeered a brush and spent half an hour combing the mare and yearling. Their beauty seemed quite extreme. I watched the brush in my hand as it moved across their smooth coats. I could feel the muscles beneath the play of dunny colours and it was as if I was again in the forest with them, and everything was again rich with mysterious meaning. They are my redeemers! I watched them being led to their boxes. Once in, they stood calmly, looking back at me. I do think they know everything about me. We are in league!

I have written this entry without a care as to its form or repetitions. It is what I feel. All my hopes are in these few words. One day soon, Catherine, you will read them and smile your frank smile, and you will doubtless chide me.

The *Manahatta* diary

AND now, following the spirit of Freyn's request, I transcribe the rest of the diary here. I set it out in its raw state. It's all I can do.

June 28. We are at sea! Catherine, Bobby, Mrs Slocumber and I stood at the rail and watched the quay float, as it seemed, away from us, as if the *Manahatta* was of substance and Temhari was not. I cannot describe how strange was my sense of proximity to Catherine. Our hands were close together on the rail and the rail itself seemed alive with her touch. We had a clear view of the horses, who showed no sign of nerves as we slipped clear of the dock. Bobby very taken with the horses and adores the yearling. He rushes up to strangers and demands to know good names for horses. Mrs Slocumber is clearly relieved to be on ship, bound finally and certainly for New Orleans.

I find myself in a difficult situation: I only want to be with Catherine, yet feel I must absent myself from time to time. I believe it is the same for her. We try not to look at each other too often. How absurd! I am determined that all should proceed perfectly between us.

Among the things we did today, in no particular order: played bridge with Mrs Slocumber and two businessmen from Belem, deck quoits with Bobby (he never smiled, so determined was he to give a good account of himself), a short discussion with Capt McCandless about the ship's history. Lunch, tea. I can't keep still. I walked round the decks when Catherine was in her cabin or with others. I talked to the mare, who looks at me uncannily. I am barely aware of the sea, only enough to report that it is fairly calm and of a very deep blue colour. That will do, as I must change for dinner.

Addendum, 10.32pm: after dinner, Mrs Slocumber allowed me to walk Catherine once round the promenade deck before delivering her to her cabin. I took Catherine's arm and, with some trepidation, put my hand over hers. She smiled! Only then was I able to turn and face her as we walked. When we were on the port side, she said how wonderful the night sky was. I looked up and noticed it for the first time. She was right, but at that moment its stars seemed to be an interruption of something much more wonderful and fragile. I will end here.

June 29, 6pm. There has been a fire and the *Manahatta* is without power. Our position is roughly 350 miles north-east of Temhari. A klaxon awoke me just before 7am. I ignored it, but it persisted. After two or three minutes there was a knock on my door and one of the stewards said: 'Please go to the starboard boat deck immediately, sir, there has been a fire:' Within seconds I could hear passengers passing up the corridor. I rushed out to find Catherine, Bobby and Mrs Slocumber. When we reached the boat deck we saw smoke rising not only from the funnel but from two of the aft ventilators. I could hear sailors calling to each other urgently, but saw very few, which was alarming. A roll call was taken and everybody appeared to be present. Then we were instructed to move to the bows, where Capt McCandless would address us from the bridge.

Capt McC did not waste words. He said that a fire in the engine room had damaged the engines and other equipment irreparably. He assured us that, provided the weather remained calm, there was no threat to the ship's seaworthiness. However, the fire had also spread into some of the ductings, burning along various electrical cables. Unfortunately, it had spread up the electricity cable to the radio room and succeeded in melting or charring much of the short-wave set. This means we will be unable to radio for assistance. Capt McC's plan is to fire off four flares per day and night (there are 24 flares in store) to attract the attention of ships passing within ten or twenty miles. He said the situation was serious but not yet grave as the *Manahatta* was near a reasonably well-used shipping lane.

It seems the results of the fire are extraordinarily unlucky. The fire had broken out suddenly at about 5am and was extinguished relatively quickly, though not quickly enough to save the engines or generators. One man is quite ill through excessive smoke in his lungs. The extent of the fire in the ducting was not realised until it was too late. Some of the passengers have been making jokes about the episode. Bobby is very excited and I have not, therefore, been able to spend much time with Catherine. We three are invited to sit with Capt McC at dinner tonight. I am confused. When I'm with Catherine, I feel both frightened about the ship yet utterly happy about her. I wanted very much to take her hand, but no opportunity presented itself.

Met Mr Lawton, who was studying the horses. He said: 'Yesterday, how beautiful the ship seemed. But today, we must rejoice instead in the wonder of these fine animals. Let us turn our eyes away from green-gloaming Acheron.' I had no idea what he meant and asked him to explain. He said Acheron was the mythical world of the dead. He said it very lightly, as if it amused him. Caught sight of Wintle, on his own. He is an odd fish. He frowns and seems only to look down.

June 30, 7am. It is odd being on a ship at sea that does not move or vibrate. My sleep was irregular, partly because of that and partly because of an attack of fever. However, the fever seems to be less alarming.

The atmosphere at dinner last night was unexpectedly convivial. Capt McC was both amusing and grave. Also rather shrewd, as once everybody in the first-class dining room had settled, he made a short announcement. Said the outbreak of fire had not been the fault of the engineers; that small fires were not, in fact, unknown in engine rooms. But its position had allowed it to do considerable damage very rapidly. He reiterated his earlier remarks about the *Manahatta*'s position and said it would take the most unusual run of bad luck for us not to be noticed within two or three days. One of the guests at his table, a Portuguese businessman, asked how much water the ship had. Capt McC said there was enough to last for five days (and nights) unrationed, which was two days more than the journey normally took. This caused a brief silence at our table.

Capt McC said that if there was no response to the flares at 3am or 9am today he planned to introduce water rationing, both for washing and drinking. Bobby immediately asked about water for the horses. Capt McC quick to point out that as the animals were not exercising they could make do with very little. It was obvious that some of the diners at the other tables were not satisfied with the situation, but were keeping their annoyance in check.

Have just returned from a circuit of the promenade deck. Stopped to look at the horses. I think they are alive in a different way to humans. They are like the sea, they flow. I must groom them today. I have Luchenne's grooming brushes with me. Bobby keen to help.

June 30, 10.24pm. I have spent a little time with Catherine. We found a quiet place to sit on the bridge deck, which is only available to first class, of course, overlooking the stern. Catherine confessed that she was afraid the *Manahatta* might not be found. At first, I thought to change the subject, only to realise that this would have been a terrible mistake. She is not fearful in a selfish way. She mentioned Bobby and looked as if she might cry. Quite suddenly, she said that she would kiss me now, rather than wait for a more proper moment, as she didn't want our first kiss tainted by the situation around us, should it worsen. How tender was that touch of her lips, their exquisite warmth and slight trembling. I told her that I loved her strange, fierce gentleness. I said my old fever had been replaced by a new one. I felt a lightheaded fool as I said it, but she only touched my cheek. (I wanted to mention the kiss

241

straight away in this entry, but restrained myself. I am obviously deranged!)

July 1, 5.30pm. Water rationing has commenced. Capt McC made his announcement three times, once to each class of passengers immediately after lunch. He said there was a reasonable stock of tinned food and fruit, but feared that the fresh meat and vegetables would have to be discounted quite soon because of the heat.

Capt McC said an experiment would be carried out after lunch, in which a container of engine oil would be set on fire, safely, in the bows to produce black smoke. If the smoke rises high enough, it will be seen from afar. He warned that the complete stillness of the air may prevent the smoke rising properly. I asked one of the stewards how the rest of the passengers had taken the latest announcement. He said second class were 'quiet as stone' and that third class 'are moaning about the gaffer, but amused like'. As for first class, I can report that there has been a mixture of ironic remarks and fixed faces – none want to show any particular concern.

It is interesting: the wits are suddenly particularly productive and rather good value, but nobody dares laugh too loud for fear of being thought hysterical. We are to have smaller meals in order to conserve water. Have just returned from the aft deck where Bobby and I groomed the horses. I was not allowed to touch the yearling! Catherine watched us. I confess that it was a luxurious experience. Just the steady soft sound of the brushes, and the sea around us, and Catherine seen out of the corner of my eye. After Catherine and Bobby left, I remained to clear the hair out of the brushes – even the clots of their hair seem magical – and caught sight of Wintle, looking down at me from the bridge deck. I said hello, but he didn't reply. After a moment or two he went away. I have more important things to do than to try to strike up conversations with Wintle. For example, perfecting the skill of washing myself efficiently with the minimum of water. It is easy to imagine the other passengers trying to do the same thing simultaneously. In our showers and baths, we are all equal! Bobby has insisted he be allowed to stay up to see the flare go up tonight.

July 1, 11.54pm. The first-class dining room was only two-thirds full tonight. We had corned beef and bananas, which gave me the opportunity to tell Bobby about the collection of the horses from El Arroyo, and my diet while travelling in the forest. There was an amusing haute cuisine lottery and the dozen passengers with the winning tickets were served the last of the edible lamb, severely grilled. Mrs Slocumber ventured to remark that, judging by the poor turnout in the dining room, sociability appeared to have been rationed too.

I suspect some of the first-class passengers could not feel comfortable dining in public unless they had been able to complete their toilettes to their full satisfaction. I wonder if they are saving up their water for a full wash only in the mornings.

None of this speculation could ever apply to Catherine. She is quite apart. She does not ration herself, and we (that is, anybody near her) can only benefit. I think she would hate to hear me say this! I am a little later to bed than usual because, after returning Catherine to Mrs Slocumber (she says 'Enter!' the very second I knock), I met Lawton on the promenade deck. He asked me to accompany him on a circuit. He waxed poetical, something about being in cabined ships at sea, and 'endless blue on every side expanding'. He also seemed to be taken up with the idea of the dead weight of the ship, 'a dead hulk, James, lying on the meniscus of a darkling eye'. He is wary. He fears that things may get worse, citing Wintle as an example. 'Within a whisker of cracking,' he said.

Lawton is an original. I think minds like his must take in and consider much more than most others. As we parted he delivered a couplet (can't remember it), and said that he might stay in his cabin tomorrow as he had been feeling unwell.

Bobby enjoyed the flare but objected that it gave off pink, rather than red, light. He said: 'If another ship sees it, they may think we're having party.' Catherine replied quickly: 'In which case they will come anyway to see if we need any more champagne.' Which reminds me that the ship is 'dry'. The last of the wine and spirits is gone.

There is a minor scandal. One of our barmen, a normally delightful man who is now quite fed up, told me that the remaining bottles of spirits had been stolen. He said that every bottle and glass was accounted for daily. He wouldn't actually say it, but his inference was that a first-class passenger had filched them.

Sea condition just before I turned in: an almost flat calm, no wind. I heard splashes aft and went to take a look. The deck hands were dumping spoiled food overboard, much of which settles on the mats of floating seaweed, and does not sink. Rather tawdry. There was a considerable smell.

The oil-smoke experiment has failed. The smoke did not rise, but only settled around the bows and over the water. It has only succeeded in making everything in the bows filthy. The deckhands are clearing it up, and doing so in an understandable surly mood.

July 2, 11.30am. A committee has been formed among the first-class passengers 'to consider additional emergency measures'. I was invited to act as secretary, but declined, which did not go down very well. I do not think a committee is a good idea as it may encourage people to question Capt McC's decisions. In my opinion, he must be supported in everything he does. The committee has proposed that some sort of de-salination plant be set up. As we have no power, I fail to see how this can be done. The committee also saw fit to discuss the timing of the flares – a patently ridiculous idea. Also, the question of security was raised. Mrs Slocumber was told that one of the committee members, a Mr Swed-Couzens of Buenos Aires, used the expression 'steerage types'. Swed-Couzens wants to know if a watch is being kept on how much water each passenger is using. Wintle is on the committee.

July 3, 11.30am. It is noticeable that there is much less conversation. The bridge deck is quiet, and so too is the promenade deck, where all classes mix. People seek out shady corners on deck, or stay in their cabins. Most of the bridge deck is exposed to the sun, so that during the day there are more first-class passengers in the public areas on the lower deck than there might normally be. It continues quite hot and the sea flat calm. Some of the food put overboard this morning has not sunk and there is a slight, but distinct, smell of rotting. Capt McC makes a full circuit of the ship three times daily, twice during the day, once at night. He has his hands hard at work carrying out cleaning and repairs. The smell of fresh paint almost covers the stink of the floating food.

July 5. There was some trouble on board yesterday. The first-class passengers committee had apparently asked Capt McC to establish if those in the other classes were using water as per his rationing regime. Capt McC refused, saying he was certain that all on board realised the seriousness of the situation concerning water. However, it seems that, after apparently withdrawing their request, some committee members, including Wintle, attempted to gain access to the second-class cabin area, demanding to make spot checks. An ugly and embarrassing confrontation ensued.

It is hard to establish the full facts. Four things are known: that Wintle struck a second-class passenger for cheeking him; that a crew member who attempted to intervene was injured, possibly by Wintle; that second- and third-class passengers have been given the run of the bow deck, which has been cordoned off from the rest of the ship. I overheard somebody say that the committee had been given a dressing down by Capt McC.

July 6. Witnessed a short, distinctly vicious argument in the saloon between Sir Oliver Stemper and a Mr Trumble, during a bridge game. Sir Oliver suddenly coloured and put his cards down, accusing Trumble of using a secret bidding system. Their partners were too stunned to speak. Trumble, a highly successful fruit exporter, calmly denied it. Sir Oliver redoubled his accusation. At which Trumble said, very coolly indeed: 'Perhaps you accuse me of secret bids because you dislike losing and because, as is well known in Roraima, you are quite a dab hand at secret bids.' Sir Oliver, quite enraged, asked him what he meant. Trumble said, very sweetly: 'Does the Temhari southern flood barrier contract ring a bell?' Apoplexy! Sir Oliver flung his cards at Trumble, who laughed at him.

Things are rather coming apart at the seams, I fear. Mrs Slocumber, who was with me, said very quietly: 'Savages in silk shirts, and more by the day.' I like her increasingly. She misses nothing. Catherine is fortunate to have her as an aunt.

July 7, 11.03pm. Catherine and I have been on deck, quite alone. We found a niche between a tidy stack of life rafts and the aft corner of the wheelhouse. We stood at the rail looking out over the still sea, when, to our considerable surprise, rain began to fall. It was not heavy, but the drops were large. Within half a minute we were rather wet, yet neither of us made to move.

To begin with, we were amused. Perhaps our glee was a release for our fears. We were soon distinctly wet. I told Catherine I intended to slake my thirst. Holding her face in my hands I began to kiss the water from her forehead and cheeks. The rain on her skin was warm. Were we not caught up in something pure and elemental? She declared that she was also thirsty and began to return my kisses.

After too short a time we were interrupted by the sound of voices. Looking down on to the promenade deck, we saw some first-class passengers, perhaps a dozen, in dressing gowns, moving to the rail. They carried glasses or cups, some had one in each hand, which they held up to catch rainwater. From the bows could be heard cheers and laughter – second- and third-class passengers up late and celebrating the rain. Unfortunately, after two or three minutes the rain stopped abruptly. The cups and glasses were lowered, as if by beggars resigned to rejection. After some desultory chat about the possibility of more rain, they returned to their cabins.

At that moment, I valued only the gift of warmth from Catherine's hand in mine, more precious to me than rain.

After escorting Catherine to her cabin (Mrs Slocumber's brisk

'Enter!'), I went aft to see the horses. The mare turned and moved elegantly towards me as soon as I appeared. I laid my cheek against her neck and thought of the forest.

There is a long final entry in Freyn's *Manahatta* diary, written on 8 July at 2 p.m. It is incoherent and I therefore decided to use parts of it in the next chapter, in tandem with additional information from him, and other sources.

This is hardly ideal, I know. I'm just trying to get it all down the best way I can.

The horses

ON July 8 the *Manahatta* had been ten days and nights at sea, nine of them becalmed and powerless. There were exactly four half-pint rations of increasingly sour water, per crew and passenger, remaining. The committee's makeshift desalination pans had failed. There was little change in the sea: its surface was flat, with mats of the malodorous seaweed rubbing against the waterline plates. The passengers were almost entirely silent. Freyn recalled the atmosphere as 'dead and heavy'. Even so, there was nothing to predict Wintle's appearance under the bridge on the port side.

Later, in a statement to police, Capt McCandless recalled seeing him there, standing stock still, trying to light a cigarette. Wintle apparently failed to light it and put the box of matches back in his trouser pocket. According to McCandless's statement to the court in New Orleans two weeks later Wintle was even less sure what to do with the cigarette. 'First, he put it behind his ear. Then he began to rub at his chin. He put his hands in his pockets and took them out again. He took the cigarette and rolled it round in his fingers, seeming to sniff at it. I'm not sure he didn't lick the wretched thing.

'Wintle seemed nervous, sure enough. But then, that runt was always in some state of agitation or other,' according to the *Manahatta*'s captain. 'I own that I could not be bothered to keep a particular eye on Wintle. I'm sorry about that now, but to admit the truth, he didn't seem worth considering. In fact, to watch him for those two minutes seemed a distasteful thing to do. It was like staring at a leper. He was still under the bridge when I turned to go back into the wheelhouse. I had a word with the officer of the watch, Slewin, and turned in. The time was a very few minutes after 1 a.m.'

Wintle's movements after that, at least until he reappeared on the aft half deck less than two hours later, remain obscure. 'But the *boy* knew,' said Freyn, frowning above his flickering candle. 'Without a doubt, Bobby knew. And if it hadn't been for Bobby, Wintle would probably have got away with it.'

Freyn had been asleep in his cabin. 'I had been particularly happy that evening,' he said. 'I think we both had. Catherine and I had not said so very much to each other. We had sat on deck, rather than risk the fickle conversation in the first-class saloon. I felt deliciously tired, no doubt an after-effect of the fever and the lack of food and water – and the uncertainty, of course. When we spoke, our voices seemed at one remove: soft, even-toned, as if from a distance. We were comfortable with each other, between those warm stars scattered low on the horizon, and the skin of the sea glowing like pewter in the moonlight.'

Less obvious were the activities of other first-class passengers that night. Their initial statements to the New Orleans constabulary agreed in one generality: that the last cards and conversations had been abandoned in the saloon at about midnight; and that Wintle had appeared once, shortly after dinner, to read alone at his usual table by the door. There had been no conversation between Wintle and any of the passengers.

'No, but you see, the *boy* knew,' Freyn repeated. 'Do you see how important that is? Bobby knew because his senses weren't occluded. He was open to the world, not closed or prejudiced against it. He was at an age when most things were new to him – experiences were tendernesses. And imagine, Walter, how those days on the *Manahatta* must have affected him; the shock of seeing adults beginning to behave so badly.'

Freyn had lost me. I had no idea what he was talking about.

He noticed. 'Do you think I'm evading the issue, Walter? Are you thinking: dear old Freyn and his little details, the old boy's at it again?' I said nothing. I wasn't going to rise to the bait and risk breaking his flow. I could see that he was deliberately getting himself worked up. 'You'd like me to get to the point, wouldn't you, eh? You sense that I'm going to describe something important and you just wish the old boy would cut to the chase?'

Freyn was stalling. The details were important, but this time I sensed that he was once again struggling to continue. His voice had developed a slightly different timbre at almost exactly the moment he began to recall what Capt McCandless had seen of Wintle from the bridge that night.

'Bobby had somehow been prepared for what happened; softened up, tenderised,' Freyn continued. 'Think how it must have been for him. To see that change in adult behaviour as the water supply dwindled. A little boy with a compass – a *soul* – whose needle had begun to whirl round wildly. You too would begin to wonder if you could ever take things for granted again. You too would look for signs with a new alertness.'

Catherine told Freyn afterwards that Bobby had woken, crying, in the early hours of the morning. 'She went to him,' said Freyn, 'thinking that he had overheated in bed. She found him shivering and gasping. She was terrified. The boy was sobbing and gasping for breath as if he were choking.' Freyn rubbed his hands together slowly. They made a rough dry sound. 'She said he had gone into a kind of spasm, clawing outwards with his hands and kicking his legs – all the while with his back arched in an alarming backward curve. Catherine couldn't hold him.'

Freyn stopped again. His eyes narrowed. He seemed to be trying to remember something, or clarify a particular thought. 'What do you think it was, Walter? Tetanus? Meningitis?' I suggested the latter was a possibility.

Freyn rubbed at his knees, nodding. 'We have a lot of meningitis here in the Delta – FDM, fulminant Delta menin-gococcus. I'm sure you've been inoculated. Know what the locals do when the symptoms appear? They drag the still-living victims off to a special part of zone 19, right up against the perimeter. There's a bunker there – seen it myself. It looks just like any of the mega waste bunkers.

'But the wide bore tubes that lead to this one don't suck out waste. Once a day, the unconscious terminally ill are inserted – has to be before 4 p.m. Half an hour later, the doors lock automatically. The tubes flex slightly and give off a faint humming sound. The humming is in three five-minute phases. The first delivers nitrous oxide into the sealed bunker; the second delivers about twenty cubic metres of neurotoxic gas, replicated from the venom of certain sea snakes; the third removes the gas and replaces it with clean air. The bodies are cleared out two hours later.

'Does that process constitute an ethical issue, do you think? Or should we simply put it down to the horror of a darkness visible? The employment of ethical thought is often a way of rationalising – one might almost say *privatising* – lack of instinct. And it's ultimately a way of justifying control.

'Ethics had no value in Catherine's cabin that night. And ethics, or even anti-ethics, certainly had no part in Wintle's thoughts as he made his way aft. D'you know, it's quite likely that he walked right past the deck-level porthole of Catherine's cabin. Maybe that was all it took to tip Bobby into his nightmarish realisation – just that wraithy feel of Wintle passing in the dead of night.'

I listened to Freyn intently, and a little tensely. He had never before talked with such vehemence.

'Bobby's condition became alarming,' Freyn continued. 'The boy began talking gibberish, whispering nonsense words too rapidly to be understood. I questioned Catherine very carefully about this afterwards, trying to piece things together. But she could remember only one of Bobby's phrases, four words: *falling down the stars*. Catherine tried to shush him gently. "You're not on the stairs," she said. "You're safe."

'She couldn't have been sitting with Bobby for more than

five minutes when she heard it. She described it as sounding like a bucket being knocked over, nothing more than that. It didn't signify. But then she heard whinnying and another sound – something vague like a heavy blanket being flapped around. And it was precisely at that moment that Bobby's delirium ceased. He looked at Catherine quite calmly for a moment – startled her. He sighed once, a long rasping sigh she said, and began to whimper softly. "The horses," he said. "Please, mummy, the horses."

'She assumed he was still feverish. She tried to soothe him, but when she wiped his forehead with a washcloth he knocked her hand away and sprang from the bed. He promptly collapsed but, to Catherine's increasing confusion, crawled towards the cabin door.

'The horror started there – for Catherine, I mean. At that point – Bobby crawling and gasping, she jumping to her feet in mounting panic – she had only one thought: to fetch me.

'Even when I heard the knock I thought it was part of a dream, part of that evening's happy tiredness.' Freyn paused and fixed me with a steady look. 'Do you have many relatives, Walter?'

It took me a moment or two to respond. It occurred to me to ask Freyn why he had put the question. But I didn't. Experience had shown that his digressions were part of a loop, tangents that invariably flicked back to the main point. I explained that my relatives had died or were dispersed. 'So if there's a knock on your door it's more likely to be the police or one of those snoopers from the social qualitat bureau,' he said. 'Yes, that's quite normal nowadays, isn't it – personal exclusivity? That's what the gauleiters want, of course. Divide and rule, or better still, sub-divide and subjugate.

'Well, then, you probably won't understand when I tell you that I had two thoughts after hearing, still half asleep, the knocking on my cabin door. The first thought: that I was at home in Kent and that my mother was knocking. Second thought: that I wanted to lie, still and warm, and listen to that little tap-tap for ever.'

Freyn shook his head. 'I'm ashamed to tell you that, Walter. Not because it's personal or sentimental. No, not that at all. I'm ashamed because, even at that moment on the *Manahatta*, nothing in me had picked up any intimation of violence or horror. Not even with Catherine and that blanket-wrapped boy standing on the other side of my door.

'I put on my dressing gown and opened the door. And still I didn't know . . . *still*. Catherine began to speak but Bobby cut in desperately. He said it was the horses and that they were dying. Catherine began to explain, at which Bobby broke away and hared off down the corridor. That was that. Mrs Slocumber had appeared by then and we ran after him.'

Freyn's and Catherine's subsequent statements to the New Orleans court were similar. They confirmed that Bobby had dropped the blanket and sprinted along the corridor, turning left through an open door to the port side promenade deck. He made straight for the aft half deck where the horses were tethered. Freyn caught him a few steps before he reached the rails. The netting separating the pen from the promenade was still up.

The mare had gone.

Catherine arrived moments later and the boy went to her. 'I stuck my head through a small hole in the netting and looked around,' said Freyn. 'I saw the yearling straight away . . . still tethered. But not the mare. Couldn't believe it. Didn't notice anything else at that point. And then I thought the netting must be down on the starboard side. I even laughed and announced that the mare had gone for a prom.'

Instructing Catherine to hold Bobby back, Freyn unhooked the netting, stepped on to the half deck, and re-attached it. 'I said something or other to the yearling and went immediately to the starboard side. The net was definitely up and secure. I looked along the starboard promenade . . . nothing.

'I turned back to the yearling and two things happened simultaneously. I saw that part of the outer cargo rail was down, and I heard the mare whinnying . . . then a splashing sound.'

For a few seconds, Freyn's lips seemed to form words, but

nothing came. It was cold in his box that night, or at least it felt cold to me, and I assumed he might be shivering.

He cleared his throat with some difficulty, his chronic bronchitis exacerbated by tension. 'I knew then,' he said quietly. 'Bobby bolted to the rail. Catherine screamed and grabbed him, but he was wailing and calling down to the mare. I finally reacted properly. I collected a spare tether and double-tethered the yearling. Then I went to the gap in the rail and looked down.'

The mare was in the water about fifty metres off the stern. At first Freyn thought he could see only mats of floating sargasso weed. When his eyes adjusted properly, he could see the mare in clear water. According to his statement to the court, it had been possible to see the moon reflected in the water.

'Just before telling Catherine to go with Bobby and Mrs Slocumber to get the captain, I bent down and grabbed the fallen cargo rail. I hoisted it with some difficulty, managed to set it into the guides and slid the securing handles home. And it was then that I understood what had happened . . . what had been done.'

Catherine's statement to the police noted that at this point, 'Mr Freyn said that I should tell Capt McCandless that somebody had deliberately forced the mare off the side of the ship and into the water. Mr Freyn said that we should run, which we did.'

As soon as the three set off Freyn examined the deck more carefully. 'I noticed that the yearling appeared to be standing over a long length of wood,' he said. 'I picked it up, saw that it was . . . it was like a crude spear. At the tip there was a point made of long nails hammered in on the skew. And there was a kind of bar bound to it just below the sharp end. It was at least two inches thick and about five feet long. Quite a piece of work – must've taken a few hours to put together. And hours more to filch the bits and pieces needed to make it. Well made, well thought out. The work of someone afraid of dying alone in a flat calm – a final deadly flowering of creativity manured by greed and hatred.'

The object was exhibited at the trial, and during the hearing a drawing of it appeared on the front page of the July 23 edition of the *Crescent City Credential* newspaper. I sourced the illustration via the Digifiche and it shows the contrivance in all its grim precision.

The thing had been formed with extreme attention to detail. It had a loop handle at one end. At the other was the point of nails on a stub of wood, perhaps two inches thick. The stub carried long, sharpened nails which protruded two inches from the rope bound round it. The drawing highlighted dark patches on the rope winding.

'The rope was wet with the mare's blood,' said Freyn. 'And then – I don't know what made me do it – I glanced up at the bridge deck above me.' Freyn's breathing again became troublesome. On the tape it sounds almost bubbly, like muted gargling. His mouth pinched shut as he sifted air carefully through his nose. 'Can't stop now, Walter,' he whispered, 'the gravity of the thing's taken over.'

He sifted more air, exhaling slowly. After waiting a few moments to judge his condition, he continued.

'Tell me,' he said, 'have you ever regretted learning a particular lesson?' I expressed puzzlement, though I'm not sure Freyn wanted an answer from me. 'I wonder how things might have turned out if I hadn't, by chance, looked up and seen Wintle duck away from the aft rail of the bridge deck.

'Perhaps it wasn't chance at all, Walter. Chance or no, it's one thing to be horrified, but quite another to experience horror in unmistakable detail. Every link in the chain revealed. Nothing left to explain.

'Well, Wintle ducked away and I knew everything at that moment. I didn't even bother to call out. I just stood, suddenly feeling faint, breathing in the stench rising from the mats of seaweed.

'I went to the rail and called down to the mare, thinking I could calm her. Then I noticed that she wasn't treading the water properly – she'd canted over slightly. I looked hard and thought I could see only one of her forelegs coming up. She'd kicked herself a little further off by now, about seventy yards I'd say.

'I had a terrible feeling then, quite terrible. I stopped calling out to her. It seemed hopeless and even cruel. McCandless arrived at a trot with a couple of mates, followed by Catherine, Bobby and Mrs Slocumber. I told him that Wintle had driven the mare overboard. I mentioned that I had met Wintle in the bush in Roraima and that he had had a pistol then.'

One of the mates was sent to rouse the purser and confine Wintle under guard. McCandless examined the cargo rail and confirmed that it was undamaged – and therefore had been removed deliberately rather than kicked down by the horse. 'The animal looked all wrong,' he told the court. 'She wasn't set right in the water. The young fellow, master Bobby, suggested that one of her forelegs was busted. The mate, Ebden, had some experience with horses and said the same. For my part, I thought straight away that it would be impossible to get the mare out in one piece.'

The second officer arrived with several more hands and within two or three minutes passengers wrapped in overcoats and shawls – blankets in the case of those from third class – began to appear. They lined the port rail on the promenade and boat decks, ignoring McCandless's pleas to return to their cabins. 'I told them to get back to bed because there was nothing they could do,' he told the court, 'and I think they would have done.

'Mr Lawton supported me very kindly and attempted to calm the assembled passengers, speaking from the boat deck. But then Lady Gwinnet-Bose saw fit to announce that she was a horse lover and had the right to see what was being done to save the animal. The majority of them got behind her and demanded their rights also. I'll wager those fine folks do regret it now.'

The captain was in a difficult position. He was certain the mare had broken a leg. 'McCandless was for putting the mare out of her misery then and there,' said Freyn. 'He kept a Remington rifle in his cabin, which he would take ashore for sport when he could. I quietly suggested he go through the motions of trying to bring the mare in: take a boat out, rope her, and begin to tow her back. The moonlight was ample. They'd be able to see what they were doing. As soon as the mare was brought alongside, everybody would see that it was badly injured. It would then be logical to shoot her from close range. It was the only way.'

McCandless set about organising the lowering of a lifeboat. 'They had taken the canvas cover off the boat when McCandless shouted at them to stop,' said Freyn. 'Then he leaned out over the rail, and froze, his eyes fixed on the mare. McCandless called for his rifle and one of the hands scuttled away to fetch it. At first, I had no idea what he had seen.'

The captain's explanation to the court of what happened next seems quite exemplary and certainly better than Freyn's attempt to explain it to me, which was dotted with repetition, long pauses and increasing confusion. His diary entry was of even less use.

This, then, is what McCandless told the court on the afternoon of July 22, 1938:

'As the boat was being readied I concentrated my attention on the unfortunate animal. It was in poor condition and tiring rapidly. Its attempts to keep above water were desperate. I resolved to put the creature out of its misery as soon as we'd rowed close enough for a decisive shot to the head.

'I was about to turn away to see if the boat was ready to be swung out when I noticed what looked like a tidy cut in the water. I thought it must be a thin line of weed in the water. But it was not, sir. I saw the fin properly a moment later and knew the worst. There came a shout from above. A passenger had also seen the shark's movement. I called again for my rifle.

'Less than two minutes passed before the lad, Settles, brought the Remington. In that time the situation changed most shockingly. Within seconds of the cry of alarm from the upper deck, the rest of the passengers on the rails realised what was taking place. A good many women commenced to scream, and the men shouted for me to do something. Some of them unlashed deck chairs and life preservers, and began to hurl them overboard in the general direction of the horse – an attempted distraction. It was pointless and they realised it soon enough.

'I turned my attention back to the struggling creature just as the first shark – I estimate at least two more had arrived by now – struck the mare. Her neck arched out of the water as if in the grip of a violent spasm, and she uttered a most appalling sound. I must tell you that it was like the sound of a pain-racked child, and it chilled me to the marrow. Quite immediately, there was pandemonium on deck.'

The *Credential*'s copious report noted that at this point in the proceedings, McCandless's last remark induced what their reporter described as 'an audible groan from many of those pressed in the gallery, and was followed by the collapse of one of their number, Mrs Marie Dutaur, in a faint. Thereafter, the court sitting was adjourned for thirty minutes.'

McCandless's description was continued later and remained precise and to the point: 'At first, the horse, by now in a pitifully distressed condition, struggled with a most terrible vigour. The otherwise calm water was, very soon, cut up by the rapid movements of the predators around the mare, which was being buffeted. A few moments later, she gave up. Her back was lost to view, and her neck and head rose straight up, the only part of her that could be seen, before slipping without further protest beneath that violent water.

'It was only at that point that my rifle was handed to me. I took it and waited for half a minute to make sure the mare would not break surface, alive, and then turned my attention to the ship at large. I noticed that Mr Freyn was standing by the yearling with the young lady and her son, and Mrs Slocumber.

'The rest of the passengers positively swarmed aft to gather round me. Several began to berate me for my failure to deal with the situation satisfactorily. I understood the reason for their behaviour and chose not to respond. But, as the great architect is my constant witness, I know that I did all that could have been done in those circumstances. Furthermore, I tell you that when evil presents itself, it may take more than a few decent folk to banish it!'

Freyn remembered McCandless's testimony only vaguely, but enough to recall the captain's concluding remark – and the chorus of approval it provoked in the gallery. But, like I said, Freyn delivered the details of the incident with difficulty, dotting around from one point to another.

By the time the passengers had gathered around McCandless, Wintle had been collected, without a struggle, and locked in a windowless second-class cabin with two stewards posted to guard the door. The hands confirmed that Wintle had put up no struggle. He had been waiting for them in his own cabin, quietly tidying his belongings. He immediately admitted to the purser that he had driven the mare overboard, using the nailed rod. 'You can't blame me,' he told them. 'I had a purpose, whereas the beast did not. I trust they have disposed of the other animal also.'

Wintle repeated the remark when questioned at the trial. 'He was quite comfortable in the dock,' said Freyn. 'I think he felt safe, enclosed by all that polished wood – on land and alive rather than dead on the deck of a ghost ship. When the sentence was handed down, he was unconcerned. I think he saw the sentence as being like the courtroom: orderly, logical. As they took him down, he grabbed the rail and called out. He said something extraordinary, I know that. But, do you know, I can't damned well remember what it was.'

The exact words, according to the *Credential*, were: 'I accept that I must be detained. I agree because I know I may depend upon others to take the necessary actions.' This induced a silence described by the *Credential*'s reporter as a reminder of the scene moments before Wintle forced the mare overboard 'into that fatal sea whose stillness concealed the stuff of nightmares'.

Freyn looked at me quizzically. 'Do you remember the obeah man, Walter?' he asked. 'In the yard at Spivey's that day? You remember that I gave my paperweight to him? Do you? Can you remember what he said to me?' I told Freyn I didn't and began to apologise, but he cut in pretty sharply. 'There's gold at the bottom of the sea; that's what he said. And what had Bobby said? Something about falling down the stars.'

Freyn shrugged. 'Well, what more can I tell you, Walter? That there was gold at the bottom of the sea? In fact, there *was*, symbolically speaking. Wintle had been driven to his extraordinary brutality because he thought the horses should not be given water. But his will to live was not pure, or even purely desperate. His was a vicious and greedy will.

'When the police went through his belongings and baggage, eight tightly sewn canvas pouches were found. Six of them were packed with gold dust. The two remaining pouches were found in one of the two saddle bags which he'd secreted with *my* luggage in first-class storage. These saddle bags would have been delivered to Morphen, with the horses. The pouches were crammed with uncut emeralds of considerable quality.

'Wintle had amassed a small fortune for himself, and contraband for Morphen – who naturally denied any connection with the business. In any case, that hoard proved more than enough to drive him to kill the mare. Do you see? Do you see how it must always end?'

Freyn yawned. 'Only one good thing came out of it,' he said quietly. 'Catherine's father bought the yearling from Morphen, who didn't want anything to do with it after what happened on the *Manahatta*. Wintle *was* connected with Morphen, you see. Found that out later. The gold and gem smuggling had been cooked up between them. Morphen, Wintle – perhaps even Spivey was involved. And Luchenne, without a doubt. The pits on his land, remember? Strictly business, eh, Walter?'

Lawton's carpentry

CLARENDON Lawton died in his cabin some time before dawn, soon after the mare's slaughter. He had sought out Freyn on deck after McCandless dispersed the passengers. Some went to bed, the remainder were restive and either walked the decks or tried to talk through the details of the night's events in the saloon. Freyn had no inkling that anything might be wrong with Lawton.

'To this day,' he insisted, 'I would swear that the man who came to me on deck looked perfectly well and quite composed. When he shook my hand to take his leave, his grip was firm and steady, the eyes bright and untroubled. I was shocked when I learned of his end. I dared to wonder if he had not actually taken in what had happened that night.'

A note was found on Lawton's bedside table. It read:

'There is peace only in movement, and in the recognition of time's hidden chime. Everything else is merely the dim recollection of an increasingly distant land. Kindly make use of the box in the usual way. Yours etc, Clarendon Lawton, aboard the SS *Manahatta*, July 7, 1938.'

Nobody understood any part of his message, though, according to Freyn, Capt McCandless remained exercised by the note for the rest of the voyage. Lawton was buried at sea on July 9. Freyn insisted that Lawton's books (a collection of poetry, novels and anthropological texts) be packed into the canvas committal sheath. His manuscripts were returned to his sister in New York State, and were accidentally destroyed in a fire at the old clapboard house in 1951.

'We consigned him to the sea in the evening,' Freyn remarked. 'It was interesting, you know – everybody, but everybody, turned out. The rails were lined. A single hymn was sung, and sung with vigour. After all those terrible days, and the ghastliness of the mare, it seemed to be our last chance to absolve ourselves – a final admission of fear and regret; or so it seemed to me.

'By the time the stretcher was lifted and balanced on the promenade deck rail the sky had deepened into a dense orange colour. I looked to the horizon pretty hungrily. The sunset was quite breathtaking and old McCandless paused for a good half minute before giving the order to tip Lawton in his weighted canvas shroud over the side. The splash was clearly heard. I couldn't look down. I thought of England in November – a cool, calm November over the Downs, slashed with the same miraculous sunset. I wasn't sure if my thoughts were born of hope or despair – not then, anyway.'

Freyn paused to try to sit up straighter. He couldn't manage it for some reason. At that moment he looked like an ancient, wizened judge.

'When I think of that sunset at sea now, I feel pain,' he said. 'I see no beauty in it. The delicate patterns of the waves seem like a carpet of fish hooks. In other circumstances I might have thought that the waves, in that light, gleamed like the scales of Achilles's armour. Instead, I can't help thinking of that night . . . that other night, over Dresden. Never mind that – doesn't matter. Connections, eh? Braids and braids and bloody *braids* of meaning . . .'

I didn't know what he was on about but said nothing. He breathed out slowly and seemed to shrink, his elbows angling out. 'I could hardly bear to be near the yearling. Forced myself, of course. Every time I touched him my hands felt cold and dead until he warmed them. And when they were warm, I felt like a traitor or a leech. That night, I woke up in my bunk and thought I could smell the mare, as if her breath was on me, as it had been that miraculous night in the forest.'

The *Manahatta* was sighted by a merchant ship on July 10, the next day. Within an hour of being boarded a gentle wind gusted up from the south-west and began to knead the water into weed encrusted swells. The merchant ship's engineering stores contained enough spare parts to achieve what Capt McCandless described as 'an ugly but effective mechanical lash-up'. And after a further seven hours of repairs, the *Manahatta* made steam and limped along within sight of the merchantman at no more than 12 knots. Kingston, Jamaica, was reached two days later, and the radio set was replaced. The ship continued to New Orleans.

'Oh, yes, and one more thing,' said Freyn, perking up slightly. 'There *was* a box! Everybody had missed the point, you see – foxed by Lawton's throw-away reference to it. But it took an accident to solve the riddle. While the *Manahatta*'s cargo was being unloaded at New Orleans one of the crates happened to slip from the cargo net and smashed open on the quay. And what do you think was inside, Walter?' I had no idea. 'A *coffin* of course! The coffin that Lawton had had made by the carpenter we called on in Temhari.'

Freyn was momentarily amused by the recollection. We both were, though I felt a bit uncomfortable about laughing at something so far removed from my existence. By now Freyn was looking extremely drained and I instinctively began to pack up my stuff. He sighed and said: 'Gravity is a heavy business, Walter . . . everything else is merely the dim recollection of an increasingly distant land. What d'you suppose Lawton meant by that?'

Freyn smiled at my bafflement and added: 'Mind if I stop there, Walter? I think the second law of thermodynamics has more or less done for me. That clock analogy of yours was truer than you think. Lord knows why you should be interested in the squeaking cogs and spindles of one very old man's life. And what is your verdict? You have the bits and pieces – the glittering tithes – spread out on the bench before you. In view of my singular history, do you find in favour of my marathon of vagrancy? Or is my current status simply the result of a deep and intractable flaw in my character?'

Freyn waited for a response from me but I couldn't think of anything to say. He began to cackle, then caught himself before continuing. 'Perdition doesn't happen overnight, but bit by bit. Not perdition, actually – that's unfair to all the others here in the Delta, and anywhere else where outcasts gather.

'You must never think we so-called degradees are simply flotsam. We are people with histories that don't fit the revised textbooks, that fail the preferred Demcorp model. I am no more remarkable than most of them – just older and more scrofulous. You might as well think of the Delta as Freynland. We're all Freyns of one sort or another here. We have chosen this; we object to the rest. We have been jettisoned and we are alone – and, if we're honest, we're happy with that. We are no longer interested in navigation. How can we be? There are no points of reference. Anarchy and filth is preferable to a flat calm in dead latitudes.'

He waited to see if I would respond. I just sat tight. I found I had been holding my breath.

Freyn shrugged. 'I suppose I must be the ghost of earlier events – or at least a *thing* that could no longer fit in,' he said. 'I knew that if I persisted in trying to fit in I would perish in a death of a thousand very stupid cuts. My soul belonged to earlier events that had gouged deep and contained a truth that was substantial; a ruthlessly delivered meaning that I would no longer try to bury.

'Did I mention that I was a bomber navigator in the war? *Navigation!* What a damned hoot, Walter. What would London Dry have made of that? True sailing was as dead for me as for the *Manahatta* in that flat calm.'

'What about Catherine? I mean, you and –'

'Expect we'd have ended up as a pair of charming bag people.'

'Yes, but what happened? I mean, with –'

'Mind if we leave it, Walter?'

The suddenly steady way he gazed at me was off-putting. 'Right,' I said.

His look softened. His eyes scrutinised mine without aggression. 'I wish you could have seen the horses,' he mused. 'They were desert horses. Did I mention that? Pure creatures in pure air, nomadic like their true masters.' And then Freyn smiled. 'I'm alive because of those horses – nothing else.'

I must've frowned.

'You look blank, Walter.'

'I thought that it was because of what happened to the mare that –'

'Don't you see that I'm still *living* for the mare, Walter? That I've been living for her all these years. Wintle may have destroyed her flesh, but I'm keeping her alive. I'm in the water with her, here in the Delta where everything is indefinite. And when I go, the mare goes. I think that's why I've told you all this. Try to think of her sometimes – in the forest, I mean. *Try.* Imagine the tug of her on the halter lead. Look for your face in her eye – it'll be there, I promise.'

Freyn held up both of his hands in what was by now a familiar gesture. This really was it: the end. I felt odd – chilled, and even a little lightheaded. I thanked him for his time and began to try to say how interesting I'd found his story.

'Please, Walter,' he interrupted. 'Not the word *interesting*. Anything but that. A life is a life. *Lichen* are interesting.'

We had a bit of a laugh about that. I was upset, though. I couldn't swallow the idea of not seeing him again. I had the distinct feeling our little contract had ended. His last remarks had been delivered with a dreamy, exhausted look: it seemed that the interview was over as far as he was concerned. I was no longer his licensed trespasser.

I asked if I could call on him from time to time, bring him bits of food and clothing. I said, probably a little too quickly, that it would be no trouble; and that I really enjoyed his company.

'Food and clothing, eh?' he said. 'Well, I am in failing health, after all – have been for, what, forty years? So why not. I've said it before, but you damned well *must* have been a parish priest in a previous life. You really are the ideal confessor for a raddled old scrap like me. Forgive me, father, for I have thinned!'

Freyn gave me a comically expectant look but couldn't hold it. His expression, which for a few seconds carried pretty much the usual amused glint, collapsed into ashen vacancy. He tried to clear his throat, which only brought on a fit of gasping. He leaned forward, shoulders raised, and managed to organise his breathing into a hoarse whisper through pursed lips. I began to ask if he was all right and he nodded and raised his right hand. I waited. It took him a minute to gather himself. His wheeze diminished into an unpleasant scraping sound. 'Who was I?' he whispered. 'What have I become? And if there has been no connection between the two then there has been no meaning . . . just more questions . . .'

A lengthy silence developed. On the tape our silence is punctuated with the vague, broken-up sounds of the Delta: barking, wavering shouts. Freyn extended the fingers of his right hand and, very slowly, touched his thumb with the tip of his middle finger, forming a decrepitly trembling circle. He studied it for ten or fifteen seconds.

I hadn't a clue what to say. I sat listening to him wheeze. After a bit, I just couldn't take it. I said I'd return his *Manahatta* diary soon, told him I'd like to hear more about his life after Roraima.

Freyn managed a laborious wink. 'You're too polite, dear boy. I appreciate it, of course.'

I said I'd be passing two days later and would definitely call in. He nodded and looked down. His hands were cradled in his lap, palms up, the thin dry fingers curled as if holding a bowl. I got out quickly.

I got out quickly. I say it twice because I need to mark that casual action. I was inadequate; couldn't cut it when it mattered.

The letters

I RETURNED to Freyn's box two days later, as arranged. He wasn't there. The interior of the box had not been disturbed and, as it was raining, I crawled in and sat on the small square of neatly folded burlap which was always laid on top of the Amtico, waiting for me.

Like I said, everything was as it should be. Everything in its place. The candle in the mortar bowl was guttering vigorously. I got the tape recorder out of my field bag and laid it beside my knee, as usual. The chrome-effect grill of its microphone was pointing at his pallet; a little left of centre, towards where he normally sat.

I waited. I did not consider that anything could be wrong. Or, to be more accurate, I did not allow that thought to gain ground. To pass the time until his return I rehearsed the day's events so far, ticked through a mental checklist of work to be done, things to be sorted. I wondered, for example, if I might be lucky on the monthly national Cash Cornucopia lottery for research grants. In the six years since completing my D Phil, I had won only one minor prize and was therefore still dependent on the Ministry of Profitability's salary rulings. It has been my hope for the last two years to narrow my specialism: pH factors in urban vegetative lesions is what I feel I could contribute most to.

I am quite phlegmatic, as a rule. But I experienced a faint

feeling of irritation after about half an hour. The evidence seemed perfectly clear. Freyn's box was obviously still inhabited and functional. He was out doing something; probably collecting an armful of magazines to make into those fuel briquettes he was so proud of. Or he was on his way back from one of the charity drop zones with a few bits and pieces. I pictured him crawling along benignly with a small plastic sack containing orange peel, potatoes, a few segments of his favourite Swiss Stylisch cheese, and some shrivelled greens.

I sat hunched forward against my raised knees. It seemed a little cold in there without him. I dozed off and woke ten or fifteen minutes later out of a dream of lights dancing through fog. It was the effect of the candle, I suppose.

There was a palpable feeling of stillness in the box, which I hadn't experienced before. The only thing that betrayed any vitality was the candle flame which still guttered, though there was no noticeable draught in the box, thanks to Freyn's excellent two-flap arrangement. It was hard to accept that the candle could burn so cheerfully without Freyn being present. It wasn't the same without his drawn face seeming to grow upwards out of its cosy, encouraging light.

I waited for the storyteller to materialise. Having been assimilated by Freyn, was I now going to be rejected by him in some way? My irritation and unease slowly turned into a distinctly uncomfortable feeling. I guess I have to admit that I felt a stab of anger.

I waited two hours. I had only intended to wait for ninety minutes, but then began the peculiar process of telling myself: 'Just five minutes more.' I did that six times and finally called it quits because I had become completely unnerved by his absence. By now, the box was beginning to seem strange to me. I almost felt like an intruder casing the joint. The only thing that I was reassured by was the candle. I thought: that's a true thing, it's part and parcel of Freyn. But it was also true that he had always been in the box when I arrived. Furthermore, he had mentioned two or three times that he always did what he referred to as his 'reccies' in the morning, well before the children began to form into packs.

I left the box, taking care to reposition the flaps exactly as I had found them. I wasn't carrying any matches or a lighter and did not want the candle to blow out through carelessness on my part and present Freyn with a dark return.

I flicked on my infrared datum locator and radiused it until it bleeped its contact with the relevant causeway beacon, and began to head back, moving north along one of the main access tracks. My feelings were contradictory. At first, I listed reasons supporting the idea that there had been some sort of mistake. After all, Freyn was ancient and was surely entitled to gross memory lapses. On the other hand, the error could just as easily have been on my side. Maybe I'd got the date wrong, and he was expecting me the next day.

But these comfortingly rational considerations were interrupted again and again by another idea: that Freyn had gone — and wasn't coming back.

I returned the next morning at about eleven. This was quite an irregular time for me and shows that I was still worried. I had not slept well that night and could not sleep at all after waking at 4.33 a.m. with a muzzy head. I had been forced to get up and dispose of a good deal of nervous energy, first by vacuuming the securispace, then cleaning the kitchen surfaces. After that, I took out the Statsol and cleaned the heads and roller guides of my video, sound cube and 3-D laser unit.

At one point, I caught sight of the neatly racked set of DAT tapes whose patterns of magnetised oxide carried the raw material of *Horse Latitudes*. For some reason, the sight of them worried me and I covered them with a scientific journal.

These details may not be strictly relevant. I mention them out of a spirit of openness and exactitude. After all, I was, as Freyn had once said, 'young Walter, my licensed trespasser'.

It was just before dusk, and after collecting my quota of samples, when I pushed my codex key into the cannula's turnstile to Causeway 3. I found that my hands were trembling slightly as

I slipped the codex back into my hip clip. My throat was dry and my neck felt peculiarly hot. I think these were symptoms of incipient adrenal exhaustion or a blood sugar glitch, or both.

My progress through the smoking shanties of the Delta's twelfth segment didn't feel like it normally did. I was not as alert as usual – twitchy rather than observant. I stumbled occasionally, not having noticed box corners or debris with my usual acuity. I pressed on and was alarmed to feel that my surroundings were not particularly familiar. I even began to wonder if I would be able to find Freyn's box.

After about three-quarters of an hour (it normally took me between thirty and thirty-five minutes) I began to recognise my surroundings and knew I was near my destination. At first, I speeded up, dodging between the braziers with my stun-baton in hand, stepping over children, avoiding the eyes of the adults, sidestepping dead animals and sludgy eddies of refuse. Then I thought how ridiculous I was being and slowed right down. Quite suddenly, I lost my desire to get to Freyn's box.

Three minutes later I veered as usual round the totem pole and saw it: it registered on my retinas with an almost palpable hit, as if the rods and cones had been waiting anxiously to receive the familiar impulses of the box's features, its varying densities of light and shade, its edges. I paused outside the flaps and listened. I was sweating and felt foolish. I thought: he's definitely in there. And then, as I squatted to lift the outer flap I knew just as certainly that Freyn was not in the box.

The candle was still just about guttering. The glossy, stiffened curl of its wick was breathing its familiar jiggle of flame. I knew he had gone – and knew he wasn't coming back. How did I know? I cannot offer a reasoned answer. But as Freyn had once said: 'Unexpected guests always arrive suddenly and, having arrived, are often unmistakable in their purpose.' His absence was, at that moment, just such an unmistakable intruder. I mean that the sense of his absence was as substantial as his presence.

I crawled in, pegged the inner flap and tried to gather myself. I felt crushed, a little tearful. It was extremely hard to accept that Freyn, in whatever way, could cease to exist. Or that his candle could continue to enliven his little space and all his tidily arranged belongings, the fragmentary evidence of his life. I felt robbed. And then I felt something else: renewal. I have absolutely no idea how these two feelings could have manifested themselves simultaneously.

And then something fanciful occurred to me. It was that Freyn had never inhabited the box. That I had, after all, been the guest of a ghost – the ghost of Main Street, Temhari, or of old Tang, waving me off into the mist with a battered jack of hearts. A ghost who had charged that dim oblong of humid, stale air with the story of *Horse Latitudes*.

I wanted more. I must have been desperate because it occurred to me that Freyn might have left me a message – a last action if, say, he'd been taken ill and been forced to crawl to one of the treatment bunkers in the sixth segment. I scanned the box. There were no notes in obvious view; nothing tucked up under the neatly folded blanket on the bed, nor any scrap slipped into the matted folds of the sleeping bag. I even worked my way round the edge of the sheet of lino lying on the pallet base in case he'd stashed a message there.

I caught sight of his machete. It was tucked down between the blanket and a metal box about twelve inches by nine inches. It was black, thoroughly dented, with patches of rust at the corners and around the simple flip-up clasp. The clasp was open and the lid of the box very slightly raised. This was obviously the fossil box he'd once mentioned to me.

The box had not been closed. What I did next was not honest, or at least not ethical. All I can repeat in my defence is that at that moment I knew Freyn had gone and wasn't coming back. I took the tin box and set it on a herniated lump in the mattress. I opened the lid, which moved stiffly and required a sharp upwards wrench.

It was by no means crammed full. It contained the following

items: an old, water-stained black-and-white photo of an Edwardian couple in their late fifties – he, a forceful figure, good-looking in a square-jawed way; she, quite pale, round-eyed, with long hands emerging from buttoned silk sleeves. Behind them was a sylvan studio backdrop, the pair of them standing on steps by a stubby classical pillar draped with ivy and surmounted by a spray of flowers. They must've been Freyn's parents.

The next item was a small specimen of quartz with two projecting crystals on one face and veins of pyrite and gold on the other. And there was another small lump of finely pitted rock which bore the signs of extreme igneity. I realised with a feeling of shock that it must have been the meteorite shard from El Arroyo. There was a small crucifix on a tarnished chain, carrying a Christ figure disfigured by a flaking coat of grey-green paint: Eglantine's parting offering. There was a Maori greenstone tiki on a leather wrist thong – a small rectangular carving of a stylised image, a human face joined to a vaguely lizard-like body.

And there was a small pipe with a stem no more than three inches long, with a thin tubular mouthpiece. Its small bowl was conical, no more than half an inch across the top and narrowing to about a quarter of an inch where the bowl joined the stem. I sniffed the bowl and recognised very slight traces of *cannabis indica* and *papaver somniferum*.

There were three further items in the box. A small quantity of stiff black hair which had been tightly braided, and two letters. The braid puzzled me. The hairs were remarkably thick, almost wiry. Quite suddenly, I realised where they had come from and felt a jolting charge like electricity in the fingers that held the braid. It was hair from a horse's mane. Freyn must've retrieved it from the grooming brushes. The mare! Right there in my hands.

I raised the braid to my nose. I cannot describe the strangeness of the smell. For a moment (or it might have been several minutes, I'm really not sure) everything seemed to stop. Or perhaps, as Freyn once said, everything participated correctly. It wasn't just a question of holding history in my hand.

At that moment, in that fusty old box, history seemed just a banal word; arbitrary, ruthlessly truncated. I felt as if I was holding a complete truth in my hand, an expanding truth. It was an almost physical feeling, like slipping your hand through the slats of a window blind and feeling the sun on your skin. Freyn, Luchenne, the *Manahatta* – they were as absolutely true as that strange warmth I felt, and they would continue to be true. I held the braid for some time and then laid it carefully back in its place in the box.

I picked up the first envelope, which was badly foxed by damp and the beginnings of a mould. The address read: J. Freyn Esq, c/o Spivey & Co, Regent House, Bay Prospect, Temhari, Roraima. The word 'Confidential', underlined twice in crimson ink, obscured the date stamp. I could make out 'rleans' but the date had faded beyond recognition.

It would be facile to suggest that Freyn's years in the Delta were the direct result of what was written in that letter. Yet the suggestion remains. Maybe Freyn had been born with a natural inclination to strip his past away thoroughly and seek simplicities instead. Or maybe the Delta is the truly natural habitat for such a person. But there must be an element of chance in the blur of cause and effect; cascades of chance which must be hard to deflect – fractals of fate. The letter must have been part of such a cascade.

This is what it said:

Dear James,
I am distraught. Your letter distressed me and leaves me feeling utterly helpless. If I could only see you and talk to you and take your hand, surely I could influence your feelings. Not only about me, but about yourself.

You say that what happened on the *Manahatta* has caused a great and crushing doubt in you, and that the doubt never leaves you. You say that you are certain that it cannot be cast aside, and that it has diminished you. You say that you believed that you were growing to love me. I accept your words, yet find it so very hard to accept your doubt and fear about yourself. Perhaps it was not me you loved, or depended upon. James, I don't write those words with any intention to hurt, but only to tell you my true thoughts.

Even if you say you are certain that you would rather remain in Roraima on your own, don't be afraid to remember me. I, too, had thought of you with increasing tenderness. That strange, painful, most wonderful night on deck when it rained, I thought then that I wanted much more, wanted your love, and hoped that you thirsted for mine in return. Though it may confuse or pain you to hear it, I must tell you that I cannot stop myself hoping for your return, or word from you at the least.

I must return your letter because I cannot bear to see it in my writing desk. I would rather think of the man I knew in Temhari, and on the *Manahatta*.

I would like to say more to comfort you but I cannot continue like this, my words suddenly feel as dry as old leaves. You spoke of thirst. Then please, darling, think of me that night with drops of rain on my face, for that is how I will think of you.

All my love and care, Catherine.

My hands felt hot. I glanced at them. They looked normal. I picked up the second letter, dated a month earlier, and opened it slowly. It said this:

My precious Catherine – I write this at my desk at Spivey's, surrounded by all that is considered decent and normal. I sit here, the fan whirrs above me, I hear the sounds of motors and carts passing in the street where you touched my hand the first time as I helped you into the taxi. How strange it feels to remember!

I cannot stop thinking of the events on the *Manahatta*. We have surely been marked for ever by them. I think of your hand, that first time I was bold enough to take it, and I think of the kiss that surprised me with its trembling gentleness. But I don't know what to think any more. Something terrible has gripped me. I cannot put it any other way.

Catherine, I am saying that you mustn't rely on me, as I have no sense of continuing at anything any more. I write this and can hardly credit it, for I am sure that I have felt a real love for you. I can see you now, as I write, and I see only goodness and beauty and inspiration. But it cannot be mine. Catherine, since the *Manahatta*, I feel as cold and set as marble. I have become riddled with doubt and it is almost a physical sensation, as if I were veined with a pernicious quartz. I can see no end to it, and therefore no other beginning. Forgive me.

I shall close by telling you that you are extraordinary, though I know it now only through a kind of mist. You must be wondering what has happened to me and what condition I must be in. Please do not speculate or seek to change my mind. I'm sorry, I can barely admit to it, but there is no point. I wonder if I will ever experience that simple thirst again.

James

I folded the letters and slipped them back into the envelope, which I put back in the metal box. I pressed the lid down on Freyn's past and flipped the rusty clasp shut.

I sat for a while longer. It was only very gradually that I again became aware of the world outside Freyn's box. I took in the usual sounds of the Delta shanties: the slap of the sheeting, wails and expletives, a ranter in the distance, percussionists, wind chimes, the amplified yammer of deejays.

There was nothing else to be done. I glanced round the box one last time and leaned forward to blow out the candle. As I did so, I pulled back with a gasp, shocked at my casual intention. I backed out of the tent, my eyes fixed on the flame, taking care not to disturb anything else.

And then I remembered something else – something ridiculous. Reaching into the front pouch of my field parka, I pulled out the bag of salt and vinegar crisps I had brought for Freyn, and placed it by the candle bowl. Before lowering the outer flap I took one long last look at that bold, playful oval of flame rising from the pale wax.

I left, turning away past the totem pole and stepping around two cirrhotic men huddled over a filthy ghetto blaster pumping out a ranting speech in German. It occurred to me that Freyn must have been very far away, or so close that he was not recognisable. In the murky, yellowish dusk, the tops of thousands of boxes and crates and makeshift tents stretched in every direction. Their wind-riffled coverings of plastic and vinyl and lino seemed to form the glistening swell of a turbulent sea.

Vaguely, through the mist, I heard the thinly echoing passage of the Norwich to Liverpool Street express: an edgy, arrhythmic ticking sound, like an old-fashioned watch winding down. Looking east in the direction of the raised track I could see only the pin-prick flashes of short circuits from the points. It was easy to imagine some of the passengers glancing out over the colourless sea of the Delta while thinking of their work targets, or apartments, or hobbies, or of the alluring set of a particular pair of lips. The train passed, its clack and whirr fading, giving way to the strange human murmur that blanketed the Delta at dusk. It was a strong sound, a raw plainsong keened by the sharply gusting wind blowing through transmission wires.

I thought of the horses. And I thought of the decrepit watch that I'd talked about with Freyn when he was about to give up telling the story. I imagined the cold metal in the interlocking arcs of brass teeth at the centre of the watch's dying mechanism.

I set my stun-baton on Ready-Max. Looking south-west towards the hazy penumbra of orange light over the dark skyline of London, I had the fleeting sense that I was heading towards something that would elude me; and that I risked losing my way.

And then, just before setting off, I remembered something. I lifted the fingers of my right hand and sniffed them. I thought

I could detect the slight but quite distinct scent of horse hair. I closed my fingers into a fist. I wanted to hold the smell for as long as I could. At that moment, as the scent coalesced into the sweat on my palm, I had it all – the peculiar gift of Freyn's history, and the mare's too.

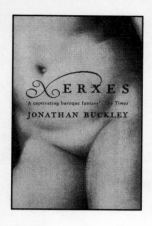

XERXES

Jonathan Buckley

Set in Munich in the 1820s, *Xerxes* traces the career of aspiring young architect August Ettlinger. Joining a salon of aristocrats and intellectuals, he falls under the influence of von Wolgast, who offers him use of his superb library. At the same time Ettlinger falls in love with Helene, one of their charmed circle. As passions intensify, Wolgast's motives become increasingly sinister.

£6.99   1 85702 997 6

JOYRIDE

Dexter Petley

From fishing for carp and trout in the waters of East Sussex, to driving the Dream Car across the cinematic America of his imagination, Josh's childhood had always been fuelled by the need to escape. Years later when Josh meets F. in a tea shop at Highgate ponds, he knows she is his last chance. *Joyride* is the story of Josh and F's journey across that vast country as they flee their separate pasts.

£6.99   1 85702 999 2

All Fourth Estate books are available from your local bookshop, or can be ordered direct from:

Fourth Estate, Book Service By Post, PO Box 29,
Douglas, I-O-M, IM99 1BQ

Credit cards accepted.

Tel: 01624 836000   Fax: 01624 670923
Internet: http://www.bookpost.co.uk
e-mail: bookshop@enterprise.net

Or visit the Fourth Estate website at:
www.4thestate.co.uk

Please state when ordering if you do not wish to receive further information about Fourth Estate titles.